THE PAINFUL STAIN OF MEMORY...

She hesitated just outside the gymnasium door, steeling herself for what came next. When she -reached- the room was empty.

"Do you want me to do this?" Jason asked.

She shook her head. "These are my people. I do this."

Easing the door open, she stepped inside. Copper and fear had left a thick metallic tang in the air that coated the back of her tongue. The high gymnasium walls echoed too loudly with the screams she hadn't heard before. She wanted to cover her ears, hold her breath, and clamp her eyes shut so hard she could erase the memory of this place. The thick ammonia smell of piss spoke of how frightened the children had been. And then there was the copper-penny scent that confirmed the worst of her fears.

Swiping her hair back from her eyes, she swallowed and paced across the dimly lit basketball court. In her vision the room had been brightly lit, the floor crowded with the terrified students. Their presences crowded around her begging for help so she felt sick to her stomach, and then angry. Mightily angry. So angry she could hurt someone. So angry the force of the earth's ley lines fizzled up and through her veins so she felt as if her skin was sparking. She fought back the need to injure something, because that wasn't her way.

There was where Headmaster Smith had stood with the other faculty. There was where he had fallen when he was shot in the leg, and there was where she had, somehow, communicated with him. The caramel-colored gym floorboards were smeared with blood—too much for just Smith's. So all of her vision had been true. The faculty—Smith, Professor Goldman in trigonometry, Mrs. Beaton in Gift control, the others—were all gone.

BOOKS BY THE AUTHOR

***The Cartographer Universe* series:**
The Warden of Power

The Cartographer's Daughter

Afterburn
Aftershock

Terra Incognita
Terra Infirma
Terra Nueva

Also by the Author
Mutable Things
Emberstone
Ice Dragon

Written as Karen L. McKee
Ashes and Light
Shades of Moonlight
Judas Kiss
Second Spring
A Different Nightmusic

Aftermath

Karen L. Abrahamson

AFTERMATH
Copyright © 2014 Karen L. Abrahamson
All rights reserved, including the right of reproduction, in whole or in part in any form.

Published 2014 by Twisted Root Publishing
www.twistedrootpublishing.com

Book and cover design © Twisted Root Publishing
Cover image: © Pavel Stobov|Dreamstime.com, ©Susan Law Cain|Dreamstime.com, © beboy|Shutterstock.com

ISBN-13: 978-1-927753-24-8

First edition: March 2014

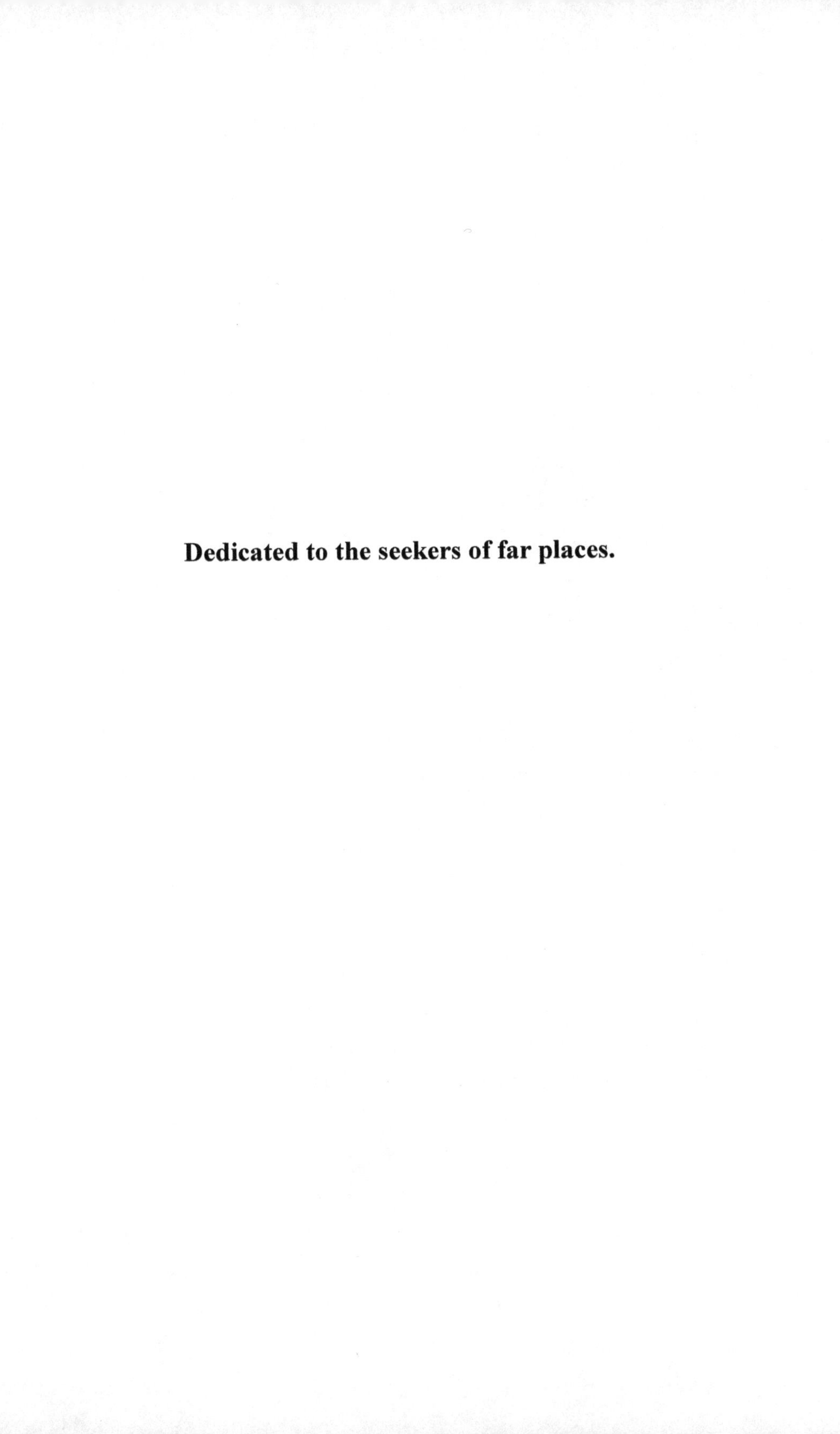

Dedicated to the seekers of far places.

Acknowledgements:

Many thanks to Kris and Dean who have taught me so much more than how to write a book.

**I stood
among them, but not of them; in a shroud
Of thoughts which were not their thoughts.**
Lord Byron, Childe Harold's Pilgrimage, canto III (1816)

PROLOGUE

Early morning at the American Geological Survey Academy was always Richard Smith's favorite time of the day. The school hummed with the incipient noise that would come with the students, but for now it was just a gentle vibration that traveled through the brick walls from the nearby dorm wing. The quiet let him focus on the papers before him: the annual state testing results. Requests for information on the latest crop of students nearing graduation. He sipped his coffee and eased his back while he contemplated just what to report about each of the students. Some had shown far more of the Gift than had been expected, while others had disappointed. That was the thing with the Gift, though it seemed to run true in families, you could never be sure what you were going to get.

A distant sound from near the foyer brought his head up from his papers and his skin prickled, but his office was its usual comfortable retreat of wood- and bookshelf-paneled walls, the aging linoleum floor, large desk and file cabinet under the window that let in the angled early morning sunlight. Everything normal, and yet all the little hairs on the back of his neck rose on end.

He -reached- with his Gifted senses and the room's walls became no barrier. Out in the office, Mrs. Shankar, his pretty new receptionist, glowed with Gifted presence as she looked towards the office door. It burst open and three men—unGifted—burst into the front office.

"What are you…!" Mrs. Shankar started to stand, her long dark hair around her shoulders, but the men swung weapons towards her.

Then the door to his office burst open and he faced three men in black fatigues holding very large automatic weapons. Richard took a deep breath to still the pounding of his heart. *Who were they? What did they want?*

Instead he said, "May I help you?"

He stayed where he was because he was a big man and his size could potentially be a threat to these men whose fingers seemed to rest perilously close to the weapons' triggers.

"Get your ass out of that chair," ordered one of the strangers. He was blond and his voice had a decidedly American accent. Not foreign terrorists, then. That was something. By their bearing they were military.

Richard eased himself up to standing, keeping his hands visible. "This is a government school attached to a top secret project. The faculty and staff are employees of an agency working with Homeland Security and have the highest clearances. I hope you know what you're doing, son."

"Shut the fuck up and get out here."

What the hell was going on? This had to be a mistake. It had to. The academy was sanctioned by the highest level of the American government.

But they waved him out of his office. Mrs. Shankar was already gone, out into the foyer where the morning's comforting quiet had been replaced by yells of protest and the running of feet as students were funneled through from the dorms, driven by more men with guns. Teachers came rushing down the stairs, rounded up by more black-clad men, and then Richard froze, his skin gone cold.

This was no mistake. This was a takedown.

A gun jabbed him in the back, but he stood his ground. He spun to face his captors. "This is my school. These students are under my protection and the protection of the government of the United States. Under whose orders are you acting?"

"Old man, your line of protection just got pulled. Now I'm going to count to three and then I'm pulling this trigger. If you want that to happen in front of all these kids, then you keep standing there asking questions."

The man's steel grey eyes said he meant what he said, and Richard's chill went icy cold. His first responsibility was to keep his students safe, but who had the power to pull the plug on the AGS school? Gleason, second in command of the AGS, would never do it. That could only mean one thing, and for a moment his knees went weak. For all intents and purposes the AGS was no more—and that meant he and the faculty were alone to deal with this. He clenched his jaw and went with the terrified children and staff, offering words of encouragement as they followed the main corridor to the gymnasium. That made sense. It was, aside from the cafeteria, the one place that could hold all the students and faculty.

The huge space echoed their footfall and the soft sobs of fear magnified to thunder. The mélange of scents of each Gifted student and faculty was masked by the sour-rust scent of fear. The black-clad men cut the faculty away from the students, himself included, and herded them to one side of the hall.

Not good. Not good at all, because the youngest students were starting to panic. The quiet sobs became louder.

"What the hell is this?" he demanded of the armed man guarding the faculty. "Since when is terrifying American children the role of the US military? I demand to speak to whoever's in charge!"

The soldier swung and Richard stepped sideways to avoid any blow. Instead, the black-clad man fired a single shot.

Red-hot pain slammed into his leg and he went down in a heap. The room seemed to telescope around him and the screams of the children and faculty came from a distance. He looked down to where his left leg bloomed bright red and blood spilled out onto the floor from the hole in his flesh. Around him the room was a sea of brilliant Gifted fishes and the small candles of the soldiers—no, mercenaries, because he liked to think that American soldiers wouldn't shoot defenseless men, women, and children—formed a net around them.

Something like silk grazed his hand and the image of one of his old students, Vallon Drake, came into his mind. Strange, he hadn't thought of her in years. She'd been his biggest problem child and the most brilliant graduate of the academy. God, he was so tired. He just wanted to close his eyes and sleep, but Mrs. Shankar was beside him, trying to stop the bleeding.

Out of the corner of his eye—*was that Vallon moving through the crowd of children?* No one seemed to see her, and when he looked in that direction, there were only frightened children being herded out the back door of the gym. The sound of a diesel engine and the clank of metal doors suggested a truck was there.

Another touch on his arm and this time he had to believe that maybe, somehow, impossibly, Vallon *was* here, because he couldn't help the children. The way he was bleeding out, he was dying. Any of the faculty who tried to do anything would be shot, too. Dammit, he needed vellum and ink, a weapon. But vellum and ink were kept locked away except during class time, against the temptation to create unsanctioned Change. It left them defenseless.

The touch came again and this time he held out his hand. The children were disappearing out the door and he had to do something. Tell someone. A tingle across his palm and he searched the air around him. No Vallon. Nothing, probably, but the imaginings of a wounded old man.

Amundson, he mouthed. *Amundson did this.* Because it could only be the Homeland Security Station Chief who had taken over the AGS and had made it clear he would never trust the Gifted.

He was cold, so cold, and Mrs. Shankar was crying as she held his shoulders. The children—the children were all gone and it was only the faculty left in the gymnasium. Even without him, the faculty were strong enough they could, even without the vellum, cause some damage to their attackers. If they thought of it. But then why would they think they needed to attack? They were American citizens in America.

That was when the black-clad men started shooting. Lovely Mrs. Shankar was one of the first to fall.

CHAPTER 1 —THE SCENT OF HOME

The dark wood stair railing had the unnaturally smooth feel of plastic under Vallon's hand as she came unsteadily down the stairs to the meeting in Elizabeth Ducharme's living room. Had she really seen what she'd seen, or was it a dream? It had been like an astral projection or—something. A dream with all the nightmarish aspects of foretelling. The children of the AGS Academy abducted in panel trucks with names like Piggly Wiggly and Cheetos on the sides. At least that was what she'd dreamed of in the overlong sleep of recovery. She'd needed that sleep after the demands of using the Gift to heal the destruction of New Madrid, Missouri. She had the Gift, but foretelling dreams weren't in her repertoire. Hell, they weren't in anyone's repertoire. Children's fairytales, that was what they were.

Her gut clenched, just like it had when she'd woken, dazed, from the nightmare and had to stagger to the toilet to empty her stomach.

The disturbing images seemed on continuous replay in her head. Couple the plastic feel of the newly recreated house with the thick tang of ozone and lightning caused by the huge task of healing the destruction of this part of the country, and she wasn't sure she could hold her nausea in check.

The ozone and ether and the plastic feeling of the house were the normal results of the power she'd used to undo the devastation of the New Madrid quake. The whole town probably felt just as plastic. Actually, given the wide swath of quake destruction, it was likely that she'd experience this fingernails-on-blackboard feeling of Change just about anywhere in the American Midwest. But it was the too-vivid images of the AGS Academy, on top of sensitivity called afterburn that came after working such massive Change, that made it feel like her head might explode at any moment.

Clinging to the railing, she felt her way cautiously down the stairs into a normal house that had previously been destroyed by the quake. Now, however, it stood right where it should be and her unGifted hosts, Elizabeth Ducharme and her daughter, Farrah, were safely back home none the wiser that their world had been destroyed one minute and restored the next. Such was the power of the Gift that Vallon and the others controlled. To the unGifted, though, they were simply guests staying at Elizabeth Ducharme's guesthouse.

The living room across from the stairs was filled with a mélange of scents—old spice, anise and mint, baby's breath, and the powerfully attractive scent of incense and cedar of Lebanon. At least it would be attractive if not for the fear-stink of her own body that tainted everything. She held onto the doorframe and took a deep breath before entering, because everyone was waiting for her—they just didn't know about the information she was bringing. The canaries in the huge cage by the front window set off a flurry of singing as she limped to Xavier's side. The whole room was like a flipping aviary, with the birds and the bird wallpaper and the feathers that seemed hung, pasted, or embroidered on everything.

Gregor Gleason, the ex-Chief of the ultra-secret American Geological Survey, the organization that was supposed to keep America safe from just the kind of attack that had occurred here at New Madrid, sat his cadaverous frame uneasily on one of Elizabeth Ducharme's uncomfortable-looking straight-backed faux-antique chairs. He'd drawn it in from the dining area at the back of the room. His skin was still slightly grey from his time in captivity when Wolf Amundson of Homeland Security had decided that Gregor was an enemy of the state. Beside him, on one end of the bird-feather patterned couch, perched Landon Snow. Her fastidious, diminutive mentor plucked at the pleats of his Colonel Saunders white trousers, but he looked up as she entered. His strange, blue-pink eyes almost seemed to glow, the way the light caught them through the gauzy living room curtains.

To Landon's right sat Fi Murdoch, Vallon's best friend, her blonde pixy cut hair scrubbed clean of the mud she'd been covered in last time Vallon had seen her at the quake epicenter. Beside her sat Jason Bryson, the tall, café au lait-skinned, Seattle Police detective who had for some reason followed Vallon here just like he'd been following her around in Seattle. It wasn't normal and it made her just a tad uncomfortable.

All her comrades. All had helped deal with the New Madrid quake, but it was the last person in the room who held her gaze. She knelt beside the feather-print Queen Anne chair and the tall, dark, and mysterious man who sat there. Xavier de Varga. His ragged dark hair hung over his collar and his forehead, and his skin was pulled tight across his hawkish features that always reminded her of Bedouins in long blue robes crossing a distant desert. But now his normally olive-toned skin was sallow and his hands made white-knuckled fists on his thighs.

"Xavier." She leaned in and grazed his lips with a kiss even though her afterburn flared with hyper-need of him as soon as she saw him. There was only one way to deal with the painful aftereffects of having used the Gift—and a most pleasurable way at that—but this was not the time. When their lips touched, she received the familiar sense of connection to this man who was everything in the world to her, but this was a wounded Xavier. She could see it in the slight wince as he moved and in the intensity of his black eyes and in the dark streaks that ran through his flaming Gifted essence when she -reached- to see him.

"Shouldn't you be in bed?" she asked. *And perhaps she could be with him.*

A single left-right of his head spoke of the tight control he had over himself. "Snow has patched me up for the moment. I will do until I can get medical attention." He frowned as his gaze met hers. "*Bela Menina,* are things well with you?"

Such a charming accent and a loving nickname she did not deserve. "Always. With you."

But she swung back to Landon and the others before he could read her any further. "Shouldn't he be in a hospital?"

Landon gave his usual slight shrug and smoothed the tip of a very pink tongue over his almost translucent lips. "With a bullet lodged in the chest, I should think so, but our mysterious friend does not seem inclined to go anywhere that his presence would have to be reported to authorities. I can do the surgery myself, but I need the proper supplies."

Xavier had been shot in the battle to stop an earthquake that would have destroyed America. Vallon's father, Francis Drake, had learned how to harness the power of Gifted and had planned to unzip the New Madrid fault lines. The resulting earthquake would have destroyed everything from Colorado to New York.

Tell them about her vision/dream/foretelling? She wasn't sure how to begin, given she wasn't sure what she'd really experienced.

"How do we get the equipment?" She reached for Xavier's hand, but then stopped herself. In his condition, the last thing he needed was to have to fend off the afterburn that must be radiating off of her. Xavier, too, simmered with his own use of power, but in his condition, dealing with the afterburn was far less a priority.

"Well, Pigeon, we could look for a surgical dealership and purchase the instruments, but I suggest that moving your friend and ourselves out of here might be the first order of business."

Gleason was nodding. "He's right. Amundson's gone nuts over the Gifted. I'd still be his prisoner if Detective Bryson hadn't gotten us both out. He'll be gunning for us now, and though we tried to cover our tracks, there's no question he'll be coming after us. It's only a matter of time before he finds this little hideout."

Her stomach flip-flopped again and she looked back at Xavier, calculating. Wolf Amundson, Chief of Seattle's Homeland Security Station, on the warpath? That could never be good. The unfortunate thing was, the news jived with the horror she'd lived in her vision/astral travel/whatever. The white-blond Chief of Station had never trusted the Gifted and had forcibly taken over the AGS. The last thing she wanted was to have to face him. But Xavier didn't look able to travel anywhere.

"Where are you suggesting we go?" She stood up protectively behind his chair.

Landon looked around the room and then down at his hands again. "I can't think of too many safe places right now, but I do know of one. It's in the desert outside of Las Vegas. A little anomaly I discovered a number of years back. Off the map, you might say, and completely safe, especially from people like Amundson." He glanced at Jason and nodded. "No offence intended."

Jason shrugged. "None taken." He was the only unGifted in the room.

Gleason shook his bald head. "I won't be going. Amundson has got to be stopped. If I know him at all, after losing me he'll be arresting every other Gifted he knows of. Given what he did to me, I hate to think what he could do to the others. If he catches them off the job, they'll have absolutely no defense given that Homeland Security required all vellum and ink be held at AGS headquarters. I sent word to scatter before I left, but I doubt everyone was able to get out—not with their families."

He hefted himself out of the chair. "I'm headed for Washington. Director Fitzsimmons might be a power-hungry fool in some ways, but he's not stupid. If I can show him that Amundson is out of control and actually weakening the country, then maybe he'll remove Amundson and put things back the way they were. Besides, he needs us to deal with the rogue Gifted who caused the quake. The destruction of their installation won't have got them all."

There was a pause of disbelief in the room, and Vallon felt her skin crawl. *If her father was still alive…* He had to be stopped, and she was the one to do it, but Gleason shook his head.

"I've got to do something, and running-and-hiding is not my thing. I'm a bureaucrat and I know how to get things done. Washington, and Homeland Security, is my job."

And what was hers? Vallon's fingertips brushed the edge of Xavier's shoulders from where they rested on his chair back, but she should be going with Gleason if he was taking on her father.

"So we're just going to allow Amundson to drive us out of Seattle?" Jason asked with a frown that placed a deep V across his usually smooth forehead. "That doesn't seem right to me. And what about the other people he's hurting? Are we just going to let him do it? Round up the Gifted in Seattle and do whatever he wants to them?"

All eyes shifted to Jason.

"Why should you care, Detective Bryson? You aren't one of us," Landon asked. His expression was one of clinical interest.

"I'd say like hell I'm not. I might not have the Gift, but I happen to have a little talent to know when your Gift is being used, and he wants that. I'd prefer to have my life back." Jason's gaze flickered around the room and landed on Vallon. "I'm prepared to go back to Seattle and try to stop him from there, but I can't do it alone. Heck, can't one of you just wipe him out?"

Vallon met Landon's gaze. It said Jason might have a point, but if her father was out there….

She swallowed and took a deep breath, because she didn't want to do this, but at this point if they didn't stop Amundson's destruction of the Gifted there'd be no one left to stop the rogues. "I think Jason's right. There are too many innocents who could be hurt by what he's doing." *Tell them about what she'd seen?* But she didn't know if it was true. Given all she'd been through in the past few days, it *could* simply be dream product of a very overwhelmed mind. It could.

But Amundson did need to be dealt with, because he could potentially lead a crusade that could destroy everything the Gifted had built in the United States. It could lead to a pogrom worse than the medieval witch hunts that had burned so many innocents. If the Chief was going to Washington and Landon was taking Xavier to the safety of his hideout to heal, then that left her to check on what Amundson was doing and stop him if need be.

"I'll go. I can rally the Agents. I have to get Maggie anyway. I can't expect my neighbor to take care of her forever. Besides, Amundson might use her as a hostage." She managed a grin. Maggie, her flirty, opinionated, black and white cat was a problem child, but had been the only constant in her life for the past five years. The little vixen might treat anything Vallon did with disdain, but she was Vallon's cat and Vallon wouldn't leave her little buddy behind.

"*Bela Menina*, non. Rethink this, please." Xavier reached up and caught her hand, pulled it onto his shoulder, and the touch of his warm dry fingers and the throb of power up through his shoulder washed over her like a heady perfume of cedar. The afterburn flared, but he somehow controlled it as their essences merged. It became a slow, banked throb of desire that was fixated on him. He wanted her. He wanted her with him where he could keep her safe.

With the deepest of reluctance she slipped her hand free and came around in front of him. "Jason's right, Xavier. What if Gleason can't do what we need in Washington? Then someone has to be on the ground to act. Next to you, I'm the best one to do it in terms of power. Besides, they won't expect me to come waltzing back to Seattle. Not right into the center of the fire, so to speak." She looked at the others. "Am I right?"

Landon thought a minute, his gaze making small leaps from her to Xavier, assessing. Finally he gave a small nod, and that was something, because Landon had the quickest mind she'd ever seen. Sometimes it almost seemed like he could read the future—or maybe it was just that he set people in motion so the future unfolded as he planned. It was an ability she wished she had. She'd create a place where she and Xavier could be alone to explore the bounds of their love for the rest of their lives. But apparently that wasn't about to happen now. She turned back to Xavier.

"It makes sense, Xavier. The Agents that are still free need someone to pull them together, and I won't be able to help Landon with your surgery, anyway. I'd just be standing around going crazy with worry until it's all over."

Xavier's fathomless gaze seemed to drink her in. Then his hand came up and he ran a knuckle down the side of her face with an intimacy that sent shock waves running through her. Everyone in the room had to see the flames erupt out of her head, the way the afterburn's lust burst forth for just a moment. She pulled back.

"You—you're not supposed to do that." At least not in front of the others where she couldn't just jump his bones.

His hard mouth quirked in a wicked grin. "You are intent on going to Seattle with a handsome man. I wished to remind you of me."

And he had. The memory of that sensuous burst seemed to reverberate inside her and was distinctly connected to his incense and cedar of Lebanon scent.

"As if I needed reminding." But she turned back to the others as Fi uncurled her feet from under her.

"What about me? Do I go with you? I've got a job to get back to, Vallon." She pressed her hands between her knees and looked up at Vallon with those huge blue eyes that, in school, had always managed to get Vallon to do whatever she needed—until Fi had disappeared as a child.

"I don't believe that's possible, Fi." Gleason's deep voice rumbled in the room. "Seattle is too dangerous for any Gifted, and Amundson knows you are one of us. It's especially dangerous for a Gifted without full training. You'd have no protection from him. No, I've given it some thought: Landon will need to focus on helping Xavier into hiding. That is dangerous work. Vallon and Detective Bryson go into their own dangers. I think the best course of action is for you to come with me to Washington."

She frowned. "But my job...."

"Fi. You should go with him. Really." If what Gleason said was true, then the students at the academy might really be in serious danger. She had to tell. "I think... I think it's already started—Amundson's round up, I mean." All eyes centered on her and she steadied herself with one knee slung on the arm of Xavier's chair and told them about her dream-vision. "The thing is, it wasn't a dream. Not really. Not the way Headmaster Smith could sense me and not the way he told me something I couldn't have known myself. If what I saw was right, then the entire school faculty is dead and all those children are in Amundson's hands. Capturing you, Fi, would just give him even more of a hold over us. I'm going to Seattle to check whether it really happened and, if it did, to find and free those kids." Which meant she was going to have to deal with Amundson. How, she didn't know; and the thought of what she might *have* to do filled her with disquiet. Killing people was not something she'd signed on for.

The whole room was silent; no one argued that what she said was crazy. Gleason paced behind the sofa. Landon seemed to stare into space as if he could read the future there. Xavier had closed his eyes, his ragged hair falling around his face as if he were in prayer. The entire room pulsed with an undercurrent of anger, but these were not men who shouted and yelled and attacked from rage. They were seasoned warriors who thought carefully about their battles.

Finally Xavier looked up, his face even greyer than it had been. "I believe Vallon speaks the truth. There is a blankness where once there was a teeming shoal of Gifted life."

Vallon's stomach felt like a stone.

Gleason's gaze hardened. "And so, young Fiona, you will come with me." He came around the end of the couch to face her. "Accept it. You cannot go back to your job as long as Amundson is looking. That leaves going into hiding with Landon or traveling with me. I think Landon will be busy enough without also caring for you."

Her friend's frown had turned into an out-and-out pout, but she finally nodded. Vallon gave her a hug. "Honey—Fi—you've made the right decision."

Fi glared up at her. "For you, maybe. So you don't have to have me around."

Vallon held Fi away from her and looked her in the eyes. "If you believe that, you're no longer the smart woman I know you are."

Finally, Fi's quirky grin came to life. She sighed. "All right. You win again."

Vallon grabbed her in another hug, ignoring the uncomfortable flare of afterburn at the touch of another Gifted. "Fi, we will always be best friends and I will always need you around—and not for cycling. What you did saved us all. We—I—will always remember that. You're a hero."

Fi's pale features brightened. "Really?"

"Absolutely. Without what you did, I couldn't have acted and none of this would be here now." She waved her hand around at the fearful aviary-feeling room and the wafting scent of fresh cookies that came in from the kitchen at the back of the house. Farrah Ducharme's happy five-year-old chatter was the kitchen background sound to their discussion. But there would be no such happy sound at the academy again.

Vallon released Fi and looked at Chief Gleason. "So it's settled then. You go to Washington with Fi, Landon takes care of Xavier, and I go to Seattle to rally the agents and free those students and stop Amundson. Afterwards we'll deal with what's left of the rogue Gifted."

The others nodded. All except Xavier. He looked at her out of desert-night dark eyes, and she inhaled his heady scent of incense and cedar of Lebanon. These people were what passed for family, and Xavier most of all. They had come together here after their whole world had fallen apart. They had thought they'd put the world together again.

Apparently not.

She leaned in to place a soft kiss on Xavier's lips. "You won't disappear again, will you?"

A small shake of his head and they touched foreheads together.

The afterburn flared painfully. Fitting, given it hurt that they were deciding to tear themselves apart again.

CHAPTER 2 — SHADE AND SHADOWS

Three days later: Outside Redmond, Washington

The sunrise over the hulking volcanic bulk of Mount Rainier was one of the most glorious sights Vallon had ever seen. The view over the Pacific Northwest landscape felt brand new, like she'd never really seen it before, but it was more like she'd never really appreciated it, given she'd grown up with it. Everywhere it was green: mountainsides, fields, yards. A miracle of verdant color compared to the parched landscape around New Madrid. When she rolled the window down on the used Buick Xavier had purchased—because they could not chance using their bank accounts since Amundson was surely tracking them—the air was smooth as wine and just as redolent with the sea and the green growth. Home. Her belly fluttered with a little nostalgic excitement.

And fear. Somehow Amundson had taken down a school full of teachers and their students. He'd known exactly when to go in and face the least resistance. He'd also managed to somehow disperse or neutralize the Seattle AGS agents because she hadn't been able to sense any of them as they drove north on I-5. That didn't mean that they weren't here, just that they'd somehow managed to hide their presence like Xavier had, when he'd lived on a houseboat so that the water masked him. Gleason would probably suggest that she abort her plans to rescue the students until she had backup, but with Amundson on the warpath, who knew when help could arrive. That meant Jason was all she had.

Well, she wasn't some unprepared Gifted Amundson could take by surprise or an untrained student. *She'd* never followed the rules about leaving all specially prepared vellum and ink locked at AGS headquarters.

Hell, she rarely followed the rules at all—at least that was what Gleason had always said about her.

But the fact she couldn't find agents to contact meant the first order of business was checking out the AGS Academy, a place she'd avoided all the years since her graduation. They exited I-405 and headed east on I-520, ending on the eastern edges of Redmond, then took one of the side roads eastward and up into the rolling, treed hills of the suburbs. There were new housing developments of ticky-tacky box houses being built among the trees, but mostly there were acreages, and the academy had one of the largest—fifty treed acres that allowed privacy for the unusual topics taught to the unusual students who attended the academy.

Vallon had Jason park a mile away from the main driveway, off the road in what was, by the discarded prophylactics, still a popular meeting place for the town's teenagers. With the engine off, she stepped out into cool, blackberry-scented air. Brambles surrounded the parking area and sent long tendrils up into the trees, so that huge juicy berries hung lush just above her. She plucked a few and sucked their sweet juice off her fingers while she waited for Jason to come around the car.

"So just what have you got planned?" He looked dubiously at their surroundings. "Back to the road and walk in?"

She shook her head, trying to get her bearings. It had been a number of years since she'd last been here. Heck, some of the older prophylactics could be the remains of some of her dalliances.

There. One of the large tree trunks split into a Y she remembered. That meant that right about here....

She tucked her fists into the cuffs of her denim jacket and reached into the brambles and pushed. Just like old times, the whole section of blackberries trundled aside.

"They are still using it!" She couldn't help herself. She grinned like a kid. "I made this back when I was in school as a way to cover my tracks when I was dating town boys." She ducked her head at the opening the rolling panel of bush exposed. "Come on. This is the gate to the back door of the academy."

She stepped through to the shaded pathways of the forest and she was young again, coming back from another secret tryst she'd had to deal with afterburn, and planning how to evade Headmaster Smith and the other faculty. Except this time afterburn rippled through her, and instead of avoiding people, she was trying to reach them.

If she wasn't too late.

Headmaster Smith mouths a word and the men start shooting.

Let it be a foretelling dream that hasn't yet happened. Let Xavier be wrong, and when I get there I'll find students tucked securely in classes and Headmaster Smith grumpy in his office. She refused to use her Gift to check.

She pushed through huckleberry bushes and third-growth brush and ferns that had grown up around the bases of the cedar, spruce, and fir. Mushrooms grew in the gloom, and bracket fungus girded some of the lower reaches of the occasional poplar. Jason at her heels, she led him down into the gulley that flanked the rear and western sides of the academy. The gulley had once been home to too many derelicts escaping Seattle. She and some of the braver students had also used the gulley as a secret place to practice with their power—much to the official displeasure of the academy. Unofficially, they always watched carefully to see who had the gumption to try it.

They reached the bottom and the trickling rill of water that ran even after a long hot summer. Small ferns coated the shallow banks of the rill, glowing where they were spotlit by sunlight that found its way through the treetops. There were the three boulders where she'd sometimes sit with Fi just to get away from the rest of the students and there was the area devoid of plants and flattened by student footfall, the place where she'd learned more about her Gift than in all the academy classes. The private exploration here and the small duels they'd fought against each other had taught her to improvise and to look deeper and for new ways to deal with problems. The fact that everyone had known about this place and the faculty hadn't stopped it, suggested that they actually sanctioned it, though they couldn't seem to be doing just that.

"Huh," she said stopping and considering. She'd never thought of things that way before.

"What it is it?" Jason came up too close behind her, sending off a pinging mass of afterburn like hot brands applied to her skin.

She stepped away from him and motioned around her. "I used to come here a lot. I just realized that all the rules that I thought the academy had were really just a figment of my imagination." She shook her head and then motioned to the steep hillside on the other side of the gulley. "This way."

A thrush cried in the forest and somewhere nearby a woodpecker began his tattoo in the treetops as she started up the steep path. Even after little rain over the past month, the soil was soft and crumbly, making it unsteady under her feet. She grabbed hold of brush and tree branches to haul herself up and heard Jason grunting behind. Sweat stung her eyes and she stripped off her jacket and tied it around her waist. Her t-shirt stuck to her and she could smell herself even through the sweet pine and underbrush of the forest.

They reached the top of the path, both of them puffing.

"You do that often?" Jason asked as he leaned his hands on his knees.

"Used to," she managed as she copied his stance. She nodded at the path. "That way leads to the circular drive. I suggest we ease around the place through the trees and come in the back. We'll be able to judge pretty quickly whether anything's happened."

She felt Jason's regard like a weight on her skin and she met his gaze. "I know. It's crazy, right?"

"Not so crazy. I know you've got special talents. As a matter of fact, I'll be more surprised if something hasn't happened."

Not what she wanted to hear. She wanted to hear the shouts of students on the soccer pitch, smell the smoke from the smoking pit. She thought of the silent screams branded on children's faces, of the pain and helpless fear of Headmaster Smith, and shivered. "Let's hope you're wrong."

She turned to the trees and the faint trail winding through the huge trunks. Please let her be mistaken.

It took another fifteen minutes to reach the rear of the school. It hunkered uncannily like in her vision, amidst the green of its playing fields. No one lounged on the green grass the way she and Fi had done way back when, and no one slouched in the smoking pit, either. The only sounds were the questions of birds and the hush of the breeze in the trees and the steady thump of her blood in her ears. She hunkered down on her heels to consider and Jason knelt beside her.

"So?" he asked.

"It's too quiet. On a day like today there should be somebody out here, because I cannot believe that every student believes that tanning is bad for your health."

She inhaled, but there was only the cedar and pine and Jason's licorice-spice scent, none of the copper fear from her vision. There was no help for it. She'd put it off longer than she should have. She -reached- and the blue and green day shifted to grey, misty outlines and the flare of living things. The forest flared into candles, a few brighter flames where the birds and small animals took cover. Beside her the flickering flame that was Jason guttered and pulsed like all humans, but for just a brief instant there was something more there, something interesting. When she looked directly at him, the 'something' was gone and he was definitely just the infuriating Detective Bryson. But there was no sign of any Gifted in the school.

Feeling sick, she stood. "Might as well get this over with."

Jason stopped her with a hand on her arm that sent the energy fields raging in her body.

She ripped loose. "What the hell do you think you're doing?"

"Stopping you. In a situation like this, you don't just go barging in."

"Oh really?" She crossed her arms and faced him. "Just what do we need to do?"

"We need to case the joint and check where people are. If something did happen here, we don't want to go waltzing right into them, do we?"

Vallon looked to the treetops and back to the infuriating detective. Why the heck she had to travel with him made no sense. In fact, she'd tried to leave him a couple of times on the drive from New Madrid, but he'd caught her at it every time, almost as if he expected it.

"You think I don't know my business, is that it? Well, I happen to have a few talents, Detective. There is no one in the academy. No one. Zilch. Zero. Nothing. There are, however, a few unGifted posted in the front—observers, I would say. So if we are careful and stay to the back rooms of the building, we should be okay. All right? Good enough?"

That seemed to shut him up. He finally nodded. "I wasn't questioning your abilities…." He looked like he'd been slapped down, but he was coming up fighting. She could almost like him for that, but not quite.

"Yes. You were." She turned on her heel and stepped carefully through the last of the brush and started across the field at a lope.

She reached the rear door of the dorms and a queasy sense of déjà vu brought bile to the back of her throat. In her dream/vision, this was where she had entered the school buildings, but it was also the most direct approach. Heat came off the red brick as if a fire raged within, but it was only the sunlight reflecting off the stone. Jason came up beside her and she resented his presence, didn't want him seeing the remains of this part of her life. He knew too much about her already. She didn't need to feed him the details.

"Why don't you wait here and I'll do a quick search. Then we can get out of Dodge and figure out what to do."

He shook his head. "I'm your backup, not your enemy. I'm staying with you, so accept it."

But there was something unfamiliar and hungry in his gaze so that she had to look away. "Fine. Whatever."

She pushed the door open and slid inside into shade and shadows.

The air was too still, with none of the frenetic turbulence that came from too much student angst. The scent of girlish perfume, of newly-discovered shaving creams and men's colognes had all faded. The childhood scent of stuffed bears and children's shampoo was barely a memory. She walked quickly and quietly down the hall towards the doors that gave onto the front foyer, the school administration wing, and the school gymnasium. If there was going to be any sign of what had happened, it had to be in one of those locations.

The grand foyer of the school had steep stairs to either side of the front hall that wound up to the classrooms. The parquet floor was dark, not with age, but from the passage of too many feet. The massive front doors with their stained glass insets gave onto the broad circular driveway out front. She -reached- and found the car out front that she'd noticed before. Two figures sat in it, radiating their unGifted nature. No surprise there. They were watchers ready to pick up any Gifted who might arrive, or to turn away anyone else. So she and Jason just needed to stay away from the windows and they should be okay.

The headmaster's office was first, so they ducked into the administrative office and the sense of displacement almost overwhelmed her. How many times had she sat exactly there, next to the door to Headmaster Smith's office, straining to hear as Landon and the headmaster discussed her fate. How many times had she sat waiting for discipline or, more likely, sat there planning how to get out of it? She screwed up her face and took a quick look at the admin clerk's desk—it looked like she'd been taken in the middle of making a student file—and then opened the door to Smith's office.

She expected him to be there, in all his ginger-haired, burly glory, but there were only slatted bars across his desk from sunlight through the half-open venetian window blinds. This room clearly hadn't been left untouched. Papers that Smith had always kept in neat piles on his desktop were strewn across the floor. Desk and file cabinet drawers yawned emptily open and books were pulled out of the bookshelves and left where they'd fallen.

Not good. So what had they been looking for? Assuming things went as she had seen, then they knew they had the children and faculty.

Families? That made sense. Smith would have records of all the children who had come through the school right from the beginning. They could hit at once and do a complete roundup of every agent's family across the United States. They could also link children to extended families.

Her legs went weak as she considered the implication. "He's really going after everyone." She glanced at Jason, who prowled the edge of the room, picking up books to examine the spine and then set them down again.

"Looks that way," he said with a shake of the head. "This is really serious, isn't it?"

"Life and death and genocide serious. So yes." If you could say that those with the Gift were a race within the race. It was like rounding up and imprisoning everyone with blue eyes. She inhaled the musty paper scent that was all that remained in the place that had once been the powerful center of the law in her universe. How many people had a chance to go back and realize just how tenuous everything they knew was? It left her stomach knotted.

"I guess that just leaves the gym." But she really didn't want to go in there. Not now, not ever again, because she knew what she'd find. It took effort to leave the office and head in that direction.

She hesitated just outside the gymnasium door, steeling herself for what came next. When she -reached- the room was empty.

"Do you want me to do this?" Jason asked.

She shook her head. "These are my people. I do this."

Easing the door open, she stepped inside. Copper and fear had left a thick metallic tang in the air that coated the back of her tongue. The high gymnasium walls echoed too loudly with the screams she hadn't heard before. She wanted to cover her ears, hold her breath, and clamp her eyes shut so hard she could erase the memory of this place. The thick ammonia smell of piss spoke of how frightened the children had been. And then there was the copper-penny scent that confirmed the worst of her fears.

Swiping her hair back from her eyes, she swallowed and paced across the dimly lit basketball court. In her vision the room had been brightly lit, the floor crowded with the terrified children. Their presences crowded around her begging for help so she felt sick to her stomach, and then angry. Mightily angry. So angry she could hurt someone. So angry the force of the earth's ley lines fizzled up and through her veins so she felt as if her skin was sparking. She fought back the need to injure something, because that wasn't her way.

There was where Headmaster Smith had stood with the other faculty. There was where he had fallen when he was shot in the leg, and there was where she had, somehow, communicated with him. The caramel-colored gym floorboards were smeared with blood—too much for just Smith's. So all of her vision had been true. The faculty—Smith, Professor Goldman in trigonometry, Mrs. Beaton in Gift control, the others—were all gone.

A wave of sorrow washed over her. Those teachers were more like her parents than her father had ever been. They, and Landon, had been the constants in her world as she grew up, even though she'd never thought herself close to them. Knowing they were dead, though, it was like part of herself was gone. Another connection to her past lost, and she hung disconnected from everything. It was worse than the meeting with her father. Since the events in New Madrid, she'd tried not to think about what her father's actions towards her had meant. He didn't love her, had never loved her. She had always been alone.

She shook herself. These people at least had cared enough to make sure she didn't hurt anyone or get hurt herself. She stood there, trying to steady her breathing, trying to hold onto the anger instead of the sorrow.

"I guess we know it wasn't a dream," she said softly, and met Jason's gaze. "I could kill Amundson for this, but I know why he did it. The faculty had the best chance of wrecking his plans. They had enough power they might have done something even without the vellum. If they did, Amundson's men might have lost the children."

Jason shook his head. "You march into Homeland Security and you're good as dead yourself."

"I don't need to go into Homeland Security to do it. I could wipe their headquarters off the face of the earth from here." And she could, even though it might not be a good idea. All she needed was pen and vellum, and she knew where she could get those—her basement, when she went to get Maggie.

"No. You won't. There are innocents there, too, remember? You don't do that to innocent people. Wasn't that what the whole New Madrid thing was about? Saving the innocents?"

He was right, but that didn't help how she felt at the moment. She studied the bloodied floor. "Where are the bodies? They didn't even leave them for a proper burial. Where did they take the children? That's the first thing to worry about."

Terrified faces in the back of a truck. The horrible slide of the rear door cutting them off.

She jerked out of the memory and bile burned the back of her teeth.

There was nothing more here to see, just dried piss and blood and vacancy.

§

A road trip was not exactly how Landon Snow envisioned himself spending his time, but a road trip alone with one of the Gifted from beyond the AGS was something beyond his wildest dreams. Well, perhaps not. Because he *had* dreamed of having time to talk to one of the great ones who must be out there according to scientific principles. If the level of Gift in the population of Gifted was a bell curve, then there theoretically had to be those people at the far upper end of the curve. People who would make the talents of the AGS agents look like children's hopscotch efforts next to an Olympic hurdler. Xavier de Varga, slumped only half conscious in the passenger seat next to him, was one of them, or at least everything Vallon had told him had indicated as much.

He tightened his hands on the jeep's steering wheel and aimed down the arrow-straight ruts that passed for a road in the desert landscape. Dust rose in a huge fishtail behind them and threatened to inundate them if he couldn't outrun it. The jeep's air conditioner blasted away, but couldn't stop the glare of the sun shining through the windshield. The bare skin of his hands stung as if they were sunburned. Thank God for the long-sleeved linen shirt and trousers he wore as protection. A panama hat, purchased in Las Vegas when they dumped the Prius and bought the jeep, made him feel like a pimp. All he needed was a gold chain around his neck—but he wasn't about to pick up that affectation.

The barren mountains and rocky desert seemed to stretch forever, like a moonscape. Except the moon had never been hot enough to fry eggs on concrete, at least he didn't think so. Southeast and behind sat the Sodom and Gomorrah of Las Vegas. No one there had ever tried to raise themselves up like Landon intended. Alchemist, researcher, and general fixer of problems pertinent to the Gifted, this was his turn to get what he had always wanted. He would learn about the Others as he had come to call them, and he would demand their help in training his skills. A lifetime of being the only Gifted in the AGS with no ability to cause Change would be over. Then he would show everyone just what Landon Snow was made of. He might not be a field agent, but he could be far more than he was. Far more. All his life he'd felt greatness in his bones and been denied it. Well, no more.

He glanced over at de Varga, slumped beside him. The man's sun-darkened countenance carried an unhealthy grey undertone. Frankly, with the bullets lodged in his chest, it was a wonder he was still breathing. He should have been in a hospital three days ago, but that just wasn't possible. Not only would gunshot wounds draw the police, they could draw Amundson and Homeland Security down on them. Landon didn't figure spending time in Amundson's care was going to do anything for Xavier's health, let alone what it would do for his own. He and Amundson had no love lost between them, and Xavier—well, Xavier de Varga was far too valuable an asset to take a chance on losing.

So Landon had bundled him into his little rental Prius, disabled the GPS in the car so he couldn't be tracked, and had headed here.

Northward, rugged mountains lifted their heads out of the military installation known to the media and conspiracy theorists as Area 51. Ahead lay the wide swath of rocky desert and low brush that was Nellis Air Force Base's nuclear testing range. Not exactly a place to be, and he'd too frequently been pursued by military patrols when he'd previously traveled this way.

Each time he'd managed to reach his secret installation before they could catch him. This time he planned to as well.

The vast plateau stretched towards the California mountains that lay like a bruise on the distance. Landon -reached- into Gifted sight and the distance between the rumbling jeep and the horizon seemed foreshortened and blurred with a heat mirage that sent radiating streaks into the sky. The middle distance became the dark ruts of the road leading forward and the wavering landscape beside it—something any mind would interpret as nothingness—just more of the same desert terrain of brown rocks and desiccated shrubs and rattlesnakes and small desert animals—fox, mouse, road runner.

Except it wasn't. The first time he had come here he sought a kidnapped girl and found her secreted in a place so secret no one without the Gift would ever find it. The original 'owners' of the anomaly were long gone to their young graves after they refused to become part of the AGS. The only two other people who knew of the place would never betray him out of respect for what he had done for them years before, and the need to protect their own Gifted identities.

He tromped on the gas a little harder and the jeep seemed to skitter and jump from pothole to pothole, and then the landscape suddenly shifted before his eyes as if he had crossed a line. He had. A line between one reality and the next. Suddenly he drove through a landscape of green grass with a small spring coiling through the verdant green. He slammed on the brakes, turned the wheel, and coasted the last few feet so the jeep stopped right next to the small installation he'd built himself. He stopped the car and climbed out.

Crickets chirruped from around the base of the prefab structure he'd hauled out here in pieces, then labored by himself to put together into the smooth-sided bungalow-sized building. Broad windows—now shuttered—filled the front of the building that served as living quarters, but around the side and back, the walls were solid—the better to keep any possible intruders out of things they should know nothing of.

Grasshoppers leapt around his legs and birds sang from the trees he'd planted next to the stream. Just because this was a working installation, didn't mean that aesthetics shouldn't be attended to.

The place—the entire hundred feet wide, mile long wedge of landscape—was an anomaly no one, including he, would ever have believed existed. It was the product of an older time of maps made by surveyors who had to cross the landscape on foot to measure the location of landscape features. Inevitably the human process resulted in human error and places where the survey lines didn't quite meet. Putting those errors down on paper had cemented the landscape in human consciousness, but left thin wedges of reality that were quite literally 'up for grabs' to become whatever the finder of one of the wedges wished it to be. In most of the world, the spread of human habitation and improved mapping procedures had erased such anomalies. Here though, next to one of the nation's most top secret installations, overhead mapping wasn't quite so careful in order to maintain national secrets. The result was that the anomaly held—for now.

It was the perfect secret base for Landon's operations and he would prefer to keep it this way. Vallon and Gleason might be good to help him, but he knew what Vallon would say if she understood his plans.

The jeep shifted beside him, the springs groaning slightly. Then the passenger car door opened and Xavier leaned out, clinging to the door frame with one hand while the other hugged his chest as if he was afraid his lungs and heart might fall out. The harsh sunlight only emphasized the lines of pain on his features and the clotted blood on his clothing.

"Where are we now? Have we arrived?" he asked.

Landon nodded and went to him. "We have. I haven't been here in a few months—too much going on with all the changes at the AGS— but I always keep a full surgical kit ready. You never know what could happen." *Like who was going take over the AGS and what Other was going to fall into his hands.* "We should get you inside and settled. Can you walk on your own?"

Xavier raked him with a night-dark gaze that seemed to speak voluminous doubts about Landon. Then a wry smile curved his lips. "I think I will have to, no?"

His throat worked with effort, but the next instant he was standing—apparently by force of will alone. He wavered there for a moment, so Landon went to him.

"Use my shoulder for balance if you like."

The man's powerful hand fell on his shoulder and squeezed, and for a moment Landon froze at the powerful sense of the man's presence. Incense and cedar of Lebanon almost overwhelmed him, as did his sense of being very small indeed. Smaller than the desert rodents that found their way into the wedge.

But that didn't mean that de Varga knew what Landon had planned. He quieted his mind, breathed out a calming breath. "Follow me."

He kept all intention other than to heal from his mind, and it must have worked. Xavier followed him passively to the front door.

An electronic key-pad protected the entry. He glanced up at Xavier's sallow features. "Anyone who doesn't know the code is in for a surprise. The entire door becomes electrified and there's a metal plate in the ground." He tapped the earth with his moccasin-covered toe, waiting for the click that would allow him inside.

Xavier raised one arched black brow. "A lot of trouble for a building in the middle of nowhere."

Landon smiled. "Literally, my friend. Quite literally. No one knows of these places between. They've been lost for centuries."

Xavier inhaled deeply and his eyes seemed to change for a moment and look beyond the landscape. "Most interesting. The place feels new, unused."

"I haven't been here for a while." Landon tapped in the secondary code and the door clicked and swung open, releasing a puff of slightly musty air. He led Xavier inside, and lights flashed on around the room to reveal his familiar living area: cream-colored leather couches and chairs, low, chrome tables, light fixtures of chrome that arched over the tables and gave a diffuse light-and-shadow pattern over the cream shag carpet. He'd virtually replicated his comfortable apartment in every way—with a few improvements thrown in for good measure. A complete kitchen filled the rear of the room, but was separated by a black granite-topped island. Landon touched a button on the wall and broad panels slid aside to reveal the windows and the view outside. Air conditioning began to hum in the background.

Xavier studied his surroundings. "You live well, but I think surgery here might damage your carpet."

The damned man was far too superior in his attitude, but Landon only smiled. Let the man think he was a useful fool, just like all the others. He knew they were wrong. He knew what was coming.

"This is the living quarters," he said cordially. "The surgical theater is through here."

He crossed the room, Xavier still leaning on his shoulder. The man leaned more heavily, so whether he wanted to admit it or not, he was getting weaker. That should make Landon's plans easier.

A door that fit perfectly into the wall was marked only by the seam and another digital key pad. Landon entered the code and touched his thumbprint to a pad. He felt, rather than saw, Xavier's brows rise.

"I planned this place with the contingency that enemies would find it. No one is getting in without my permission," Landon said as the door clicked so quietly it could barely be heard over the air conditioning.

Xavier's brow rose again. "One could almost think you were preparing to repel an attack."

Landon looked up at him sharply. "And with the state the AGS is in, that seems imminent, even likely." Even though the place had been built long before this current crisis. Being as unfavored by the gods as Landon's physical attributes were, he had always been an analytical thinker. It was not difficult to imagine the circumstances of the Gifted and the Homeland Security worsening. But that wasn't why the rest of the installation had been built. No, that was part of his private planning, for exactly this contingency.

He shoved open the door and a long line of ceiling-level lights sprang to life down the sides of a corridor. The pale yellow-painted corridor was sweetly utilitarian and devoid of the unnecessary fripperies of artwork found in most research facilities in a misguided need to 'humanize' the installation. One bare wall ran the length of the outside of the building. The other held three doors to his various workrooms: Data Collection and Analysis; Decoctions; and Pure Research.

He led Xavier towards the research door and felt the man's hand stiffen on his shoulder.

"Is something wrong?" he asked, looking up at the foreigner.

Xavier's hawk features were alive and searching, his nostrils flared as if he was some feral thing that could sense danger. Landon forced himself to relax for anything else would only increase Xavier's wariness. He glanced at Landon and held, and Landon could have sworn he felt a sweep of awareness across his mind, as if the foreign man scanned him. Landon knew he had to act. He cocked his head at the closed doorway.

"We really need to get you settled and get this done. You've lost too much blood as it is."

As if in answer, Xavier swayed and Landon bit back his satisfaction when the larger man nodded.

The research installation lay in darkness until Landon toggled the switch by the door. Harsh fluorescent light filled every corner, illuminating an operating theater and sterile cupboards and wash racks around the exterior of the room. Xavier stopped dead, his gaze wary, his nostrils wide. "What is this place?"

Could he smell it then? The deaths of the young men who had long ago kidnapped a young girl and brought her here? Landon had caught up to them, had used AGS agents to subdue them, and had brought them out here, using his own means of getting them inside and settled in this room. People who had used a young girl as they had, who had chanced exposing the existence of the Gifted to the entire populace, had posed too great a danger if they were loose in the population. Instead, Landon had found a better use for them.

A painful, lingering, purposeful use that had illuminated so much of his research into the care, feeding, and restraint of Gifted. They had died giving the AGS tools like they had not had before.

"We need to get you settled here." He indicated the main operating table.

Xavier miraculously climbed up and settled himself with a low groan as he lay down. His eyes were closed, his face pale, and his pulse jagged and powerful at the side of this throat. This was the specimen Landon had always longed for. One of the Others. One of the outliers on the bell-curve. He fished a vial out of the back of the neat chrome refrigerator in the corner and drew a syringe full of clear liquid. Then he returned to Xavier, holding the needle next to the other man's neck.

All he had to do was slide it in. Slide it in and things could begin.

He must have moved, although he would afterwards swear he hadn't. But Xavier's hand flashed out and caught his wrist so he almost dropped the syringe.

"What are you trying to do, little man? I'm not some experimental pig for you to play with."

Almost as if he knew. Almost as if he smelled.

Landon forced a chuckle, pasting the smile onto his face, but Xavier still had not opened his eyes. His breath sounded harsh and he gave off the sour scent of sticky sweat over blood. Landon eased his wrist loose. "This is a sedative. It will ready your body for the anesthetic and will reduce the pain of the procedure."

The grasp on his arm was numbing his hand, but finally Xavier sighed and Landon eased his hand loose.

"Good man. I was hoping you'd relax." And give in and make this easy, because in any physical altercation, Landon Snow was sure to be the loser.

He stepped in close and inhaled Xavier's exotic scent. Heady as wine and just as compelling. He could do this. He *would* do this. He held his breath, pulled the hard flesh of Xavier's throat taut, and slipped the needle into the artery.

The big man barely flinched.

This was it. "You're going to get very sleepy for a little while, but by the time you wake up it should all be over." In more ways than one.

His thumb shoved the plunger down.

CHAPTER 3 — RIPPLES

Wolf Amundson paced the small Missouri county airport, swearing to himself and running his fingers through his shorn, almost-white blond hair. The single line of plastic chairs in the room was an affront to his Brooks Brothers suit. The stink of cigarettes came from the overflowing ashtray in the corner. Hadn't anyone ever told these people that their smoking raised the price of medical insurance for everyone? The glacially slow, obese man at the desk sat sweating into his yellow Hawaiian shirt and the phone as he called the owners of various small planes trying to arrange a flight for Wolf.

The damned private jet he'd commandeered from Homeland Security's fleet wasn't here, and apparently wouldn't have been able to land if it were. Nope, the damned hicks in this county had built an airport with too short an airstrip for the jet, so he had to wait for this sweating cretin to arrange a small charter plane to fly him to an airport where the jet could land. Another waste of time, when time was what he had the least of.

Because the Gifted were loose in America, an event that could cause the downfall of his country. The trouble was, he wouldn't even know what they did once it was done. At least that was what the research told him. Because the demon-spawn Gifted would not only change the landscape of the country, they would change him and every other unGifted soul in the country when they did it, so that unGifted memories shifted to reflect the new reality—or so said the AGS reports.

He would not let that happen. He was Wolf Amundson, proud American son, even if the fact he'd been raised in Europe left him with a foreign accent and a penchant for precision that seemed foreign to most Americans. He was *not* some plastic toy to be posed and moved around like a plaything and to have his memories rewritten. Just the thought of being

Changed made his skin crawl. The fact that they might have done it to him already left him sleepless at nights.

The traitor, Gleason, and his co-conspirators—Drake, the evil gnome Snow, and the Seattle police detective—were loose and scheming his downfall, and with his demise it would leave his country, his America, at the mercy of these—these creatures that called themselves Gifted. Yes, he had men out searching, and yes, they'd been able to capture almost the entire American Geological Society Academy faculty and students before they could 'evacuate', but that was teachers and children, dangerous enough, yes, but not the trained agents. Unfortunately, his man Page had been a little too zealous in following orders. Amundson had said the danger of the faculty had to be eliminated, and apparently Page had used the final solution to do so. Unfortunate, but they still had the children; that would give them a huge card to play to control their agent parents.

That was a godsend given Gleason had somehow gotten warning out to the agents, and when his men went looking, most were gone. Since then, reports indicated a few had been apprehended. The rest and their families had scattered to the wind.

For a while, anyway. Just like Gleason and the others had escaped for a time. There was no way anyone could exist unnoticed in America forever. He had to hold onto that thought.

He ground his teeth and turned around at the sound of a turboprop aircraft's engine. Looked back at the bumbling fool and his telephone. He shoved open the waiting room door and strode across the tarmac to a small blue Cessna. A single woman was at the controls. Otherwise the plane looked empty.

He grabbed hold and yanked open the cabin door, much to the pilot's surprise.

"Hey!" The female pilot turned reflective shades on him and grabbed for the door. She was middle-aged, thin, grey hairs coming in at her temples.

"I need your plane," he shouted over the engine's wine. "It's a national emergency and I need you to fly me to St. Louis airport."

She shook her head, brow furrowed. "No way! I'm headed to a wedding in Little Rock."

Wolf slipped his wallet from his jacket breast pocket and flipped it open to his ID and badge. "Homeland Security. I'm commandeering this aircraft."

"But…"

"You want to be late for the wedding or get arrested for obstructing an investigation of terrorists?" Because they had to be doing that. With all the power the Gifted held, there was no question they were a danger. He eased his suit jacket slightly sideways so she could see the weapon he'd worn since he left AGS headquarters to come to this godforsaken part of the country.

The pilot looked from his badge to his face, to the gun, then back to his face again. "Cost you a thousand bucks."

"Five hundred," he countered.

"Seven fifty."

"Done." It was highway robbery, but he had to get to that plane and get back to Seattle. He wanted to be there as they began to interrogate the Gifted agents they had captured. It wouldn't be pretty, but someone would know something: what they planned, where they were going, how to detect and more fully contain a Gifted.

Yes, his researchers were on track to find some of those answers, and it couldn't be too soon. Then the purge of these dangerous people could begin.

§

Even with the windows open on the cool, musky air off Lake Washington, Vallon couldn't get rid of the stench of copper and fear in her nose. It was as if it clung to her skin, like a pall hung across the sky even though the heavens were a typical Seattle crystal blue, the benefit of westerly winds. She revved the sedan's engine and drove right up on the tail of the car in front of her on I-540 towards Seattle. The idiot was driving exactly the speed limit. She jerked the sedan sideways and tromped the gas, roared past them on the wrong side, and then ducked in front of him only to be confronted by another idiot driver driving almost as slowly.

She cursed and slammed her palm against the steering wheel. "Where the heck is a missile launcher when you need one," she muttered.

"You think maybe I should be driving?" Jason said mildly from where he'd braced himself in the passenger seat.

"I could tell you just what I think of that, but I'll be a lady and just tell you to shut up. I need this, okay? I have to do something."

"Like get us and someone else killed? Vallon, maybe you should slow down. Maybe we should go for a coffee or something? Talk this out. Figure out how to track the children. Those trucks you saw, they'd be memorable if they were together."

She glanced sideways at him. So he was trying to be helpful. Trying to talk her down off the cliff she felt like she was standing on, with a stiff wind about to blow her off. Decide to kill Amundson and his men and she'd freefall into a territory every part of her said she would never be able to recover from. "I'm sorry. I just—I just can't believe this has happened. Not in this country. Not to people I know. People like me."

He nodded, but there was something not quite right about him. His gaze seemed to skitter around her as if he would not meet her gaze, as if he looked at an outline of her. "Like I said. Let's go somewhere and have a coffee and figure out what to do next. If you aren't going to rest, you at least need food in your belly and a plan. There's a place up on Broadway, not far from where I first met you."

"Do you really think this is the time to be having coffee? There are people dead, for God's sake."

The car in front of her slowed down suddenly and she had slam on the brakes. Not good enough. They *were* traveling too fast. She cranked the wheel and slewed the car into the next lane. Eased off of the gas and sat there trying to slow the adrenaline rush that had her heart pounding. Finally she nodded.

"All right. Maybe coffee is a good thing. Broadway it is." She took the first exit when they merged onto I-5 and headed up onto Capitol Hill towards Swedish Hospital and University of Seattle. Broadway was the main commercial street in this area of well-kept older homes, before the city changed into the downtown core and its light industrial areas. Would the blue-frame heritage house still stand there as a constant reminder of the loss of her childhood? Once, the lot it stood on had held the low-slung ranch home she'd grown up in, but that had changed with the disappearance of her father. And though the blue heritage house had changed into other things a time or two, she always brought the blue house back as a reminder that nothing was permanent.

She almost looked away when its shadow fell across the pavement, because the loss of so much today was almost too much to bear. Then she pulled the car into the curb at a Seattle's Best coffee shop and climbed out, forcing herself to face the house and confront everything. Her past. The school's destruction. It felt like she had nothing, a boat loose from its moorings. She and Fi hadn't really had any chance to work out their differences. Landon was gone with Xavier, and who knew how her lover was doing? He might be dead for all she knew, though she wanted to believe if that happened she would know. And she was here with a man she had been trying to avoid in a world that felt like it had exploded.

Jason came up beside her. "Coffee?" he gave her a lopsided smile.

"You've got a one track mind, detective."

"I could try and woo you away from Xavier." He waggled his eye brows.

She sighed, and the adrenaline of all that she'd already done today had worn off so fatigue came down hard on her shoulders. "I really don't want to go there, Jason. There're a heck of a lot more serious things to worry about." She was so not getting involved with Jason again and this was what she'd spent almost the entire trip from New Madrid avoiding. He kept trying to engage her in conversation that always turned a little too intimate, like telling her about his life before the death of his wife, Cheryl.

She looked back at the house and all it symbolized. Loss—and loss seemed to be all there was in life. You think you have people traveling down the road of life with you, and then a semi comes along and runs them over. Please let Xavier's surgery have gone well. Let Landon keep him safe for her.

"Listen, you can stand here admiring that house if you like, but I'm headed for coffee. What do you want?"

She shook off her regard of the house. "I'm coming." The house was just a house. Probably not worth a lot, but the land would be. It was strange that the place hadn't been bought and torn down for commercial space. It was almost like the people of Broadway recognized something odd and special in the house just the way she did. She'd have to think about that.

Inside, the coffee shop was redolent with the rich tannins of dark-roasted coffee and the sweet scent of steamed milk with the faintly oversweet touch of flavored syrups that should, in her opinion, never grace the inside of a coffee cup. Good coffee stood on its own. Good coffee wasn't adulterated with sweeteners and flavors. The place was mostly empty, a lone old man nursing a coffee cup and reading a newspaper in the corner. He had bushy grey-blond hair that came down to his shoulders and wore a windbreaker over chinos and a rugby shirt. He barely glanced in their direction with pale blue eyes.

"Grab a table," Jason said. "What do you want? My treat?" He grinned.

She hadn't let him 'treat' on the entire trip over, but at the moment she was just too tired to argue. She nodded. "What I want is an espresso, but I think I need a latte. The milk'll settle my stomach."

She chose a stainless steel table by the window and close to the door. The better to keep an eye out for anyone who might have spotted them and to make good an escape, because otherwise they could find themselves in a scrape similar to those students—or worse. Her stainless steel chair scraped violently across the concrete floor; whoever had decorated had clearly been enamored of the industrial design look. Not exactly a place she's want to hang out with friends. Not exactly a place you could get a warm and friendly vibe going, which meant it was perfect for having a coffee with Jason.

She sat down on the uncomfortable chair and waited. Where were the children? She -reached-, but in the population of the city and without any clue where they could be, there was only the glow of humanity and the burbling bright flashes of the partially Gifted. The Gifted, those that could, had all left the city.

The hiss and sputter of the espresso machine was counterpoint to the low jazz on the sound system. Then Jason thanked the waitress and went to the sugar and cream bar. "Do you take anything?" he asked.

"Just the way it comes out of the machine, thanks." She studied the movements of the people across the brightly sunlit sidewalks. No one seemed to be paying any attention to the coffee shop as far as she could tell, and no one seemed to have come past more than once, but then a really good agent would probably be unremarkable.

Jason fussed and poured cream and sweetener into his coffee and made a show of stirring it, then brought both cups to the table, grinning. "I told her not to make it too hot."

Typical Bryson, figuring he knew what she wanted when it wasn't what she wanted at all. She liked to nurse extra hot coffee for as long possible.

But definitely not here. She took a sip and licked foam off her lips, then frowned. Lattes were always insipid, and this one had a strange acrid aftertaste as if the coffee had been burned. No wonder the place was flipping empty. She set the cup down and felt the old man looking at her.

But Jason was watching at her like an anxious puppy, which didn't fit given what they'd just been through. "Okay? Good? I used to come here when I was on the job. 'Course then it was under different management. Had a different decor, too. Back then it was all leather couches and chairs and local artwork on the walls."

Instead of the brushed steel walls that had the Seattle skyline etched into them.

A small wistful look crossed his face, but was smoothed away so quickly she almost thought she'd imagined it. The anxious expression filled Jason's face again as he looked down at the coffee cup.

God save her from anxious men. She took another swallow of the far less than flavorful coffee. "Good. Thanks. I owe you."

A slow smile bloomed on his face. "Guess I'll have to take it out of your hide."

Too uncomfortable. She eyed her drink and the foam flower on the top distorted by her lip and decided to change the topic.

"So what do we do, Jason? How do we find ten truckloads of children and twenty bodies?"

"Do we have to leap into that discussion right now? Couldn't we at least have a normal conversation for a bit?" He must have read her expression because he sighed and swirled his coffee before continuing.

"Why kill the faculty and take the children?" he asked, keeping his voice down.

She'd been asking herself the same question. "The adults knew how to use the Gift to protect themselves—if they had the time and equipment. The children—the younger they are the less control they have and the less they understand. I'm hoping that Amundson figures he can control the young ones and maybe indoctrinate them so that he trusts them." She took another sip and looked at Jason, smiled around the bitterness, and then glanced outside to the people walking down the street. No one suspicious. "That's best case scenario."

"And worst?" The hesitation in his voice said he almost didn't want to ask the question.

"He wants the children for research so he can study what's happening in their brains as they develop. He probably hopes he can find a way to turn the Gift off or to develop a weapon against it."

"Or a way to detect it. Or…or a way to give the Gift to everyone else!" His expression of excitement was way too disturbing.

"Why? You planning on signing up? You want the Gift and all the troubles that go with it? Can you imagine what it would be like, policing a country where everyone can work what seems like magic to change the landscape into what they want? Can you imagine the wars about it?"

His café au lair skin darkened. "So it wouldn't be a good thing?"

"No. It would not. The Gifted police the Gifted to prevent exactly that."

"Then I guess we'll just have to make sure that only people like you have the Gift." He shrugged. "Drink up. We'd better get to your place for Maggie and then figure out what's next."

"We just got here. We haven't decided what 'next' is."

"I could maybe use my police contacts to look for the trucks," he offered.

"I thought you weren't working with the police anymore. I thought Gleason said your ex-partner's barely speaking to you."

Jason shrugged. "Maybe. I sort of stepped away for the moment. I had other fish to fry." He tried his boyish grin but today it just wasn't working. Seeing the bloody floor at the school could do that.It made her thoughts all sluggish and muddy.

"Like what? I thought policing was your life. Maybe you should go back? How long were you with them?"

Jason's dark chocolate eyes were almost alien in their flatness. "Thirteen years. My lucky number, I guess. I was married that long, too. Did I tell you that? Thirteen long wonderful years." He shook his head. "But I can't go back. Amundson, remember?"

He was right, but his voice seemed to cut through a thick fog and she rubbed her forehead. It was suddenly far too hot in the café and the taste of the coffee, on top of everything else, was turning her stomach. Strange blue and yellow streaks seemed to cut through her vision and warp the figure of the old man patron and only increased the nausea.

"What's the matter, Vallon? You look pale as a ghost." The words stretched out like taffy and it took a moment for her to recognize Jason's voice. It was as if the world had slowed down around her, but then she'd slowed down, too. She was sliding off her chair towards a distant floor and when she tried to catch herself, she couldn't get her limbs to move. What the hell? Had Amundson's men found them? Had they incapacitated her? Was this the work of the old man?

She tried to -reach- and a flare of brightness blinded her other senses. She sagged against the table. Was falling.

"Vallon? Vallon, what's wrong?" Jason. It was Jason and he was at her arm, had hauled her up."Here. Drink this."

Something pressed at her lips and she gulped it back obediently and nearly puked at the bitter taste of copper and camphor laced through the drink. Why hadn't she recognized it before? "What?" she managed.

"You're sick. I'm going to get you out of here to a doctor, okay?"

She managed a nod, her head almost falling off her shoulders, she'd become so weak. But Jason hiked her up in his arms and seemed to move at the speed of light out the door and to the car. He slid her in onto the back seat.

"Just hold on, okay?"I'll get you help."

But the fog filtering into her brain was too much. Blinding. She -reached- but the brilliant fog hid her Gifted sight. No flicker of trees, no flame of people. Just fog and then nothing.

Absolutely nothing at all.

CHAPTER 4 — BLIND POWER

Gregor Gleason was no longer sure that they had done the right thing when they had split up after the New Madrid quake. He stood in the huge Washington Monument plaza inhaling the water-heavy air around the reflecting pool and watching the fall tourists stop to take their requisite photos. The sky was blue, the afternoon air was warm. The trees weren't in bloom, but they still held green leaves, even if a bit faded with the oncoming fall. Behind, and about one hundred feet away, he'd left Fi on a bench. Hopefully she could stay out of trouble while he met with Fitzsimmons.

It might have made more sense to all go into hiding immediately given the sporadic word he was getting from the agents who were scrambling to save themselves and their families. The horrible news that the academy had been captured had almost made him give up his intentions in Washington and return to Seattle. No one could bring the faculty back to life, but together, the agents could surely have freed the students once they found them. A number of the agents had suggested it: they wanted their children back. But then families started to disappear just because one spouse was an agent, and the agents were forced to take their remaining loved ones and run where they could, or disappear themselves. Besides, a confrontation was the last thing the Gifted needed. If they could have known what was happening soon enough, they might have done something, but the rumor was that Amundson's men had arrested the agents at the AGS installation en mass and confiscated all weapons before the agents really understood what was happening. An individual agent might take Amundson out, but to do that they had to find him and be certain they got him. Otherwise they took the chance that an attack would give Amundson the rationale to come down even harder on the Gifted.

No, he was doing the right thing coming here, to Washington. Ray Fitzsimmons, head of Homeland Security, had to be able to control Amundson and overturn his decisions. Maybe, just maybe, this would be the black mark against Amundson that would regain the Gifted control of the AGS. Maybe.

He could hope.

But it really hadn't been smart to bring the girl with him. Fi wasn't an agent. Sure, she had the innate ability of any Gifted, but without the advanced training of the last years at the academy, she could be as much a loose cannon as anyone the AGS was set up to protect against. And as damaged as Fi was, by her mother's abuse, he wasn't sure they could ever trust her mind. He glanced back at the slight figure with the wispy blonde hair seated on the park bench, her long legs bared and her face raised to the sun. She was no more than a child, really, even though she was the same age as Vallon. He shouldn't have brought her on what could be a perilous mission.

He realized that now that his telephone call to Ray Fitzsimmons hadn't elicited an appointment at the office. No, it had led to this—a clandestine meeting on the concourse. Studying the tourists and the suited men and women who were apparently hurrying about their business, he wondered how many of them were actually agents overseeing Fitzsimmon's safety.

"Gleason."

Gregor spun around, surprised he hadn't spotted Ray Fitzsimmons coming.

The man was not quite as tall as Gregor's six foot four, but perhaps that was misleading, because Fitzsimmons's hunched shoulders always made him seem to loom over those he was with. He had a hard, predatory gaze, with a long, beaked nose and leathery skin that reminded Gregor of a pterodactyl deciding when to swoop down. At the moment, all his attention was on Gregor.

Gregor shifted and offered his hand. "Ray. Thank you for coming. It has been too long."

Ray might have set the meeting place, but Gregor could take ownership of the meeting.

Fitzsimmons's hand was cool, the ancient skin dry and brittle. He eased his hand free almost too quickly, so this wasn't a meeting he wanted to treat as cordial. Gleason nodded.

"Let me get to the point. We're both busy men." *But I'm fighting for survival.*

"Yes," Fitzsimmons nodded his ponderous head. "I have congressional committees to get to."

Typical show of importance. It was all a show of dominance, and in the rarified air of Washington, a congressional meeting clearly took precedence over the potential genocide of the Gifted. But then, the various genocides around the world had never really moved the government to move quickly in the past, either.

"Then let's walk," Gleason said and swung in beside Fitzsimmons so he suddenly felt like a squadron of ancient flying animals cruising for prey. "I'm not sure what Wolf Amundson has told you, but the amalgamation of the AGS into Seattle Station has not gone well."

Fitzsimmons stopped and turned a cold reptilian gaze on Gleason. "Is that why I'm here? So you can complain about Amundson's leadership?"

It was clear that Fitzsimmons did not want to hear about it, but there was nothing to be done. Gleason had to go through with it. There was no other way.

He shook his head. "Not to complain about the decision that brought the AGS into the Homeland Security fold, but to question his methods. I'm worried that he's leaving the country unprotected." *And that we're about to enter another era of internment, but that probably wouldn't concern this ancient meat eater.*

"All right." Fitzsimmons said, the sunlight gleaming on his skin through the thinning hair on his pate. "You have five minutes. Tell me." He hunched into his shoulders and began to walk towards the capitol building. Gleason cast a quick 'stay there' glance in Fi's direction and following after.

Gleason told. About the removal of Landon from research of the Gifted and the seeming disappearance of AGS files. Of Amundson's refusal to look into the New Madrid situation and the 'almost total loss' that would have occurred if AGS agents hadn't disobeyed orders. Of Gleason's own arrest and the experimentation Amundson sanctioned on the Gifted. Of the arrest of AGS agents and shut down of the AGS. Of the disappearance of the AGS Academy's students and the murder of the faculty.

"He's now hunting the remaining AGS agents and their families, and if he succeeds in arresting all of them, the country won't have any protection." He ended there, feeling out of breath and slightly sick to his stomach at the full breadth of the issue. He didn't bother playing up the simple humanitarian side of the matter. Humanitarianism rarely sold.

Fitzsimmons had stopped walking and had turned an uncomfortable cold-fish stare on Gleason. "It was you and the Drake woman who stopped New Madrid?"

That was what he heard from amongst the litany of Amundson's sins?

"There was an installation threatening American sovereignty. It was going to destroy critical American infrastructure that would have seriously damaged our ability to protect ourselves from foreign powers."

But Fitzsimmons's cold gaze had gone even colder. "That's a trifle melodramatic. There could have been good come out of it—new roads, hospitals, etc. People rant about the aging government infrastructure." Fitzsimmons might be mistaken as thoughtful, but it was too tinged with regret, almost as if he'd wished it would happen. Something was going on here.

"Sir, what I'm concerned about is Amundson and America's safety. He murdered our people and I don't doubt he'll murder more. He's rounding up agents and their families as we speak. God knows what will happen to them. People are going into hiding to protect themselves, and the shutdown of the AGS has left us unable to monitor and protect America."

Fitzsimmons actually stopped. He turned to Gleason with a dark glint in his reptilian eyes. "It speaks volumes when agents have abandoned their posts."

As if he blamed them for running. Mother of God, didn't this man get it? Gleason took a deep breath and met Fitzsimmons's gaze. "What I'm saying is that those agents that remained at their posts were arrested, as were their families, and not just in Seattle. Amundson seems intent in interring all of the Gifted in the country. He seems to have decided that if you have the Gift, then you cannot be trusted. That you *will* harm the country, simply because he does not understand what it is that we do. That is not how you treat people who have given everything for their country."

Fitzsimmons at least had the good graces to nod thoughtfully and hunch along the mall. Blue sky reflected in the pool and the breeze rustled the leaves and skittered a chocolate bar wrapper across the concrete. Gleason waited, feeling almost as empty as the wrapper as he paced beside him. If Gleason didn't help them, what more was there to do? The presence of the Gifted wasn't anything he wanted spread around, because then other closed-minded individuals like Amundson would likely take matters into their own hands, too. Being Gifted would become a matter of death or imprisonment.

Finally Fitzsimmons checked his watch and glanced sideways at Gleason. "I appreciate you bringing this matter to my attention. I will certainly look into it and ensure the matter receives the attention it deserves.

Now I really must get to my meeting." A politic answer that meant nothing if there ever was one.

He nodded once in dismissal and left Gregor feeling gape-faced and impotent in the face of the power of the United States government. Blind power. Blind enough to let innocent people be imprisoned and potentially experimented upon while Fitzsimmons decided how to turn these events to his advantage.

The sun on Gregor's bald pate suddenly went cold and the warming run of the ley lines through the earth felt so distant they would never warm him again.

§

The operating room smelled of blood and sweat and the slight tang of excitement. The former belonged to the comatose figure on the brightly lit metal operating table in the center of the room. The latter was certainly his own as Landon paced around the table eyeing the man he had drugged and who lay at his mercy.

Xavier de Varga's shirt was off, the bloodied European cotton a shredded ball in the corner. His broad, olive-tinged chest with the light dusting of hair lay pale and marred by the stain of disinfectant and the dressings over Landon's operation. He had done good work, if he did say so himself. The bullets had been removed cleanly from where they had lodged near the breastbone. Yes, they had torn open the chest cavity and injured the outer edges of lung tissue, but once the bullets were removed, the whole wound seemed to *want* to heal. Landon had pumped Xavier full of antibiotics and prayed they'd work their magic. Which meant that now he could focus on what he really wanted from the man.

Xavier de Varga was clearly a powerful man on many levels. His long limbs showed powerful, lean muscle. His lung capacity looked like that of a runner. The calluses of his hands said he had used them in hard combat. Landon reached out and stroked a single finger down the man's hide, and a foreign surge of power eeled into his hand like a strange and wonderful creature. So much power that the top of his head might blow off with pleasure if he kept it up.

He reluctantly pulled his finger back and busied himself preparing another syringe that contained a potent mixture honed over years of research. Curare and a psychedelic combined with the antidote for the anesthetic would bring Xavier out of unconsciousness and leave him in a suitable condition. Landon needed to understand what this man was. Xavier de Varga presented perhaps the greatest mystery of his career as a researcher within the AGS. Yes, he had always hypothesized the existence of those Gifted with a greater gift, but he had never truly expected to actually have one in his hands. One with the greater Gift should be as elusive as a will-o-the-wisp, yet this man had fallen right into his grasp.

Because of Vallon, his pigeon. Almost as he'd once imagined it might happen, given her history. It was almost impossible to fathom how, in so short a time, Vallon and de Varga had formed a bond greater than he, Landon, had ever felt for anyone.

He circumnavigated the unconscious figure again. Yes, Xavier de Varga was everything he had ever asked to find—a man with so much power he could actually, according to Vallon, move from place to place simply through the power of his mind: teleportation

A tremble of excitement ran up his spine, swiftly forced to quiet with a calming breath. He needed calm and quiet to understand what he had here and how Xavier might aid him. To have the Gift and yet not— that was unfairness taken to its most horrible. Surely the Others would be able to reveal how power was developed and used so that he could regain his birthright. He was not asking for power to be simply given; no, he was prepared to practice, like other Gifted. He had spent his life readying his mind for just such a task. In fact, with his alchemical practice he *should* become a most powerful Gifted, if he could just break through the seal that seemed to block his mind. That was what it was: a waxen seal over a bottled genie of Gifted essence that was locked inside his mind.

If Xavier would only share the secret. There had to be one. All his life, his studies had led him to that conclusion, even before those with the Gift had come together. He had read the ancient texts of the Alchemists and been called to that work by the secret subtext: purify matter and purify yourself. Turn lead into gold and unGifted into Gifted. Was that what he was? Someone caught between the kinds of being?

He closed his eyes against the glare of the unwelcome thought. Was he like this secret place of his? Trapped between the parts of the human species like this installation was trapped between the edges of maps. He huffed through his nose. There was a strange symbolism in that. He lived his life *between* and that was the problem. Neither fish nor fowl. Neither Gifted nor unGifted. Just what or who was Landon Snow?

The answer had eluded him for far too many years. Now Xavier de Varga was going to tell him. And once he became Gifted, he could show the world the greatness that was Landon Snow.

CHAPTER 5 — AN UNNATURAL LANDSCAPE

arkness and a sense of movement. Soft cries and whispers and heat and the stink of fear and urine. So tired and she could no longer feel her feet. Her legs had given up long ago, but the press of the others held her up. Too many bodies, pushed chest into back into chest. Too many elbows, and she couldn't avoid them. A lurch as the panel truck went over something and someone fell. There was yelling, crying as elbows shoved them back as they fought to find enough space for the fallen one to stand up again. There'd been too many of the youngest ones who had fallen and not gotten up. If she moved her foot she could feel the softness of one of them that wasn't moving anymore. She didn't want to feel it. Didn't want to think of it. Didn't want to breathe the air that all of them had inhaled and exhaled so many times before that it was sour and rank in her throat.

Another crash over rough roads and they were all thrown against the wall, fighting to stand, clawing the walls, the older ones yelling at them to help each other. And then the truck stopped and didn't start again. She couldn't breathe in the silence and lack of motion. Had she died? Was this how it felt?

Then came the sound of muffled voices and yelling and, too close by far, the sound of rapid gunfire and screams. A rumble like thunder as the rear door of her truck rolled up and they were blinded by floodlights that lay beyond. Through the haze of light she saw the men with the guns.

It was dark where Vallon woke and for a long while she didn't know whether she was truly awake or the place was simply part of her nightmare vision. Dark silver rippled and streaked her sight and left her nauseous. Her tongue tasted like copper and bile and like something slithery was laying on it. In her mind's eye it was silvery like mercury and just as elusive. She couldn't pin it down, couldn't grab it, just like she couldn't pin her surroundings down. Or her thoughts. They skittered away like small animals away from traps. The air reeked of sweat and fear and the sour scent of something fermenting. It reminded her of the back of the truck she'd been standing in.

Truck?

The sound of her rapid breathing filled the space where she lay. She hadn't been in a truck. The truck had been where the students were. Another vision, then. The pounding of her heart drummed painfully in her ears. The sound drove a spike deep into her brain. She'd been in a car, driving, and then—somewhere else? *The scent of bitter coffee and something else.* So where *was* she?

The darkness closed in around her and she had to fight back a little instinctual terror. She tried to wipe a mat of her hair back from her eyes, but her arm was immobilized. She'd last been held down like this in New Madrid.

Terror spiked full blown. Had her father found her? Was he alive? Had he returned her to that sunken bunker and drugged her again?

No. She tried to calm herself. The bunker was destroyed. Flooded. You saw it. And then you were drugged so your limbs wouldn't work. Now you're tied. To prove it, she jerked against the bonds that held her wrists and ankles.

Besides, her father was gone. Dead. He had to be the way he disappeared. There's no other way it could be. And yet it could. She hadn't actually seen his body. And as long as he was alive there was no safety for anyone in the world and least of all her. He would blame her for the end of his plans and he *would* come after her.

But what did that have to do with children crammed into a truck, the girl she'd been? Yes, she had been with a girl as if she'd been in the girl's head, but that made no sense. She had been twelve and her name had been…. It was lost to her and, damnation, it was so hard to think with the streaks of color going off in her head and the quicksilver sliding through her brain.

What had happened to her—was happening to her? She strained against the ropes around her ankles and wrists, the rough fiber rubbing at her skin, a hard wooden surface under her cheek.

But she had to move. Had to get up, find light. Find the girl and the other children and free them. Had to at least understand where she was.

Her breath came in rough little gasps as she strained against the ropes. She twisted her body to get leverage and yanked. The ropes still held and the effort left her exhausted enough she felt like weeping. The horrible streaks sent lightning across her vision, the quicksilver slicing her brain so violently she thought she might be sick.

She lay there fighting back the nausea, and trying to slow her breathing and her racing heart. Don't act out of fear. What she felt was a natural, an instinctual fear, like a caged animal. She wasn't an animal. She could think her way through this—if she stopped panicking and focused on logic.

Eyes closed she focused on her surroundings and her breathing gradually slowed.

Her bonds were rope—something natural. Surely with the Gift she could weaken them enough to get her hands free.

It would be simple. Just -reach-. But fog, threaded with the painful silvery threads, filled her head. They clung to her and burned wherever she turned. Too damn bad. She needed her freedom.

She -reached- farther, plunging through the strands, seeking the end of the boundary. The fog went on and on and the panic seeped in again until she was racing like a panicked horse would run until its heart exploded.

She stopped. The fog lay thicker here and thicker with the slithery silver that wound around her and burned into her essence like acid. No freedom here.

Collapsing back into her body, she lay there, panting and nursing the burns on her psyche. Whatever it was, it effectively blocked her connection to the earth, and that just couldn't be. The Gift allowed the Gifted to connect to the world, but right now something blocked her and left her head throbbing as if it had been hollowed. Was this a side effect of her connection to the girl—perhaps whatever the girl was feeling—or was it her own predicament? Or was it the reason she hadn't been able to locate any agents? Had Amundson caught them all and done this to them?

Her breath sounded overloud in the darkened room, as if she was the only living being in the world. Almost as if she was in sensory deprivation, but no, she might not be able to use the Gift, but she had other senses. She wasn't cut off from *them*. She *could* hear her breathing. She *could* feel the painful scratch of the ropes on her wrists and the pressure on her ankles. She *could* taste the copperish acrid taste on her tongue, and that was more than a current phenomenon. That was a memory.

Something she ate or drank. Had Amundson caught up to her? This was the sort of thing he would do—leave a person to panic so that they were almost overjoyed no matter who came for them. But when had he captured her? She had been in New Madrid. They had dealt with her father. And then she had had a dream about the AGS Academy and the headmaster.

The memory came draining back. The aviary room of Elizabeth Ducharme's guesthouse and they had all headed out on three separate missions and hers had been to come to Seattle and pick up Maggie and check whether the dream had been real. And it had been.

Blood on the floor and the scent of fear. Trucks leaving with their precious cargo—the future of the Gifted and the AGS. All of those children born and bred to have more Gift according to her reading of Landon's files. The AGS had entered into a breeding program with its agents to try to increase the Gift in the next generation. If Amundson had known that—hadn't Landon said that Amundson's men had found his research files?—then there was no wonder he was coming after the children. They could be more powerful than the agents.

The bile exploded into her mouth so fast she barely had time to turn her head before spewing the contents of her stomach. It left her weak and almost unable to move in the miasma of her vomit.

Those children were in terrible danger and she had to help them. She'd come here from New Madrid to help them. She and Jason. She frowned.

Was he here? Had Amundson gotten him, too? And how? She remembered the academy and getting back to their car. They'd thought they'd gotten in and out unnoticed. So when had things gone wrong? Obviously, they'd been spotted and tracked—where?

A Seattle skyline gleaming unnaturally in metal. A scent of—coffee.

Coffee! She seized on the memory. It had been coffee. They had gone for coffee to decide what to do and the coffee had tasted wrong.

Excitement rushed through her and she would have done a high five, except there was no one there to do it with and her limbs felt like water. Her strength seemed to fade faster after her efforts to free herself and whatever was in her head thickened.

"Jason?" she whispered on the off chance he might be here with her, even though she surely would have heard his breathing.

His named seemed swallowed up in the darkness.

"Jason," she yelled and the force almost scared her. It left her lungs empty, and for a moment she didn't know if she could inhale to refill them. But the sound bounced back quickly, so she was in a small room; and judging by the lack of echo, it was filled with soft things that absorbed the sound.

She gathered herself again and inhaled. "Damn it all to hell! Where is this place?" she yelled.

Surely whoever was here would hear her and come to see what she wanted.

But there was nothing. No sound except the rustle of her clothing as she tried to ease her position and the not-steady-at-all pounding of her heart.

She -reached- again, seeking Jason, but he might as well have existed in another universe for all she could sense. [Xavier?] Her call was eaten up by the silver-threaded wilderness in her head.

She collapsed back to wherever her body was, sweat pouring down her forehead to sting her eyes. Whoever had her knew enough about the Gift to do something to her so she couldn't access it.

It had to be Amundson. What were they going to do to her? What did they want? Why was she alive when they'd killed the faculty of the academy?

Well, fear was what they wanted her to feel so she wouldn't give them the satisfaction. "Hey! Hey you! I want to talk to you!"

Was that a slight noise from somewhere beyond the darkness and the stench of her vomit and fear?

"Hey! I have to go to the bathroom and I've been sick in here! Come on!"

A sound like a door opening and then the clump of footfall on floorboards. Then a door opened in the darkness and a beam of light streamed in. A mass of silver threads twirled vertiginously and reflected the light right into her brain. She yanked her gaze away from the painful brilliance and the tall male figure haloed in the doorway.

"You're awake, finally," a too familiar voice said.

Not her father. Not Amundson.

Jason.

§

So it had come to this. The stink of antiseptic and blood, the bright lights, and the little man standing over him. Not so different than when the Council had bled him last time: the same hollow, helpless feeling because his mind was trapped inside his body. The drugs, though, that was something new. It brought a horrible sense of euphoria that he knew he should not be feeling.

Not when his body was stripped down and naked on a slab of a table. Not when his arms and legs were solidly strapped down with metal bands, and not when a small white gnome of a man paced around him peppering him with questions. Yes, the Council had had questions as well, but they were of a different sort—the extent of his betrayal, the danger to his kind.

This, though, was an attempt to raid his mind. The little man's questions were astute and right to the heart of the matter, and the damned drugs seemed to work so that even as he thought *I will not answer*, his betraying tongue conjured one:

He was from the Algarve, Portugal, born and raised.

Yes, he was part of a larger society of Gifted.

They estimated their population as a meager hundred thousand across the world.

No, they were not associated with any government.

Yes, they all carried the holy Gift of the Creator and mother Pangea in their blood; all of them descendents of the five First Cartos, Zim, Sang, Kron, Nga and Lazar.

Yes, they have watched the Gifted of America for a long while.

The drugs made him drowsy, so his mind floated in and out of consciousness. He knew he needed to escape before he gave up all his secrets. *All? What more was there to give?* Normally he could simply transmute out of wherever this was, but whatever concoction ran through his blood stopped him from linking with the landscape. It was like a streaked glass dome held him prisoner.

"Varga!" A tap on the cheek to get his attention. "I asked you a question."

Landon Snow was still dressed in bloodied surgical linens as if he had woken Xavier before the blood from Landon's operation was not yet dried on his hands. Given the little man's usual immaculate appearance, this was not like him. As if something had come loose in him.

Because he held Xavier prisoner. "I don't remember the question."

Perhaps that was a good sign. His mind had not simply answered the question.

"I asked you if there are people like me among you—people who have the Gift, but cannot use it?"

The little man's face spoke volumes. He craned forward until Xavier could see the rough pores of his skin, the sweat on his brow and the desperate, fever-bright shine of his pink-blue eyes. Usually the little man smelled of talcum powder, but now he smelled of sour sweat.

"There are the alchemists," Xavier's unwitting mind provided. Not too terrible a secret, but still, one of far too many.

"What? What did you say?" Landon looked like he would climb right up on the table and straddle Xavier. His lips were pressed into an excited line that showed each small pearl tooth behind it like a feral child's smile.

"Alchemists," Xavier replied, and damnation, Landon was learning too much. If his mind could just find his will again. Always he had been strong-willed and resolute, even in the face of the Council's interrogations, but Landon had used a different tactic. Bloodletting through the surgery coupled with this drug. Always his kind had avoided the use of drugs. Or at least so he was told.

A room in darkness except for bright sunlit dust columns through high windows and shadowed figures around him as he sat strapped in the chair. The air smelled of old rot and damp and the copper remnants of the last subject of interrogation. They had taken him when he came to report and brought him here, into darkness to the room that had served its owners in a similar fashion for four hundred years. Dom Gonzales and Ahmed Aziz were darker shadows in the corners, the Middle Eastern Cartos' scent of coriander threading through the stink of old pain as they inserted the lines into his veins and the slow, steady drip, drip, drip of his lifeblood as it drained into a bowl at his feet.

"You will tell us what you know, darling." Leticia's coaxing voice.

"De Varga!" The sting of a slap across the face brought Xavier out of his wandering memories. Had he spoken of the last time he was in Venice? Of the people there? Of the last time he visited home?

The little man's intense gaze drove into him. "You will answer me. What about the Alchemists? Do you mean people who practice transmutation?"

His voice was overeager. Could he be diverted from the Council and his people's history to a discussion of an almost lost sect? If he could feed Snow this information, it might save more important secrets. It might give him time to find a way out of this little man's prison.

"Yes," he answered, for it was clearly the answer Snow wanted. *Let me use your drugs against you, little man. And when they wear off you will see what a true Cartos is about and how all your petty questions, your miniscule Gifts and politics mean nothing to the world.*

"So they practice transmutation?"

"Yes." It was difficult to control his tongue, to stop it from holding forth with everything he knew. But he could at least let him play an interrogator's game and only answer the question that was posed. A simple yes or no answer was all that was required to be completely truthful.

Small furrows appeared between Landon's pale brows and he looked into Xavier's eyes as if there was something he did not trust. "Tell me about them."

So… Snow had discovered the issue of his questioning technique. The question opened doors in Xavier's mind that he could not seem to close.

"They are the lost ones. Lost during the great diaspora to hide amongst the others, denying their blood and their Gifts in order to save their lives."

Damnation, no. Do not give so much. He strained against the bonds on his mind, but the drug was like a sieve, draining it away and his words continued to flow.

"There are those who say that denouncing their Gift for so long caused the Creator and Mother Pangea to withdraw it from them, but they know that their life feels empty. And so they search for a way to reach union again."

"Have they found it?"

The eagerness was like a fever in the little man's eyes. Was he Alchemist?

The possibility set him back a moment. What did Snow already know? What would happen if all those lost ones suddenly reclaimed their power?

"No Alchemist has been seen for the past three hundred years."

A shimmer of disappointment in Snow's gaze. "Why is that?"

"They were caught in the witch hunts of the reformation. A person with the strange paraphernalia and writings of the Alchemist is always the outsider. History says the known Alchemists were among the first accused and the first to die."

Snow fell silent a moment. He paced the room in a loop around Xavier, muttering to himself, and Xavier heaved a sigh. If he could keep the man off balance, perhaps he would not think of the deeper questions to ask. Snow disappeared out of his line of sight and there was a rustle and the sound of cabinets opening.

Xavier chanced closing his eyes. [Vallon?] It took everything he had to reach out through the silvery curtain that reigned in his brain. His senses were raw and the curtain burned his mind, but he had to find her, tell her what was happening, ensure she did not come here and never trusted this gnome of a man again. [Vallon!]

There was no answer, and nothing, and that was worse than having to report what had happened. Even before he had made his presence known to her and before their relationship had unfolded, he had known her as he watched her. She was a steady light, a constant scent of ashes of roses that he caught on even the most distant wind. She was everywhere and everything to him, but the scent and the light were gone.

That couldn't be right. The bonds of his mind wound tighter as he strained to reach her, to find her. Even when he was in Europe he had coveted her steady light and had known she lived and was well, but now there was nothing. He reached down for the ley lines, but whatever Landon had given him, the lines were beyond his grasp.

He pulled back and lay there trying to quell his shuddering. He should be able to feel her, to know she was safe. But if she wasn't safe?

She had headed out with only an unGifted to help her and had intended to walk right into Amundson's city. It had been a fool's errand. Anyone who felt powerful enough to murder an entire school faculty and kidnap its students could deal with a single agent no matter how talented unless she could locate him and do what needed to be done. That was the problem. For all of his *Bela's* rough edges, she was not someone who would find killing easy.

A rustle next to his ear brought his eyes open and Landon was there again, his gaze watchful as he applied a tourniquet to Xavier's arm.

"Aah, so you haven't fallen asleep, I see. Very good." He expertly stabbed a needle into Xavier's vein, taped it down, and attached an IV drip of clear fluid "There now. You see, I can tell when you are holding back information and that just won't do." He patted Xavier's shoulder, like an owner would do with a favorite, but recalcitrant, dog.

"I want you to know I tried to do it the easy way. Now things get hard." He held up a syringe filled with a gold-green liquid. "You see, I've had years to investigate what differentiates Gifted from unGifted blood and to develop some interesting drugs to work with those Gifted who refuse to work with us." Another insipid smile with the teeth too even and pearly white, with the damp pink gums and tongue shining between. "This, my dear friend, is what I use on those who do not wish to answer."

Xavier watched, fascinated, as the syringe was inserted into the IV drip and the pale liquid entered the clear bag. It turned the saline drip a milky absinthe color streaked with blue.

Then Snow opened a valve and the milky liquid flowed down through the tubing towards his arm. When it reached him a flame bolted into his flesh, his shoulder, his back. His body convulsed and then collapsed in what felt like heated coals under the skin. Burning him from the inside out. Then the stuff hit his brain and pain ripped away all of his remaining guards. There was no thought, only reaction. No Xavier, only information.

In a last ditch chance to save himself he -reached- out for the ley lines. Find the power and change whatever this infernal fluid was. Too late. The pain cut him loose and there was no Xavier. There was no Vallon to worry about. There was just the pain and terrible need to explain the truth.

CHAPTER 6 — OCHRE AND ONYX

When the phone rang in his Homeland Security office, Wolf Amundson was just reviewing the report on the little project he'd affectionately called 'Operation Welcome' as a small, ironic in-joke given the fact that the Gifted were anything but welcome. The school closure had gone as planned except for the shooting of the faculty. Apparently the whole thing had started when the man guarding them had noticed a shimmer in the air around the wounded headmaster and the man had seemed to be talking to someone no one could see. It was a shame. The faculty were likely to be easier to deal with than the agents they were rounding up one by one, but he'd sanctioned the solution at the urging of Loadstone, the corporation that much of his security force had been subcontracted from. They had collected the bodies for further examination.

The deaths of the teachers had also left the children too terror stricken and too confused to try anything. That, at least, had gone off as planned. At least at pickup.

"Amundson," he said into the phone and turned from the report to his office window. It gave a panoramic view of the center of Seattle and Elliot Bay, the Puget Sound and white-capped Olympic Mountains beyond. Blue skies all the way, and he could breathe again now that the worst of the crisis was over, most agents arrested. Now they just had mop-up work to do. Of course, until all the Gifted were contained, he was left having to change locations frequently. He couldn't stay anywhere long enough for one of the damned Gifted to erase his location right out of existence and him with it.

"You're creating a problem," said the low, creaking voice of Ray Fitzsimmons.

Wolf sat up straighter in his chair, the view suddenly forgotten. "I am *dealing* with a problem," he said, running his fingertips over the neatly typed report pages. "I'm just cleaning up the loose ends as we speak."

Silence a moment over the phone, and then, "Then why have I got Gregor Gleason hanging around Washington like a bad smell? I can stall him for so long, but he's getting tired of waiting for me to give him a firm answer. He's going to go elsewhere. Do we really want politicians knowing what you're doing to their constituents in the name of Homeland Security?"

Wolf closed his eyes a moment in remorse, then set it aside as something that could not be helped. *Collateral damage. Friendly fire.* He looked at his report. "The school's done. Unfortunately we lost one truckload when some of the older ones seemed to be trying something at the receiving end and the guards freaked. The rest of them are safely hidden and we can decide what's best for them once the research is finished. I've managed to round up a good two-thirds of the agents here and virtually all of them in Los Angeles and New York stations. The AGS is done and closed, the building locked up tight. It's just a matter of picking up and containing the remaining agents. Then the crisis is over."

More silence on the phone, and didn't Fitzsimmons realize that he had better things to do than sit here listening to silence? But then Fitzsimmons was so far removed from the front lines he no longer remembered what it took.

"If you recall, I asked you to fill me in on your plans. It is not my fault that I did not know enough of your intensions for New Madrid. If I had, I could have been more—efficient, shall we say?—in keeping Drake and her little friends away. But that is all *water-under-the-bridge* I believe is the saying. Now the matter is containment. The fact Drake et al took out the rogues only works to our advantage. Fewer unknowns out there."

"It was a hellishly expensive bridge—all destroyed now. The investors aren't happy."

Wolf thought of what Fitzsimmons had told him of the plans for New Madrid. Make a new start for the country, one in which the corporations took the lead from the financially cash-strapped governments and built what they wanted. High time the ridiculous public and their even more ridiculous expectations were set aside in importance. A company didn't require a vote and passing of legislation when it saw an opportunity. And Drake and Gleason and the damned gnome had ruined the opportunity.

"If you'd told me ahead of time, I'm sure I could have found some excuse to get this job done before they had a chance to ruin your plans.

As it is, they'll be no problem. It's just a matter of time before they're captured, too." It could not be too soon, in his estimation. The danger these—these *creatures*—represented could not be overestimated. "I could send someone to pick up Gleason, if you like."

"Wolf."

The use of his name got his attention.

"You have taken things far enough. Clean up the debris of what you've done, but at this point do not go any farther. What you are doing reeks of genocide or, at best, Japanese internment camps. The media would have a field day with that. Our political masters don't need the headache of public reaction."

Stop? Stop now? His skin went cold and his mouth tasted of ash. "The *public* is not going to worry about these Gifted. They'll be terrified of them. They'd probably help capture any of them we don't."

"We DO NOT want the public catching wind of this. Do you understand?"

The vehemence of the leathery old pterodactyl's voice was enough to stop Wolf from vocalizing his argument, even though he had one ready. Fitzsimmons clearly had not thought things through to their conclusion. If Fitzsimmons had used his rogue faction of Gifted to do what he intended, there would be ample reason for the regular citizens to hate those responsible. Like Fitzsimmons. Like the corporations. Like the Gifted most of all; and he, Amundson, would become the champion of all normal humans. Then watch how fast and how far his star would rise. A rush of adrenaline washed up his back and through his scalp. Now *that* was a future he could endorse.

All because he was doing what was right: protecting his country from Gifted kind.

§

The blinding light through the door caught in the shimmering quicksilver haze in Vallon's brain and stunned her almost as much the man standing there.

Jason. He wore baggy jeans and a wife-beater t-shirt that showed off the muscular contours of his shoulders and arms. His café au lait features were hidden by the backlighting. His scent of licorice and spice mingled with sweat, as if he'd been working out, and sent her gagging as the truth of her situation came clear.

"*You* drugged me!" Her voice was burned-out and harsh in her ears. Harsher since she'd been worried about the bastard in Amundson's hands.

He gave a simple shift of his shoulders as if it was nothing.

"The sudden need for coffee—it was all a ruse." She looked down at herself and her bound hands and legs, exposed now, by the light. Bedroom, maybe, but no place she recognized. His place? But the walls didn't look like any city condominium she knew. No drywall. No, this was pine planking on two walls and the floor, the third wall looked like actual log. "Where the hell are we?"

Hands jammed in his pockets, he finally approached. He stood over her and the table she lay on, his chocolate gaze barely visible in the shadows, a slight smile on his lips. "I'll tell you everything if you promise to cooperate. Hell, I'll even untie you if you promise to help me." He shrugged as if it was the simplest of matters.

"Fuck you." It was a stupid, juvenile thing to say, but damn it, things were coming apart in the world and now he betrayed her like this?

His expression turned to one of distaste and she turned her head away suddenly afraid of her helplessness. He could beat her up for her actions and there wasn't a damn thing she could do about it. Fear warred with frustration at her situation, and then settled on anger. There was a twelve year old girl to help. The other children, not to mention the rest of the Gifted. Who knew how many Amundson had murdered and was going to murder?

She -reached- for the ley lines and power. If she could do that then the next thing was to burn this sucker—or undo him and the house around them. She could do it. She could.

She shivered. No, she couldn't. Wasn't that the point she'd made with her father? The Gift wasn't for killing or taking power. She'd known that ever since she'd slept with Xavier and felt the overwhelming connection of all life. Had felt it again when she'd saved Seattle and had to disperse the power through North America. No, she'd stun Jason and get the heck out of here.

Except it was all a moot point because the shimmering quicksilver encased her brain and every time she -reached- for the ley lines she knew were there, the quicksilver sent her bouncing back into her brain with something like an electric shock. Surely to God, she'd endured worse than that. Surely she could simply take the pain and break through.

She -reached- farther and the pain increased. Burned through her as she changed tactics and tried a single spear of awareness like a lance through a boil, but the silver could not be lanced. It was omnipresent wherever she went and made making a plan of any complexity difficult.

She collapsed back into herself and groaned, then turned a weary head towards him.

Jason stood with crossed arms watching. "Whatever you were trying, it didn't work did it?" Satisfaction in his voice, as if he'd accomplished something.

She didn't want to talk to him, didn't want to admit that he had it right. "What did you give me?" she finally said.

Another infuriatingly attractive shrug that flexed all of those gorgeous muscles. At another time, in another situation, she would have considered him sexy as hell, given her afterburn. But now he just looked like the enemy.

"What did you give me, please." Said through gritted teeth.

"Hell if I know. A little something I picked up from Homeland Security. I saw how it slowed down Gleason and thought I might have a use for it." Another mocking shrug. "Seems I did, given I needed your help and you seemed to cut off any attempt I made to talk to you normally about it." He edged a hip up beside her on the table and the light placed strain lines around the eyes and etched deep grooves of grief and dissatisfaction from his nose to his mouth. It was what had given him that hungry look she'd noticed before. "Now don't you wish you'd let me talk on the ride over instead of cutting me off every time?"

"You've been planning this a long time," she gritted out as she tested her bonds again. Ridiculously solid.

Another slight smile. "Let's just say since last spring." He produced a cloth and proceeded to wipe her face and shoulder of her vomit and clean off the table beside her. Then he tossed the cloth into a bucket across the room. Almost as if he'd done it any number of times.

Last spring was when she'd met him during the Rebecca Murdoch affair. He'd been there at the last as she fought to save Seattle. He'd also nearly been wiped out by Change at one point and the really weird thing was that he remembered both events—unlike any unGifted she had ever met. That was strange by itself. She chewed on that fact for a moment and then forced herself to relax instead of feeling like she would come up off this table and try to beat him into a pulp if she could just move.

"All right. What is so damned important that you'd do this?"

Another smile, and he touched a knuckle to her cheek that just creeped her out.

"Now see? Being polite wasn't so hard."

His gaze seemed to rake down her body, but it wasn't sexual— more possessive as if she was a form of treasure.

"So talk, Jason. What's so important you'd ruin our—friendship?"

His eyes went darker for a moment, and then he met her gaze so intently she almost couldn't breathe. "I've seen what you can do. The way a building can fade and change into something new. The way a mountain can move. The way you made a castle in your basement and inhabited it with tiny living people."

She froze. That had been an accident. The small building had been created in her practice sand pit during a little exercise with Fi. The building wasn't the accident, but the tiny living inhabitants had been. They should have never existed, but somehow she couldn't bring herself to wipe out something living once they'd been created. Instead she'd let nature take its course and they'd faded out of existence—or should have, just like what happened with anything created through Change unless it entered the consciousness of enough people in the population to hold it in place. That was the weird thing about the relationship between Gifted and unGifted. Gifted could work change and no one would ever know, unless enough unGifted saw the change and its results. The huge Indian Ocean earthquake had been caused by Change. No one would have noticed, except that the tsunami that had ripped into a wide swath of the coast of Indonesia and Thailand, not to mention Sri Lanka and India and so many others. So many unGifted had been impacted that the entire world had held that Change in place because they remembered it. Devastation apparently could do what simple Change couldn't.

She just looked at him. "So?"

He stood and paced to the foot of the table to a dresser that sat alongside what must be a window with blackout material and planking nailed over it. *To stop any yells for help from being heard?* He picked up something and walked over to her and held up a framed photo of a woman with shoulder-length wavy auburn hair and a million-watt smile. She was swinging on a rope swing out over what must be a pool of water the way the light reflected softly up into her face. Somehow the photographer had captured a moment of transcendent bliss.

Vallon looked from the photo to Jason.

"This is Cheryl, my wife." He touched the figure in the picture frame almost reverently. "Cancer took her. I saw what you did with that power of yours. I want you to bring her back for me."

Vallon blinked. "Pardon me?"

"I want you to bring Cheryl back. You've got power enough to create living creatures. I want you to use that power to bring Cheryl back. You do that, I'll let you go."

"No. No. No. No." She shook her head, the quicksilver blades painful in her head and she had to have misheard because there was so much wrong with this idea in so many ways.

"Are you refusing to help me?"

She opened her eyes to see Jason rigid beside her. He still held the photo, but his other hand formed a fist at his side. The muscles of his face had stiffened until his features were a mask of naked anger and need that would not be denied. A man this strong and committed could hurt her very badly indeed. She had to be cautious, to make him understand.

"No. Never. It's just—the power doesn't work that way. We don't use it on people—or dead people."

"But you created life."

She couldn't deny it, but…. "That was an accident. It shouldn't have happened. And they aren't there now, because they faded away, right? If you go to my house, you'll see. The castle and everything should be gone and I haven't been there to do it. Maybe you should go there. You could see and get Maggie for me." And she was babbling like an idiot, but she had to get him to understand. What he was talking about was just—the idea just creeped her out.

"I've already been." His matter of fact voice pulled her back from the willies. "There was surveillance on the house, but I got in the back way and got your cat. I figured that would take a worry off your mind so you can focus. I also picked up this, because I saw how much work you'd put into making it and I figured it was important."

He went back to the dresser and held up a sheaf of paper and a pen. Wait. The world reduced to the heavy black Mont Blanc pen she recognized as her own. Not just any paper and pen, her specially prepared vellum and ink made the old fashioned way with ground ochre and onyx and indigo for colors. The way to create change. Her weapons. She fought to keep her breathing steady, to clear her mind against the pulse of the quicksilver pain. With those tools she could free herself.

Now she just needed to get them.

CHAPTER 7 — NOTHING AT ALL

Three days, and he had heard nothing from Fitzsimmons. Gleason tore his gaze off the leafy street scene just outside his hotel room and turned to Fi. She was seated on the small couch with her black legging-covered legs curled up under her, a loose cream cotton tunic spread around her, her pale hair still dark from a morning shower. She had the TV on some game show, but she wasn't watching. Instead she was picking at her fingernails and pouting.

"I'm sorry," he said."Something just doesn't feel right. It's taking too long for him to get back to us and…." He shook his head and let his voice fade because he just couldn't define what it was that had him on edge.

"But all I want is to just be able to go shopping. My clothes are all wrong for Washington."

"And this from the girl who was living on the street last spring." He couldn't help but roll his eyes. Fi Murdoch was proving as much a handful as Vallon had been as a teenager. Not that he'd known Vallon then, but he'd read her file and been briefed when he started as head of the AGS. Now Fi might not be as much of a wild card, but she had plenty of attitude to make up for it. She wasn't the terrified, crazy girl she'd been when she'd been with her mother. Vallon had done that much for her, even though there had clearly been something driving the friends apart in New Madrid.

He sighed and looked down in the street again. There was nothing there to concern him. People shifted past the hotel front on Rhode Island Avenue. There were no workmen lingering. No one had been seated in the café across the street for an extended period and there were no homeless people hanging around begging. So why the persistent feeling of being watched?

"No shopping, but I'll tell you what. You wait for me this morning while I check in with some other folks I know. When I come back, this afternoon we can go out and visit some of the sights, and maybe we can visit a shop or two. Sound okay?" God save him from moody girls and young women. He blessed his dear departed wife with gifting him with a son now grown and married and with children himself. All of them were safely away and hidden the last time they'd had contact. That was at least some relief.

Fi's expression barely changed. She hunched into the tunic he'd bought her at a Walmart they'd visited on the way into the city. It was too large, but it provided an alternative to shorts and a halter and was the only thing she'd liked enough to even try on, though he'd thrown an assortment of clothes for the both of them into the car.

He went across the room to sit beside her. "Fi. I'm trying. I know you don't want to be here, but it really is for the best. Amundson is gunning for every Gifted in Seattle and he knows you. He'd have picked you up in a heartbeat and then think where you'd be. Not only a prisoner, but a weapon against the Gifted and Vallon."

She turned pinched features towards him. "You think I don't know that?" She tossed her head. "Everyone treats me like I'm stupid or an invalid, but I'm remembering stuff from school and from with my mother. I can do things, too." She looked at her hands and gave a heartbreaking sigh. "The worst thing is, I could help Vallon, and instead I'm here with you."

"But Vallon's fine. She's got Jason to help her."

She shook her head.

"She's with Jason," he assured her.

She ran her hands up over her face and buried them in her hair, the heels of her palms pressing her eyes as if she wanted to block out the world. "I know," she said, but her voice was small and shaky.

"Fi?" What was it with this waif of a girl-woman? She was one of the oddest creatures he'd ever known, and that was saying something given he worked with both Vallon and Landon. There was confusing vulnerability and strength about her that just didn't make sense. Or maybe it did given what she'd been through in her life.

"Just leave me alone and go to your meeting."

"Fi, what is it?"

She shook her head and the stubborn line of her lips said he wasn't going to get anything else out of her, which meant he was wasting his time even trying. He threw up his hands and stood. Well, he'd tried being friends and a father figure. Now he'd just be himself.

"All right. I'm going to meet with Fitzsimmons." He checked his watch. "I should be back about noon and we'll have lunch and then head out. Think about what places you'd like to see."

He grabbed his suit jacket and stepped out into the hallway, feeling just a small bit defeated—by this not-much-more-than-a-girl. He adjusted his tie and considered the closed door. Behind it swelled the flare of Fi's willful Gifted presence. He just hoped he could be more persuasive with Fitzsimmons today.

§

Where persuasiveness had failed, science had prevailed.

The lab smelled of sweat and blood and the air seemed to shimmer with pain as Landon whistled through his teeth while he pushed the equipment tray to the side of the room. He really hated to have to work this way, but the damned subject was simply too resistant to the drugs and methods Landon had at his disposal. The damned man had a will stronger than he'd ever seen in the experiments sanctioned back at the beginning of the AGS. But then he had been working with volunteer Gifted agents and a few criminals who had had the Gift, and since then there'd only been the two original owners of this wedge of undetected landscape.

Usually, the drugs alone allowed him to suck his subject's knowledge dry. Xavier de Varga, however…. Well, extreme times required extreme measures. That was what he kept telling himself but…. Landon studied the pattern of blood on his lab coat with dismay. If the damned man had just been cooperative, this would never have happened and *he* wouldn't be facing an over-long meditation session to attempt to cleanse himself of the negative vibrations of this form of action. All his years fighting for equanimity and peace, and here he was again, inflicting pain. That sort of thing could seriously impact his Alchemical endeavors. Couldn't the damned man understand that all he had to do was give up a little more information? It wasn't like he was going to try to destroy the Gifted or anything. He just wanted to be fully part of them and to take his rightful place amongst the greater Gifted in the world. Was it so much to ask, to bring science to their table?

His lab was a mess really, and so was he. That was what you got after three long days in here with barely a nap between sessions with Xavier. There was his chair, pushed carelessly against the far wall away from chance blood splatter. The tray of surgical instruments stood near the sink for washing. The bin for the disposal of medical waste stood to one side of the table where his subject lay, naked—because it should increase de Varga's sense of vulnerability—and still comatose under the drugs' sway. Better, he supposed, than fully feeling the pain of Landon's little ministrations.

The drugs had been the first layer of his actions, planned long ago in case such a subject fell into his hands. He'd begun to think that it was never going to happen when Vallon had brought word of the man she'd met. Of course it would be Vallon. She had always been his pigeon, his little bird set out so he could study her while awaiting the hawks that might circle around such a delectable possible meal. It had finally worked: an Other attracted to the powerful Gift of his Vallon. It would have been wrong not to take advantage of it.

It would have been wrong, even though Xavier de Varga had proved himself an ally in both the Murdoch affair and in dealing with the rogue Gifted. There was actually some question of whether they could have ever overcome those threats without Xavier's help.

He slid the instruments into the sink and ran soapy water over them to soak and then turned back to Xavier. Blood dripped in slow crimson drops from the table edge to splatter on the off-white floor. Of course he had neglected to put drainage systems into the room, so he'd have to mop the mess up once he'd moved Xavier to a holding cell.

He went to the table where Xavier's dark head lolled to one side. The first drug had weakened him, by thinning his blood, killing off a portion of the red blood cells that seemed to be the source of much of the Gifted power. It seemed that was the source of power in the Others, as well, so they weren't so different after all. The second level of drugs had been a powerful narcotic that attacked the centers of judgment in the brain. That burned out a subject's resistance to answering questions. And still the man had fought, and held back.

Until Landon brought out the tools.

He'd hesitated to do so. After all, he didn't *want* to maim the man. But the fact that Xavier de Varga resisted him said there was a greater reason. A greater secret that Xavier was hiding. Something beyond that there had been a race of Alchemists who had all died out or been killed off in the witch hunts. He looked down at Xavier's right hand, his drawing hand. That would be his most precious weapon if the Others shared the Gifted need to use vellum and ink to create and hold their most complex creations.

It didn't exactly look like a hand at the moment.

He had, with surgical precision, dislocated each knuckle and bone until the hand was a twisted mess. When that hadn't worked to loosen de Varga's tongue, he'd begun the careful process of flaying each finger one by one.

That had finally worked. After a second dose of the powerful blood thinner. It was like the blood was connected to everything in the Gifted. Xavier had revealed the real end of the Alchemists Landon had begun to think of as his people.

Even left to their own devices, there had been contact between the Others that he'd learned called themselves Cartos, and Alchemists, but the Cartos had done a better job of appearing like everyone else in that medieval society. They had not kept the paraphernalia of strangeness that the Alchemists had, only bits of vellum and quills. So when the purges began, many of Landon's kind had sought Cartos help. Almost to a person they'd been turned down out of fear that it would bring the purges down on Cartos heads. And so they had died—many of them most horribly. Not only was Landon alone in the world, but they had, through inaction, made sure there weren't others who could teach him what he needed to know to achieve reunion with the Creator to regain full control of his power.

Beyond that, Xavier could tell him nothing. The man passed out and Landon had the sense that he'd drained him dry in more ways than one. If he could believe him.

The problem was that thinned blood did not coagulate, and so drop by drop Xavier was literally bleeding a death of a thousand cuts through his hand. It was time to undo it.

Landon injected the intravenous tube with a pale yellow liquid that would not undo, but at least stop the further destruction of blood cells and leave what there was of coagulant. Then he pulled up a stool and set to working on the hand. First, reset the mangled joints. He took each knuckle and popped it into place, like fitting together the pieces of a cheap stereo stand. Pop. Pop. Pop. Probably a good thing de Varga was out like a light. And so on, until what he held in his two hands resembled a bloody, skinless hand again. Then he began to carefully replace the long strips of skin that he had removed and kept alive in a nutrient-rich solution. After all, he was not trying to maim Xavier for life. He just needed information that only Xavier could give.

It was painstaking work, but he had always been a stickler for details. Finally, he was able to bandage the hand. Splayed against the metal table, it looked like a white star or a flower. Something you would want to cradle close and protect, especially when injured. For a moment he even considered loosening the bonds and placing the hand safely on its owner's chest, but that would just be foolish.

"You are what Vallon says you are: an admirable and powerful man." He shifted a lock of Xavier's sweat-matted hair off of his face. Even slack in unconsciousness his features were both handsome and ruthless. It was a combination not unlike Vallon, though her features carried more beauty and unwavering determination.

The air shimmered like light on water and he staggered back. Stopped.

It could not be. The man was awake and trying something.

Landon dove for the fridge, tore open the door, and grabbed an already prepared syringe. The scent of ozone and ether filled the room as he ran back to the table. The drugs were clearly working, but not quite as well as Landon needed them to. He stabbed the syringe into Xavier's chest and the man's back arched and he roared.

Before collapsing onto the table again. The power cut out like a bubble burst and the room went silent. A rage-filled black gaze locked on Landon.

"I'm sorry," he said. "I can't possibly let you just walk away, now." Or however it was he was going to travel. And by the rage in Xavier's eyes, it was likely Landon would never be able to let him go, for the man would come for him. And being on the receiving end of Xavier de Varga's anger did not really fit into Landon's plans. That meant he was going to have to be very careful to keep Xavier drugged appropriately.

Which was a shame, actually, for he'd had other plans for Xavier—plans that would let him use technology he'd been working on for a very long time. It was also a shame that use of the drugs had the long term effects of eroding both the body and the mind of the subject. It was a problem he'd been working on before Amundson took over the AGS.

With Xavier safely contained, he left the workroom and padded in his moccasins down the hall to his private meditation chamber. The cool air was sweet with incense that cut through the copper stink up his nose. Cool enough he shivered when he stripped off his soiled lab coat, his trousers and shirt, and in his underwear sat down on a simple grey pillow in yoga position before the Azoth. The archaic drawing of a tree flanked by a man and woman, with symbols of sun and moon, the four elements, and so on, hung on the wall with its many layered symbols ready to help him in his search for meaning and transformation.

He sat there a long time, trying to quiet his mind.

It didn't happen.

If he hoped to find peace, this was going to be an uncharacteristically long session.

§

Vallon tried to keep her focus anywhere but the pen and vellum; hard to do when they were everything she needed and they were so close to being in her grasp. If she could just free her hands and arms. If she could just get free of Jason.

The acrid tanning scent of the vellum and the spice of the ink cut through the wood-scented room and felt like it started her heart beating again. She had hope; at the same time, the fact Jason had been in her secret workroom made her stomach do an unpleasant flip-flop.

She took a deep breath and looked up at Jason, where he stood by the dresser against the wall. His t-shirt gleamed in the light from the hallway, she could imagine the light fur on his pecs turning to a straight line down under the waistband of his low-slung jeans. His chocolate gaze was locked on her as if he could tell what she was thinking, could tell the effect the drawing instruments and the afterburn had on her.

She forced herself to shrug, just as a surge of incense and cedar of Lebanon-scented power burst up through the floor around her. The air vibrated and there came a sound like distant thunder and a sense of yearning and heat and unending pain. No voice. No presence, but she knew instantly. Xavier. It had to be. The power and sensations surged through her drug-weakened brain and tore her away. Her right hand was an incandescent source of pain. The room telescoped around her and Jason's angry voice filled her ears as he yelled. Was that a voice? A word? She couldn't tell through Jason's yelling. Something struck her face so hard her ears rang.

And then the power was gone, leaving her trembling on the bed with only the lingering scent of cedar of Lebanon, the wrenching pain in her hand that brought tears to her eyes, and Jason's handprint on her cheek.

"What. The fuck. Was that?" He growled, his hand about two inches from her face and ready to brand her skin again.

"I don't know. I don't know." Because if that was Xavier, where was he? Why wasn't he here?

"Don't lie to me, Vallon. I can see power, remember? I can tell when you try to play your little tricks on me."

"It wasn't me. It wasn't." Was Xavier looking for her? Then why was he in such pain? Had Landon's surgery not worked? Or had something else happened? Had Amundson's men caught them before they could reach safety? She needed to be up and away from here, now. She had to help the children and then find Xavier and Landon, because something was seriously wrong.

She fought to calm her pounding heart and drew in a breath. First things first: she needed Jason to free her or she needed access to the vellum and pen he held. "I don't know what that was, but it wasn't me. I'm sorry if you think it was. As for everything else, well, thanks for getting Maggie. The other stuff wasn't necessary." She thought a moment, trying to fight off the shaking that just wouldn't seem to stop. "So just when did you start searching my house?" Had he started during the Murdoch affair? Had he known all along what she could do?

"A week or so ago. When you left for New Madrid, I took over caring for Miss Maggie. Before then I got the idea when I saw how you *changed* things. I've been trying to talk to you about it for months, but you wouldn't give me the time. Remember?"

She did. All the brush-offs because she'd thought he wanted to talk about their very brief, but torrid, relationship.

"If you can change a mountain, surely to God you can give me one woman. I was sure of it when I saw living creatures in your basement."

So the past few weeks he'd had the full run of the house because no one was there. Her skin crawled at the thought of him searching her rooms, touching her things, and the taste of bile rose in her throat. In so many ways, this man had violated her.

She took a deep breath because she had to deal with him to get through him. "I can't do what you ask. It's impossible. The Gift is tied to the earth, not to people."

Jason's expression hardened. "Don't try your lies on me. I saw your eyes when you saw these." He held up the pen and paper again. "You wanted them almost as bad as I want my wife."

She knew it was no good to deny it. The damage was done. She closed her eyes trying to get her arguments in order, but the damn drugs, the worry for Xavier, and the quicksilver sliding over her brain made concentration almost impossible.

"Jason, don't do this." She opened her eyes. "There are people dying out there. That burst was from Xavier. Something's gone wrong. And I had another vision and there were screams and gunfire. The children are dying, Jason. You don't want that. Please just let me go, and I'll forget all about this. Please. For the children."

His implacable expression never changed. "Funny thing. Once upon a time I'd be right there with you. That was my job. But I left that job because there's only one thing I really care about: Cheryl. They're your children. Your kind. I never met them. Seems to me, the longer you fuck around refusing to do what I'm asking, the more kids will probably die. The choice is yours."

The cold glare of his gaze was so far removed from the dedicated Seattle PD detective she'd met barely six months ago, it left her almost gagging.

He left the pen and vellum where she could see them and went to the door. "I'm a reasonable man, Vallon. Just give me what I want and I'll let you go." The sound of a cat's cry came from somewhere beyond the door. He looked around at it and checked his watch. "Sounds like my star boarder wants dinner. I'll let you think about things for a little while and then I'll be back. Hopefully you'll make the right decision and I won't have to drug you again."

And then the door slammed shut leaving her in darkness that was streaked through with sickening quicksilver threads and the knowledge that she was helpless when too many lives depended on her.

"Jason!" she shouted and fought against her bonds.

No answer.

"Jason, please! For the children!" And Xavier. She wrenched at the ropes around her wrists and ankles, arched her back, and fell back on the table frustrated.

Nothing at all.

CHAPTER 8 — LIKE VALLON WOULD DO

Wolf Amundson slid out of his chauffeured town car and stretched his back. An hour and a half from Seattle to inspect his handiwork, and the warehouse hunkered down in the midst of a nearly abandoned light industrial area lodged between farmland and the edge of the ocean. Suitably isolated and yet suitably close to major transportation. The small Washington town of Anacortes lay about five minutes down the road, but since the recession gutted the town's businesses, the locals were leaving and the tourists just didn't come like they used to. Even when they did come, a warehouse with high barbwire fences wasn't about to capture their attention. The men stationed inside the fences had weapons concealed against the casual passerby's inspection, and the subjects, well, they were apparently suitably subdued inside. It was almost a peaceful scene, with the hush of cars from nearby Highway 20 and the quiet lap of water on Fidalgo Bay. Why anyone would put industrial buildings on what could be resort land, he'd never know, but it had served his purposes.

He turned to Page, his hulking number one man on contract from Loadstone. "Looks good. Impressive even, and right under everyone's noses. I like that."

Page inclined his head. He was a big man, through no taller than Wolf. He had the hulking shoulders of a football player or a man who spent too many hours at weights, and the rough-hewn face of a man with limited patience who had managed to transcend that limitation. Self-possessed and self-controlled. Both qualities that Wolf admired in a person who always got the job done.

"So how much is all this going to cost me—us—the government?"

"Couple of mill a month." Page shrugged.

"A couple of million." Amundson thought about the appropriation meetings Fitzsimmons was going to. "That may be a little steep."

Page's blade-grey eyes caught and held on him. "If you want, we can just release all the subjects, or maybe we should just cull them. We've got enough spares."

"Jeezus Christ, Page. They're children, even if they are Gifted. I want tools I might be able to use, not dead bodies that I have to explain to Washington. That little shooting was about the last thing I needed. They're kids, not terrorists."

"Yeah, so? One of the men got spooked by the mist rolling around the students and he thought they were trying something. He's been removed from the detail. Okay? And it was you who was moaning about costs. I was just laying out options like you pay me to."

Killing children was not what he'd created this installation for. He had created it to hopefully gather some answers about the Gift. Like what part of the brain the power came from and how the hell to turn it off. If they could turn it off, then no one would have to be hurt and maybe, just maybe, he'd feel like he could breathe again. But in the interim, a couple of million a month wasn't the proverbial 'chicken feed' and he seriously doubted that Fitzsimmons would in any way sanction this installation. His own decision to shut down the AGS might just about cover it, but right now that money was being used to fund the extra agents he'd brought in to track down the missing AGS agents. He was going to have to make some cuts elsewhere in Seattle Station. Well, some of the other domestic terrorist threats were about to be downgraded for the moment and any wages for AGS agents were suspended. That should help.

He lifted his chin at the building. "You going to show me around?"

Page lifted one eyebrow. "Of course. You're paying for it."

They entered through a small side door near the neatly parked industrial forklifts and light trucks.

"Nice touch." He nodded at the equipment.

"Came with the building. Owner couldn't give them away after the economic meltdown."

They entered and Wolf found himself in a loading bay area with doors at either end. Page led him through one of the doors into a short hallway.

"This hall is able to be locked down and gassed in case anyone tries to break in. The hall at the other end is the same."

He led Wolf through another door and inside. The place smelled of not-quite-eradicated engine oil and antiseptic and air heated by newly installed, rank upon rank of white lights that hung down from the ceiling. Electrical cabling swung in thick, twisted mazes between them. Below the lights, what looked like modular walls divided the floor of the warehouse into smaller mesh-ceilinged rooms separated by narrow corridors. Openly armed men patrolled those hallways. More armed men guarded a stairwell that led up to another level.

"As you can see, we had to jury rig enough power for our purposes. The kids we have upstairs because someone suggested that having the electrical power between them and the ground might act as a barrier to them accessing whatever it is they do from the earth." He shrugged. "So far it seems to have worked. Seems to me, if they try something, we have other ways of dealing with it." His hand unconsciously reached for his concealed weapon.

It was that attitude that had lost them a full one quarter of the young people picked up at the academy, and their deaths left him feeling not a little sick to his stomach. But they'd already had words about it, so Wolf wasn't going there again, just so long as they had the understanding that it wasn't to happen again.

"You've gotten a lot done in such a short time." Wolf said.

That curved Page's lips in a look of satisfaction. "Let's just say we thought a place like this might be useful someday."

Wolf took that news in as something to consider another day. A major corporation had a facility like this just sitting empty until Wolf asked for it? "How convenient it just happened to be so close to Seattle."

But Page's closed expression suggested that similar sites might be elsewhere in America. Near every major center? They *could* serve as internment camps for a host of possible subjects. Or research facilities. A foresighted move, then, but one that made his skin crawl a little.

"So show me what we have so far."

"This way." Page led off into the maze of corridors to a door marked V1, knocked once on the door, and entered.

The room was clearly a security control room, smelling of heated electronics and stale coffee. Banks of computer consoles controlled monitor screens covering the walls, with four burly men seated in semidarkness, watching, their fingers playing across keyboards.

"This is viewing room 1. We have three of them in the building as a means of double-checking what is going on and ensuring that if one set of eyes is distracted, another will catch it if something is wrong. Each of the viewing stations has identical monitors, except for one." He pointed at a monitor showing a room with a long line of unoccupied beds. "This is the viewing room that focuses on nighttime activity in the subject holding area. They have infrared to track whether there are any groups meeting together."

Amundson's gaze slipped from the screen to Page.

"We want to ensure that there's no plotting going on, so we don't have another episode like the last one at the trucks."

So he was still holding to the belief that the students had planned something while in the trucks. He was giving a bunch of terrified students a lot more credit than Wolf would have.

"Each of the other viewing rooms has another view of the rooms the subjects reside in, eating area, bathrooms. Each has responsibility for all of that area. We decided to go this way after we discovered that watching that many subjects continuously raised the fatigue level too high. There was too much possibility of missing something."

Amundson turned his attention to the screen. Though the room of beds was largely unoccupied, three of the beds held what looked like slumbering figures. No one moved. Nothing happened, and frankly, he would rather slit his own wrists than do this very boring job.

But there was something about the scene that bothered him. He leaned in close to the monitor and still wasn't sure if he saw anything. "Have you got the room wired for sound?"

"Of course," Page said and nodded at one of the four men, who removed an earbud from his ear and held it out to Wolf.

"All here, but there's nothing going on. Like a grave in there, ya might say." Page nudged the man's chair with his foot. "Sir."

So not company men, this lot. Amundson gingerly accepted the earbud with distaste and held it up to his ear. There came only the sound of empty air and a light crackling. And yet…

He looked back at the video again. "Zoom in on the face of the boy in blue."

The man who had shared his earbud nodded, his fingers flickering over his keyboard in the semidarkness.

The boy in question lay on his side, short curly blond hair tousled, his legs curled up and his hands curled up towards his face, a position mirrored by the other two youth. But when the camera zoomed in, Wolf was even more certain.

"Zoom in again, and close up on his face."

More clicks of the keys and the camera flickered, and suddenly the boy's face filled the screen and it was clear that the men had been mistaken, because the boy's lips were moving.

"Show the faces of the other subjects in the room."

He had the attention of the other people in the room now. Swiftly three monitors changed from views of hallways to bring up the faces of the other 'sleepers'. On each of them, their lips moved, but not in unison, as if there was a whispered conversation with each person taking their turn.

"Shit," Page said. "They've got a conversation going on right under our noses." He grabbed a phone off one of the consoles and stabbed a number. "I want the students in the sleeping room brought out separately. Now. Each strapped down in separate examination rooms. Now! And check the fucking microphones in the room. We're not picking up anything."

He slammed down the phone and turned to Amundson. "Thank you. Who knows what the little bastards could have cooked up together? They were old enough to work some serious damage from what the reports from the school indicate."

On the monitor the three faces suddenly disappeared from the screens, but not before Amundson saw one of the faces, a girl's, scream.

Then the camera's pulled back to show three struggling teens in the hands of twelve well-armed men. Overkill, he was sure. But then a haze seemed to lift off the floor.

"Aah, fuck," Page swore as one of his men screamed and sank into the floor. He grabbed a microphone on the wall. "Knock 'em out! Get them out of there!" Three rifle butts slammed into three temples and the kids collapsed. The shimmer in the room stopped and Wolf blinked and wiped his eyes. What was going on? A weird sort of buzzing seemed to ring in his ears for a moment and then was gone. Page seemed dazed and so did the others, but slowly fingers got back up to speed on the keyboards. Page took a deep breath and shook his head as if to dislodge something.

Wolf stepped up to the bank of monitors. All showed the busy movement of people in a busy installation. Then three new monitors lit up as armed men dragged three comatose bodies into separate rooms and strapped them onto what looked like examination tables. Three other monitors showed an empty room of beds and that made no sense at all that one room should get so much attention. Except for one thing that drew his gaze like the gore scene at an accident, and made his skin crawl. A man's torso stuck up out of the metal decking of the room as if it had grown there.

He had no idea how it got there. His gorge rose in his throat at the seamless way the man joined with the floor.

Page, white faced and furious, turned to him. "Kids? You see, Amundson? These aren't just kids. I'll be worrying about my men more than these little bastards."

§

The stupid television was playing yet another mind-numbing game show and Fi thought her brain might explode. Here she was trapped in a hotel room, and darned Gleason thought the TV would keep her entertained. As if she was a child or something. Everyone seemed to think of her that way, even Vallon.

Actually, especially Vallon, though she'd said all the right things when they last saw each other in that hole, New Madrid. A place like that, aside from Farrah and Lizzy Ducharme, they might have done the world a favor by just leaving the place in a pit caused by the New Madrid fault line. But Vallon had done more than treat her like a child—Vallon had *used* her like a tool to control the afterburn and then had dumped her like a hot potato when Xavier had shown up. He must be a better tool—*or have one.*

Her cheeks burned briefly. That was Vallon—always looking for a better tool. But Vallon did have a good side. She was dedicated to her work. Always had been, at least she had been in school, to the point where she'd break the rules to practice. She was always pushing the envelope. And she *had* saved Seattle and the entire Midwest. Not bad for a kid abandoned by her father.

In fact it was pretty darn good, and really good compared to what she, Fi, had done with her life. Panhandler and street person, that's what she'd been. She *had* painted a bedroom. And gotten her first job. The first two were all she'd ever done by herself. She'd never have even had the possibility of the second two if not for Vallon. So maybe Vallon wasn't the problem. Maybe she was. Maybe she needed to grow up so that they'd stop treating her like a child.

She clicked off the TV and the inane chimes and boings and the excited shouts and the stoopid music cut out and left her in a breathless silence. She stood and paced to the window and looked out on the leafy Washington street. A few people walked past, business men mostly, along with a few women obviously shopping. Like she could be, if Gleason only trusted her. But he'd never trust her as long as she acted like a child.

It looked like one of those wonderful September days when the summer was just thinking about fading into fall, warm with cool notes in the evening. But this was a different kind of city than Seattle and a darn sight different than Hicksville, New Madrid. The shorts and t-shirts she'd worn both places just weren't going to cut it here, and the pretty dresses and so on she'd bought for the 'holiday' she thought she was going to have with Vallon had all disappeared in the devastation. They were some of the little things that a Gifted didn't think about when making a Change. Come to think of it, how many empty closets were there around the Midwest right now? Now that was something funny to think about. Something to tease Vallon about.

She rolled on her heels and pressed her lips together as she considered her plight. What would it hurt if she went out just to the shops across the street and at least took a look? If she found what she needed, then it would leave so much more time for sightseeing with Gleason this afternoon.

But he'd told her to stay put in no uncertain terms. Terms a child could understand.

She scrunched her eyes shut and balled her fists. Darn it! Gleason wouldn't try something like this with Vallon. If he did, what would Vallon do?

She opened her eyes and looked out the window; the answer was so easy.

The wrinkles in the stoopid Walmart tunic didn't quite come out when she tried to smooth them, but it would have to do. She slung her fringed purse over her shoulder and, humming the stoopid theme song from the stoopid game show, she went to the door. "Sorry, Gleason. I'm not a little girl anymore."

Outside, the warm air was like a balm after the air-conditioned stuff in the hotel. It smelled of summer—warm asphalt and sprinklers in the air and the scent of coffee from a shop just down the way. She inhaled and closed her eyes. Sooo much better than the room, and even better because she was doing this on her own.

Her shorts and the tunic stood out on the street just as they had in the plush carpeted hotel lobby. She really needed the clothes, but first maybe she'd just stretch her legs a little. She missed the walking she'd done as a street person and all the good food she was eating was putting flesh on her bones she wasn't sure she liked.

So a quick walk and the shop and then back to wait for Gleason. No, make that shop first—you never knew how long that could take. Then a quick walk and back to the hotel. She could already feel the Cheshire cat grin she'd give him as he arrived and took in her new clothes.

The traffic wasn't heavy so she jaywalked across the street, figuring this was a tourist town and drivers would be used to people diving into the street. It was shady on the other side and the air was cool enough she shivered. Across from her, the hotel's windows bore blinding reflections of the sun that made the entire building look like it burned, and suddenly she really didn't want to go back there.

She wouldn't. She'd shop and walk and then have a coffee and meet a surprised Gleason at the front entrance. It would save them time.

Okay. And now to the heavy task of shopping. Xavier hadn't given *her* much money at all. Not like he'd given Gleason. Another example of how she was treated like a child. And just what was she supposed to do if she and Gleason got separated, hmm?

Well, it was enough to maybe pick up a couple of things she needed.

She marched down the sidewalk and into the first store. It had a blue awning and the name *Sophie's* in a lovely script that spoke understated and expensive. A tiny bell tinkled over the door and she straightened, brushed her hair back from her face, and tried to imitate the haughty attitude of the well-heeled women she'd seen on the streets of Seattle. The air smelled of light citrus perfume.

"May I help you?" asked a perfectly coifed and made-up brunette, who appeared from the back of the store. She wore an azure suit with a white ruffled blouse and pearls that were probably real. The woman's gaze ran her top to bottom and clearly wasn't impressed by what she saw.

Fi had to fight back the urge to turn and run, but she was emulating Vallon, wasn't she. She swallowed and took a deep breath. "I'm looking for a top and trousers. I was traveling and the airline lost my luggage." She was proud of herself for coming up with that excuse for her appearance.

The woman's pink tongue touched her lips briefly and then her lips curved into the practiced smile of a saleswoman. "I'm sure we have something. Can you give me an idea of what you're looking for?"

Fi stammered through that one, but managed to save herself by saying she'd prefer to just look around. The woman left her then—but not totally. Her dark, sales person eyes were like hawk claws on the back of Fi's neck as she browsed. She fingered the fabrics and surreptitiously scanned the price tags and finally settled on a pair of turquoise capris and white sweater set that would just fit within her meager budget. When she modeled them and asked for the woman's opinion the woman's gaze changed almost as if she could see Fi as a worthy customer. Fi bought them and wore them out of the store, her tunic and shorts in a cloth shopping bag that made her purse look shabby. It was ten thirty: still time for the walk and coffee before Gleason returned.

She struck off down the street with the sun on her left shoulder and, far ahead, the spike of the Washington Monument like a torch against the blue sky. She'd been there a few days ago when Gleason had his first meeting. Hey, maybe she could surprise him and meet him there. Yes, that would be a Vallon thing to do!

Happily contemplating how her actions would change her relationships with Gleason, Vallon, and the others forever, she lengthened her stride and started humming as she swung her new cloth bag beside her. She felt good. She knew she looked better. The saleswoman had even said so.

The man strode past her just as many other pedestrians did, but he was tall and sandy-haired and blue-eyed and he actually smiled at her like they had a secret joke about the day and then he was gone in the other direction. She felt special about that smile. Maybe even that smile made her feel a little pretty. A pretty woman, and she thought of the movie. Maybe she hadn't been a prostitute, but she was hauling herself up by her bootstraps, too.

The same man—or she could have sworn it was the same man— hurried past her in the direction she was going. He sped about ten paces father on and then stopped and turned around and smiled again. She looked to either side, because he couldn't be looking at her with that lovely smile could he, and she felt a blush rise up her shoulders.

She tore her gaze away to the memorial that she was using as her compass but suddenly a pair of bright blue eyes blocked her way.

"*Fi?* Fiona Murdoch?"

She stopped dead in her tracks and let her gaze be drawn up to his. She was almost sure she didn't know him, but he knew her name and spoke it with such authority. Still, she'd spent enough years on the street to be wary.

"Who are you and what do you want?" She stepped back to put a safe distance between them, but there were enough people on the sidewalk that was difficult.

"It's me, Karl. Karl Heibert. Remember? I'm a friend of your mother's." Said with the right ring of familiarity, but there just wasn't any recollection of a Karl Heibert to be had.

She shook her head and backed up a step farther. "I don't know you."

"Sure you do." He grinned at a couple staring as they passed by. "The old swimming hole by the Robert's farm out next to that old private school of yours."

There had been a swimming hole that the kids would escape to from the academy, but she didn't remember any Robert's farm. She wished that Gleason was here, but the memorial was still too far away and the safety of the hotel was too far behind.

"Were you a friend of Vallon's?" she asked.

"Vallon, of course. We were great friends back then." He said and took a step closer. "How is ol' Vallon."

She'd never met a soul who would call her friend "ol' Vallon." And to her recollection, Vallon had no friends—except for her BFF, one Fi Murdoch.

Fi managed to plaster a smile on her face. "I haven't seen her in the longest time. We lost touch after school, you know?"

Edge back into a place where there are lots of people. A restaurant. A café. A business. Anything. She'd done it on the streets of Seattle when bad things had threatened to happen. There was a little bistro with some cute French-sounding name beside her. Maybe the lunch crowd would be busy enough. Maybe she could tell someone he was harassing her.

She backed up again and there was glass behind her. Grabbed for the door as Karl dove for her and barely managed to get inside the slam the door.

"Fi!" he yelled, his blue eyes flashing, no longer so guilelessly friendly.

The place smelled of melted butter and onions and garlic. She skittered away from the door feeling like some stupid, foolish animal. "Help. Someone!"

A woman with straight, black, shoulder-length hair and dressed in a sleeveless black dress and black fishnet stockings stepped out from behind a bar. "May I help you?"

"There's this man…" Fi began all the terror suddenly filling her as Karl stepped up beside her.

"I'm *so* sorry," Karl said, his calm deep voice cutting through her protests as he caught her arm, and *squeezed* so hard she almost fainted. "My sister. She has mental health problems. We thought she was doing better and brought her out on a day pass to go shopping." He sighed so realistically Fi almost believed.

Then he looked down at her and the welcoming blue of his eyes had gone cold. "Come on Fi. We'd better be going. Dad's going to be so upset this happened."

And before she could do anything but turn helplessly back towards the woman, he had her out the door, his grip so hard on her triceps she thought she might cry, and all she could think was that she so wasn't like Vallon.

CHAPTER 9 —THE BITTER TASTE OF FAITH

The room was white-washed, with metal cabinets on three sides and the only door—also metal—on the fourth, but even the too-white paint couldn't hide the copper scent of blood and the sense that someone had died here.

The metal bands bit into her wrists as she lay helpless on the cold, hard table in the center of the room. With her arms stretched wide and the horrible lights overhead, she felt like a specimen ready for dissection. She felt more like that when the men were in the room. The cold man with the ice-blue eyes and white-blond hair had looked at her like she was no more than a frog. He'd even acted like he hadn't heard her when she talked to him. It was like she—the person inside—didn't exist, and that was the most terrifying thing of all after all the terror of the school, the trip, and this place.

Well, maybe not the most terrifying. That would be the way the screams had stopped in the room next door and left her listening to the pounding of her heartbeat and the clatter of rain on the metal roof. Billy Newman's screams. Billy, the senior who had said they could break everyone out if they'd only work together. But most of the other seniors had been too afraid. Only she, a grade seven student, and Brett Horseman, a junior, had agreed. She'd been the least trained, the lowest in school grade, but she'd also been in an accelerated class for the truly Gifted, and she'd seen these people mow down a truckload of students as if they didn't matter in the least. She'd seen Cathy Bristol and Trevor Haines and Shakira Jones and so many others, both younger and older than she was, scream and die, cut down by gunfire. She hadn't wanted to stick around waiting for these people to come for her like they were slowly picking people out of the dorm room that was more like a holding cell.

So she'd agreed and everything had gone hopelessly wrong and so she was here. From the next room, the harsh men's voices and Billy's moans started again, like nails across a blackboard. She wanted to scream, she wanted to cry, but she'd done enough of both and they'd got her nowhere. The worst was that she couldn't stuff her hands in her ears to cut out the sound.

So over the sound of the rain she had to lie here listening to Billy dying—she knew he was because when she -reached-, his Gifted flame was streaked with horrific grey. She had to inhale the air scented of death and sea salt and maybe, just maybe, someone with the Gift would hear her sending. She was trying, though she didn't really know how to do it. Billy had said it was only a little possible and mostly only possible with the assistance of the map console.

Poor Billy.

The moaning had stopped.

The door to her room clicked open and then the three men stood there, including the ice-eyed man. Now it was her turn.

∫

Vallon jerked awake, a part of her still reaching for the connection. Her heart pounded so fast it took her a moment to realize where she was, who she was, that it wasn't her own terror she felt. She hadn't meant to doze off, but here in the night-dark room with the drugs placing the quicksilver streaks across her vision and her brain, she couldn't help herself. It was like everything conspired to shut her down, hold her in place, and smother her will to get free, just when she most needed to get out there to help those children. To save that little girl who had been brave enough to try to save her friends, from the same ending her Billy had faced.

One deep breath, then another. Blow the breath out slowly and clear her mind. Her heart slowed to its usual slow metronome cadence. She tried futilely to yank her arms loose of their bonds. Damn Jason. Damn him all to hell because she now had a sense of where the girl might be. Still in the Pacific Northwest most likely, because she'd smelled the sea. The metal roof on the building suggested a barn or a warehouse, and given the number of children taken, she'd bet on it being a warehouse. And wherever the girl was, she was—north!

Knowing it, feeling the remnants of the connection, was a triumph in so many ways. Most of all it was a triumph over the drugs. She could feel the connection; it had been there, though it no longer existed. The giant pulse of the ley lines came up through the floor though she could not reach for them yet.

Jason might see the Gift's actions, but he sure as hell wouldn't even see it coming, until she was done with him.

"Jason! Jason!"

Sure she'd agree to help him. Anything to get her hands on that pen and vellum, and then watch her work.

She lay there inhaling her own sweat and filth. She'd needed a shower when they'd arrived in Seattle. After sneaking into the school and then being here for however long, she was pretty well ripe and turning to rot. Jason had allowed her up only once to relieve herself, and the drugs had been such that she could barely stand, let alone summons enough strength to even consider attacking him.

"Jason!" She screamed it at the top of her lungs. Damn him. Where was a good one when you needed them? Like Xavier. Where was he?

A fading whiff of cedar of Lebanon reached her nose. Had he truly tried to come to her? Or was it just wishful thinking? Jason had seen that something was happening, so it must have been Xavier. But if so, why hadn't he come through? Why the strong sense of pain?

She closed her eyes and -reached- and slammed right into the invisible drug-induced wall around her head. Her stomach heaved and she turned her head, but managed to swallow her gorge again. Damn drugs. Damn Jason. She never should have let him into her house the first time. If she'd just left their relationship as professional....

Nice time to finally recognize that, Drake. She could hear Landon's prissy diction as he lectured, because he would lecture, albeit briefly. Then he would proceed to analyze all the things she had done wrong in her life that had resulted in her making whatever bad decision he was faced with.

But now that she was here, she had to find a way out of the predicament and she could think of only one way.

"Jason! I'll do it. I'll try!"

Would he accept her offer? More importantly, would he believe her?

Footsteps sounded from elsewhere in the house-apartment or wherever this was. Then a key sounded in the door lock and suddenly the darkness parted. Jason, silhouetted, leaned against the door frame, stroking a little black and white cat that he held in his arms. Maggie.

"You said something?"

Again, she couldn't see his face and didn't like the way he held Maggie. There was something powerful and not quite right about it—as if the cat was here to prove something. But she had to do something to get out of here and help that child—all the students—and Xavier. There were too many potential victims out there.

"I said I'd help you. I'd try. It doesn't mean I'll succeed, but I'll give it my best shot in return for my freedom. I have to save those kids, Jason." He wouldn't give a damn about Xavier.

He stepped farther into the room and a level of tension seemed to ease from his body. His chest expanded and release in a huge sigh. "So let's get to it."

Damn it, didn't he understand?

"I can't do a darn thing like this." She writhed in the ropes to get the point across. "I need to sit up. I need my hands to use, and most of all I need a clear mind."

Jason came around her so the angled light hit his face like in a Rembrandt painting, and all his features were in high relief. "I see. That might be a problem, given I don't trust you, Vallon. Give you the tools and you're just as likely to blow me away like dust, like Rebecca Murdoch tried. Remember?"

"Not likely I'd forget. I tried my best to save you. To hold you, but I would have failed if Fi and Xavier hadn't arrived." Remind him of all they'd survived together and of how she'd tried to help him. What did they say in hostage situations? Build rapport with your captors. Well, she'd give it the old college try.

"Jason, I can see that you love Cheryl. I can see she's your passion and that you'll do anything to have her back. That's how I feel about those children. I'll do anything to make sure they survive. If it takes fulfilling your wish, so be it. But I can't guarantee it. Please understand that."

His gaze felt like a heavy weight on her face. Finally he sighed. "You really think you can get by with trying? That's a no go, for me, I'm afraid. So how about we give you a little more incentive? How about Maggie, here. Succeed and you and your little friend can go your own way. Fail and maybe Maggie doesn't do so well." He pointed to a chair half hidden in the darkness of a corner of the room. "There's a sac there and there's a lake not too far away. Seems cats can't swim too well when they'd confined."

She almost quit breathing. Sure, Maggie was a brat, but it was Maggie. She loved Maggie. "I thought you liked Maggie." She could barely get the words out.

"I do. Quite a lot, actually. But if it comes down to Maggie's life or Cheryl's, my wife wins hands down. So I guess you better make sure this works, hadn't you?"

She closed her eyes where she lay. Knowing Jason, if she did nothing, he'd drown Maggie anyway, as punishment. She had to get free, and the only way she could see was to get at least one limb free and/or an undrugged mind. Neither was apparently something she could do for herself. At least not in any timely fashion.

When she looked at him, she met his gaze. "This has never been done. How can I promise something I don't know I can do?"

And he smiled. "Vallon, you've been doing the impossible ever since I met you. I have complete faith you can do this."

It was a smile of such charm and humor that she thought she might be ill.

§

Landon rinsed his mouth again and spat into the rushing sink water of the single small bathroom that existed in his desert installation. Repeated the action for the third time, but it still didn't relieve him of the taste of vomit, nor of the stench that had finally forced him up from his meditations because he could not stand himself.

He leaned heavily on the clean white porcelain, trying to stay upright, but his knees kept buckling, wanting to return him to the undignified embrace of the toilet.

All his doing. Just what was he doing? *What he had done to Xavier's hand.*

A cold, clinical part of himself was properly satisfied that it had all worked so well. He had left the hand reassembled as best he could and had gained a reasonable amount of information for his efforts. But another part of him was filled with horror, and the whole time he tried to meditate the image of Xavier's hand kept breaking his concentration. He'd finally given up on the Azoth and had tried to meditate on Xavier's injured hand, but that had just led him to even darker places in his mind.

And that had sent him scurrying for the bathroom.

That Xavier might never have full use of that hand again—well, that was the price to be paid for holding out on Landon Snow. The clinical part of him thought this physical illness entirely ridiculous.

It was just a hand, and far and away the least the man could give up if he was going to try to hold onto secrets he shouldn't have. It was a symbol if nothing else; and symbols, as he knew, were important.

It wasn't as if he'd come into this wanting to do anything nefarious. He simply wanted access to what was his by right of blood. He eased up to the small medicine cabinet mirror over the sink and leaned there shakily. Too pale, too-pink skin, and watery pale blue-pink eyes met him. A thatch of askew white hair atop the head, but that was thinning. Not attractive. Not at all, which was why his love had been unrequited years ago. He knew what others called him—the White Gnome. The Twisted Dwarf. But he was none of these. He was a just a man with the unfortunate genetic luck to be born albino and unforgivably short. He had no twisted limbs and was within the bell curve norms—just at the low extreme. A fair trade for the brains he received in return.

But no one looked past the exterior. Not even Sylvia, the woman he had loved forever and probably always would. But she was elsewhere—

Portland, if his tracking of her was up to date. Not exactly a safe place given what Amundson was doing, but then no one knew about Sylvia's Gift. He'd seen to that years before.

He had hoped that Xavier would reveal things he needed to know to gain his Gift, to become a full-fledged Gifted instead of someone who was tolerated like an ugly, but useful, dog because of his other talents. But the news had been less than stellar.

Alchemists. How odd that the Others had called the long lost ones of their people this, given he had been drawn to Alchemy ever since that hot summer day when the grasshoppers and cicadas hummed in the tall grass that grew around the base of the library. He'd found the topic mentioned in a book crammed at the back of a top library shelf in the small Midwest town where he'd grown up. The book hadn't belonged there. It had no library stamp, no check-out card, and no library number on the spine, so he'd taken it—his very first crime. The book had discussed all sorts of esoteric beliefs—crystals, tarot cards, astrology—not your usual reading in a small farming town like his, but it had got there somehow, so someone had read it and wanted others to find it. From the moment of reading about how ancient people had tried to transmute lead into gold, he'd known Alchemy was not only for him, it was *about* him. About transforming his small white body into something wonderful and important. He'd stolen the book and still had it, the first in his collection. Finding the Gift had almost convinced him he had achieved the transmutation.

But that wasn't enough. Not after he'd realized how much more the Gift could do that he couldn't. When he'd tried, it was like a wave of nausea rose in him. A fire burned along his limbs and into his hands and then dissipated into nothing. Was that what had happened to those other Alchemists?

The Alchemists destroyed in the witch hunts of Europe. Could that be what his family was—survivors? Escapees from those purges who had willfully forgotten what they knew in order to live? Or was he some kind of genetic throw-back, a mutation?

Somehow that fit with the rest of his lovely physical attributes.

Had those ancient Alchemists gone to the pyre having found the answer they were looking for? Or were they like him, caught in a nether region of desperate, hopeless experimentation to find an answer that would always elude them.

Xavier had suggested it was so—that the source of the Gift was in the blood and that the Alchemists, loners all, were the product of indiscriminate breeding with unGifted, so the blood was too thin. That made sense, because any community of Alchemists would be destroyed by people afraid of the knowledge and beliefs the Alchemists had. Thus, over centuries, their Gift was squandered.

This was as opposed to Xavier's people, who had lived in small enclaves that were more outwardly alike to the unGifted around them, but able to keep the blood true through pure breeding. And in today's world they simply fit in, with their secret intact—until now. And there were still secrets he needed to uncover. Thinking about it, he realized he had left so many questions unasked. Like: Where did the Others came from? How did they know to become secret enclaves? Were there secrets to the use of power? What were the Others capable of? And why not contact the Gifted in America? Why not warn them if living openly was a danger?

But then he thought of Xavier.

Had the Alchemists before him gone so far as to hurt another to find the secrets they sought, or had they gone to the pyre still as purified as all Alchemists sought to keep themselves?

His stomach heaved for the umpteenth time since he'd left his workroom. He crumpled towards the toilet and retched, bile burning his throat, tears stinging his eyes.

His only saving grace was that he had nothing left inside him to give up.

CHAPTER 10 — LILY WHITE, PETAL PINK

Gregor Gleason swept in the doors of the glass-fronted Holiday Inn. He crossed the faux-marble floored lobby with its quaint waiting area of faux-vintage chairs and its inviting burgundy couches—also faux, because everything in this damned city was faux.

He stabbed the elevator call button and his anxieties vibrated through him. He should have known that Washington was false before he came here. So was his hope. Ray Fitzsimmons had never been an ally. Ray Fitzsimmons and the entire U.S. government had sold him and the other Gifted a bill of goods, because they weren't prepared to do anything to stop what was happening in Seattle. So far, no one had noticed the families suddenly disappearing from their houses. The people picked up on the street. Because it *was* happening. He'd taken the chance of attempting to contact some of the agents and had managed to contact his ex-Executive Assistant Moore. She had told him things with Amundson were getting much worse and that she was hoping to be able to get away and out of town in the next few days because she didn't know how much longer she could last. The contagion of Amundson's arrests were spreading farther, beyond Seattle to the relatives of the Gifted who lived elsewhere. It was only a matter of time before he got rid of her, too. There'd also been hints that he might be going after the partially Gifted. Then she'd had to hang up and he could only fear the worst.

Not good news at all. It meant Amundson had some means of reading the Gift in people. And that could mean that there was no running and hiding.

He rode the elevator up, listening to a ridiculous New Age version of something that sounded suspiciously like In-A-Gadda-Da-Vida, and strode down the hallway, dreading telling Fi that their little excursion this afternoon was off and they were heading out west to Landon and Xavier as fast as their little used Ford Focus could carry them.

He took a deep breath as he slipped the card into the reader and the door clicked open. Thankfully the TV was off and the inane bings and bongs of the game shows Fi seemed to prefer were silenced.

"Fi?" No sound from the sitting room, but maybe the girl had decided to nap rather than sit here rotting her brain.

He went to the closed door to her room. Knocked.

"Fi? We need to talk about this afternoon."

No sound, and the girl had never been that sound a sleeper from what he'd seen. Survival instinct probably, given where she'd been.

He hesitated, a part of him saying surely she wouldn't have. It was a completely illogical thing to do when there were people possibly looking for them. Hell, with Fitzsimmons' loyalties so in question, he could turn them in himself. He -reached- as he opened the door and knew the answer before the door swung open onto a room already tidied by housekeeping. No Fi.

A sweep with the Gift said she wasn't in his room either, and not in the hotel. A sick sense of dread filled his gut as he extended his reach. The tidied state of the room said she hadn't been here for a long while. No sense of Fi's Gifted flame out on the street, nor in the shops across the way. He opened himself to the City and there was a scattering of partially Gifted, like glittering bits of fool's gold in a beach of fine sand. Here and there, a bright pillar spoke of someone with Gift enough to register. Agent? Someone on the run? Because the Gifted in this country, when identified, were recruited into the AGS.

But of anise and mint-scented Fiona Murdoch, there was no sign at all.

§

Two hours of sitting up with her feet still tied to the table, but even though Vallon's hands were freed, her fingers still tingling a little with the free rush of blood. And she was still waiting for the drug to pass out of her system. The light had been turned on in the room, revealing a place that made her think of summer cabins: Braided rug on the floor; cobwebs high up on the faded log walls; kitschy photos on the wall of families hamming it up at a barbeque, a lake in the background. One of the figures in the photos looked like it might be Jason. With him was Cheryl. A log cabin and a lake made sense. A retreat he could take a prisoner to and do what was needed, with less likelihood of being caught. Given the faint scent of cedar she'd had since she got here, she figured it couldn't be that far from Seattle.

Or was she confusing the scent with the cedar of Lebanon scent of Xavier she'd sensed? She closed her eyes. Oh God, give her release from this drug. She was muddled enough as it was with competing priorities.

When she opened her eyes, Jason was there, slouched and slit-eyed in the chair opposite her, his long legs stretched out in front of him. "Admiring the family photos?" he asked. "I figured this place would be the best to do this. It always makes me think of Cheryl. This was the first place I think I understood just how much I really loved her."

He wore the same jeans, but had pulled on a worn denim shirt and had his police issue Sig Sauer resting in his lap, just like he'd had since he freed her hands. Maggie, unfortunately, crouched unhappily in a cage beside his chair, and the look in his eyes had said he really would do her harm if Vallon didn't do what he wanted. If she didn't succeed.

And the trouble was that just the thought of trying to create a person made her feel like losing the meager meal he'd given her of a baloney sandwich on white bread. How was she supposed to create a person she'd never met? Not just a figment of her imagination, but this person had to match Jason's expectations, when she hadn't known Cheryl Bryson. And how could that be done, even if she had known the person, because when do you ever truly know the heart of someone?

Jason looked at his watch. "Almost time, I think. Gleason started to recover after about twelve hours. How're you feeling?"

She tried -reaching- for the ley-lines and the quicksilver was still there, but fading like an aurora borealis as the sun rose. Beneath the floor and the sandy soil and the bedrock lay a deep, glowing vein through the earth's lower crust.If she reached out to touch it....

She did, and the power flushed up through her like the killer of all blushes, until her stomach did a flip-flop and she had to swallow back bile.

"Good enough I think." Good enough she would try this insanity as soon as possible. Good enough she could erase the bonds on her ankles even now. But not before he could loose a bullet at either her or Maggie or both. Stupid, maybe, to put her cat's life up against the creation of something that every part of her said was a travesty, but this was Maggie. Maggie might not love as people loved, but she depended on Vallon and trusted her. She wouldn't let her down, anymore than she was going to let the children down. Doing this would get her free to help them.

"I need the vellum and pen and something—something of about your ex-wife's *volume* to use as a source of material."

Jason stood up. "Why didn't you tell me that before now? I'm not leaving you alone in this room."

"If you think I'm planning something, maybe I would have if your flipping drugs hadn't muddled my brain so badly." She nodded down at the rug. "That'll do. Just roll it up for me."

So he did, scowling distrusting glances up at her. As if she had done something to bring them to this point, not the other way around. She was the prisoner here.

The braided rug lay in an uneven loose roll on the floor. "What else?" he asked.

"I'd like to at least see a photo of your wife."

"Her name is Cheryl," he said, his lips white around the edges.

Was Cheryl. "Fine. Cheryl. And tell me about her. What do you think I need to know?"

For a moment his expression went hazy, all the anger replaced by longing. He handed her the photo off of the dresser. Cheryl smiled up at her from dark eyes amid a glorious mane of dark auburn hair. Her aquiline nose made Vallon think Mediterranean, and yet her skin was the alabaster of an Irish milkmaid. A good multicultural mix, typical of America. She had a nice smile with a fulsome set of teeth and a spark in her gaze that said she was keeping secrets. *And what secrets would those be, Cheryl Bryson?*

"What was her maiden name?" she asked.

"What difference does that make?" Jason snarled.

Vallon put the photo face down on the bed beside her. "Listen. You asked me to do you a favor by trying something I've never done before. If you want the slightest chance that this is going to go right, then you have to give me every bit of help you know how. Now what the fuck was her maiden name?"

Jason glowered at her, then glanced down at Maggie, who had hunkered down at the back of the cage. Clearly the little cat didn't like what she felt in the room.

"Renaldi. Her maiden name was Renaldi. Her family came over from Venice and her Dad was a clothing designer. We met and fell in love and got married and then she got cancer and died. Okay? She loved espresso and American pizza and hamburgers and tiramisu and going to baseball games and camping on the Olympic Peninsula and curling up with a good book after a walk together in the rain. Okay? Is that enough? She was kind and gentle and cared a great deal about absolutely everything. She used to say that the world was our mother Pangea and we had to care for her just like she cared for us."

The words had exploded from him and left him slumped and looking like there were too many more words ripping at him to be let out. But he yanked away and turned. His shoulders worked and then he shook himself and straightened. He turned around and glared at Vallon. Then his eyes narrowed.

"What? What is it?" He demanded.

"Nothing." She swallowed and scrabbled the photo back up to look at the image. Because there was something. Pangea was not a word used frequently. Pangaea was the word use in New Age discussions, but Pangea was the term Xavier had used for the Earth during the transcendent moment when their bodies united and gave back to Pangea to deal with afterburn. Just what did this mean, and what did it mean for any attempt she made to meet Jason's demands?

"Vallon? What the hell is going on? I've jumped your stupid hoops. Now do this or lose a cat and any chance of ever getting loose to help those children."

His fingers worked around the grip of the Sig Sauer. He stood back between the door and his chair.

When she didn't move, he lifted the pistol and took aim at Maggie.

"All right. All right. Just give me a moment."

She closed her eyes and the queasy quicksilver iridescence had faded farther. Was she being asked to not just create a person, but a Gifted? Her stomach flip-flopped in protest. If one was difficult, the other had to be impossible.

The pulse of the earth—of Pangea—lay below her. Maggie was a small spark of life crouched on the floor in her cage, and Jason was only the ruddy flame of the unGifted. Or… there was something different there. A slight off-color tinge she'd never noticed before. Was it just because the man had gone off his rocker and done what he'd done, or was there something more to it?

But she had no time to go probing the essence of Jason Bryson.

"Jason, what did your wife smell like?"

"What the fuck does that have to do with anything? I'm warning you, Vallon."

The sharp report of his pistol and the awful scent of cordite threw her forward in terror. "Maggie!"

But Maggie only cowered farther back in her cage. The floor in front of her enclosure held the neat hole of a single bullet embedding itself.

Vallon's heart beat a wild tattoo at the dead black look in Jason's eyes. She'd never believed he'd do it. Now she wasn't so sure.

She swallowed. "What did your wife smell like? It's important."

"Like apples and dusty vineyards full of ripe grapes." His stone gaze never left her face.

She nodded and looked down at the photo again. Her hands shook as she -reached-.

Down into the earth and Pangea's veins. Ozone and rose-tinged ether filled her lungs. Then deeper to the lavender-scented lines she'd sensed in New Madrid. Heat all around and the pressure of the earth's crust above her, below her the shimmering vein of the earth flowing westward before dipping down beneath the ocean. She opened herself and drew the power inside her so that her body felt bigger, fat with the essence of Pangea and her life-giving force.

Then she pulled back and sat there panting around the queasy remains of the drugs. When Jason went to say something, she barely managed to shake her head. This was not going to be easy, given how sick she felt. But she had a plan now. Use the power as Jason wanted, but at the same time send a small amount to the ropes at her feet. Release them and she could be out of here running so fast—correction—she could be out of here with Maggie running so fast.

"The pen and vellum." Her voice was barely a whisper, but Jason did as asked—handed her weapons of his demise.

She began to draw, the vellum balanced on one thigh, as she glanced down at the photograph she had resting on her other leg. "If you came closer you could tell me whether I'm getting close."

Jason did as she asked, shifting the pistol to his other hand and stepping in close enough to look over her shoulder. Farther away from Maggie, at least.

"Her face was longer, narrower," he said.

She adjusted the drawing and kept on going, her focus now split between the drawing she made and the roll of carpet. The scent of ozone filled the air and the carpet shimmered with its own inner light as the power entered its fibers and worked Change. Auburn, slim, but with a feminine softness in all the right places. Up to Jason's shoulder, so she fit under his arm in a comfortable way. A laugh like a brook and a voice deeper than most women's. He whispered these into her ear as she worked. As the air above the carpet began its own tornado whirl and small tendrils of power coiled unnoticed through the ropes at her ankles and at the sides of Maggie's cage.

Her ankles were for all intensions free, and so was Maggie. A final small push and the cage would be gone and Maggie would scoot out of here as fast as she could, Vallon right on her furry little black and white heels. She reached out and grabbed Jason's arm. He jerked back, but she wouldn't release him.

"Think of her. Think of everything you know of her."

She flowed power into him, praying it would imprint his longing, his knowledge onto it, then dragged it into her. The whirlwind was a column and the room filled with wind. The carpet came apart like sand and like sand it whirled up and around, around, around.

Became finer, like skin. Pulled moisture from the air like flesh. Bonding matter together into forms it had not intended to be. Legs, slender, over-long fine feet, hips full, waist waspish, breasts like lush peaches and broad shoulders.

The tornado spun harder, in a tight column.

The face, the hair, but more than the body, the heart, beating solidly with the beat of Pangea's pulse, the soul—the soul pulled from the air and from Jason's desire.

She sent a final great surge of power and the whirling column exploded. Dust blinded her and filled the room as she kicked free of her bonds, as Maggie yowled and ran, as an auburn-haired figure collapsed in a heap where the carpet had been.

A moan. Vallon froze. It wasn't supposed to work.

Jason stood immobilized, his gaze locked on the huddled figure that—moved. She was lily-white skinned and her hair like copper. Her lips were rose-petal pink, her breasts pale. The scent of apples and ripe vineyards filled the air. Jason fell to his knees beside the woman as she mewled on the floor. Maggie screamed and all her fur stood on end.

Vallon dropped to the floor, the pen and vellum still clutched in her hands. Move now!

It was a command to her body, but limbs held immobile for a day don't move like they should. Where she should have leapt for the door, her feet stumbled and she almost went down. Jason jerked up and raised the gun. She threw herself for the door and felt/heard the bullet's concussion over her head. Another shot and she rolled into the hallway, a blur of black and white fur disappearing down the hallway in front of her. She shoved herself up and ran, heard a scream behind her, heard Jason yell.

Nothing she was going to listen to. Just get the heck out of wherever this was. The reek of ozone and ether filled the air as she pounded up to a closed door. Old. Wood. Painted faded blue. Maggie frantically scratched at the barrier, mewing plaintively. Vallon scooped her and tried the door.

Locked, damn it. And any moment Jason was going to be coming. She threw a shoulder against the door. Again. Again, but the old metal held. The frame, however, gave with a horrible wood-splitting sound. From behind her Jason was screaming. "No! No! No!"

Damn it she was out of time. She shoved against the door again and the frame gave the last bit and the door's bolt swung free. She half fell into a living room. Cabin, her mind sorted. Log walls. Old couch pulled up before a lit stone fireplace. Small kitchen with old fashioned appliances. Two front windows, curtained. A door.

She ran for it, fumbled it open, fighting a squalling, scratching cat, and leapt out onto a wide front porch that overlooked a forested lake. The scent of cedar and pine and growing things was like a punch in the gut, she'd been denied freedom for so long. If she wanted to keep it, she sure as hell had better get going.

Where?

Didn't matter. Just get the hell away. She leapt down onto soft forest soil of old pine needles and fallen leaves and turned west and ran into the trees. Where was the road? Where was the car?

She chanced a look over her shoulder. The car Xavier had purchased was parked behind the cabin. There had to be a road there. But just then Jason stumbled out onto the porch, gun in hand, fury on his contorted face. "I'll kill you for that, you bitch. I'll kill you!"

Then he spotted her in the trees and leapt down after. All that was left were terrorized cat claws and a terrified retreat on drug-fumbled feet.

CHAPTER 11 — IN THE WIND

The bag over her head made it impossible to see more than shadows, and the musty air in the bag carried the stink of her fear. Fi fought it back again, reminding herself to be strong like Vallon. Resourceful like Vallon. Vallon would never be caught by anyone—unless it suited her purpose. If she was caught, she'd be pretty quick knowing where she was. The trouble was, Fi didn't know anything about Washington DC other than what she'd seen in pictures and read about way back in school.

So she sat very still in the back of the car with the blond man beside her and tried to remember each left or right turn that the car took. Unfortunately it wasn't working as well as it did in the movies. She'd lost track about six turns in and had totally forgotten the earliest part of the ride now that they'd been on the move for what seemed like forever. She was small and incredibly stupid for venturing out of the hotel and for not being able to remember all the twists and turns. Vallon could probably do it in a heartbeat. The only thing positive was that her hands weren't tied. Mr. Not-So-Cute Blond Guy must figure she didn't pose any danger.

"Where are you taking me?" she asked, finally finding the courage to ask, but afraid of the answer.

"You'll see soon enough." A gruff answer in a gruff voice that sounded nothing like the nice young man who had approached her on the street or who had convinced the restaurant hostess that she was his sister.

"What does it matter if you tell me, then? It's not going to help me get outta here."

The big car turned right off the pavement and rumbled over potholes. The scent of growing things reached her even over the artificial smell of the air conditioning. Were they taking her out in the woods to kill her? They did that in the movies. A shiver of fear drilled even deeper into her core. But...

"Why are you doing this?"

Darn it, if she was trying to be like Vallon, she should have used the Gift to get free way back in Washington. But the option to try it had just slipped her mind, given she'd had no control over her Gift for years, until Vallon started helping her. Well, not really helping her. Vallon had used her to help with the afterburn, but the process of 'cycling' had helped Fi, too. It had put her more in touch with the Gift she possessed, but she hadn't used it on her own—not until Vallon's father had trapped them and Vallon needed help. *Her* help.

So if Vallon had needed her help and it had worked, then maybe she could do something on her own. They'd never even see her try with her head hidden under the bag. She grinned to herself. Wouldn't they be surprised? Wouldn't Gleason and Vallon be impressed that she'd freed herself. *Then* they'd have to quit treating her as a child.

Darn it. If she'd only thought of it sooner instead of trying to memorize sounds and road turns.

She -reached- and the power of the ley-lines scorched her so she jerked back, but Vallon wouldn't do that, so she tried it again. Bit her lip against the pain as the heat ran up through her body and sweat beaded her brow.

Okay, do something, but what?

Destroy the car? She might be able to do that—soften the metal so all the parts melted together. Would that cause an explosion? She wasn't sure.

Just holding the heat and power inside her took all her concentration. She'd lost the ability to really focus on what she was doing during the time her mother abused her by stealing power from her, but once, in school, she'd been pretty good.

The car crunched over more pot holes in gravel as she sent the power out into her surroundings. Soften, metal and everything melting. Tires melting, too.

The car seemed to lower, then there was a small lurch as one of the tires gave way and a wind seemed to pass through everything and set it vibrating. The seat under her had too much give—she was falling through it. She leaned forward and her feet sank into the floor. The car lurched to a stop and Mr. Cute Blond Guy stirred—or didn't. A strange moan, a strangling sound, and Fi worked up the courage to tear the sac off her head, ready to kick and claw and scream if the guy tried to stop her. A painful heat ran up over her limbs and curled an insistent ache around her private parts. Afterburn.

But he didn't try anything. She still sat—well more like knelt—in the back of the car, but the seat back in front of her had melted half onto the floorboards and around her feet. The doors were half melted, too. The windows had flowed down over the metal and the metal looked like it had flowed down into the ground.

A mewling sound beside her turned her around and Mr. Cute Blond Guy sat there—or what was left of him. Blond hair now grew from melted flesh on his cheeks and where his ears should be. His face—wasn't. Features had melted, the slight bulge of eyeballs covered. Mouth melted shut by the flow of the nose down over it. A single hole spoke of where the nose might have been. Shoulders slumped inward, like the side of a hollowed-out candle, arms melted into chest, so that only small flipper-like appendages worked the air at his sides.

She might scream if she could catch her breath. She wanted to scream. She wanted to push herself right out of the side of the car and run-run-run as fast as she could go and as far away as she could get from what she had done. It was supposed to be the car. Not him. And where was the driver? She couldn't see his head over the top of the driver's head-rest anymore.

Her breath came in short, desperate gasps. She needed to get out of here for so many reasons. She hadn't meant to hurt them. It was like she'd thrown acid on them.

A small moan escaped her and she tried the door. Melted shut, it seemed. Beyond the warped side window glass lay a warped countryside of trees and meadows. Something moved beyond the white fences that ran alongside the road the car stood on.

She craned around to the rear window. The roof of the car had run down over the glass to form narrow bars there. The windshield had melted totally away and there was nothing there, but she didn't want to think about crawling next to what must be pooled in the driver-side seat.

But she had to get out, and right now she'd apparently used the power only to trap herself more securely. The afterburn ache stopped her from trying the power again. If this was what Vallon had felt like, she now understood why Vallon had begged for help and why she went with those men. And Vallon had always used so much more power. Still, she wanted to wipe the car right out of existence given what it contained. It would be a kindness.

But get out first, and that meant climbing into the front seat. She pushed the melted passenger-side seat back forward as hard as she could.

Maybe she could just slide right from the seat back onto the dashboard and out onto the hood and be gone before anyone discovered what she'd done.

That was the plan. She pushed herself up onto the seat back that apparently had had all it supports melted away. The dashboard was within easy reach, so she got her knees under her and went to crawl up and out of the empty window to where melted glass covered the sagging engine hood. But not before her gaze skittered like an unruly mouse over to the horror in the other front seat.

Looked like a wet bag of flesh in a suit. Head melted down between what used to be shoulders, two terrified eyes staring up at her. No mouth. Nose hole like Mr. No-Longer-So-Cute Blond Guy. Tufts of brown hair growing here and there across his face and out of the fabric of the suit that was now part of his flesh.

Her stomach clenched and she couldn't help herself. She vomited into the driver's side wheel well and then clawed her way out of the car onto the hood and clung there, stomach still heaving.

Then, on unsteady feet, she slid off the car and looked around.

A farm. The air smelled of clean grass and clover and sun-warmed dust—and horse. A fresh wind blew in her face and she could have bathed in it, it felt so good. She was on a farm with white fences and fancy-looking horses in the fields on either side of the lane they—correction—she stood on. It ran down an easy slope towards a lovely grey stone house and what looked like a huge horse barn and maybe an indoor arena.

So not what she'd expected, and so not anywhere she wanted to be.

She turned and nearly fell, but caught herself against the melted metal and jerked back at the slippery touch like new-made plastic.

If she didn't want to be caught, she needed to get going before they discovered what she'd done. Clearly her two captors hadn't picked her up on their own. Someone had sent them. She headed back up the road to where there had to be a main road. They hadn't turned onto the gravel road that long ago.

The afterburn throbbed unpleasantly, though she could think of pleasant ways to get rid of the sensation. The lane ran in through tall pine and maples that showed the faintest hint of red around their edges as a sign that summer was over. Ahead was the road, paved, but narrow. Not a main thoroughfare like she'd hoped. She reached it and paused. Left or right. The car had turned right so that meant she'd turn left. She started trotting down the pavement.

Cool air filled her lungs. Trees shadowed the road, sunlight flickering through leaves. She was free, and the way she wanted to get away from that car, she could run right back to Washington if she had to. She'd beg Gleason to help her get the heck out of Washington and to teach her how to use what she knew. Or she'd promise never to use the power again. It would be an easy promise to make given what she'd done, what she'd seen.

A sound like a car engine came towards her. Hide in the woods until they were passed, or ask for help? Help would be so good. They could drive her back to Washington, or at least loan her a phone to use so she could get a message to Gleason about where she was.

She stepped out into the middle of the pavement and waved her arms as a navy blue sedan cruised around a curve. The car slowed, came to a stop in front of her, and the driver-side window purred down.

"You have to help me," she said. "Some men were trying to kidnap me, but I escaped. I'm afraid they're going to come after me." Well, maybe *they* wouldn't, but someone would. "I need to get back to Washington. Please. Can you help me?"

The man looked up at her from clear hazel eyes that reminded her of the bottom of a pond through ice. "Sure. We can help you. Climb in and we can take you to the farm and call it in."

The farm. She backed up a step. 'Call it in' was the kind of phrasing police used and she wanted nothing to do with police. None of them, even if Vallon did hang around with Jason Bryson.

"Come to think of it, maybe I need the exercise. I'll walk thanks."

She turned and started walking hurriedly away. A door opened behind her.

"Hey! Wait up. We can help you!"

She ran, sprinting up the road as fast as her legs would take her. Heard racing footfall behind her and knew there was no way she could outrun a man. She leapt in amongst the trees, forgetting she wore her expensive new clothes. Just run. Just lose herself so they lost her, too.

Bang into a tree trunk, bounce around it and keep on running, leap over the low bushes and ferns and fallen logs. He was after her. She heard his swearing, the crash of his passage as counterpoint to the moan of her breath. He was too fast. Too fast. She slid down an embankment to a stream and started up the far side, but it was too steep, her feet slipped and slid and then a hand fell on her shoulder and dragged her back. Grabbed her hands and pulled them behind her so hard her shoulders wrenched and she cried out as he pulled something plastic from his pocket and twisted it around her wrists.

"Can't have some poor little girl running loose in the woods, now can we? She might get hurt."

He half shoved, half carried her back up the embankment she'd slid down and then marched her out to the road, then down the pavement to the car. Her clothes were covered in dirt, her shoes in mud. At the car he yanked open the back and shoved her in. The car stank of men's florid aftershave and the coppery scent of her fear.

She wasn't alone. A man she recognized sat there.

"Hello, Fiona," said Francis Drake, Vallon's father, the man who had imprisoned both her and Vallon and countless other Gifted. The man who had caused the New Madrid quake. The man who would most likely kill her.

§

The whirlwind in the bedroom sent off dim sparks of fire that mesmerized Jason where he stood next to the table with the improvised shackles that held Vallon Drake. Finally, *finally* the damned woman was doing as he bid. A good thing, too, because any longer and he really would have killed the cat, even though he was fond of little Maggie. But a cat's life was a small price to pay for the life of Cheryl. Even the lives of some hypothetical children at some hypothetical school were nothing.

Vallon's eyes and hands seemed to glow as she sketched on the oily feeling paper that she called vellum with the ink that filled the room with the unpleasant scent of sour wine and something acrid. Then the tornado began to collapse in on itself. The whirling slowed, revealing a smooth shoulder, a hip, a flick of long auburn hair in a familiar shade. Cheryl. She was truly, before his eyes, reborn. He could almost grab Vallon, hug her, shout his joy to the moon, but the tornado still spun in his bedroom and he held a gun to make sure the job was done and done right.

The spinning stopped and the whirling dust collapsed onto the floor around a pale-skinned figure he would know until he died. The woman huddled on the floor, her hair spilling forward covering her face, and shoulders the color of new milk. Skin smooth as silk, she would have aureoles the color of pale peaches, lips the color of cherries, and hazel eyes that would haunt him all of his life. Like his life blood, and he was finally given a transfusion.

The woman stirred, moaned, and he was on his knees beside her, the weapon, the cat, the other woman with the vellum forgotten. There was only his beloved Cheryl.

He pulled her into his arms, warm, the scent of apple trees radiating from the dark spaces under the fall of her hair, the scent of sunshine on her skin. He could drink her in, get drunk of her. He had kept her clothes and slept with them for months after she died to try to recapture this scent. He realized now what a poor substitute it had been. Cheryl was here. In his arms, as he pulled her into him, her sweet face with her eyes clamped shut as if she was afraid of him.

Vallon suddenly tore loose and leapt across the room, the cat burst from a cage that was suddenly only three sided. Both leapt for the door and were gone, stumbling down the hallway. Let them go. He had Cheryl. Beloved Cheryl.

She looked up at him with her strange and wonderful hazel eyes and he leaned in to kiss her on the forehead. She tasted of dust. When he pulled back his lips were coated with it and flakes of it fell from her forehead, from her cheeks. Dust ran through his fingers where he held her shoulders, slowly at first, then like sand through an egg timer, and then faster still.

She looked at him, terror in her eyes, and her hand came up, fingers turning to sand stroked the side of his face. Her mouth opened, and, "What have you done to me, Jason?" she said before her tongue, the lower part of her face melted away and he was holding cascading sand and screaming and Cheryl was a heap of growing dust on the floor that he could not seem to put back together and *Vallon Drake had tricked him.*

With a roar, he grabbed his fallen gun and leapt for the door. From the hallway came the thud, thud, and crash as she tried—no, broke down— the locked hallway door. He roared again as he leapt over the dust that was all that remained of Cheryl and into the hallway. Empty, but he would get her. He knew this cabin, this area like the back of his hand.

He plunged down the hall and into the main part of the cabin. Not here. The front door hung open and he ran out onto the porch. The silence of the lakeshore always overwhelmed him. He stopped, suddenly immersed in the wind in leaves, waves on grassy shore sounds and the scent of cedar and damp earth. Where? He scanned the small lawn running down to the lakeshore, the small pier for a rowboat that had been dubbed the Cheryl, that he had long ago sold after his wife died. Turned towards the car, at the rear of the cabin, but there was only silence and more wind in that direction. The forest, then. He looked at the trees and there—pale face with a strangely silent struggling cat in her arms. Good thing she had the cat, because he *would* kill it now. In pay back. Oh, Vallon Drake deserved payback in so many ways.

He pulled the gun up and took a casual shot, just to see her run. Then he went lightly down the steps and set after her at an easy lope. There was no question he would catch her.

CHAPTER 12 —THE WATERS

Vallon ran, dodging tree trunks, leaping fallen limbs and tree trunks and thick clumps of ferns. It was stupid, really. She could just use the power to wipe Jason right out of existence, but she'd been trained all her life that the power was used to preserve, not kill. So she ran. Get some distance between them and she'd do something to stop Jason. Just not kill.

Thankfully Maggie had quit fighting. The little cat cowered, shaking, in Vallon's arms. If only she had something to carry her in; it would be so much easier to run if her hands were free, but she was not leaving Maggie. Not for Jason to shoot, because clearly he would, given the screams she'd heard. Something had gone wrong, just like she'd known it would. The Gift couldn't just create a person. That the Gift might be able to—that someone might even try—made her feel sick to her stomach. And she had tried. Her skin crawled.

And Jason would make her pay for that failure. If she ever wanted freedom, to be able to help the children or Xavier or anyone, she had to evade him.

Her breath tore through her lungs as she, gasping, struggled up a forested ridge. Maybe when she got to the top she would be able to spot a landmark that would tell where she was. Then she wouldn't be running mindlessly like this. Hell, she could be running *into* the wilderness with a cat in her arms and nothing else. Not even a jacket. Well, maybe she had something. She still had the vellum and pen she'd stuffed in her pocket as she headed out of the cabin.

The air was heavy with cedar and pine sap. As she climbed the ridge trying to be quiet, a crow flapped cawing overhead. Behind her, Jason crashed through the forest, redoubling her efforts to go faster, farther. She would get away from him. She would.

"We will, Maggie. Just stick with me, kid."

The little cat shivered in her arms, but she pressed into Vallon like she never had before. "Silly kitty. You think I can save you. Well, let's hope, shall we?" She used one hand for balance on the steep slope and scrambled up the last of it.

It really was just a ridge—a sharp tectonic up-thrust had shoved a layer of rocks up on edge where they had then weathered away leaving only a thin wedge overlooking the land and rough crevasses of rock that had, over eons, filled with soil, allowing the trees to grow. She looked out over trees and more trees, and thrusting up out of them like a god stood Mount Rainier.

She knew where she was. Still in Washington State, at least, but a darn sight farther out than she'd thought she was. She must have been passed out for some time. *How long?*

She -reached- for Xavier, but there was only a strange echo of pain as if he was lost in a deep canyon. The young girl? No, that poor child had enough problems without worrying about some woman lost in the hills.

A sharp snap behind her told her Jason wasn't far behind. She had to make a decision about which way to go. There was straight on towards the mountain that stood miles away, or down the ridge and then follow along it either north or south.

Another snap, closer this time. She leapt down the far side of the ridge like a deer running, though she wished she had something other than Sketchers on. Her Daytons, how about. They'd protect her legs and give more support. At the base of the hill, she looked back and caught a glimpse of Jason's furious face as he topped the ridge. He wasn't far enough behind her. She needed to get moving.

"Which way, Maggie?" she whispered, because she really had no idea herself.

"Mew." Soft, as if she knew her voice would carry.

"Left it is." She turned northward and tried to be careful of where she stepped, hoping to leave no sign of her passage.

"I know you're out there, Vallon, and I know you're close." Jason's voice rained down over her, thick with hate. "Do you know what I'm going to do to you and your cat? I'm gonna set that animal on fire and make you watch, just like I just had to watch my wife come apart like a sand castle in a wave."

She crept from shadow to shadow, praying he wouldn't see her, but then something crashed halfway down the ridge and she positively flew across the forest floor.

A shot ran out through the forest. He'd seen her. There was nothing else to do but run.

Down along the base of the ridge, where rain water had washed debris that cracked and crackled under her speeding feet. A stream flowed into the space between ridge and forest and trickled downhill beside her. At least there was that. She wouldn't go thirsty. If she dared pause long enough to drink when Jason was out there, gunning for her.

She kept running, falling into a ground-eating lope and thankful for all her years of running over the hills of Fremont. Maggie squirmed in her arms, but for some reason the little cat seemed to stay where she was. If Jason caught them, she'd let Maggie go. Better the cat took a chance in the woods than meet certain, horrible death at Jason's hands. Every now and again she heard the crash of bushes and an oath that told her Jason was behind, but he was coming on—and fast.

She just had to be faster.

The slope gradually increased and she kept up the pace, stumbling, half leaping down the side of the mountain, to what she wasn't sure, but given the way the creek had grown from a bare runnel across the ground to something three feet across and growing, there was every likelihood there'd be water involved. And where there was water, there were very often people.

She held onto that hope, the light through the canopy of cedar and pine gradually dimmed into late afternoon, shadows swelling around her. She had to reach something soon, damn it. Her lungs hurt, her chest hurt, her legs were torn from brambles and branches and falls, her arms marked by cat scratches. The only good thing was the way her head cleared of the drugs until she could feel the steady pulse of the ley lines beneath her like a constant beat of her heart. Of course the drug's passing also left her open to the afterburn the attempt to bring Cheryl Bryson back had caused.

Her hands shook a little and her legs didn't feel quite solid. Flashes of heat ran through her even though the day was cooling. A crash and oath too close for comfort said all her efforts weren't eluding Jason. There had to be something. In her state she wasn't sure she could do much without a focus. That meant she needed the vellum and ink, but if she was going to use them, it had better be now.

She hesitated. Change always had consequences, but if she didn't do something, she was going to die and then there would be horrible consequences for those students and for Xavier, if what she felt was true.

One handed, she dug in her pocket and fished out the vellum, then reached for the intoxicating rose-scented ley-line power. The pen was slippery in her sweating, Maggie-fur-coated palms. Fear had the little cat dropping fur like crazy.

In the past she would just cause a hole around the person's feet, but she didn't know exactly where Jason was. That meant she needed a bigger intervention. She drew the power into her and the air tinged with ozone as she almost tripped over a fallen log. Caught herself before she and Maggie and the pen and paper went flying.

She headed right, away from the ridge and the creek to where the land sloped more steeply downhill, and kept going, leaping and bounding down through the trees and trying to be as soundless as possible. At the base of the slope, she stopped. Listened. Couldn't hear Jason at the moment, but that didn't really mean anything. The athletic nature of the man and the fact he said he knew these woods suggested he had woodsman's skills. She could just bet he'd move silently.

She knelt and, switching Maggie to her other arm, much to the cat's displeasure, spread the vellum on the ground. The sketch of Cheryl Bryson was fading like old ink, a sure sign that the power hadn't worked well, but that was the problem with the power. Whatever was created never lasted unless the maker concentrated and held it in place, or unless the greater populace experienced it en mass and accepted it. Thus a disaster like the Southeast Asian tsunami could become part of the landscape, while a change like Vallon was considering would not. At least not after she quit holding it in place.

She glanced up slope and began to sketch, the sloping the earth, the array of tree trunks, then she scored it through with a deep rift, a ravine so straight-sided, wide and deep, there was no way Jason could cross it and long enough the end of the rift met the steeped part of the ridge so it would pose a problem to go around it.

The air reeked of ozone and ether as the slope above her shimmered. Trees turned to mist and the earth sank away. A curse from above her told she all she needed to know. She scrambled up, stuffed the pen and vellum in her pocket, and kept going, hurrying through the cedar-and ozone-scented air and holding the ravine in her mind. Her urgency, the afterburn, and the effort of holding the rift conspired to unsettle her footing. She stumbled, twisted an ankle, and kept going. Heading north again, in the same direction the ridge ran. Hopefully she could reach civilization before Jason could figure a way around her barrier.

An hour farther, the ground flattened out and she suddenly found herself walking in a forested area without underbrush. Stone-encircled, grilled fire pits stood out black against the red-needle-covered earth. A campground. Civilization.

She rushed along the narrow rutted road that linked the campsites along a winding, rock-sided river. No occupants. A closed gate greeted her when she reached the sign. Pleasant River Campground. She hadn't been thinking when she worked the Change. She could have brought civilization to her if only for a little while.

But the consequences of doing such a thing was one of the reasons the AGS was created—to stop inadvertent and intended change from occurring in the United States, just as similar secret organizations were known to exist in other nations. In some countries, however, the governments dabbled in making their own changes. The Russian government tried it when they diverted rivers that fed the Aral Sea, and the consequence had been an environmental disaster. The awareness of the disaster had been so great and so gradual that the Changes had stuck. Now, to undo the changes, they would be noticed by too many.

She didn't want to cause something similar.

She climbed over the single metal bar that blocked access to the campground and started jogging along the dirt road. It ended at blessed pavement and she stood there a moment, listening for the approach of a vehicle. There was only the wind sighing in the trees and her own rapid breathing. She looked down at Maggie, who seemed quite content right where she was.

"You're heavy, little girl. We might have to consider putting you on a diet."

Maggie just gave a not-on-your-life chirrup and looked at her with don't-mess-with-me golden eyes.

"All right. So you're just big boned." Vallon sighed and started trudging along the road. Civilization might not be close, but it was at the end of this road. All she had to worry about was Jason thinking to go back for his car. He'd know that down the hill was the river and the campground that would lead out to somewhere. So any car from behind her, she'd hide, and any car from in front of her, she'd be safe.

That was the plan, anyways.

§

Swimming up to consciousness, the waters of Xavier's mind glowed thick and red and viscous as if he swam through his own depleted blood stream. Not blood, no, though the room stank of its copper. The white glow of the omnipresent fluorescent lights in the infernal white room burned through his eyelids. That was all. The light placed a red glow over his life, his being, his world. Red, like blood, and yet he had not enough of it. The little man, Snow, had seen to that. First the drugs, then the pain, then the slow, drip, drip, drip of bleeding to carry on where the destruction of his hand had begun. So many ways to ruin a man, and Snow seemed intent on trying every one.

In the throes of drugs and pain he had told—what? Everything? At least the basic answers to whatever the little man had asked. The Alchemists. The Council. The existence of another race of beings in the world. All things the Council had expressly forbidden to be shared with anyone. As if he did not have enough to atone for with the Council.

But first he must get himself out this place. The surgery, the drugs, and the bloodletting had all left him weak, but the drugs had faded from his system, the little man obviously depending more upon what was actually the traditional route—the bloodletting—to control an errant Cartos, as his people were called. These American Gifted—they were not Cartos. They were throwbacks—the few wherein the diluted blood of age-old Cartos-human interbreeding had finally distilled enough to allow the power to Change. The Council had foreseen such a thing occurring eons before and had made the decision not to welcome the upstarts into their order. They were not pureblood. Not that there were any truly pureblood Cartos anymore. The Diaspora of his people after the cataclysm had left too few of them. Many had intermarried with the humans who had once hunted them down and remembered them as the demons of legend.

Whether Snow was the result of such distillation of Alchemist bloodlines remained to be seen, but the little man had no power, and that meant that the least of a full Cartos' power should be enough to get him free. As long as he could keep the little man guessing as to the amount of blood Xavier could afford to lose.

He forced a weak moan and let his body go slack, then listened. No sound of stirring like their usually was. No over-warm fingers on his wrist or neck urgently checking for a pulse. Which could only mean that this might be his chance.

Slit eyes revealed the painfully white room and the gleam of chrome counters and cupboards on either side of the metal door. His gaze sloped lower and caught the metal cuffs of the shackles around his right wrist, the bandaged hand down below. He tried his fingers and a groan escaped him. The little man had much to atone for after this was all over. If he lost the use of his writing hand, there would be much indeed.

He -reached- for the warmth of mother Pangea's depths. Filled himself with the rose-petal-scented *kata* and let it wash over him. Far better than the copper-penny scent of his blood. With his blood so thinned, the rose-petal power could do little for him. He needed the strength of something stronger. -Reached- deeper, through bedrock and down to the lavender scented *heret*. His poor veins sizzled as his depleted blood struggled to hold the power, but the *heret* ran from him like water through a sieve. No, that would not work. *Platiqua,* then. The deep magic.

Down beneath the crust of the earth where the *kata* and *heret* ran like capillaries through Pangea's body, ran the great veins of *platiqua.* Though they were not the deepest, they carried great power and were the deepest his people dared to go—and that only by the most powerful and the best trained because the *platiqua* was risky in so many ways. The crust's weight bore down on him as he sought through thermal heat. Down, and then one of the great, wending blue-gold rivers appeared out of the darkness and the scent of saffron overwhelmed him.

He hung there, above the rushing gush of power, as this had to be done with the greatest of care. To plunge in would be to be ripped away and drown in the power, the body a husk left above. His awareness barely touched the surface and the heat soared through him, almost turned him to ash. He ignored the painful heat and sucked in the power, almost solid except for the heat that kept it running in thick veins from east to west beneath the continents.

When he could stand the pain no longer, he yanked back into himself and lay there panting.

Power that would burn metal and melt diamonds burned in his veins. Smoke lifted off his skin and his vision clouded, both signs that his temperature was up in the danger zones. To be expected, and more so with less blood to spread the power through. But he would not hold the power for long.

He closed his eyes and the metal shackles turned to dust that ran off the table edge. The blood surge into his hands and feet was painful, but no more than the burning sense of his organs. He sat up and the world momentarily darkened. He swung his legs over the side of the table, then slipped down, bare feet against the praiseworthy cool floor. Wings of darkness crossed his vision again and his legs gave. He clung to the tabletop and fought with his betraying limbs. Blood loss could apparently do more than simply drain away his power, but the *platiqua* helped. The viscous power spread out from his blood and into his limbs until they tingled. His thinned blood frothed in his lungs and heart and brain. High on it. Giddy enough it was hard to control the snigger that curled back his lips.

The time for laughter was later, when he was free of this place and with Vallon, once more visiting that mystical place that only their mating could bring them to. He held onto the memory of shimmering rainbow light and the peace of being with Vallon at Pangea's heart.

[*Bela Menina*, I come.]

Even with the *platiqua* he wasn't sure she would hear, as weak as he was, but it was a sign to the universe that he was rising again, a phoenix from the ashes of this trip with Snow. No one would stand in the way of him reaching Vallon again. No one.

He forced himself upright and released the table, waiting for his legs to accept his weight. Step one accomplished. Now he must walk. He used the table as a protection against falling and shuffled around the table until gradually his strength returned. The *platiqua* was a double-edged sword, filling him with temporary strength. The downside, however, was the painful afterburn that awaited on the other side. Just let him get some place safe to recover and he would deal with the pain. He had dealt with Snow's torture and the Council's interrogations. He could deal with this.

He was walking more steadily now, his stride lengthened, the *platiqua* singing through him. He stretched out his arms and back and took three long breaths of quiet meditation. With his blood intact he could simply transmute from this place, but now a goodly proportion of his blood lay in a bag hanging off the side of the table. If he knew how, he would drain it right back into his body, but that would take too long. If he did not have the use of his blood, then Snow would not either. He ripped the bag from the table, found a scalpel, and slashed the bag into the sink, letting the crimson copper scent fill the room as it circled down the drain.

Dared he try transmutation? It would take most of the power that he currently held in his body. He would need to go someplace safe. Somewhere that he could easily reach Vallon or she could reach him, because he was not going to be to full strength for a while, not unless she helped him. The houseboat he had kept as his refuge on Lake Washington was long destroyed. That left only one place he could think of. It would, hopefully, be empty now.

He closed his eyes and pressed palms together, then drew in deep, centering breaths, drawing his awareness into his core, where the oneness with Pangea rested. He -reached- for the rose-petal-scented *kata* and visualized his limbs, the elements of his body, folding in around him, becoming a missile of Xavierness that flowed deep down into Pangea's *platiqua* veins and along them.

Heat all around him, tearing him far from the confines of Landon Snow's little house of horrors and on towards where the veins of the earth formed a bright glowing road map, a nexus of power before draining down below the oceans for the long lingering travail across to the other side of the world. He fought to slow his plummeting race through the veins of the earth, bur the *platiqua* never liked to give up that which it held. He grabbed for the earth, tried to claw his way up to the slower moving *heret* and then the *kata*. But the *platiqua* was there, dogging his heels, clogging his veins as he threw himself up to the surface of the earth. His legs gave. His naked body collapsed onto concrete, and the faint mélange of ozone and ether, newly tanned leather, and dried herbs joined with the fresh scent of rose petals. It took everything he could do to open his eyes.

Wooden workbench. Sand practice pit. Cracked basement concrete and the soft glow of the *kata* that leaked into the basement.

He had made it. Almost.

Then the *platiqua* took him.

CHAPTER — 13 THE WEIGHT OF CARING

Bitch!" Jason stood in the cedar and pine forest, the dark canopy of boughs laced above him and the damned broad ravine that no one in their right mind would try to climb down into and out of again. Undercut sides of slippery mud gave onto a rushing stream that flowed down the ravine's length away from the ridge. It hadn't been that way before. Before, the stream had run right down to the end of the downward-sloping ridge and into the small Pleasant River that ran down from Mount Rainier's flanks, steadily gathering water.

But it wasn't doing that now, because Vallon had blocked him. The bitch hadn't used all her power to bring him Cheryl; she'd faked him out, stolen Cheryl, and run. Cheryl hadn't deserved to die and she sure as hell hadn't deserved to come apart into sand in his arms. How must that have felt? How terrified she must have been. How horrifying it *had* been. His stomach still rebelled when he thought of it. Her beloved flesh falling away, collapsing into herself as he fought to hold her.

Yes, Vallon Drake would pay, and so would everything she loved. Things he could do. Oh yes, there were.

Holding to that thought, he turned back the way he had come and retraced his path up over the ridge towards his cabin, the cabin he and Cheryl had built together. The place he had hidden out just after she'd died. It was after dark when he reached it. He stomped back into the cabin and flicked on the lights, looked at the main room, the overturned chair he'd knocked over as he tried to catch Vallon. He uprighted it and then headed down the hallway, past the ruined door and into the back bedroom where he'd confined Vallon.

No, it was not a dream. A heap of the finest white sand lay in the middle of the empty floor. No wife and no rolled up carpet either. He knelt down and ran his hand through the fine grains. Like lightest snowflakes but warm. Almost ash in consistency and yet it weighed him down with caring and hurt and pain. No. He had cremated Cheryl once before, laying her remains to rest in Queen Anne's cemetery.

He pulled back, backed out of the room and locked the door. It would be a memorial to the crimes of Vallon Drake. The crime she would pay for. But first he had to get ready for his revenge. He went into the bedroom that he and Cheryl had lived and loved in, and took a shower to wash some of the rage off. He took the time to steady his hands and shaved. Then he pulled fresh clothing out of the closet that had been stored here years before against an emergency call into work.

Dark grey trousers, a dress shirt that Cheryl had ironed for him so long ago and yet it still carried the scent of her hands. A dark blue jacket— more winter weight and a little out of fashion with its wider lapels, but it would have to do. He shrugged the jacket on and studied himself in the mirror. Same old same old. Jason Bryson, SPD detective, even if his eyes looked a little darker and haunted and his cheeks looked a little gaunt.

He headed out in the car Xavier de Varga had bought them and thought about Landon Snow and the dark man. Vallon cared about both of them. She cared about Fi Murdoch, too, and maybe even Gleason. Yup, there were a lot of casualties he could put in play here.

He started the car, then fished out the phone and dialed as he headed for Seattle's downtown.

§

Wolf Amundson ran his fingers through his hair as he studied the scientist before him. The meeting room at the Homeland Security headquarters was a far cry beyond the makeshift warehouse research facility the woman was used to. Broad, floor to ceiling windows gave a view onto the glorious view of Elliott Bay, Puget Sound, and the tall, iced peaks of the Olympic Peninsula. That was what kept capturing the scientist's attention, not the closer view—the one Wolf was most concerned with. That was the view onto the street far below and the countless people Wolf was committed to protecting.

He sat on one side of the gleaming twelve-foot long meeting table, his facial silhouette reflected in the gleaming walnut finish. The woman, Rona Fujikawa, stood before him—he had not invited her to sit. She was the chief scientist responsible for the research at the warehouse, and so far she had failed him. She wore street clothes, a simple, ill-fitting suit of pale grey that washed her pinched features and graying hair out even further than they normally would be. A nondescript woman, which, he supposed, was the best sort when you wanted one to do a job. They worked harder to please, wanted to show that they might not have gotten the looks, but they certainly *had* inherited the brains.

Now prove it.

He shifted the file on the table before him, before meeting her gaze. Held it. "Reading the old AGS research, it seems to suggest that there is an age of onset of this Gift. I'm told that suggests it's a biochemical effect. Have you found a means to neutralize it, or am I to be forced to take a more final solution to the problem posed by the—shall we say 'residents'—of your facility?" And you, but that went without saying.

He watched the throat bob in the woman's neck. The way her hands seemed to flutter a moment before she found her self-control.

"Sir. As my correspondence told you, we are having a challenge obtaining the specimens we need. The continued environmental stress and hyper vigilance of the children impacts their body chemistry. It is difficult to know whether the differences we're seeing are the results of the stress of their situation or of the incipient Gift. We have, however, made significant progress in the management of those with the Gift. We've used a number of the older students and have been solidifying our understanding of the process needed to totally submerge the Gift. We're just trying to address some of the side effects now."

Wolf suppressed the need to shout and straightened the folder edge against the table edge. Didn't the woman realize she walked treacherous ground? There were other, equally well-qualified biologists and biochemists who would jump at the chance to work with Loadstone and earn their rates.

"I don't really give a damn about side effects, Rona. What I want is control. A means to control the damned agents when we catch them so that I am not forced to take the flak for dispatching them. And a means to stop their fucking children from becoming another generation of predators on society. Finally, I believed I asked your team to find me a solution to the problem of detection. Just how are my agents supposed to arrest these people without knowing who they are?"

He looked up at her and forced a smile on his face. His smile became real when she had to look away and actually took a step back from the table and shook her head.

"I'm sorry. The team hasn't had much luck on that front either."

But there was a satisfying fear in her eyes now. Good. She understood her place. That always seemed to bring better results.

The buzz of the cell phone next to his hand stopped his response. Damn it, he had specifically had all his calls routed to reception so that he would not be disturbed. He chose to ignore it.

"So, what? We're to just arrest everyone until we can run an endocrine test on them? We're to implement such testing at birth and just leave things as they are for now?"

The damned phone continued to buzz, and then went blessedly silent as the woman hemmed and hawed her way through an unsatisfactory answer.

"Damn it, I hired you for complete understanding! For results! Top of your class at Michigan State! You expect me to believe that?"

A soft knock on the boardroom door and the woman spun around. Wolf came half up out of his chair as the door pushed open and his Executive Assistant, Moore, stuck her lovely, doomed, Gifted head in. Unbeknownst to Gleason and Snow, Moore had been working for him these past four years, providing eyes and ears inside the AGS because he happened to have enough concocted evidence on her favorite brother to send said brother away for a very, very long time. Their relationship had led to a rather pleasant affair as the woman apparently thought that was the way to gain freedom for her and her brother. It hadn't worked, and he still had conjugal rights whenever he wanted. A shame it would be over when this whole thing was finished. One does not leave loose threads like that lying around.

"Sir." Moore's lovely Eurasian face showed signs of the stress that only came when she was truly troubled about making the right decision. "There is a phone call I think you should take."

"Who?"

Moore glanced at Rona Fujikawa. Then looked hard at him. "A detective with Seattle PD. He says he knows you and has visited this facility."

Bryson. It could only be. Bryson, who had the talent to tell when the Gift was in play. Bryson, who was friends with one Vallon Drake. Bryson, who had escaped from Homeland Security once, taking with him former AGS chief Gregor Gleason.

Wolf levered himself up out of his chair. "Ms. Fujikawa, I believe we are done for today, but I expect results. Understand?" He said it mildly. The fact he said it at all was warning enough. He gave a hand signal to Moore and let her usher the visibly shaken scientist out the door and then picked up the cell phone and touched talk.

"I'm listening," he said. Unprepared to commit to anything that would end as badly as his last dealings with the man. If he could keep the man on the phone long enough to trace, that would be worth a great deal.

"And I'm dealing. I happen to know Vallon Drake's whereabouts and the general locations of Landon Snow, Gregor Gleason, and Fiona Murdoch. I thought we might be able to come to some agreement." The detective's voice was harsh with emotion.

Amundson let the conversation lag as if this decision took a great deal of thought. The offer was almost too good to be true, but the raw emotion suggested it was.

"And just what is in it for you, Detective Bryson?"

"The chance to see Vallon Drake and her kind burn."

An outcome that would undoubtedly please him, too.

CHAPTER 14 — IN THE COMPANY OF MEN

Vallon hadn't believed her luck when the beat-up Ford pickup had stopped for her. She'd walked in the cedar-scented woods just within sight of the road, afraid to walk on the pavement for fear that Jason would see her. The warm afternoon had disappeared into a long, cool evening, and finally she'd seen his car cruise slowly past towards town, almost as if he wanted her to see. Almost as if he could sense her.

Perhaps he could. All she knew was that she'd counted to one hundred after he passed and had stepped out onto the road when the beater pickup had stopped for her. Its owner, Larry Zarka, a greying, back-to-the-land type with a bushy grey-blond head of hair and pair of intense twinkling blue eyes, had offered her a ride as far as Tacoma. She'd climbed into the scent of wet dog overlaid on weed, newly tilled earth, and mornings. A large chocolate lab, Treacle, in the back of the truck had hung her head through the open rear window and given Vallon a wet doggy kiss on the ear. Maggie had not been pleased.

"So," Larry said, with a sideways glance at her and Maggie, who was finally curled asleep in her lap instead of crying. They'd just passed through Olympia and were bouncing their way north on tired shocks in the rusted-out frame of the vintage truck. "You mind me asking what you were doing walking down the road in the middle of a forest with nothing but a cat?"

He had a good voice, deep and rumbly, and she had the weirdest sense she knew him from somewhere, or had at least seen him before in some place that made her think of a cold city skyline, but her poor scrambled brain came up empty.

She looked up from where she'd been leaning her head against the door post. Her head ached. Her body burned with afterburn and throbbed with general fatigue. So far she'd managed to avoid responding to any of Larry's meaningful looks, but the man had been terribly kind, sharing bottled water and what was obviously food intended as dinner for him and saying nothing when she'd sniffed the water suspiciously and wolfed the food down like she hadn't eaten in days. But even with the food and the rest as he drove, she couldn't stop the shaking in her hands, a combination of the aftermath of fear and adrenaline and afterburn.

She shook her head and looked out at the long line of trees siding I-5. "I'm not sure what to tell you. Let's just say I was in a bad situation and the only way I could get out was to just run." She caught him looking at Maggie. "There was a good chance they'd kill her if I left her behind. I couldn't do that."

Larry's lips made a curve in the bush of his beard. "Sounds like the right thing to do all 'round. Good thing for you I was coming to town to visit friends. Don't do it so much anymore. I like my bit of a farm up in the hills. Quieter. Not the nastiness going on in the city. You know?"

She nodded. Nastiness was a very nice way of describing what was happening right now to students of the AGS academy and to any Gifted Wolf Amundson could get his hands on. This was very dangerous territory for her. "Sounds like the kind of place I wouldn't want to leave, either."

They were passing through the swath of landscape that was the Fort Lewis McCord military installation and on into strip malls and suburbia.

"You got a place in mind for me to let you off?"

"Anywhere's fine. Anywhere at all."

Larry turned to look at her. "You sure? You could come with me, have a safe place to sleep before you head out on your way?"

She really looked at him then, ugly suspicion twining through her brain. Could he be a set up? Had Jason set this whole thing up? He said he knew the area around the cabin. She managed a casual shake of the head. "Thanks, but no. You've been a huge help as it is. I can take it from here."

The highway exit sign said the Tacoma Mall exit was coming up.

"Why don't you pull off here and I can get out at the mall. Go in, make a call, and head out to friends." She tried for a confident smile, but the sudden suspicion that Larry wasn't what he seemed had spooked her some. The sense she knew him from somewhere was growing.

"Nah. That's no place to leave a damsel in distress. You come on with me and we'll fix you right up."

Okay. Now she was getting concerned.

"No. Take this exit. Please. I truly appreciate your help and I'd pay you if I could, but I would rather do this on my own." She said it with force, hand on the door handle.

Larry just looked at her, looked at her hand. He shook his head. "Jeezus. Whatever happened to you really spooked you."

But he took the exit and the truck rattled its way into the expansive mall parking lot with its BMWs and Audis. He stopped at the main entrance.

He turned to her. "You sure you want to do this?"

She nodded and clicked open the door.

"Hold on a minute. He leaned over her and fished in the glove box through a mess of old napkins and what looked like fishing gear and came up smiling with a length of twine. "Thought I had one." He held it out to her. "For your cat. Mall Security might take exception to her."

She just looked at the string, then back at him. Maybe she was wrong to be suspicious. Maybe. She accepted the string and carefully tied it in a figure eight around Maggie's neck and body behind her front legs. Not that it would do much good. The cat would either fall over at the confinement or do her Houdini impersonation and be gone. But it might help to keep mall security off her back.

"Thanks." She climbed out of the truck and thumped the door shut, feeling both sad to leave the truck's relative safety and relieved that Larry hadn't turned out to be the enemy.

She walked around the front of the truck and headed for the entrance.

"Hey, Vallon." Larry called. "You might need this."

She half turned to see him holding out a twenty dollar bill, just as a dark sedan that looked exactly like government issue agent vehicles rolled up behind him. So maybe he hadn't been in on it, but someone had put Homeland Security on Larry.

She turned and bolted into the mall somewhere between Nordstrom's and JC Penny's and found herself near a play area. Maggie was squalling at the abrupt wake-up call and fighting hard to be put down.

"Sorry, Mags. Not going to happen." She stood in an almost rotunda, the mall Muzak echoing around her. There was only one way to go, and she'd better take it and get the hell out a back way before HS agents had the whole place locked up solid.

She ran down the hallway to the intersection with the mall's main corridor. Left and she'd hit Nordstrom's. Right and she'd find Sears and Penny's. Given she was heading to Seattle, it made sense she'd head right.

She turned left and sprinted down the hallway to where Macy's flashy, wide-open entrance stood among the smaller shops. There had to be an outside exit to the store. She slowed and, snuggling her squalling cat to her shoulder, slipped hurriedly down the aisles of cosmetics and leather goods towards the last vestiges of daylight through the rear glass doors.

She was almost there when a black van pulled up outside. She stopped. Checked behind her and saw two suit-clad men and a woman enter the store behind her. No way out.

"I'm sorry ma'am, but you are going to have to take your cat out of here. No pets allowed in the mall. It's posted on the door." The woman, was pretty. Young. Clad in the latest pastel fashion, and please, Louise, was she *ever* that young.

Vallon shouldered past her and scanned the store for an alternative exit. Nothing. The van might be nothing, too, but she didn't give it a lot of hope. Which meant she had only one option. Fighting back a sick feeling in her stomach, she hooked Maggie in her arm and pulled out her pen and vellum because, as exhausted as she was, they would help her focus.

She closed her eyes and sent a prayer for forgiveness out to whatever Powers existed. Then she sketched a garden area flanking the doorway, the van gone. The vehicle smoked and the smoke coiled down and became earthen flower beds. The van and its contents shimmered and faded and trees grew up and spread shady leaves. Flowers appeared out of nothing.

Ignoring her rebelling stomach, Vallon bolted for the door. Heard a shout and knew the agents were behind her.

Outside, she paused and drew on the ley lines, pulled the power up into her and turned back to her pursuers with her vellum and pen. Sent a bolt of power up through the floor and a quick three lines created a wall blocking the three running figures. Good enough.

She started walking rapidly down the exterior sidewalk, fighting back tears and the sick feeling in her stomach about whomever was in the van.

How many of them were there? A screech of tires said another one of the vehicles was hurrying to help the agents she'd just taken out. She leapt across the road and into the parking lot, ducked down behind a BMW. She could unlock it in a moment and then she'd just have to figure out how to get it started. She waited for the car to cruise past, but it stopped by the door and the agents got out.

"She was here. I'm sure of it. She worked the Change. I'll bet you'll find you're missing some agents."

A voice she'd know anywhere, but not one she'd expected. She chanced a look over the hood of the car and her stomach sank.

No question. Jason. And working with the HS agents.

§

The room in one of the outbuildings of the farm Fiona had seen was small, no more than six feet by six feet square; walls, floor, and ceiling were of cold concrete and bare of anything like furnishings. A single black metal door with a small, sliding viewing panel was the only thing that broke the monotonous grey. Fi huddled in a corner as far from the black panel as possible and tried to keep her face averted from the camera that hung just above the door.

They were watching her. They hadn't quit watching her since they picked her up on the road and gave her to Vallon's father, Francis Drake. There were just too many enemies in the world, it seemed. She clenched her eyes hard against the tears the memory brought. There was no way she was going to let these bastards see her cry. Not when Vallon wouldn't. Thinking like Vallon might have got her in trouble, but it always seemed to get her out of trouble, too. So what could it hurt to think like her best friend?

Aside from getting her dead, she couldn't think of anything, so think like Vallon it was, because Francis Drake was likely going to kill her anyway. So what would Vallon do in this situation?

Certainly not just crouch here with her hair pulled over her face trying not to cry. Okay. She swiped her face and glared up at the camera. She was no little girl anymore. She was friends with Vallon Drake, and Francis Drake was going to hurt her very best friend.

That meant she needed to find a way to warn Vallon. Heck, she needed to warn of the simple fact that Francis Drake was alive.

Vallon had told them that she'd seen the stanchion of the horrible machine in Francis Drake's hell pit wipe clean the spot where her father was standing. She'd believed he was dead and had almost seemed relieved at that fact. Almost like Fi had been when her mother supposedly died.

Had she been wrong, too? Was Rebecca Murdoch somewhere out there plotting against them?

A shiver ran through her, because she might be brave enough to meet Francis Drake, but she knew she couldn't face down her mother.

So to warn Vallon she had to get out of here, or at least have access to a phone. That meant she had to convince them that she'd cooperate with them, and that meant she had to convince them that she didn't pose a threat. For once the fact that everyone thought of her as a child seemed to be in her favor. So she needed to pretend she was Vallon pretending she was Fi.

Much too confusing, but she knew what she had to do. She kept looking up at the camera and let her glare gradually crumble into tears. Then she covered her face and sat there rocking, huddled in on herself. She'd done something similar often enough when Vallon had first taken her in. Sometimes tears really were a good weapon.

It seemed like an incredibly long time before she heard something from beyond the door. At least it sounded like something. A footstep perhaps. Or maybe a scrape. After so long in the room with no change in light or dark to tell her what time of day it was, she wasn't sure of much anymore. All her senses seemed a little off. But if they were coming, she wanted to be strong. She -reached- like they'd taught her in school, down to the power that always reminded her of roses and gardens and elegance that she would never achieve.

Its scent filled her up and she funneled a small amount up into her body so it fizzled and popped under her skin like carbonated water. Maybe—maybe if she had the chance she could use it to get free.

A click and the ugly sound of metal on metal hinges brought her to her feet as the door swung open. One of the suited men stood there. Not Gifted, at least, and that was surprising given what she'd done to the car and escort before. She might actually have a chance, even if her knees were shaking.

"Why am I here? What do you want of me? I haven't done anything."

The man's piercing grey gaze said that that wasn't exactly the truth.

He silently motioned her to the door and caught her arm and half-led, half-dragged her down the long corridor that ran the length of the building. The sweet scent of hay and the musty scent of horse filled the air. A barn. That was what this was. A barn with an ultra-secure holding cell. Who built such a thing?

Vallon's father for one, or at least he had the barn fitted out with one. The man hurried her past stalls with expensive-looking horses and then out a door and into darkness.

Night? It was night? But she'd thought it was mid-morning. Confusion and sudden fatigue stopped her until Mr. Grey Eyes dragged her forward. Vallon's father couldn't control the time of day, could he?

Could he?

The fact she didn't know made her want to curl up in a ball with her arms wrapped around her head. Why, oh why, had she been so stupid as to leave the hotel room?

She was still asking herself that when her guard marched her into the main house that smelled like last night's meal of steak and mushrooms. Her stomach growled. Then she was shoved into a room that looked like a library, with a huge desk settled like a behemoth in the midst of an oriental carpet between the stacks of shelves that lined the room. Seated at the desk was Francis Drake, looking fresh and alert in a pair of navy dress trousers and a cream-colored polo shirt that set off his newly-tanned skin. He had a thin sheaf of papers in front of him over which he steepled his hands as he watched her enter the room. He nodded her towards a chair that faced him.

No way Vallon would do as he said.

"I think I'll stand, thank you," she said, trying for defiance.

Vallon's father only shrugged. "Suit yourself. I just thought you might be more comfortable seated for our little talk."

She kept a stony eye on him, but shrugged off Mr. Grey Eyes' hold and gripped the back of the chair for strength. "What do you want? You have no right to hold me here."

That seemed to bring a smile to his face. "You sound just like Vallon. I wonder how deep your defiance runs. As deep as hers, do you think?"

How was she supposed to answer that? She'd never be as strong as Vallon. Or as brave, or as smart, or as anything. She was just an imposter gaining strength by pretending to be something she could never be.

All the fortitude she'd held onto seemed to run down her spine and into the floor, and she was a scared, silly, little girl, just like they'd always treated her.

"It's okay, Fiona. You can be afraid. You aren't Vallon and never could be, but you are her very good friend."

She jerked at his use of her name and the fact that he seemed to know what she was feeling.

"She's very lucky to have a friend like you. Someone she can trust to look out for her."

Fi found herself nodding.

"You'd do anything to protect her, wouldn't you?"

She just looked at him and crossed her arms over her chest. The room felt chill, even though the rose-scented power ran warm in her veins.

"I agree with you, you know. Vallon's special. She needs to be protected, and right now I think she's in very grave danger." Francis Drake said softly.

"If she is, it's from you," she said.

He just shook his head. "I wouldn't hurt Vallon. I feel terrible about what I did before. I should have given her the time she needed to make a decision to help me. If she'd really understood, she would have."

Fi straightened. "She wouldn't help you. Vallon believes in the AGS mission. You—don't. You're rogue."

Francis Drake's gaze fell away and he ran his hands up through his thinning blond hair and sighed. "It hurts me to hear you say that, Fi. May I call you that? Fi? Or would you prefer Fiona?"

He looked up at her, his grey eyes enquiring as if he really cared to know. As if. She rolled her eyes.

"Fi. Fiona. It doesn't matter. What matters is that you're a liar. You forced Vallon because you didn't care, just like you didn't care about me or any of the other Gifted at New Madrid. You forced us."

Darn it, her voice had risen and she knew if she kept talking like this, the tears pressing at her eyes would begin to fall. She hugged herself harder and dug her nails into her arms to remind herself that this man wasn't nice. He didn't care about Vallon or anything.

"You're wrong, and it pains me that my daughter and her friend feel that way about me."

She glared at him. "You don't care. You left her when she was eleven and never even let her know you were alive. What kind of father does that?"

It was like she'd shot him. His shoulders slumped. He fell back in his chair with the bleakest look on his face she'd ever seen. He met her gaze and finally nodded.

"It was a bad decision. The worst decision I've ever made, to leave my Vallon behind. Your mother had the right of it, for all her actions were wrong on so many levels. But I left because of what the AGS was becoming. Government was interfering with the purity of our work. Eventually the bureaucrats were going to take over. The Gift—it's something the unGifted can't fathom and it will terrify them if they try. So I left to do in secret what the AGS was trying to do openly. Don't get me wrong: I respect the agents in the AGS. I just think there is more opportunity for wrong decisions at the top."

She looked at him—the middle-aged man who looked so sad about, well, everything. It didn't fit with what had happened in New Madrid, at all. Had Vallon been wrong?

"Like now?" she said.

Her words seemed to rustle around the room.

Francis Drake nodded solemnly. "It's bad out there, now. Very bad with Wolf Amundson at the helm. The man knows nothing and is terrified by that fact. He's been picking up agents all over the country unless my men get there first. That's why you're here, Fiona. I wanted you safe."

Something about his story just didn't seem to fit. She frowned, remembering the room she'd been held in.

"I'm sorry about the room, Fiona. I was concerned for your safety, given what you did to those men. A tragic accident, I know, but something that was likely to garner retribution from my men. I wanted you in the one place they couldn't get to you."

"You did?" But that still didn't quite make sense. It was cold there, and he'd left her there so long—days, it felt like—but she realized she really had no idea how long she'd been held there. Maybe her whole sense of time was wrong. Maybe he was trying to help her.

Still, he nodded at the chair again. "Please sit down, Fiona. I need to talk to you about Vallon. I'm terribly worried about her, what with all that Homeland Security is doing, but I can't find her anywhere to offer her refuge. I was hoping you might be able to help me."

She sat. Everything felt wobbly. Her knees, her thoughts, her resolve to be angry in the face of this very soft spoken man who had only been looking out for her.

"I—I'm not sure I should tell you anything. You did so much bad stuff before. Why should I believe you now?"

Vallon's father nodded sadly. "I was afraid of this. You don't know me and I've made a very bad first impression."

That, she could believe was the truth.

"So what can I do to convince you otherwise?" He leaned forward, a look of earnest desire in his eyes as he placed his hands palm up on the desk.

Darn it, how was she to know what to do? She wasn't sure of him, but she wasn't sure of much else either, and she certainly wasn't sure of Vallon and Gleason and Landon's plans to go running off into danger without her.

"She's in Seattle." It came out without thinking. "Or at least that's where she was heading. She should be there by now. I'm worried about her, too."

She held her breath. Had she done the right thing?

Francis Drake only smiled, but it wasn't like most smiles. His didn't feel friendly and happy. No, his was more the cat that ate the canary kind of smile, and she wondered if she'd just ruined things for Vallon.

But Francis Drake only nodded. "I can see you're worried about her as much as I am, so why don't we work together to find her, okay?"

Biting her lip, she finally agreed and he gave a great sigh and looked over her head at the grey-eyed man who still stood at the back of the room.

"Good. Now that that's settled, let's get Fiona, here, some place more comfortable to wait while we roust old Fitzsimmons for a jet out west. We don't want Vallon falling into the wrong hands, do we?"

CHAPTER 15 —THE WEIGHT OF EARTH AND TREE ROOTS

The oil-stained cement was hard under Vallon's knees as she chanced another peek over the front of the red beemer. The bright Macy's light reflected on the hood and windshield of the dark SUV parked by the entrance. Three men—no, agents—stood there along with Jason Bryson, looking all hair-slicked-back, spit and polished in a suit, no less.

One of the agents was busy talking on his Bluetooth, coordinating agents converging on the mall, while another was on the phone. Still another was grilling Jason about just where she might be going. Thankfully, Jason didn't seem to be that helpful, probably because he didn't *know* anything.

"Friends?" He said. "There was me, the woman next door who fed her cat, that little albino fellow, Landon, but he's not here." He shook his head and shoved his shoulders back.

That's right, you bastard. You try to stand up with the big boys. Just see how long before they knock you down again.

"If she doesn't have friends, where would she go?" asked the agent, another clone of the big-man-broad-shoulders-dark-suit that Wolf Amundson seemed to prefer to surround himself with. They weren't even Homeland Security agents—more contracted men from Loadstone, as if the government couldn't protect itself anymore, so it had to hire help. It was a frightening concept. More frightening still when she realized that with Amundson's apparently unwitting help, these people and the big corporation they represented were taking apart one of the last means the government had to protect itself.

God, she wished Xavier was here, not because she needed help to protect herself, but just because he seemed to fill her with confidence just by being around.

Jason considered the agent's question a minute. "I really don't know. She knows Seattle well. She wouldn't go home. There's nothing there she wants. I already went there and got it for her." He shook his head. "Not quite how I intended things to go down. Maybe go to a hotel, or crash with the street people. She knows where they hang out. But that's just short term. Ultimately, she plans to go to where Amundson has those kids—those students. She plans to break them out."

If she could have blasted him off the face of the earth, she would have. Well, maybe she could have, but if she had, it would have left her in no condition to get the hell out of Dodge. It just went to prove that you couldn't trust any unGifted. Not like Xavier. Him she would bet her life on and, she believed, he would do the same with her.

So now they'd be waiting for her wherever the students were. That meant she's better have a darn good plan, and she wished again that Xavier was around, not recovering from the bullet wound with Landon. But Xavier *wasn't* around, and that meant she needed a place to go to ground so she could figure out a successful attack plan on her own. Not her first choice, but probably the best one given her current situation. The question was where? Flopping with the homeless people was definitely something she'd considered. But now that Jason had alerted Homeland Security to that possibility, it was out of the question. So the poorest of Seattle's poor were going to be rousted unmercifully and she wouldn't even be there. But Jason *had* given her a destination. Maybe. Her house. It was both the most obvious and least obvious place to go, because it would undoubtedly be watched. But she had ways she could avoid watchers that no one would ever know. At least no one unGifted. Ways that Xavier's little disappearing acts had helped her come up with. Now she just needed to get there.

The car in front of her would help. She placed her palm on the door lock and sent a tiny runnel of power into it until the locking mechanism melted away and the door pulled open, releasing the scent of warmed leather and clove cigarettes. She climbed in behind the wheel, released Maggie, and slouched low in the cushy leather seat while she considered the steering column and the skills she'd developed during her misspent youth.

She placed her hands over the ignition and closed her eyes and -reached-. Thankfully this was an older car without the electronic ignition. She caught hold of the wiring and used it against the car's key mechanism by splitting the ignition wire and connecting it so that the ignition turned over. And over. And caught. She tromped on the gas and got a warm purr in response. Whoever owned the car had treated it well.

Maggie, taking cover in the back seat, yowled.

Still slumped low, so her full five foot eight wouldn't show, she dropped the car in gear and eased out of the parking spot away from the entrance and the HS agents and Jason. Please let them not spot her. Please.

In the rearview mirror she watched as Jason's gaze tracked her car's retreat down the line of parked cars. The trouble was, most drivers would take the route that led them right past the agents towards the exit, instead of driving farther into the parking lot. Trust Jason to notice, but he still hadn't realized just what it was that didn't seem right to him. At the end of the row, she sped up across the lines of cars and then turned back towards the mall and the nearest exit that would take her onto I-5.

A sudden flurry of movement behind her said the penny had dropped for Jason and her head start was over. She gunned the car out of the lot and up and onto the overpass that would put her on the highway northbound. From the mall came the red and blue flash of police lights.

She swerved around a car and cut across traffic against a light and onto the highway on-ramp. Maggie was giving gut-wrenching feline screams. Then she put the pedal to the metal and kicked the beemer into overdrive.

It was a sweet set of wheels, quickly responsive to a touch of the wheel. She only hoped the brakes were in as good repair as she swerved in and out of traffic, trying to put as much distance between herself and her pursuers as possible. The trouble was, Jason had seen what she was driving. A custom-paint-job deep ruby beemer was not exactly an unmarked car, even if he hadn't seen the license plate. And with HS resources, they could easily put a road block in place. Which meant she'd need to get off I-5 as soon as possible and take the back roads. It would add hours to her trip. Hours she didn't really have, because the longer she was out in this car, the more eyes HS would have out there looking for her. She needed to lose this car, and quickly because she didn't think she had the reserve power to Change it.

Ignoring the squalling cat behind her, she took the next exit fairly confident that they wouldn't have seen her take it and ended up in an area of car dealerships and casinos near the port of Tacoma and turned into a casino parking lot. This would do nicely. A huge neon sign advertised concerts by aging rockers and lit up the dusk-filled parking lot. It wasn't full, but still, several hundred cars waited for their owners to return after they were fleeced of their money. She found a likely looking Audi next to a vacant spot and pulled in, then sat there a moment getting a feel for the rhythm of movements around the lot and trying to coax Maggie onto her lap. Darn cat wasn't having any.

Other cars followed her in, but found their own places to park and emptied out couples who headed into the bright lights of the casino's entrance like moths to flames, or the way Gifted were drawn to Seattle.

When the area around her was empty, she got out of the car and stepped up to the Audi. The car was a few years old, but in good condition, with that slightly iridescent cream-colored paint job that had been popular with the older set. The fact it was an Audi and older meant it likely wasn't a police bait car, but the fact it was an Audi meant it likely had some spunk.

She placed her hand over the locking mechanism again and sent a thread of power into it. The metal heated under her fingers and the afterburn flared again after she'd fought it into submission on the long ride in from the mountain.

She swayed and pulled the car door open, then went back and retrieved a protesting Maggie. After all this, it was highly unlikely the little cat would ever speak to her again. She half fell, half lowered herself inside the Audi. Leather seats again. Nice. But the interior of the car had the horrid pine scent of a cheap air freshener that hung from the rearview mirror. She ripped it off and tossed it onto the pavement, then repeated her ignition trick and sat there with closed eyes, trying to quiet the painful burn in her bones and the migraine forming behind her eyes. Please just let her get somewhere safe before the afterburn all came crashing down around her. She hadn't really dealt with it since New Madrid, before she'd had to face down her father and stop the quake's devastation.

Xavier where are you?

But there was only a quivering sense of presence, immediate enough it was almost as if he was someplace nearby.

The car smelled strange with the pine scent no longer permeating the air. Musty. Old and copper. Well, it would have to do.

She eased the car in gear and carefully drove out of the parking lot, then got back on the highway, a deep sense of relief escaping her as she settled back to drive. If they set up roadblocks, she'd know well ahead of time by the slowdown in traffic. She could get off the highway then. More likely they'd simply have watchers set up on the highway seeking the red beemer. Once that car was spotted, they'd move in. But her current ride they didn't know. She'd cruise right past and down to Fremont, if she was lucky.

She held her breath when she saw the first of the spotters—a dark sedan pulled onto the shoulder of the highway. She cruised right past and the dark sedan stayed where it was. She passed three more of the spotters, both on overpasses and along the highway, before she took the Mercer exit and headed downhill into Seattle towards the space needle, then turned onto Westlake Avenue and followed the shore of Lake Union to the Fremont Bridge.

"Hello, troll," she said, still imagining that a troll like the one under the Aurora Bridge also sat under the Fremont structure. And then she was in Fremont and almost home. She didn't dare leave the car in the main part of town because it was entirely too likely that she'd be spotted. She didn't want to drive directly home, either, because it was possible they had a trap set up for her. That meant she had to use another way.

She cruised up Fremont Street past her turn and suddenly made up her mind. On her right lay the BF Day playground, its trees and playing field caught in the first blush of streetlights. Most of the ballplayers had gone their way, so when she eased the Audi into the curb and climbed out, she was almost alone. Just like she wanted.

The air smelled of heated turf and leaves as she strode into the deeper shadow of the trees, Maggie once more cradled in her arms, happy to be free of the horror of cars. In a small clearing where a flat rock lay exposed in the grass, she knelt and, one handed, dug the vellum and paper out of her pocket. She flattened the vellum on the stone and opened the nib of the pen. The faint scents of vinegar, copper, and tanning fluids wafted up to her nose.

Maggie looked up at her with huge amber eyes and squirmed. "Hush, little one. Not much longer."

She checked over her shoulder for watchers and, when there were none, she closed her eyes and -reached- into the earth. Her pen touched the vellum and the ink began to spread. She began sketching. The park around her, the spot where she knelt, and beneath the roots of the trees beside her, a tunnel in the earth.

In her mind the tunnel traveled below Fremont Avenue and the basements of the houses across the street. Beyond the laneway and on to Dayton Avenue, where the tunnel sloped up. Her pen sketched again. Square foundation. Half wall. Workbench and broken floor. The end of the tunnel was a plain brown door in the foundation.

She opened her eyes, and the afterburn flamed up her arms and into her brain. Maggie meowed in protest and began to squirm in earnest. Vallon lost her balance and sat down hard. Maggie used her claws and fought loose. She dashed through the darkness and Vallon scrambled to her feet, barely grabbed the pen and vellum before racing after her cat.

Maggie was a black and white streak towards the trees. She gave a great echoing yowl and disappeared. Vallon stumbled and fell—right into the tunnel she'd made. She slid down the incline and came to a stop in darkness, the vellum and pen lost in the fall. The place smelled of moist earth and old rot, and Maggie's protest mews echoed back towards her.

Perfect. Just plain perfect. She could hold the tunnel in place for a while. She could probably even replace the vellum, but the pen was irreplaceable. She scrambled on her knees, running her fingers through the loose dirt. She came up with the vellum lodged where the dirt floor became the wall, but the pen eluded her. She looked back up the tunnel to where a vision of shivering leaves against a night sky filled the opening. A whiff of cool breeze reached her. Well, there was no way Maggie could go but forward and there was nowhere the pen could be but near her. Life would be perfect if she had a flashlight, but that was beyond her. She began to crawl back towards the tunnel opening, running her hands over the soil. Nothing was there. Not even when she reached the grass of the park.

She climbed to her feet and returned to the stone. She had been right here. She had leapt up and turned, then leapt forward. She was sure the pen had been in her hand.

It was nowhere around the stone. She looked back at the tunnel. A faint meow wafted up to her. The air was filled with the scent of earth and a light mist filled the space under the tree eaves.

Not mist—at least nothing natural. It was the mist of the tunnel unmaking. New Madrid, the horrible attempt to create life for Jason, and efforts with the cars all conspired to drain her of strength so that holding even the simple tunnel was causing sweat to run down her brow. If she was going to get to her house, it had to be now. If she was going to save Maggie from smothering, it had to be now.

"Damnation," she swore and ducked back to the tunnel and down into the darkness. If she'd missed the pen in the tunnel it was about to be buried, but she had no time to worry about it at the moment.

The moist dirt walls became her guide as she hurried blindly down the tunnel. At least it was straight, even massive tree roots cut off and cauterized by her change. Everything would go back as it had been as soon as she released the image of the tunnel from her mind and the power of the earth from the vellum she held. Why vellum worked and plain paper didn't, she didn't know, but someone had discovered the old fashioned vellum and what it could do.

The breeze from the park disappeared and mist seemed to fill the darkness around her. The tunnel filled with the sound of her footfall and the rough sound of her rushed breathing. The weight of the earth over her head seemed to fall on her. Sweat slicked her face and back and a sour bile taste rose up her throat to choke her. Why the heck was she always ending up in tunnels? The Seattle incident had been bad enough, but New Madrid had been over-the-top. Apparently it had left her a little claustrophobic.

She didn't like it. Didn't like it at all. Her palms were slick and she could hear her breathing hitch higher and higher in her throat. Not good. Not good at all. She knew the tunnel was relatively short, but at the moment it felt like it went on forever and she was trapped and the ceiling was about to come down and the walls move in as soon as she lost the will and the strength to hold them and she'd be buried alive and breathing in dirt to smother and lay here as food for worms.

Her breath came so short and rapid she felt faint. Cold beads of panicked sweat stood out over her body and she stank of rank fear.

Then came a *mreow* and something soft rubbed her ankle and she almost screamed.

"Maggie. Thank God." She grabbed the little cat and hugged her, much to Maggie's discomfort, but the fact she was here said they had to be close to the end. The door. If it still existed.

Damn it, it still existed. She'd made it. She held it and would hold it no matter how tired she was, for as long as it was needed. She just hoped she was right in deciding to return to her house. There could be people waiting on the other side of the door right now.

She stopped where she was and closed her eyes. Where had all this fear come from? Usually she was cold and clear as a triangulated survey site. Usually fear was something she just assessed and set away.

She slowed her breathing, burying her face in Maggie's fur, and gradually the fear subsided. She opened her eyes and straight ahead saw a glimmer of light in the form of a rectangle, like faint light leaking around a door frame.

"Thank you, powers that be." She hurried forward, the mist in the tunnel multiplying until the darkness masked the hint of light as well as an ocean fog might. But her hand found a wooden door, a metal doorknob, and she twisted and the door pushed open.

Onto the faintest light leaking only from under a doorway at the top of the stairs.

To be expected when it was nighttime and when all the basement windows were blacked out, yet it still seemed brilliant after the tunnel's utter darkness. The pungent odors of leather tanning and the more subtle scents of ink making—verdigris, cobalt, indigo, cedar, and so on coalesced around her like old friends. She stumbled out onto the concrete floor—*her* concrete floor—and went to her knees. Maggie yanked loose and disappeared into the darkness, then meowed mournfully.

"Shh. Maggie. Shh, girl." Vallon crawled on hands and knees over the cracked concrete towards the crying cat.

Her hand banged into something soft and she yanked back.

There shouldn't be anything soft here. There were only her workbench on the far side of the room and the practice sandbox against the neighboring wall. Unless Jason had left something down here for her.

All the little hairs on the back of her neck prickled on end. Would he be so sure she would come here if she got loose? Or was he counting on her not coming? After what he'd said to the HS agents, her first inclination was 'no,' he didn't think she'd be here. So what was down here?

She tentatively reached out again and this time touched something smooth, like skin. Yanked back and tried again, holding her breath. A cool shoulder. She followed the shoulder up and came to a tangle of hair that released the scent of sweat, cedar of Lebanon, and incense. Her heart leapt.

"Xavier?" she whispered. How the heck had he got here?

He didn't move.

"Xavier?" She shook the fallen figure and ran her fingers down over his face—definitely Xavier—with the craggy features and hawkish nose of a man of the desert, and down over his well-muscled chest—bare. She stopped.

He wasn't breathing.

CHAPTER 16—BLUE GOLD

The white room really was a mess, and it was going to take some effort and time to clean up—time he probably didn't have if Xavier de Varga was half the man he appeared to be.

Blood dripped and dried onto the floor in a line from the procedure table in the center of the room to the sink against the wall. Bloody footprints on the linoleum elsewhere. Blood caked the sink and smeared on the right side of the table and the heap of bloody clothing on the floor. The air reeked of fading copper and cedar.

Yes, rather a mess compared to the pristine environment his meditations required. Landon ran his manicured fingers through his thinning white hair and frowned down at his tan moccasins. Not exactly the footwear for such a clean-up job, but one must expect a mess from time to time if one was going to advance his agenda as Landon had done. The ruin of his shoes was probably very little to pay.

So first things first. He stepped carefully across the room to the heap of clothing and bandages and gingerly picked each piece up and shook it out. The spicy scents of cedar and incense were released by the cloth, but nothing else. He tossed the clothing on the table and rolled a metal bucket and mop out of a cupboard.

So, his plan of catch, tag, and release had worked. He should have tagged while he did the hand; that failure had required he knock out de Varga a second time. He'd been concerned that Vallon's reports of the man's appearances and disappearances might mean that what he was going to try wouldn't work, but apparently the little biological tracking device he'd implanted in de Varga's chest in place of the bullet had been transported with him. Interesting.

He pulled a computer tablet out of a locked drawer and used his thumbprint to open it. The machine and a modified edition of Google Earth sprang to life, the globe spinning in space and then gradually rushing up towards the observer. Western hemisphere, North America, America, the Pacific Northwest, Seattle. A blinking red light at the northwest end of Lake Union just north of the locks.

A little thrill of satisfaction ran through him. It was true. De Varga could teleport himself across great distances.

So. The destination shouldn't be a surprise. De Varga had gone to join up with Vallon. That was going to pose a bit of a problem, but given the growing situation in America, he had no doubt things would move in the direction he planned. Xavier de Varga had made Landon work for his secrets, and though the mysterious man might not have given away everything, the little tracking device would soon address that issue. Set de Varga running and he could track the man right back to the people who sent him.

Landon filled the metal bucket with water and cleaning fluid and began mopping. Pinkish water slopped over his shoes, but he still couldn't stop himself from humming.

§

The assassin found Gregor Gleason just as he entered the Henry J. Daly building for the sixth time in three days. The grey stone building at 300 Indiana Avenue stood in a sea of concrete parking lots and green grass. With its multistory, narrow, art-deco windows, it looked as if it modeled the bars of a jail cell—whether to keep the public and criminals out or in, Gregor couldn't say. Either way, he felt like a stranger in a strange land every time he entered, regardless of his position with the AGS, now Homeland Security. He wondered when a hand was going to fall on his shoulder and lead him away to lockup along with every other known Gifted. Amundson wouldn't be happy until things were that way.

Gleason paused on the grey steps to look out at the summer-burned lawns and the art deco eagles by the red brick walkways. He'd studied them too many times the past few days, and each time they made him aware of the passing of time and reminded him of his helplessness.

He closed his eyes. He was not used to feeling helpless. Helpless was something the public might feel when their house was broken into. Helpless and violated. But he didn't feel violated. Not unless you counted the helpless rage he felt because the country was falling apart for the Gifted and there didn't seem to be anything he could do about it.

He fumbled his phone from his pocket in case Reitsma had sent him a text message. Reitsma, an old university buddy and the assistant to the head of the Congressional Security Oversight Committee, had said he would talk to the Congressman about what was happening and see if there was anything to be done. Reitsma had said he would get in touch with Gleason as soon as he had something to report. It had been two days, and his old school chum was his last resort. Fitzsimmons and his ilk seemingly had a lock on Washington decisions regarding the AGS, and no one was prepared to do more than sit back and watch Amundson do his thing and then assess the damage.

"Dammit." Gleason went to slide the blasted phone with its lack of messages back into his pocket. The traitorous instrument slipped from his finger and clattered with an expensive sound onto the concrete.

Swearing, Gleason bent to pick it up, and felt the wind of the bullet pass over him just as he heard the weapon's report.

He threw himself backwards and into the building, seeking the source of the shot. There. In the police parking lot—a grey sedan that had simply pulled up amongst the police cars as if it belonged. A man was just pulling a rifle barrel back into the car, as the vehicle leapt back out of the parking spot and sped out of the lot and was gone.

Not a surprise. He'd known Amundson would eventually get word of where he'd gone. It made sense that Gleason wasn't getting the decisions he wanted. Amundson would be working the backroom deals to consolidate his power, regardless of anything Gleason did. He wondered whether Fitzsimmons was backing him or just too smart to get in the way. Was it Amundson who had abducted Fiona, or was there another power in play?

After six days there still was no sign of her, just a vague recollection of a restaurant hostess that perhaps the girl whose photo he showed her *might* be the crazy girl who'd been escorted by her brother. She didn't know where.

It wasn't much to go on and the only hope he had was that Amundson wouldn't bother coming after a girl like Fi, not when he had other, bigger, fish to fry. Like himself and Vallon and Landon.

"May I help you, Sir?" A uniformed police woman had come up to him while he stared out at the street. She was a pretty woman with deep coffee-colored skin and her hair cut in a skull-hugging afro. She wore her uniform with razor-sharp creases and spoke with just as sharp an inflection in her voice.

He shook his head. "I was going to check on the status of a missing person's case, but I'm thinking that me interrupting the investigating officers isn't going to expedite the case. I think I'll be on my way, thanks."

He pushed out of the door and into the car-exhaust-scented air that was a darn sight better than the just plain exhausted air-conditioned air of the building.

Washington had yielded nothing and had only taken his time, his pride, and the woman-child he was supposed to be looking out for. It was time for him to go where he might do some good.

§

No! Xavier couldn't be dead. Not here. Not now.

She ran her hands over the rough hair of his chest. Through the tangle of damp hair on his head. No injuries she could tell. Roll him over? Had someone shot him in the back? Had Jason?

She needed light. Stumbling up, she fumbled her way to the stairs and crept up them to the light switch just inside the basement door. Come to think of it, she shouldn't be able to see a lighter area under the door. After the incident with the castle in her basement, she'd nailed a towel at the base of the door to stop the little people she'd created from possibly getting out of the basement. She hadn't been back since. She ran her fingers down the door. No towel. She found it torn loose and shoved aside, and swiftly stuffed it back in place and flicked on the single bare bulb that hung in the basement. Ghostly light shone up at her and she hurried down.

A naked Xavier lay on his back across the cracks in the concrete. The sandbox lay smooth beside him, so the castle and all its surprising little residents had disappeared back into the sand again. Signs Jason had been here showed in the open cupboard doors above her wooden workbench and the scattering of vellum across the workbench top.

She went to her knees beside Xavier.

"Please be alive. Please. Please. Please."

But when she checked his pulse she didn't feel anything. When she lay her ear against his too-cold chest, she heard nothing. Or maybe a single thump that she couldn't be sure was real.

"No. No. No-no-no-no-no-no-NO."

She closed her eyes and-reached- for him. The barest flicker of light surrounded him. None of the brilliant bonfire she was used to. She yanked back. What was the matter with him?

His features were devoid of the intense black gaze she knew and loved. His body looked battered, but healing. The wounds in his side had been closed and neat sutures were clearly Landon's work, though there were no bandages. His right hand, though—unbandaged, it was covered with shredded skin, the entire thing swollen and bloody almost beyond recognition. What the hell had he and Landon run into? Was Landon okay? She looked more closely. The hand wasn't shredded. The flesh had been methodically flayed off the bone.

Her afterburn-upset stomach did a slow drop and roll at the agony of what it must have felt like—must feel like still.

Who would do such a thing—and then rebuild the hand again? That was—sick. Totally sick, but it took a great deal of skill to actually put the hand back together so that it actually looked like a hand. A surgeon? Landon?

He would have such skills, because everything he did was a quiet show of excellence. But Landon would have no reason to do something so vile.

She -reached- for Xavier again and his scent of cedar and incense filled her awareness, though the fire of his life force barely burned.

[Xavier?]

Something quivered in the low fire, almost as if it heard her.

[Xavier, can you hear me? You have to come back to me.]

Another quiver, and surely she wasn't imagining the way the flame suddenly sparked and turned blue at the edges. She reached out to the flame, hesitated, and then touched it.

And fell.

Torn away, down and down and down into the earth. Past the deeps that had held the magma chambers of Mount Rainier. Past the depths of the lake under New Madrid. Below her, a web of power channels spread beneath Seattle. She grabbed for them, but was ripped past and down, down into the darkness of earth.

Her head filled with lavender and then a huge river of power flowed east to west and swept down under the Pacific tectonic plate. It burned as she was dragged lower still, the pressure and heat of the earth's mantle compressing around her. She hadn't known such power existed so deep in the earth. Was this the secret to Xavier's power? Where was he taking her?

Because wherever he was, whatever had caught hold of her was still dragging her deeper. Terrifyingly deep. So deep she wondered if she could find her way back to her body.

Was it possible to be lost from your body?

Panic spread wings around her and set her heart racing harder. She tried to stop her downward spiral and couldn't. Was she collapsed on the basement floor beside Xavier, trapped by whatever force had caught him? Because if he was trapped, what hope did she have of freeing herself?

She tried to slow her breathing, and surely that was her body responding, her heartbeat slowing. Yes, she was still connected, even as the force dragged her lower.

A blue-gold light seemed to grow around her, revealing stone compressed due to massive pressure, and yet she floated through it, down to strange structures of towering diamond and ruby and sapphire crystals, all refracting the deep blue glow that came from a massive power flow far below.

[Xavier?]

[Vallon.] A faint voice from far beneath her.

[Xavier!] She dove down towards his voice, his presence.

[Don't!] His voice rose like steam off sun heated stone. [The *platiqua*. It is too strong, *Bela*.]

She tried to slow her descent, but a powerful force had caught hold of her and dragged her towards the brilliant blue-gold river to where it fell away under the oceans. She fought, as a swimmer might fight a riptide, and slowly, slowly stopped herself just above the surging surface of the flowing power. The world reeked of something deep and earthy as saffron and pulsed with so much power just being this near she thought she might explode.

[Xavier, where are you?]

A brief sensation of direction and she sped along the blue-gold surface until it plunged deep beneath the ocean. She hesitated, then plunged with it, falling as if the fall had no end, the heat of the earth and of the blue-gold power sizzling through her until her skin felt crisped and blackened. Her brain sizzled in her skull.

And then the fall ended as suddenly as it had begun. She couldn't stop herself in time and plunged deep into the rushing blue gold.

She couldn't breathe. Couldn't move, because power blasted inside her nose, her ears, her pores, and became one with her. She with it. So much power she felt ten stories high, a mile wide, and still growing, her skin stretched thin and near to bursting. She was as large as the world and almost giddy with the influx of power, even though it seemed to burn right through her.

[Vallon! *Bela*!]

His presence was near. Somewhere close and she brought back her focus, tried to bring herself in check, tried to stop her rush under the ocean's floor.

Easier said than done. She scrabbled at the crystalline structures, tried to hold on, but the power seemed to melt them from under her hands; each time she was torn loose again, until suddenly a force reached her, reeled her in, and she was caught against a spur of bedrock, the warm cedar of Xavier all around.

[Xavier.] She pressed into his essence, but it was not the rich presence he usually had. This was thin, like scraps of cloth on the wind, barely holding together. [Xavier, what's happened to you? I saw your hand.]

There was silence a moment and the sensation as if he held her in his arms. [Landon happened, *Bela*. I do not think he is my friend—nor yours.]

She pulled away not fully comprehending. [Why are you here? I thought you were dead. Your body… I couldn't find a heartbeat. What's happening? Are you dying?] Just thinking the words brought a deep echoing grief until Xavier pressed his presence into her again.

[Not dead yet, *Bela*. Does the saying not go, 'whatever does not kill us, makes us stronger'?]

[But why are you here?]

She felt/saw his amused smile. [It is simple, *Bela*. Because I cannot seem to get myself free. Your friend Landon bled me to the point I could barely get free of captivity. When I transported myself here, I had not the strength to get my essence free of the *platiqua*.]

He motioned so she understood the strange word to mean to blue-gold glow, but she could not get past one word. [He *bled* you???? *Landon*?] But Landon was her mentor, had always been there for her…

[It is a means of controlling the—Gifted. It strips away one's ability to use the power."

Jason had made similar threats. He and Gleason had talked about how HS had bled Gleason. They had to have known about this technique of dealing with the Gifted by reading something in Landon's files. She felt sick to her stomach, she had trusted him as a father. How could he do such a thing to the man she loved? She thought back to the conversation in New Madrid. Had he planned such a thing all along?

[We need to get you out of here.]

A caress of presence ran through her. [Easier said than done, I believe. The *platiqua* does not give up what it holds easily, *Bela*. In my condition it may not be possible.]

[So, what? We wait until you regenerate your blood? Or better yet, until we can get you a blood transfusion—because that's not going to happen. Amundson's men are hunting us and I don't know how long it will be before they think to check my house again. Hell, they may have rigged it so they already know we're here.]

She could imagine his dark visage go thoughtful in the pause, then: [It is most difficult. The *platiqua* I can hold in my blood, but that makes me too akin to the power stream, it seems. When I try to pull loose, it pulls me back in. This is as far as I have managed to get, and the current continues to drag me slowly farther under the ocean. The more distant I am from my body, the more tenuous my connection to it.]

She thought of the almost imperceptible heartbeat. Much less connection and he surely would die. But it was also true that even in this small eddy of power, they were being tugged slowly, inexorably, deeper and farther under the Pacific.

[What can I do to help?]

Another caress of his presence and she wanted to melt into him, but she had to be the strength for them, because Xavier almost sounded as if he'd given up.

[Perhaps there is a way if your power can be enough for both. Perhaps you can feed power into me when I am depleted, at least enough to get free of the *platiqua*.]

She could almost laugh if his situation was not so dire. She *was* big as the world and still expanding with the blue-gold flow around her.

She reached out a virtual hand and he answered with his, then opened herself to him and felt their essences merge and bond. In response she ripped herself upwards from the blue-gold flow, then jerked back when the weight of Xavier fell on her. She came up out of the *platiqua* sputtering.

[Like this, *Bela*.] Humor colored his voice like honey, as he showed her how to send the power into him so that he could escape on his own. [Preserve yourself. As we go higher, it will be more difficult.]

She didn't ask why, simply obeyed and funneled power to him as she strained to lift herself. The *platiqua* was viscous and clung to her skin and to her insides as she tried to pour it into Xavier. The stuff grasped at her like quicksand, refusing to release, first her waist, then her legs, but finally she wrenched free and turned back for Xavier. His form—a simulacrum of himself—shimmered, as if it was fading in and out of existence. As if his body died above him?

She poured power into him, absorbed how it seemed to flow out of him almost as quickly. She had to do something, because she would not let him die. Would not! Poured the power she held into him and felt her strength waver. She sank towards the seething blue flow. [No! Damn you! You're not getting me back and you're not keeping him.] She grabbed the power and sent a mighty burst of it into Xavier that sent her flying back from him so far, so fast, that their connection broke. She fell deep into the *platiqua* and it swept her away. Deep.

CHAPTER 17 — NOT ALONE

Wolf Amundson paced beside the panoramic office window and could barely stand to look at the man standing beyond his desk. The desktop was bare except for a pen holder and a closed silver laptop. The air was cool and yet he could smell the man's sweat and a slight sour tang of fear. Good. He looked away from the panorama of the Space Needle and, beyond the blue waters of Elliott Bay, the green hump of Queen Anne Hill with its trendy eateries and treed residential avenues. Beyond it would be Puget Sound and beyond that the Olympic Peninsula and then the breadth of the Pacific Ocean. At least the ocean provided some protection from the damned Gifted. At least that was what the research through the white gnome's files had said. The Gifted power could not cross open water, so the coasts were at least protected from attack from that quarter.

But there was still too much danger from within, not to mention the danger of these—these creatures—crossing the Canadian or Mexican border, or worse, sitting across the border and wreaking their destruction from beyond his reach. The worry about it kept him up at night. And now this man had failed him and left a more immediate danger loose in the city.

He turned back from the view and rested his fingertips on the top of the cherry wood desk, leaned on them, and flexed.

Jason Bryson looked nothing like the smug detective he'd first met a few months ago, at a certain AGS agent's house. He didn't even look like the man who had helped Gregor Gleason escape from HS headquarters research facilities less than three weeks ago. Now he stood like a suspect from a crime drama in the middle of the oriental carpet Wolf had had laid in his office, his rumpled, slightly out-of-fashion suit looking more disreputable in the midst of the regimentally neat rows of photographs of

Wolf's various meetings with dignitaries and the various recognitions he had received for his work.

But the change in Bryson was more than the rumpled suit; the man appeared thinner, slightly more stooped in the shoulders. His handsome face had taken on a haggard look, with hollowed cheeks and dark crescents under haunted eyes. He did not look a well man and that was interesting, too, for the last time he had seen Jason Bryson he had been the epitome of health—and defiant, too. This man had the hat-in-hand expression of a man facing his last chance at redemption.

That was about where Wolf would place him, too.

"So," he said, his slight accent from his years growing up overseas casting a slight 'zzz' over the S. It was a fault he still had not been able to correct. "I am having difficulty determining what your game is, Detective. And that makes it difficult to decide whether to hire you or have you confined with the rest of the anomalies—or as you know them, the Gifted." He raked an assessing gaze over Bryson and waited to see the man's response. Would he flare in anger, or had something happened so he'd simply given up?

Bryson only shrugged. "You can do what you want, but I'm still your best bet at finding Vallon."

"Agent Drake, yes. We estimate about sixty percent of agents have been repatriated to AGS holding facilities along with their families, but she still eludes us. I had high hopes when you contacted me, but that doesn't seem to have brought us any farther forward than we were before your little offer to help."

He let that sink in a minute. Drake was a problem, yes. And there would be a personal satisfaction to bringing in the agent who had been a thorn in his side since before he had used her performance as an excuse to finally take over the AGS. Drake had been too central to Gleason and the white gnome's plans—at least it looked that way. That meant she was the kind of agent who had to be contained before she could do damage to his cause.

"You at least know she's in Seattle. That's more than you knew twenty-four hours ago," Bryson said.

The interesting thing was that it was a simple observation of fact, not the words of a man pleading for his life. Wolf sighed and nodded. "There is that."

"Yes. There is. And I know her better than you or any of your men. Possibly better than any of your personnel files, too. Because I know her secrets."

That was more like it. Squeeze the man a little and see what he sweated. Wolf waited for Jason to fill the quiet.

"She's here after the children—to free them."

Wolf slipped into his ergonomic high-backed leather chair and clasped his hands on the desk's smooth top. "And this I already know."

Jason stirred and straightened his shoulders, no longer the slumped man. "Did you know that she has a connection to them? She said she had a vision of when you rounded them up. She knew. She's had more of the visions since. She says it's like she's connected to one of the students. A girl."

Wolf quelled a shiver down his back and a sick feeling in the pit of his stomach. He didn't like these stories of what the Gifted could do. Didn't like the fact he had yet to find a way to control it other than a final solution. Not even with the full weight of Lodestone's research facilities behind him. At least not yet.

He nodded. "Interesting, if true. But you could have just made that up."

Jason stepped forward and, without being asked, sat down in the chair facing Wolf. An almost admirable sign that he was not going to be intimidated.

"Then maybe you can explain how I know that your men wiped out at least one of the truckloads of kids. Vallon saw that. She heard the screams and the gunfire from the point of view of a young girl in another truck."

Wolf straightened and wiped suddenly sweaty palms on his pants legs. "That may be true. But you could have gotten word through other means, I suppose. You were a police detective. Such a thing could even be a bluff if you thought such an event was within the realm of possibility."

"All right. If that's how you're going to play this, you don't need my help. I'll find Vallon Drake and deal with her myself."

The detective stood up and started for the office door as if he had permission to leave. That wasn't right.

"I don't believe we've finished our discussion, Detective. I believe there's the little matter of your certain talents?"

Bryson spun around, his dark eyes flashing. "I offered you my 'talents,' but you don't seem inclined to take them in a trade. No, you seem to expect me to just give them to you, while you prepare a place for me in your—just for the fun of the pun I'll call it a finishing school. Because that's right, isn't it? You and your little band of thugs are murdering people.

Families of them, if I'm hearing you rightly. Or else you're offering me a guinea pig role. Neither option seems particularly attractive to me." He chuckled. "Funny thing is, you don't really have a hope in hell of standing against Vallon Drake if you go up against her alone, and if by some fluke you do succeed in catching her, well, then you'll have the really big guns to deal with." A mean smile. "I suppose I haven't mentioned Xavier de Varga yet, but you've met him, or at least your men have. He was there during the Seattle event. He's got as much Gift as Vallon and probably more."

That *was* news. He slid his laptop in front of him and opened it. When the screen sprang to life, he touched a few key and ran a search. It came up with nothing.

"There's no mention of a Xavier de Varga in either AGS personnel files or case records."

"Well, I can't help the fact that Vallon and her little band of helpers were hiding things even then. He's real and he's her lover. I don't know where he's from and I'm not sure anyone else does either. I ran a search on him through SPD channels and he comes up on Interpol. He's a Portuguese national. He works for some company called *Cartos National* or some such. He's apparently been in and out of this country for years."

Wolf's mouth went dry. Here was the connection he needed. A foreign Gifted coming into the US and secretly fomenting the Gifted. All he needed was to catch him. "Are you telling me you know where this man is?"

Jason turned around and strode back to the chair. "I might. Just like I might be able to find Vallon for you through my little 'talent,' as you call it. If it's worth my while."

The chance to prove his case beyond a shadow of a doubt and wake the government up to the danger in their midst was almost too good to be true. Too good. "How do I know what you say is real?"

Jason started to laugh, a soft, harsh sound that grated like fingernails on blackboard. "Now that is funny given we're talking about people who can fuck with reality. You either want my help as an equal and you'll provide me the resources to do my part in finding Vallon and de Varga, or you don't. No more threats of imprisonment and no more talking down like I'm some peon. Partners."

Wolf considered the fire in the other man's eyes. If what he said was true, that fire would spread across the country and the Gifted would be finally dealt with. No more worry his mind was being tampered with as reality shifted. He hesitated, then stood and came around the desk.

"Perhaps I have underestimated what a committed patriot you are,

Detective Bryson."

He held out his hand to his latest partner.

§

The burning saffron-scented *platiqua* filled Vallon up, but it also sucked her down, as if it would claim her as its own, as if it would burn her essence away and there would only be one thing. *Platiqua.* She fought to free herself, scrabbling for a hold on the diamond spires it flowed through to no avail. Fought to leap free, but it was as if she was a cat and someone had hold of her tail; she kept being pulled down into the omnipresent rushing like water over rocks or—voices?

If she quit her frantic fight for freedom, she could almost hear it. At least one voice like a quiet thunder that pulsed through her and even into her body's bones. But the connection to her body was growing thinner and harder to hold. The *platiqua* was dragging her away.

[Vallon! *Bela!*]

[Here. I'm here, but don't come after me. You're too weak.]

She cut off his response and almost snagged a metallic boulder so dense it would explode if brought closer to the surface. She flowed past and deeper under. The ocean was like a weight over her; it made her laugh as she thought of her concern in the stupid tunnel she had made. The trouble was, the ocean's deep water made it more difficult to maintain contact with her body. Much farther and she would be cut free, even though she was not injured and depleted like Xavier.

More sounds in the *platiqua.* A rush like voices wound around the deep throbbing resonance. As if a conversation occurred between the earth and something else, and then suddenly a presence appeared beside her, not cedar-scented like Xavier, but of sandalwood and smoke. It ripped her up out of the Platiqua, up out of the earth, and she came to herself in a body tumbled onto the floor beside Xavier, who stirred.

She scrambled to her knees as his eyes flashed open, their dark depth full of pain—and then joy as he saw her.

"*Bela.*" His uninjured hand came up to trace her face and she threw her arms around him.

"Thank God. Thank God. But you're hurt." She pulled his hurt hand between them. "What happened? The shots you had, but this?"

"Snow wanted my secrets. As I said, I think he is not your friend."

"Landon? But…." Totally impossible. She felt him stiffen and pulled back. His face was even paler than it had been as he tugged his hand free. His gaze turned bleak as it locked behind her.

She turned. They were not alone in the basement.

CHAPTER 18 — OUR KIND

Jake Murphy checked over his shoulder and scanned the campground one more time. The tall, moss-draped trees of Olympic National Park surrounded the motorhome. The nearby river placed a lulling hush over the scene of green trees, green underbrush, and mountains. Rain patted the cottonwood leaves where the huge old trees hung over the river. Otherwise all was still, except for the wind stirring the tops of the tall cedars. The air was clear, scented of cedar and fresh water, and tanged with the propane-scent of the motorhome's furnace and stove.

But something didn't feel right. Maybe it was a scent on the wind he couldn't quite parse out, or maybe it was just the whole situation that had sent him, his family, and every other AGS agent heading—literally, in his case—for the hills. When the bug-out code came through from Gregor Gleason, he'd almost missed it. He'd been about to leave on holiday with his family, so thankfully Gwen and the girls had been loaded up and ready to go when he'd taken the last minute phone call. A cryptic voice had only said *bug-out* and the code that told him the AGS had ceased to exist and had hung up; and for a moment he hadn't been able to move.

A joke? But no one in the AGS would play one of such poor taste. Gleason had drilled into them all that such a day could come, though it hadn't seemed possible. They worked for the government, for God's sake. They protected the country.

Apparently that wasn't enough, because when he finally got through to someone to make sure it wasn't a hoax, Agent Sam Burns had told him to get the hell out because Homeland Security was coming for him, for all of them, and that he'd already heard that Marilyn Ricardo, Jake's partner, had been picked up. So he'd headed, not for Disneyland, his original destination, but for here. Hopefully no one would find them here until the whole thing was sorted out and over.

The wind rustled in the trees and sent raindrops pattering over the motorhome's roof. Just what the hell was it that had him so spooked? They'd been here three days and hadn't seen a soul.

"Jake? What's the matter?" Gwen came up beside him, her dark head as sleek as a seal with her hair cut so it just skimmed her skull. Her slim body slotted perfectly against his side, but her face was worried. She wore one of his old flannel shirts left permanently in the motorhome, and a pair of old jeans that had holes in the knees, like a teenager. She was lovely, and though not Gifted, she understood that he worked in some ultra-secret organization and that his cover had been compromised. She just didn't know that it was their own government coming for them.

He shook his head and gave her a squeeze. "I don't know. I'm not sure. I couldn't sleep last night and I've felt restless all day—as if a storm is coming."

He -reached- and the forest around them turned a spectral white with gleaming candles at the hearts of the living trees. Each bush and fern and fungus had a smaller spark so that the forest was awash in burning fireflies. Through it came a phalanx of sullen red flames. Not what he wanted to see. UnGifted moved through the spectral forest with military precision towards the campground, their presence like vivid embers.

"Shit. Get inside." He shoved her ahead of him and leapt up the stairs and slammed the door, then fumbled the motorhome keys from his pocket.

"Mom? Dad?" Gwyneth, the oldest, asked as Gwen went to her. At eleven, she had her mother's dark skin and her intelligent eyes and was just starting to show signs of the Gift.

"Daddy?" Zoey, the baby at eight, had his rounder face and tawny skin. She was distracted from readying the board game they'd figured to while away the drizzly afternoon.

Jake just shot a look at Gwen. *Deal with them.*

Her soft voice was a balm as he climbed behind the wheel and cranked the engine on, then drove with a lurch, straight off the leveling jacks and headed for the narrow road. Trees branches whapped the metal sides of the vehicle, but it didn't matter. Neither did the antenna he'd so carefully adjusted so the girls could get television and he could get the news. He just had to get out of here. Back on the highway they might stand a chance. Alone, here in the wilderness, there was no telling what the bastards who were doing this might do to his family.

With his Gifted vision he tracked the others. The phalanx of intruders had changed direction, were headed for them. He tromped on the gas and the motorhome shuddered over a creek bed and onto the potholed roads. The brush was heavier here—something he'd eased the vehicle around on their trip in. Heavy branches and foliage buffeted the side windows. A sudden shudder ran through the motorhome and the vehicle almost stalled. He gunned the engine and a huge, metal-ripping sound said he'd hit something and a piece of siding was being torn away.

Too bad. They'd spent a fortune on the damned thing only last year. *The perfect family hideaway, but we won't be trapped by a single location,* Gwen had said in bed before they went down and signed the papers.

This wasn't quite what they'd intended.

Damnation, the intruders were getting closer. They moved swifter than he'd expected through the underbrush. He gave up caring about the vehicle and drove his foot home, ignored the crashing sounds and the screams behind him.

Just reach the road. Just get free and head south-north-anywhere but here. Maybe Canada. They couldn't follow him to Canada, could they?

Then pitted road gradually smoothed as if it had been graded not too long before. Not much farther and it would join the larger road to the main government campground. The motorhome swayed around a corner and the wider road was there. He sped up, his heart racing.

"Hold on, everyone." He swung wide to take the corner, came around it onto the road, and slammed right into a tree felled across the road. Impact sent him soaring through the windshield. The sound of breaking glass, of screaming, and then the ground came up and pounded into him.

Still screaming.

"Jake! Jake!" Gwen's shrill cry. His daughters screaming as he pulled himself half up, almost choking on coppery blood, to face a sea of fatigue-clad legs around him, the business end of automatic weapons trained on him. The men wore body armor and had camouflage paint on their cheeks and foreheads. Insertion and extraction team, his mind supplied. But why here?

Because of you and what you are.

"Gwen." His voice was a choked moan. He tried to move, but his right leg wouldn't obey him. He -reached- for the pungent rose-scented power and sent it coursing into the soil under the men's feet. Take them down. Stop them. He'd get rid of the tree in the same way and be gone with his family.

"Jake!" Frantic now.

"You better think twice before trying any funny business. Anything seems funny, I've got orders to put a bullet in their heads," a stranger's voice said, and suddenly Gwen and the girls were pushed into his field of vision by another man in body armor holding a weapon on them.

Gwen hugged the girls to her, her fear sour in the air. Jake tried to get up again, but pain rocketed through him. It stole his breath and made simple vision almost impossible. Black streaks formed bars across the scene as Jake looked at the armed man with his finger on the trigger of the weapon trained on his wife. He nodded and raised his hands in the air, even though their chances of survival in the hands of the HS were slim to none. If he could just get his feet under him, maybe eventually he could do something to free them all. He had to hold onto that thought.

Then the ground erupted under the armed man and his figure collapsed into the earth up to his hips at the same time as his body seemed to come apart like sand in a high wind.

Weapons fired, and Jake threw himself sideways towards his family. "Get down! Get down!" He screamed helplessly at Gwen.

The other armed men wisped away like smoke, and suddenly the forest went horribly silent except for the rain falling on the leaves and the sound of sobbing. Jake managed to get to his knees and crawled toward his wife and children. Gwyneth and Zoe clung to their mother.

A man stopped him. Tall, with greying blond hair thinning at the temples and an ice-blue gaze, and vaguely familiar. He wore a hunting jacket over a flannel shirt and jeans, but the flare of the Gift radiated off him with a scent of almonds.

"I'm sorry we weren't here sooner."

Jake ignored him and kept crawling for his family. Why were they still down? The shooting was over. At least he thought it was.

"Mr. Murphy, you need to come with us. HS will know something has gone wrong when they don't hear from their agents."

He glared up at the man. "I want my family." And kept on crawling.

The cold air went colder when he reached them and the day seemed unreal—the crying sky, the trees of tears, the steady rush of the river, the stench of copper, all made it hard to think as the girls came to him and clung like blood-covered limpets. But not Gwen. Half her chest was gone. Dead on impact.

He sat there, numb, disbelieving. It was all a mistake. A trick. A horrible mistake, because he'd given everything for his country. But not his wife. Never his family.

"Jake!" The man grabbed his shoulder. "Jake, I'm sorry, but she's gone and we need to get moving."

"He shot her. He shot her because of you!" Jake came up off the ground before the pain in his right leg stabbed him again and he fell, still holding his sobbing daughters. He looked up at the man. "Who the hell are you and who asked you to help?"

Beyond the stranger, other similarly clad men came onto the road. Each of them bore the scent of the Gifted.

The vaguely familiar man stuck out his hand. "Francis Drake. There's a war going on, Mr. Murphy. I'm here to make sure our kind win."

§

When Vallon turned, two sets of bare feet stood at the bottom of the basement stairs. She followed the feet up to bare ankles and thighs, to torsos—also naked—and finally up to two faces. The man bore the look of someone who lived his life in the sun, with fine lines woven through sun-browned features on his face. He had the same broad chest and shoulders and hawk nose as Xavier, except this man's powerful thighs made her think of olive trees and goatherds wandering hillsides. The woman was raven haired and olive skinned and as pale as the man was dark, though she might have been of any age. The barest of lines showed around her eyes, but that could have just been the frown of disapproval she wore. She had high, perfect breasts and a figure that could have inspired Mother Earth carvings. For a moment Vallon felt both overdressed and inadequate in comparison.

The woman cast a disapproving gaze over the basement and then said something fluid that almost sounded like Spanish.

Xavier answered in the same tongue, and then shook his head. He looked pale and more exhausted and weaker than she'd ever seen him, but his black gaze still managed to flash with impatience. "I thank you, and Vallon does as well. But this is Vallon's home and we are in America. We speak English here."

The woman sniffed and stepped away, as if seeking. "A fine place this is. Not even robes for travelers." Her accent was thick, but still comprehensible. Italian, maybe.

"This is her basement, Leticia. Not her living room or bedroom. Besides, how many guests arrive at your home without clothing?"

She returned to the silent man's side. "Is this her, then? The one you have ruined yourself for?"

Xavier shot a sideways glance at Vallon. Was that warning, or acknowledgement? Either way, the glance felt like a caress across her skin.

He was as hungry for her as she was for him, no matter his physical state. *No matter what Landon had done?* The time in the *platiqua* had just increased her already overwhelming afterburn until just the touch of her jeans and t-shirt were enough to send her over the edge. She needed him.

"No matter," said the man. "It is clear what is between them. Xavier, brother, por favor, think hard on this. She is just a woman, although lovely. Would you give up your people and family for her?"

Xavier struggled to stand and Vallon gave him a hand up and her shoulder to lean on when he wavered when he faced them.

"After all these years, you would deny me what you two have found?"

Vallon studied the couple in light of this information. Xavier's brother and his wife, and they were not pleased at Xavier's choices.

"You go against the Council and your people," Leticia said with a too-lovely headshake, as if she would use her beauty to chasten Xavier. "You leave me no choice but to report it. You have gone against everything that has preserved us."

Her gaze turned to Vallon and was dark as a pit, with a slight hazel ring on the inside of the iris that gave the impression that her gaze went deep. Vallon knew accusation when she heard it. It left her with a queasy feeling. Had Xavier truly chosen to do the things he'd done, or had she compelled him to do it? Yes, he had intervened to her aid, but that had been to save Seattle and the Midwest. She hadn't forced him, had she?

And there had been their times together, the sublime union of bodies, his touch, like fire that she could recall instantly and that sent the afterburn raging.

"*Bela*, don't," Xavier murmured.

She swallowed back her lust and met Leticia's gaze.

"It is not wrong to care for another. That's what Xavier and I have. I've never felt for another like I feel for him."

She brought her hand up over Xavier's on her shoulder and their fingers intertwined.

Leticia's gaze followed the action, her gaze like stone. "How sweet. She thinks she loves you and for this you throw away your life and the lives of those who care for you." She looked at her husband, whose dark gaze held on his brother. "We should not have helped, Carlos. The Council will suspect us now. There will be repercussions."

"He is my brother. I could not leave him to drown in the power." Carlos waved her insights away. "But she is right in many ways, Xavier.

You place us all in jeopardy, for these upstarts do not have the years of knowledge we have. They have not felt the humans' destruction. They do not have our history. You may decide to throw your lot in with them, but do not expose your brethren. That is a sin that the Council will not forgive. *Você entende?* Do you understand?"

"No matter what the Council thinks, I will protect you with my life. I have sworn it." Xavier bowed his head.

"Then see you remember that before you call for aid. It will not come again, *Cunhado.*" Then Leticia turned to her husband. "We must get back. They will have felt our leaving and there will be questions asked"

"Wait!" Vallon stepped forward. These were people with the same powers as Xavier, part of Landon's outliers. "Please don't leave us. Help us. There are people here—Gifted people—children who have been and are being rounded up and used for experimentation. Please help us help them. For the children."

"Impossible," Leticia said with a firm shake of her head.

"It is not allowed, young woman. No matter how tragic, for to expose ourselves would lead to a blood bath."

"How can you say that?" She left Xavier's side and faced off against Carlos. "We are your people. We're the same. We have the Gift."

Leticia had the poor grace to titter. "We are *not* the same, you and I. You—upstarts—do not even know the name of your people. You are children building sand castles, unlike we who once owned a world. Not us at all. Perhaps you have some modicum of power, but you are not the— how do you say—the lost tribes of Israel to come back into the fold. You are too young and dangerous to us all because you do not know how to control your own." She caught Carlos' hand. "We must go. Xavier, please do not call on my husband again."

Carlos bowed his head as the room filled with the scent of lavender and roses, then a whirlwind of light shot up through the floor, inundating the couple. Transfixed by the flow of power, their forms dissolved away, their essences stripped into the power flow.

The light winked out, leaving only the stink of ozone and roses.

Vallon turned back to Xavier. "*That* was your family?"

His hair hung lank around his face. His shoulders collapsed around his broad, bare chest "Part of them. The best part, I had thought—wrongly, it turns out. But they helped."

"This time." And at what cost to Xavier? "She went to him and put her arms around his naked chest, and inhaled the cedar and incense of him. "I'm so sorry. If I hadn't messed up getting you out of there, you wouldn't have needed to call them. You did call them, right?"

She looked up at him. His arms had come around her and his cheek rested on her hair, his breath soft upon her face and scented of saffron. The *platiqua* he had taken in. She leaned up to kiss him, intending a chaste kiss.

Soft lips against hard, but his mouth opened and demanded. His good hand slid up her back and caught in her hair and held her to him. He groaned and used his bad hand to pull her into him. There was nothing chaste about it. Nothing injured and depleted, either, by the way he ground into her, the way he pressed her back until she stumbled over the sandbox and fell, pulling him on top of her.

"*Bela.*" His voice was breathless as he pulled back from ravaging her mouth. "I have dreamed of this. It was you that I held to while Landon...."

She pulled his injured and bloodied hand up between them and he winced at her touch. Not what she wanted. Her times with Xavier were joyous, not times of pain. She shoved back the afterburn and knew she'd pay for it. "I want you. God knows I do. But you're hurt and I'm afraid I'll hurt you more. Tell me how this happened while we get it bandaged. It cannot stay like this or it will get infected. Surely there was a mistake. Landon would not do this."

She gingerly held his shredded hand and wanted to cry for the pain he must feel. She looked up at him again when he hesitated. "Tell me. I'm not some child that needs to be protected."

"He is your guardian. You have trusted him."

Her heart hardened. "Wrongly, apparently, if he did this to you. Now tell me what happened?" Could she not make it anymore clear that she needed to know, to understand what Landon had done? For some strange reason it did not surprise her. He had been so distant lately, almost as if he was awaiting something. A chance to get to Xavier, apparently.

Finally, Xavier sighed. "I think—I think he planned it from the start in New Madrid. He was so careful to make a case that only he could take me to safety for help. And so he had me alone and I trusted him, but after he drugged me for the surgery—" he motioned to his injured chest, "—well, he did not ever release me. Instead there were days of drugs and torment. He used this as a means to get me to speak." He hung his shaggy head. "Carlos and Leticia were right. I have already failed them. The Council will never take me back."

The basement had taken on an ice-cold chill that seemed to radiate right into her core. Landon—her Landon had done this to the man she loved when he knew how she felt. Had he ever intended to release Xavier? Would he have bald-faced lied that Xavier had died on the operating table? She would not put it past him.

With a sick feeling in her stomach, she realized she didn't know Landon and never had. He had always been a cipher, a mystery as deep as the Alchemy he practiced. The knowledge left her shaky, as if the soil was giving way beneath her feet.

Reluctantly she pulled away from Xavier and pulled her clothes back into place. "I need to go upstairs for the first aid kit. I might have some clothes you can wear, too. Speaking of which, why the nude bodies?" She lifted her chin to where Carlos and Leticia had stood. Think about mundane little facts and figures. Those she could handle while her world exploded.

Xavier looked up at her from where he sat on the edge of the sandbox, his injured hand cradled against his chest. "We can only transmute ourselves, not our clothing."

"Too bad. I'd get you to show me how to do it, but I can't imagine transmuting naked as a jaybird into wherever it is that Amundson has stowed the children. Wait right here."

She headed for the stairs, head too full and heart too frozen with thoughts of Landon, when a soft meow stopped her. Maggie came creeping out from behind the furnace half-wall, her fur still half on end.

"Poor little one, did that nasty lady scare you?" She chucked Maggie under the chin and then started up the stairs, Maggie on her heels. At the top she stopped her. "Sorry, girl. I'll see what I can do about food."

Then she -reached- to make sure no one was waiting on the other side before pushing open the door onto a lit only by street lights and a fading moon and scootching out while holding Maggie back with her foot. When she closed the door, the cat meowed mournfully from the other side. Great. Just great. If anyone was listening, they'd know something was here.

She ducked down against possible observation through the rear window and went to the cupboard under the kitchen sink. Thankfully she kept a first aid kit here. She pulled it out along with a couple of tins of cat food. Found Maggie's dish and grabbed a box of granola bars from a cupboard and took her booty back to the basement door. But Xavier needed clothes. Heck, she could use a change of clothing, too. Focus on the small things while her unconscious brain sorted out what Landon's actions meant in her world.

She left the kit and food by the door and, bent over, left the kitchen for the living room. The living room curtains were, thankfully, closed, so she straightened and climbed the stairs silently two at a time. Down the hall past Fi's newly painted bedroom that she might never see again and into her bedroom. It looked eerily unfamiliar in the darkness, the white bedspread a canvas bare of life, the empty picture frames over the bed just increasing that lifeless sense. Pale, French Provincial dresser on one wall, window framed in white sheers on the next. She eased open dresser drawers and dug down to the bottom of her t-shirt drawer and hauled out a Seattle Marathon volunteer shirt, a freebie for her help a few years back. The shirt was an XL and far too large, so she'd saved it for yard work.

She grabbed it and a clean t-shirt and a fleece for warmth, then stopped. Something—a sound—turned her around.

At least she thought it was a sound. Something so faint she almost wouldn't have caught it if she hadn't just been at that odd spot between inhaling and breathing out. She crossed to the window and stood to its side to peer out through the gauzy curtain she'd made.

Dark street. The digital clock on her bedside table said it was two o'clock in the morning. The rhododendron bush in the front yard spread a pool of shadow over the lawn and the picket fence. Overhead the night sky was clear, the stars few due to light pollution and the half-moon setting over the ridge of the houses across the street. There were no lights on inside the houses, but most had porch lights on as if to reject the darkness. That light, and a few meager streetlights, coalesced around the pavement and the line of cars parked along the curb.

She followed the line of cars up the street. They all looked like they belonged here, but the light caught the rear bumper of something dark parked around the corner up a block. Big, like a humvee and dark in color. No one in the neighborhood drove anything like that—they were far too environmentally conscious.

Movement below her snapped her attention back to her yard. A figure separated from the shadows of the rhododendron. Man, tall by the look of him. He stepped close enough to the street that the light caught him, and then turned back towards the house. Jason, dressed in a dark suit, with a telephone to his ear.

His gaze reached her window and looked right at her as if he knew she was there.

CHAPTER 19 — BLUE-BLACK

The empty white walls of Landon's windowless office pressed in on him like an avalanche on a snowmobiler—not that he had any idea of why anybody would want to ride a machine that was made for nothing but taking noise deep into the pristine silence of a dangerous wilderness. No, give him the order of home and the mystery of how things worked. His was not the adventurous way of the explorer. No, his was the way of the Van Gogh or the Rembrandt, looking through reality for the mysteries beneath.

Except the damned mysteries weren't cooperating, were they?

He slammed the sweaty palm of his hand down on his metal desktop and dragged his gaze away from the inscrutably, inexplicably never-changing fifty-two inch computer screen that sat on the desk. He dug his fingers into the corners of his weary eyes. The recycled cool air was exactly seventy degrees and still inexplicably tasted of de Varga's cedar scent. He tugged on his collar and unbuttoned the top button of his polo shirt against a flush of heat. The filing cabinets, with their neatly labeled drawers, and the empty chair across from him were just a source of irritation, as was the fact that his feet still didn't comfortably sit flat on the floor, even though he'd had both the desk and the chair altered to fit his smaller frame.

It had been five hours—five hours!—since the man had done the almost-miraculous and somehow 'teleported' himself free. At least teleport was the only word he could come up with to explain the ability Vallon had first hinted at when she spoke of seeing de Varga. But teleportation as described in science fiction did not seem entirely consistent with the skills of the Gifted, so all he could say was that Xavier de Varga had an ability to travel that he did not understand. Even the cameras and readouts of the activity in the holding room had not been able to tell anything other than that the Gift had been used. It was based on the same principles as the huge AGS maps—the self-same maps Amundson must be using to locate the Gifted and potentially the partially Gifted in the Pacific Northwest. Given the number of people with a partial Gift, Amundson could be arresting half of the population.

The scare that would cause nationally, he didn't want to think about.

He leaned back in his chair and stared at the offending computer screen. He did not like not knowing what the man was doing.

He'd implanted the tracking device because he knew de Varga could and would lead him back to the other outliers that existed in the world. The man was a watcher—therefore he watched *for* someone, and those were the people Landon was after. The people, according to Xavier, who had for all intents and purposes allowed the genocide of his people.

The little interview he'd had with de Varga had not yielded up all the secrets he was looking for, like how the power worked and how he could get more. Instead, the foreigner had gone on and on about Pangea, as if the power was somehow linked to his religious beliefs. Perhaps for de Varga they were, but there had to be someone amongst the outliers who understood the scientific truth. Those were the people he wanted to talk to. Those were the people de Varga could lead him to.

Except the damned tracking device remained a steady blinking presence north of Lake Union. Vallon's house, it had to be. That was an issue on a couple of levels. First of all, there was the possibility that de Varga had been captured. He could have transported himself right into a trap, returning to Seattle—and that was about the best of scenarios. The second interpretation of the static tracking symbol was that de Varga had been far worse off than Landon had known, and had died or was dying wherever he had arrived. It *was* possible. He'd bled the man significantly, using the results of the research on AGS agents. Perhaps the outliers were physiologically different enough that they could not afford to lose as much blood. Of course, the fact that the man had been able to get himself out of Landon's little research station made that less plausible.

The last possibility, and it was the one that left him feeling a trifle more uneasy, was that de Varga had linked up with Vallon and the two were doing what their natures demanded. That in itself was fine, but what they did afterwards was the question. Given the state of the news out of the Northwest—reports of a new disease and people—entire families—being detained for testing had the newswires all ablaze with Center for Disease

Control spokespeople fielding questions from acres of microphone and camera-wielding reporters.

The story was that it was a strain of particularly virulent bird flu that had a longer than usual incubation period and that they were trying to round up the carriers, many of whom were linked to worksite contamination caused by a visiting foreign diplomat.

The news reports talked about people refusing to be tested because, they said, it violated their personal and religious freedom, and the news anchors were all over the angle of personal freedom versus societal responsibility. It was going to be interesting to see how this went, but man-on-the-street interviews were clearly on the side of societal responsibility. The AGS agents weren't going to be getting much public help at this rate.

But the bigger worry if de Varga and Vallon were together again was that de Varga might uncover and disclose all of Vallon's background. That would end what might be the greatest social experiment Landon had ever embarked on. Because if de Varga left the country and took Vallon with him....

Beep.

Beep-beep-beep.

Landon sat up, the glare off the room's walls onto the computer screen momentarily making him less sure of what he was seeing.

Beep-beep-beep.

The red dot that was Xavier de Varga was on the move again against the blue-black expanse of the map.

§

Somehow, inexplicably, Jason had found her, and his ravenous gaze looked up at her through the darkness and he knew she was there. She held her breath and eased back from the sheer curtains, trying her best not to disturb them. In the blue-black shadows of the half-moon's light, she let her breath out in a sour-tasting rush. He was here, standing beside the rhododendron in her yard, and she had no doubt who he was on the phone to. Amundson or his men would be here any minute. She needed to get Xavier, herself, and Maggie out of the trap that was her basement, pronto.

She grabbed the clothes, added a pair of overlarge shorts she'd somehow inherited, and a duffle bag from the closet, then ran down the darkened stairs, no longer so worried about silence. In the kitchen she stuffed the food and medical kit in the duffle and opened the basement door, caught Maggie before the little vixen could get past her and out the cat door. The very last thing she wanted was for Jason to get her cat. She had no doubt Maggie would pay for her mistress's failings.

She slammed the door behind her and clattered down the stairs to where Xavier waited, head hanging, as he slouched on the side of the practice pit.

"They're here. Jason's outside and he's called the others."

Xavier looked up at her with a world-weary gaze, his bloody hand cradled against his wounded body. For all the man normally radiated power, at the moment he didn't look like he was going to be taking on anyone. It was all Landon's fault that he had to use his good hand to support himself to standing.

"Then I suppose we must make our exit," he said. "But I fear it must be through a more mundane means that transmutation."

She nodded and set the bag down and tossed him a granola bar. "That's what you call it, is it? That thing you do to travel?" She hauled out the first aid kit. "Sit."

She pushed him down on the stool and grabbed his injured arm, pulled open the kit, and apologized as she covered his poor flayed hand with antiseptic salve, then wound a bandage around it. It came out looking like a white stump. "Sorry. Best I can do at the moment, and we need to get going." She helped him on with the marathon shirt and blue athletic shorts and stepped back to look at him critically. Smiled.

"You almost look like a Seattleite. All it would take is a Gore-Tex jacket or a fleece, and a set of running shoes. We'll have to take care of that when the stores open." She stuffed her pockets with cat food and energy bars and then placed Maggie in the duffle and zipped it up into a makeshift cat carrier. Maggie let her displeasure be known.

She went to her workbench and pulled open the cupboards. Thankfully, Jason hadn't emptied them out. She grabbed sheets of vellum and pots of her specially made ink, then turned back to Xavier.

"I don't have a pen."

He quirked a grin that took years off his face. "There were not always pens, *Bela*. A twig or anything natural will do."

A twig or something. She rummaged in the cupboards and found nothing, but then her eye caught in the herbs she had drying, hung from hooks in the ceiling. She pulled down a bunch of basil and untied the string that held them together and found one that had a sturdy stalk. She stripped the dried leaves off the stalk, unfolded a piece of vellum, and opened a pot of ink. From upstairs came a thud and a crash. Undoubtedly the end of her front door.

She fought her racing heart and closed her eyes and took a long calming breath, then dipped the stalk in the ink and visualized the door in the far basement wall. The room filled with the scent of roses as she fed the drawing power.

Footfall overhead heading for the basement door.

Xavier grabbed her arm and dragged her across the room, still clutching the vellum and ink and stalk of basil, still drawing the tunnel beyond the newly formed door in the basement wall.

She kept drawing and Xavier released her to open the door. She stepped through, a slam, and all light cut out. She sketched the tunnel and tried to remember the tree and rock and park where the other end needed to be.

Footfall like thunder behind her. They rushed through the tunnel.

"Let the door go, my *Bela*. Let it be concrete again."

Swiftly she drew over the sketched door and felt the wall settle in place again, heard shouts, pounding and Jason's threatening voice. Let the tunnel go behind her and heard screaming—cut out. They kept going, following the tunnel through the earth, Maggie's squalling echoing down the tunnel along with the sound of their breathing. And then suddenly the scent of night air and growing things intruded into the place of damp earth. Xavier led her silently up and out of the tunnel, but not before he knelt and picked up something that he handed to her.

"Yours, I believe. I stepped on it."

Her pen. Her father's pen. She didn't know whether to be happy she had found it or not. She decided on happy and stuffed it into her pocket as she climbed out of the tunnel and into the park.

"This way." She led him out of the trees and across the night-darkened grass of the ball diamond towards the Audi. "This is stolen, so we'll have to change cars today."

"Not necessary. I still have resources." He climbed in the passenger door and settled Maggie on his lap. He opened the duffle zipper and she poked out her head and quit yowling as he stroked her head.

"Well, would you look at that." Darned cat was always better for everyone but her.

"Perhaps she just likes men." He cocked his head. "Perhaps she is like her mistress, no?"

Vallon rolled her eyes and started the car, then pulled smoothly out from the curb and began to wind her way slowly towards the Aurora Bridge and hopefully away before Amundson could have all the streets blocked.

They were just across the bridge when police car strobes came barreling towards her and passed towards the bridge and Fremont. Vallon held her breath as the vehicle pulled to a stop on this side of the bridge, but it didn't pull a U-turn to follow them. She blew out in relief.

"I think we're okay. For now."

When Xavier didn't say anything, she glanced at him.

His head lolled on his shoulders, and streetlights placed blue-black bruises all over his heavy fiveo'clock shadow.

Exhaustion, she hoped, because there was no way she could afford to stop now and no way she could afford to ask anyone for help.

CHAPTER 20 — REVERBERATIONS

G o! Go! Go!"

The well-armed Extraction Team poured down the wooden stairs into Vallon's basement, Jason hard on their heels. The warm vibration he had come to associate with whatever it was the Gifted did radiated up at him like sun on his face. Something was happening and it was happening right now.

Amundson's men filled the small space before the workbench, their shadows distorted on the wall by the swinging overhead light. Nothing in the sandbox. Cupboards over the workbench open. A door firmly closed in the far wall.

Door?

"There! That's new." He lunged for it, but two of Amundson's men got there quicker. They yanked it open to reveal a tunnel, and ducked heads and weapons inside. A third man waved Jason back. But something wasn't right. The vibration seemed to fade, like a cloud passing over. Mist came off the door like sheets of paint.

"Get outta there! Something's happening."

One of the men ignored him and stepped through as the door seemed to telescope in on itself, leaving behind concrete wall. He grabbed for the man who was halfway through the door and ripped him back.

"Get the fuck outta there!" The others yanked him out of the way. The men in the tunnel began to scream, the scream muffled out suddenly, dirt probably already sifting into their lungs. The concrete ate the edges of the door until it was gone. The vibration stopped, leaving a bunch of heavily armed men milling in the basement.

"Nothing here," proclaimed Cee Brown, the man leading the team, a bruiser with shaven black hair and a body builder's shoulders under his black shirt. He cast Jason a disgusted look and started for the stairs, his men parting around him.

"There *was* someone here and we just missed them. Vallon and her foreign friend, I think." Because the air did smell of Vallon's strawberry scent with a hint of cedar, now that he thought of it. That and a sense of lightning. He'd never actually thought about his sense of smell before, but his senses were always sharpened around Vallon. They'd been that way with Cheryl, too. It was like he knew he was alive when his sense of smell became almost electric. "They were here and they escaped through a door into a tunnel that likely doesn't exist anymore. You lost two of your men inside it. You just don't remember it."

Brown wheeled back to him, his foot on the first stair. "Like hell. I was in Iraq. I never leave a man behind." He looked around the room. "All here. All accounted for."

Jason glared up at him, but finally sighed. This was going to be the ongoing issue with being the only person who seemed to recognize Change outside of the Gifted. "Fine. Have it your way. But if you break through that wall and dig a few feet, you'll find two men dressed exactly like you. Maybe you'll remember them then."

Or maybe not, too. He didn't understand how this worked at all, nor why he remembered when others didn't. But Brown was eyeing him as if he was crazy; the big man shook his head and stomped up the stairs, his footfall heavy across the floorboards above as his men thundered after.

It left Jason alone in the basement he'd last visited when he pulled together supplies so that Vallon could bring back Cheryl. He crossed to the workbench cupboard and examined the contents. The neatly stacked pile of handmade paper was gone—vellum, she'd called it. Some of the jars of ink looked like they might be missing, too. So it was definitely Vallon, and she had built a tunnel to get in and out of here. He turned around and studied the wall where the door had been and the floor in front of it where the large crack snaked across the foundation.

Something dark there. He bent down to touch it and his fingertips came up red. Too thick to be ink. So blood. He'd lay money on it.

He climbed the stairs and switched off the downstairs light, then followed Brown's men out of the destroyed front door and pulled out his phone. It rang once and was picked up. No introduction on the other end.

"She was here, but she escaped out a tunnel she made, then unmade. You lost men inside because your man Brown didn't listen. I'm going to track her, because there has to be some trace of her around here, but I thought you should know she'll likely be heading for the kids now. She got what she needed from the house."

"The guards at the warehouse will be alerted." Amundson's voice sounded low and unhappy.

"If you want to protect that place, you either need Gifted there who'll work with you, or you need me there to tell you when the attacks start."

"I can give you the location."

He did. But his readiness to do so said that he still didn't have Gifted under his control whom he totally trusted. Interesting. But then Amundson seemed to have blinders on when it came to the Gifted.

"There's something else. That foreigner I mentioned: Xavier de Varga? I think he might be with Vallon."

"What are you basing that on?"He could almost hear Amundson sit up and take notice.

"Blood spatter on the floor and a certain scent in the air. Someone other than Vallon was here, and whoever it was, was injured. I don't believe it was Vallon. If de Varga is mobile, he'd try to reunite with Vallon. How he got here, I'm not sure. Last I heard he was heading for Vegas."

"Vegas? Why?"

Shit. He'd planned to hold that little bit of information to himself. "No idea. Listen, if it is him, you've got a hell of a problem. He's got a hell of a lot of power from what I can tell."

There was silence a moment and then, "I'll warn my men. Forewarned is forearmed. Is that not the saying?"

Jason hung up and headed for his car. Warn them, sure. For all the good it would do them. He had to get there first.

§

Vallon pulled off I-5 North into the rest stop and parked as far away from the washrooms as possible. The tall cedar and poplar placed patterned moon shadows across the windshield. When she opened the window, the breeze brought the scent of diesel from the idling long-distance trucks on the far side of the rest stop, but there were no voices, none of the far-to-loud tourists that were around during the summer. Of course, maybe it was that they were here in the dark, bathed in the sound of the rush of highway traffic and the insects in the trees.

She turned to Xavier, still slumped in the corner, the car console lights placing red and mint green brands on his features. His chest rose and fell in a slow, steady rhythm and when she -reached-, his essence was safely inside him. Sleeping then, and sleep was a restorative—when you couldn't have sex.

Her gaze lingered on his face, his forearms as they rested across him, still cradling his injured hand. The hand Landon had destroyed. How could he have done it when he knew how she felt about this man? What was Landon thinking?

The answer was *nothing at all*, because she meant nothing to him. She swallowed back emotions she didn't want to feel.

It didn't work. He was the closest thing she had to a father. But look what her real father had done. Neither had ever cared for her. Not really. She was truly no more than a tool to them. In Landon's case, he had used her to get to this man—the proof of his hypothesis about the others. How many other ways had he used her over the years? How many lies had he told her to set her in motion to do his bidding? Only Xavier had never lied to her.

She stroked a stray piece of his black hair back from his face and his eyes jerked open, instantly aware and assessing.

"I'm sorry. I didn't mean to wake you," she said softly, pulling her hand back.

Xavier' hand caught her wrist and held it, the force of his power, even in his weakened state, crashing into her like a wave. She sagged next to him and he used his good arm to half drag her up and over the console. His injured arm came around her as he settled her in his lap, and he closed his eyes and sighed as she rested against him.

"You are sad, my *Bela*."

She shook her head, not meeting his gaze. "I'm so sorry, Xavier. I feel responsible for what Landon has done."

"It was his choice, not yours."

She met his gaze then. "But he would never have met you if not for me, and you would never have trusted him if I didn't tell you he was okay." She shook her head. "How could I be so wrong? First my father and then him. I'm obviously a terrible judge of character."

"Aah, my *Bela Menina*, that is the problem, is it not? We are all strangers in this world." He stroked her hair and she fought his soothing.

"How do we ever live together if we know each other so little? How do we ever trust when we don't know what each other want or need?"

He leaned down and kissed her forehead. "This is what I need, *Bela*. The dangerous world is out there and we may not be able to rest in Pangea, but at least there is this."

He rested his cheek against her forehead and the spice of his cedar of Lebanon and incense filled her head. The essence of him flamed around them both and mingled with her like a lacing of fingers, only more intimate. She knew they should be talking and making their plans, both to deal with Landon and to rescue the students. She knew they should be driving and getting farther away from Amundson. But for just this moment it felt so wonderful she would rest her eyes.

Instead, her cheek against Xavier's chest, his arms around her, and his chin resting on her head, she slept.

White light and pain and fear.

She still lay on the table, her arms and legs tightly strapped down. An effort to erode the girl's will. She wore only a thin patient's gown and the air was cold against her skin, just as the metal table was cold. For all her hours here, it seemed like her body couldn't warm that horrible metal that looked blue-black against the pallor of her skin. Actually, the metal matched the bruises up and down her arms and legs from all the needles. Blood. Tissue. Bone marrow. What else, she couldn't say. They had bled her a bunch until she felt she might faint, and had pumped her so full of drugs she could barely think.

Which was a good thing because it numbed the knowledge that they were going to kill her, just like they had Billy and Brett. Of the three of them who had tried the plan, she was the last. She wondered what had become of the other students. Had their captors told them what had happened?

What was she thinking? Of course they had. The kids were no longer children, just as she wasn't. You grew up a lot when you saw your friends and teachers killed. The others were probably doing whatever they were told. If they didn't, they'd join her down here. Actually, given the frantic fear of the researchers and the way they seemed so dissatisfied with her, the others might be down here soon enough anyways.

There had to be a way out of here—someone to help them. Someone had to know where they were, surely. Their parents must be looking for them. She allowed herself a tiny bit of hope.

You're being stupid. If they come after you, they'll be killed, too, if they haven't been captured and shot already, because Mom and Dad would do anything to keep her safe. Anything.

Which just made the table harder beneath her shoulder blades and bum and heels, and the chill air just made it harder to hold back the grief and the crying.

The sharp sound of knuckles on glass brought Vallon blinking awake into too bright sunlight that reminded her too much of white ceiling lights and a chill metal table. But she was warm in Xavier's strong arms and the car redolent of his cedar and incense.

The rap came again and she looked around. At the driver's side window a young state patrol officer in mirrored sunglasses peered inside the vehicle, his knuckles poised to rap again.

She froze. Not only were they both likely wanted, they were sitting in a stolen vehicle. Start the car and run, or…?

She slid across the console back into the driver's seat, Xavier protesting sleepily. Plastering a faux-embarrassed expression on her face, she powered down the window and combed her hair with her fingers. "Yes officer?"

"I'm sorry to wake you miss, but this isn't a camping area. I wanted to make sure everything was all right."

She scrubbed the sleep from her eyes. "Sorry. Everything's just fine. I just was falling asleep driving, so I pulled over and thought I'd take a nap. I guess it was a little longer than I'd intended." She tried for sheepish smile. "I must look like heck."

The officer was looking from her to Xavier, awake now and looking a tad past ridiculous in the t-shirt and shorts. With the blood-drained pallor of his skin, his tousled black hair, and hawkish features, he could be the most disreputable of men. Or a terrorist.

"Where you two headed?" the officer asked, peering into the back seat of the car where Maggie had raised her head sleepily to blink big golden eyes.

"Vancouver," she said. "He's got family up there. A brother." She felt Xavier's gaze on her and found the wherewithal to look the patrolman right in the eyes. "I'm really sorry to have caused any trouble. We'll be moving on now. Okay?"

One Mississippi, two Mississippi, as he considered.

He straightened, his gaze never leaving her face as if he was memorizing it. "Okay. Have a good trip."

He turned and walked back towards his cruiser. Vallon turned back to Xavier.

"He will remember you," he said.

"He'll remember *us*. If he runs the plate number, we're in big trouble."

"Then I suppose we should be on our way before he gets the plate results."

She nodded and -reached- and the car started. The trooper might be suspicious when they just headed out instead of using the rest stop facilities, but they just couldn't afford to take the chance. She guided the Audi out onto the highway.

"We need to switch cars again."

Silence a moment and then, "I have a car. It is not stolen, but I cannot drive it with this." He hefted his bandaged hand. "At least not well."

"Where?" She checked her rearview for the trooper and pulled off at the next exit.

He nodded back to the highway. "North of Everett. There is a large boat dealership along the highway. I rent a boathouse from them."

"A boathouse."

He smiled. "It holds more than a boat. Perhaps we can be safe long enough to determine where we are going and what we are going to do."

She raised one eyebrow as she guided the car back onto the highway. "You mean make a plan? Since when have we ever needed a plan?" She glanced at him and got a never-before-seen confounded expression. "Okay, we need a plan, or at least more of one than we've had the last two cases going in. But I already know where we're going—sort of."

"And that would be?"

She guided the car around a semi and joined the flow of traffic heading for Everett and Bellingham and the Canadian border.

"North. It's like I have a connection to the girl I told you all about back in New Madrid." It felt like forever ago, but the girl's fear was like her own, a stone weighing her heart. "She's somewhere ahead."

They drove in silence a few minutes. "How are you doing? Did the rest help?" she asked.

"A little." He sighed and laid his head back against the head-rest and closed his eyes. "I feel as if I could sleep for a year and still need more rest. But you are here, my *Bela Menina*. That gives me hope and the strength to go on."

As if he had once considered not going on. She swore grim revenge against Landon. How dare he do this to Xavier? She shook her head and glanced at Xavier as he rested his eyes. His shaggy head of hair fell around his haggard face and she wanted to touch him, to hold him as he slept, just the way he had held her.

"You know, one of these days it would be really nice to just have time together. To sleep, to eat, to laugh together. I might feel like I've known you forever, but I hardly know you, you know?" She cast a glance at him.

He had opened his eyes and was watching her, and the heat of his gaze made her skin flush. "Is there so much more beyond where Pangea brings us?"

The afterburn flared at the thought of their one moment of peace on his houseboat where they had found each other. Her skin tingled at just the memory of the heat of the encounter.

She tightened her hold on the steering wheel because otherwise she was going to pull over and have him right here. "I was thinking about things that are a little more mundane. Like, that guy was really your brother? Where are you from? How many siblings have you got? Where did you grow up? Who are your friends?"

His expression turned troubled and he looked as if he was going to say something, but then thought better of himself. "Carlos? Yes. We share the same bloodlines, but not the same temperaments."

"And not the same beliefs, I think."

He nodded. "They, like we, have drifted apart over the years—a product of my job for the Council. I see many things as I travel. Carlos—does not."

His cautious words told her a lot. He was not about to expose everything to her. A small stone formed in her gut. So he did not fully tell her the truth, either. "And Leticia? What's she to you?"

"My brother's wife and not my friend, for many reasons."

She heard a grim smile in his voice as she guided the car past the main Everett exits and down the hill towards the slough that held the marine equipment facility Xavier had mentioned.

"Like what?"

A weary shake of his head. "Like I did not approve of his courtship of her so long ago. She controlled any man she had been with, or had tried to."

She glanced over at him. "That sounds like personal experience talking."

He gave a small head shake and a shrug. "A very long time ago we were together for a short time. I broke it off and she never forgave. Instead, she hooked Carlos and still uses it to wound me when she wounds him. She refuses him children and has been unfaithful many times, even though their union means wounding me should no longer be necessary. Carlos loves her very much. But most of all, it is the way she comes between my brother and me." His head slumped back against the head-rest again. "You will take the next exit."

She did, allowing him to change the subject, and followed his circuitous instructions to wind down into the Steamboat Slough area of Everett, along Ross Avenue past the log yards and concrete factory, and past a boat launch into the slough and into an area of acres of boats and dry-land boat sheds. An old barn with outbuildings was her destination. Near it, Xavier pointed out a building the size of a roomy two-car garage, but with a second story.

"The code is 396421," he said, and she jumped out of the car and ran up to the door. This early in the morning there were still plenty of people around, getting boats ready to go into the water. She ignored them, found the keypad lock, and punched in the code. A low click told her the single large sliding door was unlocked. She gave it a push and it slid smoothly back with a rumble, exposing darkness and the dimly seen draped shapes inside.

The Audi passenger door thumped closed and Xavier limped across the gravel looking strangely even more exotic in his ridiculous getup. Her skin tingled as he neared her. He led her inside to where the bullet shape of a very large speed boat loomed over a tarp-draped form. He motioned for her to remove the tarp and expose a black Porsche Cayenne SUV.

"Ohmygod." She ran her hands over the hood. "I've always wanted to drive one."

"Well, now you shall. The keys should be in the glove box."

"It's not locked?" She looked at him in surprise.

"If someone can get past that door, then they can bypass any lock on the SUV," he said. "I will drive the Audi inside."

She climbed in and sank into the smooth leather seats and inhaled the scent of new. Well, maybe not quite new. If she turned her nose to the leather, she got a hint of Xavier's heady scent. She started the engine and the car rumbled under her and obediently grumbled its way out the door. She parked the SUV and waited as Xavier pulled the Audi in, then climbed out and went to him, sliding the door closed behind them.

He nodded her to follow him to a narrow set of metal stairs that climbed the outside wall at the rear of the building and led up to an open loft that looked down on the boat's cockpit, with its white leather seats and a massive transom that hinted at a huge and powerful engine. The loft itself surprised her. What she'd expected to be a storage space for marine equipment instead held a narrow cot, a small fridge and stove, a table and one chair, and a cupboard. She set down the duffle and let Maggie loose, then filled food and water dishes, and the little cat chirruped and dug in as if she'd never been fed.

Xavier went to the cupboard and pulled out a bundle of clothing. Then he stripped out of the shorts and t-shirt and stood there, for all his injuries, looking like a magnificent warrior.

The afterburn flared and Maggie was forgotten. Vallon licked her lips. The way his broad shoulders tapered down to his hips, the ripple of muscle under the skin of abdomen, buttocks, back, and thighs.

He turned towards her and she knew he'd felt her arousal. His dark gaze swallowed hers.

"*Bela*." Low. Guttural and full of yearning.

It was all he got out before she had crossed to him. She threw her arms around him to revel in this moment of safety together.

"I missed you so much," she said.

His bandaged hand came lightly under her chin to lift her face.

He took her mouth with passion, his good hand pressing her into him with so much need that the afterburn burned away the need to be away, to rescue the children, to stop Amundson. The world fell away in ashes as he tugged her t-shirt over her head and ran strong fingers down over her back and lower, into the top of her jeans. His fingertips teased the top of her crack, plunged lower and pulled her into him as he pleasured her from behind.

"Wait! Stop! We can't do this. You're injured."

His low, wicked laugh almost made her come by itself.

"Aah, *Bela*, you are so young. You do not know the Cartos kind, nor the powers of Pangea." He took her mouth again, his lips and tongue ravaging it, then he pulled back again with a quick kiss on her mouth. "Get out of those clothes or I shall rip them off you."

Get out of them she did, swiftly stripping off her shoes and jeans. She barely got them off before he stepped up to her again, flicked her bra loose. She slipped it off, slid her panties down, and stood there seeing that he clearly wanted her, regardless of the wounds on his chest and the bandages on his hand.

Then she was in his arms again, flesh against flesh the way it was meant to be, and he pulled her back with him towards the table, lifted her up, one armed, and sat her down, her legs spread wide around him as his head came down to nuzzle her breasts. His tongue found her nipples and she trembled. His good hand found her softness and teased. She groaned.

"I want you so badly," she said and pushed his good hand aside, caught him in her hand, and shifted her hips for his access. "I have since New Madrid. Since before. Since always."

She locked her legs behind his hips and moved. He complied, and his entry arched her back in pleasure. She cried out in need and his low groan was an echo.

"Creator," he sighed as he began to move in her.

She bit her lip and moved with him, each surge sending sparks flashing through her. Each ebb, like the tide, leaving her barren and wanting more. Waves of pleasure flooded through her and she leaned up to kiss his chest, caught his nipple in her mouth, and felt his groan through her teeth. Ran her hands over his hard shoulders and chest and down to his hips, the fine muscle of his buttocks. Lifted herself onto him so he found his way deeper. Would that he could bury himself inside her, impale her, become one with her.

The slow strokes picked up speed, became deeper, harder, and he pushed her back so she lay on the table, his dark gaze burning into her as he buried himself in her, as the universe constricted around them to the room, to the echoes of their cries, to their flesh, as he stiffened, as her body convulsed and his with her, and the world and the flesh fell away with a great bell's chiming. She jerked upright into his arms and the universe wheeled darkly around them.

Great stars burned holes in the darkness, a blue planet whirled underneath, and they were one with the planet, the Great Mother. Her power flowed into and through them as if they were organs of her flesh, just as it flowed into flowers, trees, forests. The animals, too. And humans.

Humans?

But she was....

There was another kind of being, spread across Pangea's loving face. Beings like she was. Like Xavier. Pangea's children, and she was one with everything and with Xavier and that was good and it was all that mattered.

At the moment.

CHAPTER 21 — PERSPECTIVES

Francis Drake looked up from reading his report in the office of his makeshift headquarters at the AGS Academy. He had chosen to camp in the abandoned remains of the headmaster's office. Amundson had seen fit to confiscate all the student records, but he hadn't bothered with the furniture or even to turn the utilities off. Perhaps it was to leave the sense that the school remained open. And so it had been an easy task to erase Amundson's men and walk in unnoticed to take up residence. The scarred desk was likely the same one that Vallon had stood in front of so many times. The pool of light from the open window placed a warm patina on the wood walls and the bookshelves—empty now because Amundson's men had taken those, too, along with the computers, though they'd left behind the printers and other office equipment. It had been simple enough to come in, hook up his laptop, and be back in business again.

Right under Wolf Amundson's nose, and there was a certain satisfaction in that. Amundson didn't know he existed, and so he wasn't even looking. The fact whatever Amundson was using to locate the Gifted hadn't indicated Francis's presence spoke volumes of the H.S search methods. They had genealogical charts and they had good old fashioned investigative techniques. At least so far. It was Francis' job to keep it that way. He'd be damned if he'd let Amundson destroy the talent blossoming in America, and he damned well wasn't going to stand by and watch him round up Gifted to practice genocide.

He closed his eyes against the heated rush of anger. He should just wipe the man and the entire HS structure off the face of the map—the trouble was, he wasn't sure of Amundson's location. The man had gone to ground at the same time as his teams of men were busily tracking and picking off the Gifted who had managed to elude his first wave of arrests. Word of the action had come from Moore, a longtime spy within the AGS, and once Gleason's trusted Executive Assistant. It had brought him into action again, even though it had actually been time for him to lay low after the disaster at New Madrid.

He'd barely escaped with his life, leaping into the flood of mud as the stanchion wiped out where he'd been and then escaping out the door after it was clear that the installation was in ruins as a result of his daughter. His hands fisted on his lap. Vallon was now experiencing the repercussions of not agreeing to help him. There was no way the unGifted and Gifted could live side by side like the proverbial lion lying down with the lamb. The unGifted would always resent the Gifted once they knew of them. They would attempt to get rid of them out of fear. That was why he'd assisted the corporations in their attempt to control Middle America by taking control of the country's Midwestern heartland. Because it was the perfect way to become a power broker for those who currently held the power in America and beyond. And once they were dependent upon the Gifted, well, then the power would have transferred and the Gifted would be in control, just as they should be. It would place him on equal footing with the others in the world who had so far refused to make contact even though, over the years, he'd done everything in his power to arouse them.

But Vallon and her little band of helpers—Gleason and Snow and the others—had undone his plans and set in motion Wolf Amundson's purge. This situation required a different approach, fighting fire with fire. Their first success had been the rescue of the family in Olympic National Park. Since then, three other families had been extracted from the hands of one of Amundson's teams. The funny thing was, Amundson didn't even know it, because once his team was erased, so was his memory of it.

The challenge, now, was to find Vallon, because he needed to have a little discussion with his daughter about her choices and her allegiances. His flight across the country with her friend Fiona had been quite enlightening, talking about what Vallon had accomplished and about the mysterious stranger she had linked up with. This Xavier de Varga presented the first link to the others he'd had in years, and he was not going to lose the chance to use it.

A knock, and the presence beyond the door announced himself as Max Carver, a longtime AGS agent and one of the first they'd rescued from Amundson's men. He was a good agent and clearly committed to doing whatever would help the Gifted, given his wife had been one of the teachers here at the academy. He'd been picked up by Amundson's men, running with his two toddlers.

"Come," Francis called.

The door opened and the big black agent stepped inside. He was a tall drink of water with a basketball player's build and hair shorn short over his head, but dyed a dreadful shade of red that on anyone older would have looked ridiculous. On him it just looked modern.

"I thought you'd want to know. The team just got back from your daughter's house. The place had the front door broken in and had been searched. There was no one there, but in the basement we found this." He handed over a piece of crumpled vellum. "Your daughter had clearly been practicing and making her own vellum, even though it contravenes AGS policy. I know, I know, not your problem. But there'd been power use there—actually, quite a bit of it. Some of it was your daughter—her ashes of roses scent came through loud and clear. But there was other scent as well, at least one, possibly two or more, and a feeling of power the men report as being something they'd never felt before." He shook his head and shrugged. "Bottom line, she's gone. The team thinks she made a tunnel and escaped that way. There was evidence of change on one wall. There was no clue as to where she was going."

"I know where she's going. If she's on the move, then she has to be trying for the academy students. Fiona said she was deeply disturbed by her vision. Given my daughter's penchant for helping the weak, I'd bet that's where she's going, if she can find it. Set the searchers on that, top priority. I'm betting it's somewhere in the Northwest, because Amundson wouldn't want to take a chance, transporting truckloads of kids too far. Too much chance of something happening and someone catching wind. It wouldn't look good in the media."

He thought a moment. "Maybe get Toby on it while you and the others keep on with your extractions." Toby Watts might not be Gifted, but he was resourceful as only a corporate heavy could be, and he'd hung around Francis like a pet after digging out of the mud and destruction of New Madrid. He had enough research skills that, given the logistical needs of housing the children and a research facility, he could identify potential locations around the Northwest.

"I'm on it," Max said and left the room, the door closing quietly behind him.

Francis swooshed his finger over the mouse pad on his laptop and the screen sprang to life with a smaller version of the AGS map software like that used in the huge AGS map pits. At present the huge map was probably as much use as lump of stone because Amundson and the unGifted couldn't read the darn thing. This miniature version in no way allowed the level of detail, nor picked up the small changes of the partially Gifted, though it did show their presence with miniscule golden pinpricks. Here in the Pacific Northwest, it was like there were shoals of them glittering along vague lines that stretched east to west. He'd bet money those shoals lay above the ley lines. Here and there, a brighter flare spoke of those with more Gift, and brighter still, the white-hot flare of agents. Right now, there was a flare where Vallon's house stood, but that flare began to move, heading off on another assignment or coming back in for a rest. Up on Broadway, another group of agents was going in to repatriate a Gifted who had apparently holed up in a room above one of the shops along the street. Apparently Amundson's men hadn't sniffed him out yet, but better to bring him in safely beforehand.

Yes, things were looking up. Agents who would previously have abhorred Francis Drake's perspectives had suddenly had their minds changed when Amundson's men came to pick up their families. At the school, their numbers were growing, and soon he'd have enough resources to take the battle directly to Amundson.

There was no way the Gifted wouldn't win.

§

Something clearly wasn't right.

Wolf Amundson rubbed his forehead and studied the reports again. His office was filled with silver-grey light from the cloudy day outside his floor to ceiling office windows. He preferred not to work with the overhead fluorescents because lately they reminded him too much of the research and interrogation rooms. For all he liked the information slowly percolating its way into the HS mainframes, he didn't particularly like the sensory input that came with it. Coppery blood and those moans and all the injuries to limbs—those he'd rather not remember. So he used the natural light as long as he could, and it went well with the chrome and black lacquer of his office.

He swiveled his chair to look out the window at the grey skyline and the grey waters of Elliot Bay beyond.

He'd had excellent leads as to the locations of the missing AGS agents. Some had come from other, captive, agents through interrogation. Others had come from just good old-fashioned police work tracking the use of credit and bank cards. And yet, not one of the excellent—no, perfect—leads had led to an arrest in the past two days. Before that they'd been picking up the scattering agents like shells on a beach. Many had been caught unaware; they had missed the warning Gleason had apparently sent. It made no sense that they'd suddenly become wiser and more difficult to catch—not that there weren't low hanging fruit and all that.

He stabbed his intercom. "Yes, Sir," came Moore's crisp voice, ever obedient. He liked that about her—his first Gifted servant. Holding her brother hostage had proved to be the perfect way to keep the lovely Eurasian tractable, and had supplied a proven source of information about the Gifted. After all, they weren't war-hardened men and woman like the contracted agents from Loadstone. No, these were talented individuals trained as mapmakers and surveyors, who just happened to also bear the mutant gene for the Gift.

"Where's Bryson? I asked for him to be brought in an hour ago." He'd thought better of his decision to let Jason head to the students alone and had, for a moment, suspected all of Jason's actions to have been a ruse to get the students' location.

There was a sound of keyboard keys and silence, and then, "C team says they're just pulling into the garage with him. They caught up to him at the Anacortes turnoff of I-5. He is apparently not happy."

"Too bad."

He hung up and stood, because immobility was driving him crazy. Not that he wanted to be out there bringing in the Gifted, but he wanted this phase of the operation to be over. He wanted a means to undertake his bigger plan, to rip the Gift out by its roots from the American population and to establish a perimeter that would keep them from coming in from outside nations. Otherwise the country would never be safe from incursions of these monsters who tampered with the minds of those around them.

It was five minutes before Moore knocked on the door and admitted a slightly steaming Jason Bryson. The good detective glared at him from a face that was greyed with exhaustion. Thick lines had formed from his nose to his down-turned mouth. His five o'clock shadow gave him a dissolute look and his suit hung on him as if he'd dropped weight.

"What the hell's so important that you pulled me off waiting for Vallon and dragged me back here? We know she's coming for the kids. Just how the hell are your people even going to know they're under attack without me there?"

Wolf controlled the urge to slap the man down. "Sit down." He motioned to the chrome-and-leather guest chair in front of the desk, then settled himself in his ergonomic chair. "I needed you here because I have a nagging feeling that something's not right."

Jason crossed his arms, his lips firming into an aggressive line. "A nagging feeling. That's enough to put your entire research facility in jeopardy and to chance losing Vallon?"

Wolf chose to ignore the attitude. Instead he laid out his concerns regarding how the pickups had gone the past two days compared to previously. "I need you to do some checking for me."

"And just how the hell am I supposed to know whether something has gone down when I don't even know where it was supposed to have happened? It's one thing to be present where an event is going down, and another to come into a place after something has happened. I can sense it in both cases, but I can't just pull it out of the air. I have to have a specific place to check."

Wolf swiveled his chair around to the grey view and closed his eyes a moment. How could he say where agents might have gone? Where pickups might have occurred only to have them Changed by the Gift, when he couldn't remember it himself? The feeling of violation, of being tampered with, left him sick to his stomach. Or else he was developing a powerful sense of paranoia.

He swung himself around again, because he really couldn't think of anything else to do. "Check me, because I would have had to have been changed. Check this." He slid his lists of team assignments and reported results across the glass desktop to Jason.

The detective just looked at him, then dropped his gaze to the paper. A muscle worked in his jaw, and then he looked up at Wolf and nodded.

"Change. The paper's shiny like plastic, so something's changed on it. I've got no way to say how it's been changed in the past, but I can monitor it now."

Wolf's stomach did a rapid roll. So he *had* been changed, was no longer the child of his parents, because he didn't remember things that he should, and that made his skin crawl. "I want you monitoring it 24/7. I want standby teams so when a change occurs the standbys can move in, aware of what they're up against. I want you to brief them."

Jason sat there a moment and then nodded. "And Vallon?"

"When we catch her, she's yours to play with—anyway you want."

A slow smile thinned Jason's lips further as he stood up to leave.

"Thank you," was all he said.

CHAPTER 22 — CAYENNE, CEDAR, AND ALMONDS

Xavier woke to the mingled comforting scents of saltwater slough and of ashes of roses that came from the damp tangle of Vallon's hair. Somehow they had ended up on the cot built for one, their limbs tangled together with the thin cotton sheet over them, dark and light and lighter. Her smooth skin was silken under his palm, the slow rise and fall of her breasts against him enough to arouse him again. She had had this effect on him from the moment he saw her as a young woman, the magic of her profile, the sweet yearning to meet her. He was sure he would always feel this way: protective and hungry, both at the same time.

"You're not sleeping," came her sexy, after-sex voice, muffled by his chest. Her breath was warm on his skin.

"We have had so little time together, do you begrudge us this?"

She moved against him and brought her head up, blonde hair tangled around troubled brown-green eyes. "Never. I could stay like this forever—except my foot's asleep and…" She leaned up to kiss him. "The kids are so near here and she's in horrible pain and afraid and…."

"And how can you lay here in bliss when that is occurring," he finished and stroked her hair back off her forehead and out of her eyes and leaned in to kiss her back. "I understand, my *Bela*. You do what is right and I love that about you."

She went utterly still, her great dark eyes studying him.

He ran the side of his hand down her face and smiled. "Yes, love, *Bela*. That and too many things to name about you. Like the shape of your elbow, though it digs into my side, no?"

She hurriedly removed said offending elbow and scrambled up beside him, her breasts pale and delicious-looking in the dim light, but he caught her around her naked waist and pulled her, protesting, back beside him to nibble on her ear. "You are like a feast, my *Bela*. A feast that fills me up and completes me."

She squirmed around to face him, her breath, scented of roses, on his face. "We need to get going, Xavier, and you need to rest. They'll know we're coming and so they'll be prepared."

He nuzzled her ear and caught the lobe in his teeth. "Rest, *Bela?* You forget the rejuvenating aspects of Pangea's bliss."

His good hand cupped her breast and she responded to him. She turned and kissed him, a long, lingering, passionate kiss that swiftly stole his breath. His flames submerged her in cedar and incense essence. The pleasure of her skin, of her touch, was enough to set an inferno loose in him, but….

She pulled back and looked at him. "Is it fair for us to have such bliss when those children are dying? We have to get going. Every moment we delay, someone else may be lost or tortured."

The concern in her gaze drew him in with its warmth and secrets, but he shoved back his ardor to a simmer that he knew would boil at the slightest provocation. His hands came up and held her head, then he leaned in and kissed her hard one last time.

"That is to ensure you will remember me no matter how far apart we become."

She placed three fingers over his mouth. "Not going to happen. I'm not losing you again. Understand? We stick together like Elmer's Glue."

For a moment he was puzzled and she shook her head. "Don't worry about it. A colloquial expression that means we're not splitting up."

Their clothing was scattered on the floor, and Maggie had nested in the midst of Vallon's clothes. Thankfully there was a small shower down by the boat and they enjoyed the sensual soaking together, then toweled each other off, him marveling in the delicate strength of her body. It was enough to make him forget his injuries.

Xavier dressed in his usual dark trousers and rugby shirt. She pulled on clean underwear and white t-shirt and the same forest-mud-spattered jeans. It was the best she could get here, but at least their afterburn was a thing of the past. When they were dressed, she rebandaged his hand. At least this place had a more complete medical kit. She placed salve over the sliced flesh, then covered it in gauze and a wrapped bandage. "The color seems better. It looks like the flesh is healing," she said.

"Yes. And the bones knit, as well. For all your Landon Snow did this, he seemed intent on healing as well. A very strange man."

She glanced up at him as she finished wrapping. "Strange, yes. He always has been. But just yesterday your hand was a mass of mashed bones and torn flesh. I've never seen anyone heal so fast."

"And I suppose that is a good thing." He smiled down at her, not telling her everything, and hoping it didn't matter.

She placed her arms around him and planted her cheek against his chest. "We'll have more of these times together."

It felt like both a question and a wish as his arms came around her.

The knuckles of her spine stood out under his palm as he stroked her back. "There will be many, many times, *Bela Menina*. You are mine and I am yours, remember. Pangea showed us." His lips grazed her forehead, but then he released her. "So, where do we go?"

Vallon closed her eyes and he felt her -reach-. "She's not far. I feel her like a cinnamon-scented banner, northward, calling for help. A great cloud of churning terror surrounds her, along with the essences of the other students. That no one has come for them breaks my heart." She opened her eyes. "Farther north, but not far, I think."

Xavier pulled packages of military-style meal packages out of a cupboard. "Eat. The body needs fuel to keep going."

They sat at the table, at least Vallon did, while Xavier perched on the side of the cot as they gulped down self-warming pouches of stroganoff with rice and peas. It tasted better than it looked, but looks didn't matter at the moment.

"How do we go in?" Xavier asked. "I don't dare try transmutation in the state I am in." He looked at her and saw her sudden worry. "Pangea can heal many things, but not all. Some things take time, though being with you makes me feel new again." He smiled. "Do not worry. I am still good for many things."

He waggled his eyebrows playfully, but he could see it didn't resolve her disquiet. To rescue the children and take down Amundson—it would be difficult at the best of times, but now the effort was very risky.

Still, she found the strength to smile as she herded Maggie back into the duffle bag and headed for the stairs, then back down into the dimness of the boathouse, the graceful length of the powerboat coming up beside them.

"Why a powerboat?" she asked. "I pictured you more as a sailboat kinda guy."

He cocked a brow and patted the red hull. "Let's just say that sometimes options to leave the country are a good thing."

"It sounds like you never really trusted the Gifted," she said as he passed her by, headed past the Audi for the locked door.

"The Gifted were never meant to know I existed, *Bela*." He keyed in the code for the door and it slid open far enough to expose a fading day beyond. Vallon breathed in the sea air and sent an apology northward to the children. She had dallied an entire day away, and for what? Sex with a man she lusted after? The guilt was overwhelming.

She turned back to him as he set the lock from the outside. The sunlight pasted her long shadow over the building's side, like the stylized pattern of a shadow puppet. "Then why expose yourself to me, Xavier? It doesn't make sense. Why help me like you did?"

He caught her by the Cayenne, his hands on her shoulders. "Because it *was* you, *Bela*. I had watched you too long to let you die that way."

She shook her head. "But why? Why watch me? Sure, I work for the AGS, but there are a lot of female agents. Why me? Why pick me to help—and don't tell me it's because I'm beautiful, because there are lots of beautiful girls in the world, and I'm pretty sure you could have any of them you want."

She looked him in the eyes, but he could not reveal himself. He looked away and felt her stiffen in front of him. She pulled away.

"What is it, Xavier? What aren't you telling me?"

He sighed and looked over her head and over the SUV's roof towards the water, seeking a route of escape. He felt the heat of their intimacy fade from her gaze.

He shook his head. "Now is not the time, *Bela*. But I will tell you. When the time and place are proper. Please believe me." He looked down at her, pleading. "For now, I believe we have some young Gifted to help."

When he left her for the passenger side, he saw her shiver and rub away the spots where he'd touched her. After all she had been through, he knew he risked everything to hold back from her, but some secrets were too great to bare in the midst of everything else going on. Xavier knew almost everything to know about her. He'd known much when he met her and had discovered more, and yet he revealed almost nothing of himself. Such inequity could not go on for long.

She climbed in behind the steering wheel and started the car. It rumbled and then settled into a steady purr, which should have delighted her, but she sat there with a frown etched on her face as if something preoccupied her. Under her guidance, the Cayenne grumbled over the gravel lot and back onto Ross Avenue.

Please let her remember I have helped her in two very difficult cases and in both instances I have risked my life. And not just my life. My place amongst my family, my people.

They reached the highway and she set the Cayenne loose. The lovely vehicle leaping forward like a race horse until Vallon eased up on the gas

I-5 North cruised up through hilly, undeveloped areas, and then back down into farmland turned ripe with harvest in the setting September sunlight.

"The feel of the girl has shifted westward." She took the Anacortes Ferry turnoff and followed the long, straight road through the fields of corn and last-cut hay. "I want to send to her that we're coming and to be ready, but I don't dare. Wolf Amundson is crafty enough anyway, and with Jason's help, they'll be waiting."

She -reached- and he followed her, the landscape filling with the sparks of the hayfields, the glow of the people in the cars around them, and in the houses scattered over the fields. Through Vallon he felt the girl and the miasma of fear that surrounded her flowed like a mist out over the otherwise normal-looking landscape. She was—there. Beyond her burned an inferno of candles.

The Cayenne flashed past an old salmon canning factory on the shore of a shallow bay. The road curved up into a forested area, splitting to travel down to Whidbey Island. Vallon continued on to Anacortes and followed the road down into the quaint little town and pulled into a grocery store parking lot.

"Did you feel them?" she asked. "Did you see the building? It looked old."

He nodded. "I felt them. But I felt others, as well. Gifted. There were many, and they were not in the building. They surround it."

"What? How could I miss that?" her gaze went distant as she -reached-. And then suddenly doubled over.

"Something's about to happen. Oh my God, almonds! My father!"

Alive and here.

CHAPTER 23 — DECISIONS

The news was not good. Since Jason had been called in, three teams of HS extraction experts had not just been destroyed—they had simply ceased to exist. At least that was how Bryson interpreted the way Wolf's lists suddenly changed, even though Wolf neither saw nor remembered the previous list.

Wolf sat at his darkened glass-topped desk with the offending list before him looking ridiculously innocent. He didn't want to touch it in case it infected him as badly as American society was infected. The trouble was, they didn't even know they were infected. He shook himself and ran his fingers through his hair, then turned his chair to the view over Seattle. His beautiful emerald city, and at any moment it could be written off the face of the earth by those—those creatures.

His fingernails bit into the leather chair arms and he imagined the dark towers smoking and withering away, the people lost like ash in the streets, and raucous cheers from non-human thugs who would no doubt dance in the ashes and send them dissipating on the wind while they *took over*.

It could not be allowed to happen.

He swung his chair back and looked at the man seated on the far side of his desk. Jason Bryson still looked gaunt, and for a moment Wolf wondered what had brought the man to this. He had been Vallon's ally once upon a time and had risked his career to help her. So what had changed for the man that he was now her enemy? He almost asked, but the situation was too dire and Jason needed to get back to the installation, because there was no doubt that things were coming to a head there. Even the researchers reported tension in the air. His men were on edge and there had already been one incident where Wolf's men had shot a student who was having a seizure.

"We can't let them win, Jason. We can't let them change things right under our noses. It's the ultimate terrorism. Can you imagine what would happen in the hands of *al Qaeda*? What they could do with impunity?"

"It's what the Gifted and the AGS were supposedly for—to protect from just that kind of thing," Jason said.

"They would say that." Wolf shook his head. "But think about it. There've already been cases of homegrown *al Qaeda* terrorists—American soldiers, some of them. What's to stop these Gifted from doing the same—working with international terrorists? Think of what they could do—and we'd never even know it was happening. They could turn this country into an Islamic state and we'd never even know it."

Jason looked doubtful. He shook his head. "I think the Gift is over the landscape and people, not over their beliefs."

"But you don't know that. You don't know that at all."

Jason sat forward on the sling-shaped chair and looked down at his hands. "Maybe it's not my place, but maybe you should take your concerns to Washington. Maybe they need to know. More than me, anyway."

Wolf swung his chair away before Jason could read his face. He turned back to the view that could be wiped away at any time, and a frisson of fear ran through him. How many times had it happened already? Was he a creation of one of them?

"I've been on the phone to Fitzsimmons since this whole thing began." He shook his head and stiffened at the memory. "The man thought he could laugh at me the last time that I called." Laughed? Fitzsimmons had told him to get a hold of himself or it might be necessary to rethink his posting. He closed his eyes and clutched the chair arms. "I bring him warning of the greatest threat to this country this generation has ever seen, and he's fool enough to laugh." And threatens me. "I should just let them change him. Wipe him away."

He stood up, unable to be contained by the chair. He paced behind the desk, feeling Bryson's gaze on him. He turned to the man. "When the government won't act and won't give warning to the people of the danger in their midst, our leaders look for a fall guy. I've seen it before in law enforcement: something goes wrong; they look for someone to blame. But the righteous man must act to protect those people regardless of the Ray Fitzsimmonses of the world. He will need to look for a different scapegoat."

He grabbed hold of the back of his chair to stop the trembling in his hands. Well, at least to stop the detective from seeing. They were busting their asses out here. But the detective's guarded gaze said he might have already seen. And judged.

"What about going above Fitzsimmons' head. You must have connections."

Amundson ground his teeth. Connections? He had dirt on half of Washington, but apparently not dirt enough. Fitzsimmons has gotten to them. Washington was locked down tight. He inhaled. "Connections. Yes."

The room went silent, the quiet hush of recycled air the only sound.

"So what are you thinking?" Bryson asked quietly, as if he was trying to sooth an agitated beast.

The man's fresh-air-scented aftershave seemed too potent in the room. Amundson swallowed and turned back to his window, seeking the strength and purpose the view always gave him.

He squared his shoulders and straightened his tie. That was how he always appeared ready in the face of disaster. He rubbed his face and left his uber-competent expression in place, then turned back to Bryson.

"If the government won't do its job, there are other means. We've done it for years when the police couldn't. *America's Most Wanted* has been successful in catching people the country's finest couldn't."

Bryson's disbelief was clear, but Wolf had made his decision. Correction, Ray Fitzsimmons and his Washington cronies had made it for him. He picked up the phone and stabbed reception. "Moore. I need you to set something up. Call the local media and tell them we're doing an urgent press conference. We're going public."

§

"My father!?" In the vehicle idling in the little supermarket parking lot, Vallon collapsed bath against the smooth seat leather of the sweet Porsche Cayenne and turned to Xavier. Beyond him, out the passenger-side window, the parking lot was going through a little rush of morning shoppers and the quaint-looking coffee shop was busy with what looked like tourists grabbing a coffee before lining up for the ferry to Canada. It all looked so normal that it made her father's presence even more surreal.

She -reached- again, but the strong scent of almonds was unique amongst the Gifted. She remembered how her nose had crinkled at it when she was a kid and how she had known him in an instant when she finally met him in New Madrid. And how he'd imprisoned her. "But I saw him die."

"Apparently not," Xavier said. He caught her hand and squeezed. "He is a man like a cat, yes? He has many lives."

She shivered where she sat, because he had supposedly died twice that she knew of. "But why here? Why now?"

Xavier looked out the SUV's window and shook his head. In profile, his hawk nose gave him a dangerous, predatory look that made her swallow. "Perhaps he has come looking for you." He paused. "Or perhaps he knew of the children and wished to help them."

She shook her head. "My father never helped anyone without there being something in it for him."

"Could he not feel threatened by Amundson's actions? Might he not intervene?"

She had to agree it was a possibility. "But he'd be doing it to expand his own influence. He'd be taking refugees in to convert them to his way of thinking."

She thought a moment. "Crap. That's exactly what he's doing. He's using Amundson's craziness as proof that people with the Gift can't trust the unGifted. Oh my God! He's trying to start a war!"

Xavier gave her a look that said she might have not just jumped, but *leapt* to an overblown conclusion.

"Listen," she said. "Think of what we know about my father. He was trying to take down the country. What better way than to gather the Gifted around you until you have enough force to attack and make change on a massive scale? Think of what he did with the few Gifted and partially Gifted in New Madrid. With the entire force of AGS agents behind him, he'd have a reasonable chance. It makes sense that he'd try for the students. It would be a way to prove to the agents that he's on their side and cares about their children."

And no one would know what a lie that was. Her father didn't give a damn about those kids. Her father was *only* about the power they might bring him. "It won't matter a damn bit to him if those kids are killed in the fight he's going to start. In fact, that will work to his favor. The kids will be martyrs and a rallying cry. He'll have created a band of furious, grieving Gifted and will be able to build on that. There's nothing like grief to lead to revenge."

She could see the scenario playing out. Her father feigning grief and inflaming anger. He'd end up with the most highly trained Gifted to work with him on a rampage against the very people they'd been trained to protect. That in turn would lead to Amundson taking the gloves off. There'd be a witch hunt the like of which the country hadn't seen since— well, maybe there really wasn't precedent. At least not in this country. It would make the Salem witch hunts and McCarthyism look like a Sunday School picnic.

"We have to stop him."

The question was, how?

She -reached- again and studied the situation. The blaze of the imprisoned children was like a centerpiece to an encircling cordon of other Gifted. Her father, meanwhile, was settled in what must be a fisherman's shack along the water. So far they hadn't attacked, but that could end at any moment.

The scent of anise and mint caught her nose and she stopped her pondering to look more closely at the mélange of Gifted with her father. It could not be, but it was.

She slumped back in her seat and knew for certain that this wasn't about the children. They were only pawns, as were the Gifted her father had recruited to help him. This was only about one thing. Her.

She looked up and found Xavier frowning. "You have realized something."

She nodded. "He has Fi. He must have remembered her from New Madrid. He knows I'll come for her as well as the children."

Every part of her tingled with an adrenaline rush as she dropped the transmission into drive and abandoned the parking lot.

CHAPTER 24 — DIRTY LITTLE FUTURE

Vallon. *Bela*. Perhaps we should discuss this first." Xavier placed his good hand over one of hers that white-knuckled the steering wheel as she pushed the Cayenne beyond the speed limit, out of the quaint town of Anacortes and eastward.

She would not listen to him—only shoved his hand away. "He's got her as bait, Xavier. He has to know she's important to me. He won't hesitate to put her into danger. I won't have her hurt. Not after all she's done for me."

"Then why fall right into the trap he has set for you, *Bela*? That is no way to defeat the man." Please let her listen to him.

She tossed an angry glance his way. "No? Then what's the plan, Xavier? What big plan do you have to save my friend and those children? Stand back and watch for a dozen years? Somehow I don't think we've got that much time." Her eyes flashed like cold steel as she and her shoulders were hunched and stiff in determination as she accelerated out of Anacortes and back to the highway that led to the warehouse.

"*Bela*, please. This is not meant to stop you. It is meant to urge caution. To think before you act, perhaps. Think of consequences."

She slowed long enough around a curve to throw him a glare.

"I'm thinking about consequences. Like the consequences for everyone if he succeeds in starting a war. There're going to be a hell of a lot of innocents hurt if that happens, starting with those kids and Fi. If I go in now, there's a chance I can circumvent it. Use the agents to get the kids out without any bloodshed. Then we and the kids and their families can take cover until we take out Amundson. Simple as that." She flashed him a triumphant grin that only sent a deep chill through him.

Since his escape from the *platiqua,* he had been weak and cold and wounded. His time with Vallon in the boathouse and the bonding with Pangea had reduced some of that depletion and had certainly allayed the afterburn that had been an insistent pain since New Madrid. But he was in no shape to face down a cadre of trained Gifted, and that was not why he was here. Keep Vallon safe was one thing. The Council might forgive that once they knew the truth about her. But reveal himself enough to stop these Gifted—that would be the unforgivable.

And there was little way he could defend Vallon if the Council destroyed him. "I do not think this is a good idea, Vallon. Let your father attack and use the confusion of battle to get in to the children."

"And have them murdered before I can get there? Or Fi? Not on your life, Xavier. No way."

The road curved downhill towards the warehouse and the shallow bay. She cranked the Porsche into a side road, the wheels sending up a spray of gravel from the edge of the road. If anyone was watching, and undoubtedly there were watchers, they'd know someone was on their way. "You advertise you are coming?"

She flashed him a glance. "Do you really think they can stand against us?"

"And what if I will not help you with this? Or cannot?" He held up his injured hand. Surely that would give her pause. "Vallon, this is a bad idea."

She made a show of stepping down on the gas and the Cayenne leapt forward. "I'm not letting my father start a war and use those children and my friend as fodder for it." The SUV shot past the warehouse and down to the water, to a small shed along the shoreline that, given the rotting pier, might once have been a fisherman's residence. She skidded to a halt amidst more flying gravel and leapt out, the engine still ticking as she marched to the front door. Xavier stepped out behind her and watched her go.

So much for a careful, planned approach. At times Vallon was too ruled by emotions and impetuousness. Terrifyingly so.

Xavier sighed and inhaled the briny air. At least he could try to save her from herself.

But the person who pushed out the grey-painted door to greet her, before she reached the stairs, was not her father. Instead a familiar, slight, pixy-cut, blonde person leapt down the three rickety stairs and across to Vallon to throw her arms around her friend. Fiona, the wild one who had come far from the half-mad girl-woman he had met in Seattle. Now she looked older, more in tune with the world. And ecstatic to see her friend.

She pulled back from Vallon and shook her head. Tears glistened in her eyes. "I was so worried, Vallon. There I was in Washington and Gregor couldn't seem to get anyone to listen to him. I-I guess I got tired of listening to him, too, 'cause one day I went out for a walk instead of staying in the room like he said, and your Dad's men picked me up." She shook herself like a wet dog.

Vallon held her arms. "Are you okay? Has he hurt you in any way?"

Fi frowned and the child came through in her gaze. "I'm okay, I guess. At first I was really afraid, because he locked me in a room. I didn't fall apart though, I kept asking myself 'what would Vallon do?' and that kept me strong."

Vallon looked like she was about to protest, but Fi carried on. "But your dad—he said we'd come back here and find you and now here you are—just like he said." She grinned broadly and hugged Vallon again while Vallon looked back at Xavier, confusion in her face.

Fiona might be fine, but something did not feel right. He shook his head.

The front door opened again and a tall, athletic-looking man with grey-blond hair stood in the doorway, his gaze focused on Vallon. "I'm glad you decided to join us, Vallon."

Behind him stood a muscle-bound blond man who had shoulders and chest that could only come from years of rigorous weight-room training and a cool, steady gaze that spoke of time in the military. He was also the same man who had, once upon a time in New Madrid, shot one Xavier de Varga. He wore a red t-shirt and faded jeans, and slouched by the entrance in a studied way that belied his casualness. His gaze caught on Vallon and his lips curved in the kind of smile that could only mean he *knew* Vallon too well and in too many ways. A low snarl snagged in Xavier's chest.

Vallon set Fi aside and faced her father with her hands on her hips, too-studiously ignoring the younger blond man. "I did no such thing. I came to get Fi and to tell you and your people to back off. We don't need this situation going up in flames. Fi, come on. We're blowing this pop stand."

Fi hesitated.

"Really? So soon? But Fiona and I have become fast friends." The blond man barely shrugged, but his gaze strayed to Xavier and froze. His eyes seemed to widen and his throat worked a moment. "This must be the mysterious friend Fi has told me about." He stepped to the side of the door. "Please, come in. We have much to discuss and more to plan if we're to save those poor children." He nodded in the direction of the warehouse and half-empty equipment lot that stood in an unmown field set back from the ocean.

Vallon hesitated as Xavier studied her father. Blond, like her, but otherwise there was nothing else like her—except perhaps the stubbornness that kept Vallon going far past the place others would give up. He suspected that was not a good thing in this man, just as it often got Vallon in trouble. Francis Drake had the look of a zealot in his eyes, and zealots had caused so much trouble in the world.

"Do not accept his invitation," Xavier murmured, coming up behind her and resting a protective hand on her shoulder.

"I have to stop him. I can't just leave him to start a war," she said, turning to him, a single palm on his chest sending a surge of welcoming warmth into him. "I don't think you should come in, though. We don't want him getting a better read of who and what you are. I'll go in and talk to him and then we can decide what to do."

Xavier glanced over her head at the way her father and the blond man watched them. It sent a chill down Xavier's back. Her father might not have Cartos skill or power, but he was still a formidable foe, with the cold, calculating look and the number of Gifted he had working with him. They surrounded this area like a malevolent cloud. The anger was palpable. And the other man had the physical prowess to do Vallon physical harm.

He shook his head. "Don't go with them. You cannot stop him, Vallon. He has made up his mind and has fueled the anger in others just as you said. You do not just turn such emotions on and off. Depose Amundson and there might be a way to stop this, but as long as your father and Amundson lead their people, the fear and the anger will be explosive with the potential to spread."

Her stubborn grey gaze said his speech made no difference. She nodded. Her hand came up to stroke his cheek "I know you're probably right, but someone has to try to diffuse the situation, and I can't very well go strolling into Amundson's office."

It was the truth, and perhaps Francis Drake was the lesser of two evils, but he could not believe it, even though he had not met Amundson. There was something chill about Vallon's father. Something that made him wonder how the child this man had raised to age eleven had turned into the woman before him. Sometimes, apparently, there *were* miracles. Praise the Creator that Vallon Drake had not turned out like her father.

Unlike him. He looked up at Drake. "We will not be separated."

Vallon caught his hand and leaned in to talk to him. "We need to know what he's planning and this is the best way to find out." She nodded up to him 'Please, Xavier. I need to do this. We're not really separated. Not by any distance at all."

She was so certain, so determined to go. He glanced up at her father again. "If harm comes to her, there will be nothing left of you to beg for mercy." He crossed his arms and flexed his muscles, as much for the blond man's benefit as to put Drake on notice that he did not trust him.

Fi clutched at Vallon's arm. "Come on. I've been telling him all about you and how I helped you in New Madrid."

Vallon linked arms with her and let herself be tugged across the gravel and up the stairs. At her father, she stopped and looked up at him, and Xavier felt the currents of testing from both father and daughter.

"Hello, Toby. I was hoping you were dead," she said. Then she stepped past, into the building, and was gone, the others on her heels

Xavier toed the ground. He should not have let her go. After freeing himself from Landon, he'd promised himself that they would not be separated again. That he would protect her. He'd risked everything to come back to her and now he was letting this happen.

He kicked the gravel with his heel and had the satisfaction of stones clattering against the old building's time- and worm-pitted siding. He opened himself to the cinnamon, apple, wet earth, coriander, damp fur, and so many more sensations of the Gifted and busied himself identifying the location of each of Drake's men and women, but most of all he paid attention to the building. Vallon's brilliant ashes of roses flare, Drakes too-sweet almond, and Fi's anise and mint scents. The man called Toby was a dull human glare—Drake's muscle, obviously. Silence fell except for the low hum of traffic from the highway and the rolling hush of the nearby ocean.

The usually soothing sounds could not calm him, because the rose and ozone scents of *kata* power built around him.

Go in? Get Vallon?

The doorway beckoned.

Something was about to happen.

§

The old building smelled of mildew and wood rot overlaid with her father's too-sweet almond and Toby's pungent floral aftershave. Toby's scent alone was enough to send her retreating to the car and Xavier. She didn't like that she'd left him out there alone, nor the fact that she was in here with only Fi beside her. Fi, who seemed ridiculously comfortable in Francis Drake's presence. Toby's presence just made her grit her teeth in anger. The man was a corporate agent who'd worked at her father's side before and had been the person who'd shot Xavier. She'd had sex with him once to deal with afterburn and wasn't proud of it, which just made his presence that much more offensive. She'd been much happier when she thought he was dead.

The walls of the dim corridor were painted the same chill grey-blue as the door, and years and the brush of people's shoulders had worn through in places. Elsewhere, chips of the paint lay like confetti on the floor. Side doorways, minus the doors, gave onto rooms, some with signs of squatter habitation—old mattresses and newspapers against the walls, tin cans and plastic bag debris, and the stench of urine—others where the floorboards had simply given way, leaving a view of muddy soil below.

The wood-worm-eaten floor joists creaked and sagged under each stride as she -reached-, but there was no one else in the house that she could sense. The other Gifted were situated like sentinels around the warehouse that radiated with the heated presence of the terrified students. Wrapped in amongst the bright flares of the student's fear came the dim lights of their captors. It made her shiver.

Fi led her to the rear of the building, to a single large room that might once have been a kitchen or a work area. Either way, it had a broad counter and double sinks and a large broken window that someone had recently nailed sheets of plastic over. The placed smelled damp and the floorboards seemed patterned with ancient fish scales. A door, probably from one of the other rooms, had been laid across two sawhorses to form a table, and two plastic patio chairs sat beside it and a laptop computer stood open on the top. Before Vallon could stop her, Fi went to one of the chairs and sat down while Vallon stepped inside and let her father pass her. Toby stationed himself at the doorway behind her, his muscled arms crossed across his hard-body chest. She tried to ignore him and stepped just inside.

"Not exactly a palace. Must be a real hardship for you, Dad. After your last plushy digs, I mean. Haven't you got any corporate backers to help you this time?"

He swung around towards her, his gaze hard and unyielding. "Actually, no. I don't. Toby here has decided it's best to run with the winning side, but that's about it. But if this is only to give you a chance to gloat, I would have left you waiting out front." He motioned to one of the chairs. "We need to talk."

She crossed her arms and leaned against the doorframe, too aware of Toby just behind her. "Fine. Talk. I can hear just fine from here."

Her father closed his eyes and his lips formed a frustrated line. Then he inhaled and looked at her again. "I mean it. We need to talk. We're on the same side, Vallon. We're both Gifted—the same kind."

"Wrong. I'm an American. I'm not so sure about you." She hefted herself away from the wall. "If we're going to have a talk, then that means you have to listen, too. There are things in play here. If you and Amundson start a war, there'll be no stopping it. The Gifted are so few that they can't afford to be public enemy number one, and that's what will happen if you take out that installation."

Her father stood by the table, backlit by the window so that she could barely read his expression.

"So? What? We just stand around while Wolf Amundson and his ilk round up our people? You're sounding an awful lot like the people who said it couldn't happen in Germany before the Second World War."

"Dammit, Dad. You know better than that. This is America. We don't round people up like that. We have laws. We're civilized."

"Are we? I seem to recall Japanese internment and the McCarthy years and, oh yes, let's not forget racial profiling. That's your America for you, Vallon. And didn't young Fi here just tell you that your old friend Gleason went around Washington looking for someone to turn Amundson off and no one would listen? You think someone in Washington is going to make things right, think again."

"No." She shook her head. "That can't be right. He just hasn't reached the right people yet."

"Really? What if I told you that Gregor Gleason is right now running for his life across the states, with Amundson's men in pursuit? From what I know, he's somewhere in Utah. Seems like he's headed for Nevada. You know any reason he'd be headed there?"

Landon. She knew Gleason had to be headed there. Was he in on what Landon had done to Xavier? Whether he was or wasn't, he didn't deserve whatever Amundson would do to him. He was a good man who had served America well. But if Washington had refused to do anything to stop this…. The thought left her shaken, her stomach knotted.

"You don't know that. You're making that up."

"And now you sound like the child you used to be, not the skilled agent you are now." Almost as if he was proud of her skills, and she knew that, along with the rest of what he'd told her, was probably a lie. She dug her fingers into her arms to remind herself.

"Then prove it." She lifted her chin up.

"I cannot produce the agent who contacted me. He has gone into hiding in case Amundson's men noticed his presence."

She thought about that and her skin prickled in concern. "Are you saying Amundson has a way to detect the Gift?"

Her father simply chuckled. "Think, girl. Perhaps not yet, but it's only a matter of time. We gave him the technology ourselves with the maps. If they can change the technology enough to allow unGifted to read them, his research teams could have also created a mobile device. I suspect they have been stealing the AGS technology and preparing for this for some time."

"Loadstone," she said and saw the man who was her father nod. The private corporation had become rich contracting with government and taking over many of their security operations by luring away the government's best agents and researchers and then contracting the service back to the government—for a higher price.

"Then they already know we're here." Exactly what she didn't need if she was to stand a chance of getting those children out. "Their guards will be on alert."

"There's that possibility."

"Damn it, Dad." She had to move to deal with her frustration. "Are you purposely being obtuse? It'll be that much harder to get to the kids."

"Vallon?" Fi broke into her thoughts.

"Not now, Fi." She waved off Fi and continued to face her father.

"Vallon," Fi insisted. "He wants to help you get the children out. He has their parents and others who are afraid of what Amundson does here with him. It'll be good, Vallon. That's why I helped him."

She did a slow swing around to Fi, suddenly afraid, and then looked back at Francis Drake. "My father is not a person you can trust, Fi. He is not a good person. Remember New Madrid and being a prisoner?"

"But…." Fi's uncertainty made Vallon look at her, and there was fear on Fi's face. Fear that shouldn't be there, unless….

"What did you do, Fi?"

Fi shook her head and slid her chair back behind the computer for shelter. "Didn't do nothing."

Her voice was the same sullen voice of a teenager she'd had when she first showed up at Vallon's. A girl who didn't like being caught doing something wrong. Because there were things Fi knew about Vallon and about the Gift that no one but the two of them and Landon knew.

Landon. Damn.

"What did you tell him, Fi?" She kept her voice soft and nonthreatening, as if she was talking to a child again.

Fi came right up out of her chair. "Stop it. Just stop it. Everyone including you treats me like a child—except your father. He sees me as someone with expertise and he treats me as an adult. A full person. No one's treated me like that ever!"

She fell back in her chair and looked up at Vallon's father. "I'm sorry. I know you didn't want this to be a confrontation, but I just don't want to be treated that way anymore." Her gaze turned to Vallon. "You taught me that, you know. Vallon Drake never acts like a child and never accepts being treated as one."

Vallon's knees went weak and she would have liked to sit down. Fi had trusted her and she had taken advantage because Fi had been like a child—until the end of New Madrid. Vallon had thought things had blown over between them. That Fi knew Vallon saw her as an adult now, because she did—mostly. But she and Gleason and the others hadn't acted like it. No, they'd foisted Fi off on Gleason because they wanted her out of the way like a nuisance kid.

"Fi, I'm sorry, I betrayed you. I didn't mean to."

"Yeah. Sure. Actions speak louder than words." Fi crossed her arms in finality and studiously looked away to the computer screen, leaving Vallon feeling helpless. What more could she say or do?

"She told me about your little problems with afterburn, Vallon. And how she and Landon Snow helped you. Just where is Landon these days, by the way? Fi mentioned he went out west with that friend of yours. Is that him?" Her father nodded toward the door.

"This isn't about me and my friends or Landon or anyone but you and what you are going to do by attacking Amundson's installation."

"Fine. Fine. Fine. We can discuss it all you wish, but it does not negate our situation. Amundson left alone will wipe us out. He'll use whatever he can to conduct his research and find weapons against us. We have to act now, before he's successful."

"You sound like some idiot Cold War general recommending a preemptive strike. What I'm concerned about are the kids."

Her father paced around the table, his hand gently grazing Fi's shoulder like a supervisor might touch a familiar employee. Vallon's skin crawled.

"Those children are the subject of Amundson's research. He wants to learn what causes the Gift and how to stop it—root it out. If it means killing us off or burning out minds, he'll do it," he said.

Hearing it articulated almost took her breath away, even though she'd thought it since she knew the students were abducted. "You think I don't know that? That's why we have to get them free."

"And that's why we need to work together. There is enough to do for all Gifted. We have children to rescue, Amundson to take down and…."

"Francis?" Fi interrupted with barely a glance at Vallon. "I think it's happening."

Happening?

But her father went around the makeshift table and peered at the computer screen as if Vallon didn't even matter anymore. She followed more slowly, and peered over his shoulder at the small screen.

It showed an NBC newsfeed with the ubiquitous peacock on the left corner and a streaming banner that read *Breaking News* at the bottom. On screen was a miniature representation of Wolf Amundson's pale Teutonic features. His mouth was moving, but his voice was almost impossible to hear.

"Turn it up," her father ordered.

Fi obeyed.

"I am a patriot. I love America and would never consider breaching Homeland Security secrecy if not for the danger to this great country." Miniature Wolf's throat worked as if he was overcome with emotion. He shook his head and played directly to the camera. "But Homeland Security cannot address this threat alone. It will take the will and the effort of the American people. You see, for years this government has allowed a group of people in our midst to develop unspeakable power. I know this will sound like something out of a science fiction novel, but they can reshape the landscape with only their minds and a pen and paper. They can wipe out cities and everyone in it, and worst of all we—normal Americans—will never remember that things were different before." He swallowed and held up his hand to stop the explosion of questions from the reporters in front of him. "I know. I know. The question is how can I prove such a wild story and how can I even know that such things happen. On the one hand I had the fortune to be handed control of this secret arm of Homeland Security. I immediately began to shut it down, and to take the agents into custody, but many escaped. We are tracking them down, but we need the public's help. We need the public's help in identifying those people who have these skills within the population. And as for how we know these changes occur, one man has been identified as having the talent to tell when a change has occurred. He is a patriot and has come forward to work with us."

He turned and the camera angle shifted to show Jason Bryson standing uncomfortably behind and to one side of Wolf Amundson as he was introduced as a Seattle Police detective. Then the camera swung back to Wolf.

"Our most immediate concern is in the Pacific Northwest." He nodded at someone and a screen projection flickered on, revealing an aerial image of a large fenced building near a large body of water. She knew immediately what it was.

"This is a real-time image of a facility in Washington State where we are detaining a number of these dangerous subjects for the safety of the rest of the country."

"But they're children!" Vallon protested.

Her father waved her to silence. A highway near the facility showed tiny vehicles speeding along it, but then the camera zoomed in and Wolf nodded again. The image changed to something far too similar to the AGS map, so Loadstone had managed to read the maps. On the screen, the dark facility bloomed with the brilliance of Gifted presence.

"This is the signature of these 'Gifted' as they are known. The facility glows because they are being held there." He nodded again and the unseen person changed the scene again. The image pulled back and showed the same AGS type map, but this time the area viewed was wider and showed the brilliant cordon of Gifted surrounding the facility. There was a rush of murmurs from the reporters.

"Yes. Those are Gifted as well. They have come to break out their brethren and wreak havoc on our country. I have called in the National Guard to help stop them, but I have no doubt they will attack."

The news conference room was in an uproar and Wolf and held up his hands. "Please! Please! What we need is for the American people to be vigilant. To report anything suspicious to their local Homeland Security office, and if that does not get action, to contact my office directly. The situation is dire and the worst of it is that we no longer know who our friends or enemies are. Please. For America, work with me to preserve this great country. God Bless America."

Wolf stepped away from the microphone and to Jason's side, ignoring the barrage of shouted questions. A communications person stepped up to the microphone. "Mr. Amundson is sorry, but he must get back to dealing with the situation in Seattle. He does, however, have information on agents at large that I will be distributing. This information is also now available online. These people are dangerous and should not be approached. Contact the number provided in the packet of information." The newsfeed clicked off and NBC commentators started talking and Vallon stood there stunned. It hadn't been her father to start things, but she knew he'd sure as heck plan to finish it.

It was her father who turned to her, a smug smile on his face. "Too bad, Vallon. But it had to come to this. We have our dirty little war, it seems."

CHAPTER 25 — THE DIE IS CAST

The heap of Las Vegas rose out of the desert like a nightmare oasis—flattened by the sun, reeking of car exhaust, clanging with casinos, and grotesque for the display off so much unnatural water in a parched landscape. Gregor Gleason threaded his car through the heavy traffic, praying that maybe here he could be anonymous instead of standing out as a stranger as he had in every small town he'd passed through on his rapid drive across the country. Some rest and then try to make contact with Landon. That was the plan. Then sit tight until they saw the lay of the land and Vallon got the kids free.

He scrubbed at gritty eyes and scanned the strip for a likely hotel. It had been a hellish drive across the country, and to prove it Gleason's eyes felt like too much desert had blown into his eyeballs. Too many hours behind the wheel. Too many miles and too little rest and too much sun's glare. At least there was too much glare now, and had been since he'd driven the long stretch of straight road through Monument Valley with its huge, red weathered outcrops and cliffs and through the pine forests north of the Grand Canyon.

Too much sun and heat and the knowledge that time was running through the proverbial egg timer, so he'd dared not stop and dared not sleep. Just pop another keep-awake pill and keep on driving, because the bad times were coming and no one was going to stop it. Washington had made that clear. Someone, somewhere, had decided to let the Gifted question answer itself and let the chips fall where they may.

It was obviously someone who didn't understand the actual power of the Gift.

A three-story moderate-sized hotel came up on his right—The Bonanza. Bright lights even in the midday heat advertised a midsized casino that probably existed only due to its budget guests and low-income locals looking for some action away from the bright lights of Mandalay Bay, the Venetian, and the other big name players on the strip.

Just the kind of place he was looking for. The parking lot wasn't jammed with tour buses, so maybe there was a chance of getting a room.

He pulled in and found a parking spot in the far back of the lot between a couple of motorhomes where it would, hopefully, be less likely to be spotted. Then he wandered inside into frigid air conditioning and the hum of air circulators that could never fully remove the stench of cigarette smoke. The not too distant inane musical chatter of one armed bandits, the TV turned on above the reception counter, and the way the people around him moved more like sleep-deprived zombies than he did, added to the surreal feeling lack of sleep caused.

His nostrils curled, but it couldn't be helped. He'd run out of stay-awake pills and had to sleep and soon, or he was going to kill himself and possibly someone else in a car accident.

Thankfully, they had a non-smoking room and he carried his one small bag down the maze of hallways and locked the door behind him. Inside, it still carried the same cigarette haze and he swore he could still hear the chinks, chimes, and bleats of the slot machines, but he just pulled down the blackout curtains, turned on the television for company, stripped, and headed for a shower.

The blessed water almost revived him, but his latest pills had worn off about an hour ago by his watch, and he could barely keep his eyes open. When he'd done letting the water run over his head and shoulders, he toweled off and came back into the room with a towel around his waist and his sights set on the bed. The TV announcer was just interrupting whatever silly game show was on for a special bulletin.

"A Homeland Security department head has broken the cone of silence surrounding the organizations' operations to issue a major warning to the American public. Wolf Amundson, Seattle Station Head and oversight of the American Geological Survey department within Homeland Security is blowing the whistle on the top secret operations involving operatives apparently with the incredible power to alter the landscape around them."

Gregor sank down on the end of the bed, his body gone numb.

"Yes, that's right. Alter the landscape—and he's not alone in saying that these people exist. Amundson says that a rogue faction within the agents is, as we speak, attacking a secret government prison being used to house these dangerous people. The National Guard has been called in to assist Amundson's men, but in the meantime he is seeking public help locating other rogue agents who have so far eluded capture."

He closed his eyes and rubbed them, knowing what was coming but praying that when he opened them again it would all have been a figment of his imagination.

"The following photos are of known extremists. Do not approach them. Do not call your local police. Instead, call the number on the screen and someone will be standing ready to take your call."

He opened his eyes in time to see Vallon Drake's photo flash on the screen, to be replaced by his own cadaverous countenance. There was no way in hell someone wouldn't recognize him.

He stood up, pulled on his recently removed trousers and polo shirt, and tossed everything else back in his bag. A last look of regret at the bed and he headed out the door again, praying the front desk hadn't already made the call to Amundson.

§

It was working, and Wolf Amundson could barely contain his glee as he walked through the room of agents set up to field the calls. Fifteen agents, contracted from Loadstone using money he had arbitrarily reallocated from the AGS budget, had been set up at the table in the large boardroom overlooking the city with telephone consoles and computer screens in front of them. Their voices were a comforting drone as they took information and fed it to the computer that would then come to him and Bryson for decisions regarding action. Who knew the meddling detective would turn out to be such an ally, just for the chance to get Vallon Drake securely in his hands?

Beyond the wall of windows, the sun had come out from behind a cloud and filled Seattle with a golden light that could only presage his victory over the AGS and its agents. His chest felt filled with light at the prospect of ridding the country of the creatures that had populated the AGS. Then America would be secure. All Gleason's years of fear mongering that the country needed to be protected from terrorists with the Gift had just been a ruse to build his own little comfortable empire.

But now the empire was gone. Phone calls were beginning to come in from all over the Pacific Northwest and as far away as California and Montana, with sightings of the missing agents. They had run, yes, but few had been imaginative enough to recognize that he *would* catch them no matter where they went in the country.

Each agent on the phone gathered information on another agent or on another suspected Gifted from around the country. Funny how many people had noticed things over the years, but had held back saying anything until now, for fear of being ridiculed. All of the callers reported knowing something was wrong, so perhaps Jason was not as unique as they'd all thought. Perhaps the awareness was there, but we just self-censored it out.

That *was* an interesting thought.

"Sir!" That was Vega Tyson, the lovely young agent from Baton Rouge with a southern accent and just a hint of Cajun. It went perfectly with her café au lait skin and her mane of black hair that she kept tied back in a constrained ponytail. She wore a tailored blue blouse, tan trousers, and tiny diamond earrings that matched the small cross she wore around her neck.

"What is it, Tyson?" Keep it formal. Keep it professional, even though the woman's light scent of oranges fascinated him and seemed to get stuck up his nose.

"Sir, I just took a call out of Las Vegas. The woman on the line is positive it's Gregor Gleason. She says he just checked in and then left the building right after the PSA from the local ABS affiliate. She was a brave woman and followed him outside to the parking lot. She got a description of the vehicle and the plate number."

Amundson had to stop himself from clapping. Instead he bowed his head momentarily in thanks, and then smiled at Vega Tyson.

Gleason, the bastard.

"Get a team on it, stat." Yes, he really did like it when a plan came together.

§

The news commentator's voice was a drone that seemed to drill right down to Vallon's bones. It set her teeth on edge, but also started a vibration that could only be real fear. She needed to sit down. She needed to get going, but she still couldn't believe the announcement Amundson had made. The Gifted's existence was known. The lie about their purpose had been told, and in convincing enough fashion she had no doubt that the public would by it.

She stopped herself from leaning on the makeshift door-table and upsetting the laptop onto the floor. The stink of saltwater tidal flats came through the plastic stapled over the vacant window, the hint of mildew and rot came up through the floor, and Toby's sweet aftershave turned her stomach—and still the shock wouldn't seem to let her make a decision about what to do. She'd always been a runner-inner in times of crisis, but right now it was all she could do to move at all, while Fiona, her father, and Toby all seemed just fine.

Her father had elbowed Fi aside and was doing something on the computer. Fi was beside him, talking at his elbow. Every once in a while she'd look back at Vallon as if checking on her. Toby just loomed across the room.

What was the matter with her? She'd been in bad situations. Nothing was holding her here, and Xavier was outside.

"Vallon."

Her father turned back to her, and it was like she could suddenly hear again, or hear something other than the sound of her own breathing and the rush of her blood.

He caught her biceps. "It's done. And you saw that I had nothing to do with it. Amundson's started it. Now, if the Gifted want to survive, we have to stand together. Even you and me."

Work with him? She yanked loose and ran her fingers up into her hair. After everything he had done to her? To others?

Fi was doing it and seemed happy with her choice.

But Fi was a child—or not much more than one. No, that wasn't true, given how Fi had helped in New Madrid. Without her, there wouldn't be a New Madrid anymore. There probably wouldn't be a Wolf Amundson anymore, or a US government as it was now anymore, either.

So what was right and good? Had the AGS been wrong all these years? Had Fi read the true nature of Vallon's father while she, Vallon, was too caught up in old wrongs to really see what he was trying to do?

She looked back at her father. The longer she dithered, the more chance those students would be killed.

"Fine. You do what you have to. I'm going in to get the students. Have your people ready to help when I bring them out. Have you got that?"

She pushed past Toby and started for the door.

"Vallon." Her father stopped her with her name.

She swung back to him. "Don't slow me down. I could change my mind."

"Take—take care of yourself. We'll do everything we can to support you from out here."

She nodded and was gone. As if her father really cared whether she lived or died, just like she didn't give a damn about him. But Fi. She stopped. She should have demanded Fi leave with her.

But Fi seemed happy where she was, and she was as safe with Francis Drake as she was with anyone in these perilous times.

She burst out the front door and heaved in a breath of salt and mud flats and seaweed drying in last afternoon sun. The sun had sunk westward over the low treed hill that hid Anacortes and the ferry terminal. The water of Puget Sound would soon be turning coppery with evening. Closer in, the Cayenne still waited; Xavier, all in black, leaned up against the side like a prince of darkness. Beyond the parking lot and the lone sedan she assumed was her father's, there were only fields of grasses, low brush, and fledgling poplar growing in the abandoned spaces. Good enough for some cover, but not enough. She could change that, of course.

She clattered down the stairs to Xavier. His face was still pale, but breathing the clean ocean breeze seemed to have helped him. He looked stronger, more solidly 'there'.

When he tried to put his arms around her she avoided his embrace and stepped back, looked up at him and shook her head. "There's no time. Amundson has declared war." She told him about the news feed and the call to the American public to report anyone suspicious.

"If Homeland Security didn't have people scared and looking over their shoulder for terrorists before, they certainly do now. The trouble is, there'll be accusations against people who haven't done anything. They'll be rounding up people who don't even know they're Gifted, along with people who don't have a lick of Gifted blood. We have to stop it, Xavier. Stop the bloodshed."

As she told her story, his face darkened with anger. Then he started to pace. When she finished, he turned to her, with fury and sorrow blended on his face. "*Bela*, this is the great fear of my people and always has been. We have lived in secrecy for millennia to avoid just such a thing. This—this exposure—it will run rampant across the world. Millions may be killed if we cannot stop it."

"There's no way to stop it. The awareness of us has entered the public mind. I don't know what it will mean other than that they'll try to hunt us down."

"Once our kind held dominion over the earth, but some still wanted more. A war between our lords led to devastation, and the unGifted rose up against us. They hunted us down and killed us by the millions. Only a few survived, hidden. But the memory of those awful days lives on in both us and the unGifted. The stories of demons are a memory of those days and our kind." He shook his head. "I do not think our kind can survive a worldwide purge again."

"Can you warn your people?"

"I am sure they already know."

"While you make sure of that, I'm going for the children." She started across the parking lot towards the half mile of fields separating them from the transformed warehouse.

"What do you think you are doing?" He caught her arm and swung her back to him.

She arched a brow. "Like I said. Going after the kids. You've got other duties to attend to."

His jaw flexed, then he pulled her into him. "No. I will not let you do this alone. I said that we would not part again. I meant it."

"You have to warn your people. You can't wait, and I can't wait, either. Amundson's National Guard contingent has to be very close." She tried to pull loose, but his arms stiffened around her and his embrace became fierce.

"You will go. I will give warning, and then I will come after you. We will meet before you enter that place and plan together."

Pressed into his chest, she inhaled his cedar and incense, and his adamancy was almost a relief. She leaned up to place the barest of kisses on his lips. "Then let's get this rodeo started, shall we?

He released her and it was like a vacancy in her life. She wanted his arms. She wanted time to just be with this man and learn his moods, his seasons. She ran her palm down over his face. "Come quickly, then."

She turned and loped to the barbwire fence that surrounded her father's headquarters, gingerly climbed over, and then turned back to Xavier. He stood there as if watching her, but there was already a faraway look in his eyes that said he was elsewhere, conversing with his kind.

She turned back to the field, fished her vellum and pen out of her pocket, and -reached- for the rose-scented power. Her pen scratched across the vellum and the acrid scent of the wine-and-vinegar-based ink filled the air. Then came the ozone and the air shimmered and the grasses wisped away, their essence transforming until they gradually solidified before her. A pine and cedar forest coalesced in the field. Something that would provide cover.

She stepped into the woods and the air was cooler after standing in the sun. Behind her, Xavier still stood like a statue as she started to run. The appearance of the forest would warn Amundson—or rather, Jason would recognize the change and would warn him.

That meant she had a very short window of opportunity to do what needed to be done. Weakened as he was by Landon's treachery, if Xavier didn't catch up to her, that was fine.

CHAPTER 26 — IN AND OUT

After living for so long in Seattle, the Las Vegas landscape was barren and parched, trees a sad facsimile of the tall stands of timber surrounding the AGS installation in Redmond. Gregor Gleason missed that place, missed even the verbal jousting with Amundson, but Amundson was no one to joust with verbally now. He needed to be run through.

He just needed to figure out how. The first order of business, however, was to get to cover. He steered the brown sedan around the motorhome lumbering along the highway north out of the city. Beyond the road, miles of ticky-tacky houses had filled up the desert landscape so that the valley that held Las Vegas looked like an unfriendly maze of streets that all led to the funhouse glitz and madness of the strip that glittered behind him in the early evening light. It was a surreal image in a surreal time, so it almost felt like the cityscape was an image projected against his windows. Because he was suddenly public enemy number one. Well, perhaps not number one, but close to the top. Surely if he just opened his car door, he could step out of this madness and things would be the way they were before.

And that was a fool's wishful thinking.

He glanced in the rearview mirror for the millionth time since leaving the Bonanza. So far, everything looked good. No one had approached him and no one seemed to be following. At least that he could tell in the heavy traffic.

He pulled his car in front of the lumbering motorhome and sped up a little, keeping watch behind him. A red SUV sped up and passed the motorhome and an alarm went off inside him. He'd spotted the vehicle about fifteen minutes ago, but nothing had suggested it was following him. Until now. Would Homeland Security have a red SUV?

Anything was possible.

He forced himself to take a deep breath and wished he had more recent experience working in the field. *Sit back and keep on driving, that's all you can do.* He fought the urge to white-knuckle the steering wheel. The red SUV in the fast lane kept pace with his car, but that could be because of the traffic that was slowly dwindling as the city diminished behind them.

Space opened up on the road ahead and he slowly increased his speed, then changed into the fast lane with three cars between him and the red SUV, and sped up again, pushing traffic to get out of the way.

There was no movement of the SUV. He exhaled. *Being stupid, Gregor. You're so spooked you're about to bug out at the slightest suggestion.* Which wasn't quite true, but he felt more vulnerable than he liked.

He looked down at the cell phone on the passenger seat. This phone and this alone was programmed to ring through to Snow. Years ago the man had told him he had a hidey-hole. Before he left New Madrid, Gleason had demanded Snow give him a way to contact him in case things went sideways. He hadn't even begun to fathom just how sideways they'd go.

He'd been putting off phoning Snow until he was out of the city and closer to the general coordinates Snow had given him—not enough to pinpoint his location in case Gleason was compromised, but close enough Snow could guide him in the last ways once he was close.

The traffic slowed around him and Gleason swore and stepped on the brakes. The cars converged around his and together they crawled along. What the hell was happening? An accident? A roadblock?

Another surge of adrenaline and he swerved the car over towards the median to see ahead. A red construction sign urged traffic to merge due to construction. Another exhalation. He was getting too old for this, he really was, but there had been no one at the AGS who had been ready to take over. Once he'd had hopes for Vallon Drake. The woman was smart and resourceful, but she'd proven to be too much of a loose cannon, like her father. It was going to take more years and maturation than he might have to give before she'd be ready. Something to discuss with Snow, when he saw him.

The traffic inched along, the red SUV now five cars behind as Gleason merged into the other lane and sped up a little as the cars began to stream past the construction site, with its huge paving machines. A flag person stood there waving her slow sign around, and Gleason touched the brakes, just as a large black SUV roared out from beyond the equipment to block the road right in front of him.

He slammed on the brakes and knew what was happening. The hotel had called him in. They'd used the construction to corner him. He aimed the car for the space behind the black SUV, slammed into construction pylons, and slid towards the back of the SUV.

Doors flung open and then something shattered Gleason's side window. The padding on the passenger side door exploded. A gust of hot cement and cordite filled his nose and he slammed his foot onto the gas amidst the sound of more gunfire.

The rear door window shattered and the thud-thud-thud of bullets came from his door. He was past the damn SUV, but the traffic was still snarled up ahead. He couldn't get away fast enough. He aimed the car for the rough desert beside the road. It might tear the undercarriage out, but it also might let him bypass this bottleneck. The rear glass imploded and something stung his left shoulder. Something else slammed into his back and he felt something warm running down the back of his shirt and into his trousers. The hot air through the window suddenly seemed cold. He hit the edge of the pavement and dropped down into gravel and sand. The car skidded sideways, seemed to bury his right wheel up to the axel.

No. This could not happen like this. He was going to make it.

He stepped on the gas again and the car lurched forward. More bullets slammed the metal, shattered his windshield. Something caught his left arm and his hand went numb, dropped off the steering wheel. He fought the slewing car one-handed.

Another thump into his back threw him against the steering wheel. He uprighted himself, but the damn gas pedal seemed almost impossible to push. He started coughing—bright red gobs that spilled down his front and splattered the dashboard. The evening sunlight had gone hard white, with flashes of lightning through it. He winced against the glare, winced against the pain that finally reached his nerve centers and sent them screaming.

No. It was not happening. He kept the car going, aimed it where the construction seemed to end. Drove the car up onto the pavement again and almost was t-boned by a sports car trying to pass on the wrong side.

The car leveled out and he headed north, driving faster than he should, given the way his vision wavered in and out of focus and it was hard to breathe. The hot air slammed into him and sucked the moisture from his skin, just as his car seat and clothes absorbed his blood. He was bleeding out, or would unless he got medical attention, but turning in to a hospital wasn't an option. He glanced in what remained of his rearview mirror. A large black SUV was on his tail.

A small gasp of desperate pain escaped him. He had to keep going and he had to lose them. Life reduced to each labored breath and to reaching Landon to plan the comeback of the AGS.

§

Vallon ran through the forest she'd made. Pine and cedar branches caught at her clothes, the air stank of ozone and lightning. Her breath came in great inhalations, and not for the first time she was happy she ran for pleasure. She stretched her stride a little longer. The bare mile to the warehouse should be nothing for her. Long muscles stretched, joints took the concussion and gave. Through it all she was humming, her mind racing. It was finally time to do something. She was here. She -reached- for the girl she had touched before.

[I'm coming. Stay alive.] She sent calm. Relaxation.

There was no response, but that didn't mean that the girl was dead. It could just be she didn't know how to answer, young as she was.

The late sunlight sent golden columns through the dark foliage to illuminate the forest floor. Red needles had covered the soil and long ago turned into loam. Or so it looked. Sword fern sprouted on great splashes of green. Mushrooms and bracket fungus glowed palely, the fungus rotting the hearts of the trees, much like Amundson had rotted the heart of the AGS.

The bright glow of the imprisoned Gifted came from up ahead and she slowed to a walk. Best to gather her breath before she got there. Sea wind rippled the trees so their hush and groan became part of the quiet. A bright glow off to her right and the familiar scent of woodsmoke spoke of one of the Gifted—someone she should know.

But she had no time to figure out who. Hopefully her father would have included mention of her presence when he warned his men and women. She had no time for explaining what she'd decided to do during the run. The warehouse was ahead: its barbwire fence showed through the trees.

She slowed further and crept through the timber, keeping to the ever growing shadows as the light fell. The warehouse stood in the midst of its large parking lot, the concrete cracked and overgrown at the edges with dandelions and purple thistle. The warehouse itself was two-story, concrete-sided, probably as a result of being so close to the concrete factory down the road. What had once been yellow paint was stained the color of rust from rain on the old metal roof. The main door into the place faced toward the highway, but she faced a bank of loading docks—

the perfect place to unload truckloads of children and wounded or dead agents and their families.

Vallon's nails bit into her palms as she fisted her hands. Damn Amundson. All of them were innocents. None of the AGS agents ever thought of harming anyone. She knew. She's grown up among them.

She remained where she was, still and watching the rhythm of the guards Amundson had placed around the warehouse. There were plenty and they patrolled in pairs—as if that might save them from the effects of Change. All were of a type she'd become familiar with during the Murdoch affair and when she'd returned to work after convalescing—the big, brawny type who worked for Loadstone, the corporation to which Homeland Security had contracted most of their security and intelligence work. Mercenaries, in other words. Men who, for a price, really didn't give a damn about the people involved. It was all about the job, and if the job was to contain the students and other Gifted they'd picked up, then they'd do it at any cost.

Not good. Vallon swallowed. In the greying afternoon, floodlights flared on from the roof of the building, illuminating the parking lot and sides of the building like the sides of a fortress and effectively eliminating any hope of a stealth entrance. The only good thing was it made her slightly less queasy about what she was about to do.

She placed her palm on the moist earth. *Pangea, if you're out there like Xavier says, now's the time to really work with me.* She -reached- and pulled the rose-scented *kata* to her.

[Vallon, *Bela*, I am coming.]

She swung around from the warehouse. There was no sign of him, but the not too distant rumble of engines and clank of equipment suggested the National Guard were nearing. Once they were here, her task would be that much more difficult.

[I have to go now.]

She knew he would protest, and so cut their link. Then she turned back to the warehouse and pulled the vellum from her pocket. Sweat ran into her eyes as she tried to not only hold the forest in place, but also focus on what she would do to the warehouse. She sketched the fence gone, its ends now bowing inward to connect with the side of the warehouse, the forest extending inwards to its side.

Concrete wisped up like fog. The fence in front of her melted. Rusted equipment wisped away and reshaped to become young pines, whipping in an unnatural wind to either side of one of the warehouse truck docks.

The rose and ozone scent was so powerful it almost seared her lungs, but when she was done, the bitter ozone on her tongue and the first pangs of afterburn weighed on her shoulders.

But time was a-wasting and she had to get this done at all costs.

Keeping low to avoid being seen, she sprinted across to the warehouse door. The young trees rustled on either side of her and she took cover in their branches and looked over her shoulder. The bright flame that was Xavier was coming, but too slow to wait for him. The rumble of the soldier's vehicles was far too close and she needed the kids out of here before they arrived if at all possible. Guns and bullets could still cut a swath through them too easily.

She turned to the truck dock and closed her eyes, and flattened the vellum against the metal. She swiftly drew the truck dock and placed a small door in the center—unlocked.

The texture of the metal went soft and then hardened under her hands, a burst of ozone and roses went up her nose, and the afterburn increased like painful little cuts to her skin. She could deal. She opened her eyes and cautiously pushed the door open a half inch onto the loading dock. Listened.

There were distant sounds but nothing close. She pushed the door open further and checked inside, even though her Gifted senses said no one was there. No cameras either, at least from this angle. From behind her the sound of voices calling said that whoever was responsible for the building's security was sending men to protect this now-vulnerable part of the warehouse. She glanced down at the vellum. Hold the forest, the shifted fence, and the door in place, or let them go? She'd have better focus and better ability to deal with whatever she faced ahead if she wasn't holding them.

She let them go and the door went soft again, then melted into itself, leaving behind a sensation of new plastic; but that would be detectable only to a Gifted—or Jason. She shivered at the thought of him and how he was working against her and all her kind. She'd known when she first met him that there was something different about him. Now she realized that he was one of those people who was literally haunted by the loss of his wife to the point where he would do anything to get her back. If she was caught, she had no illusions that his deal with Amundson probably included an opportunity to have her back in captivity again. Apparently it didn't matter to him just how many people he hurt to get what he wanted, or to pay her back for her previous failure.

So the trick was to not get caught.

She -reached- and felt the glow of the Gifted students. Most were in a large group to her left and above, their mélange of scents carrying the iron scent of fear. Five others had been separated and were somewhere in the center of the building. That was where the young girl was.

She hesitated. If she went for the group of kids first, she'd be hampered by herding so many kids while she tried to free the other five. If she went for the five, she might never get a chance to get the larger group of kids. The young girl she'd connected with glowed like a light in the dark. For some reason the girl had been able to reach her—that had to mean something. But she'd always been taught to work for the greatest possible good, and if she didn't get the group of students out, there'd be that many more children potentially subject to research. For a moment she regretted that Xavier or one of the other agents wasn't with her. Call Xavier in? If she did, it would put him in more danger, when he was barely recovering from his ordeal with Landon.

Up and left it was. She padded along the concrete floor. The lack of dust said this route was used regularly. Ahead was a metal door, complete with security locks, and voices came from beyond it. If they came this way, the jig was up. Maybe she needed to rethink this. The large group of children were just above and to her left. She could create a staircase and get them out of there quickly once she had the others free. And she could do so without leaving them like sitting ducks in the loading dock area.

So change of plans.

She closed her eyes and leaned against the wall, -reaching- out to get a sense of the layout of the warehouse. Through the presence of groupings of people's flickering candle-like essences, she could trace where hallways were and where people congregated. She turned back the way she'd come and jogged quickly to the other end of the loading bay. Another metal door and another high-security electronic lock.

Changing the lock just might set off some kind of alarm. She stopped and considered. When she -reached- there was no one in the space beyond. She flattened the vellum against the wall and sketched the door with a narrow opening through its center while focusing the power there. The door shimmered and its center faded. She stepped through into a corridor and let the door reform behind her. She stood in a long white corridor with no doors except the one she'd come through and one at the other end. Harsh white light came from fluorescents so bright she winced. The air carried a strange metallic and almond tang, but not like her father's scent—like...

Poison.

Crap. She whirled and a security camera bubble was above the door. Her stomach clenched and she vomited, retching up bile that burned her throat and tongue. She forced herself upright and hoped that gave them some satisfaction. They were watching her. Well, let them watch.

She brought the vellum up but her breath hitched in her throat. Her lungs wouldn't work and she was gagged for air. Draw. Damn it. Hold your breath. She ignored her body's craving and sketched—hole in the door. Her knees gave and she fell. Pulled the vellum to her and clutched the pen so hard it hurt. Hell, hole in the wall, let the outside breezes dissipate what was in this air. The white light faded, vision contracted. Put a hole on the inside wall and send the poison out to inflict damage. She rolled on her side, pushed herself up to her knees as clean ocean wind filled her nose, but her strength wavered. The wall misted into place. No. She had to hold it, but the strength it took… Her fingers were barely able to move.

[I have you, *Bela*.]

The break in the wall solidified again and Xavier's powerful sending allowed her to release her concentration. She focused on moving her body; pushed herself to standing. The vellum fluttered from numb fingers. The pen clattered to the floor.

She retrieved them, holding them against her body, and limped to the wall that was open to the outside. Inhaled great gouts of sea air, and gradually her head cleared. She looked back at the camera. Bastards. Let them get their enjoyment of poisoning her, would they? Well, she'd see about that.

She hauled on the power and walked to the door, reached up, and placed her palm over the little dome over the camera lens. So just how would she do this? She'd never done anything like it before, but she'd once tried to use the power like cardiac paddles. It hadn't worked to revive the dead person, but it had sent a shock through the body. Well, let's see what it does to electronics.

She pulled power up from the earth and into the camera. The dome melted and ran hot plastic down the wall. The scent of frying wiring filled the room. She stepped back and staggered as an alarm claxon sounded. Not what she needed. And the sound drilled into her afterburn-fatigued brain and the painful muscle throb that came as afterburn increased. Okay. Maybe she'd gone a little overboard, but at least she didn't think they could track her with cameras anymore.

She turned.

The girl and the four other Gifted students were through the inner wall and still further inward. She stepped up to the hole in the wall, but a barrage of bullets sent her stumbling back for cover. She didn't know how many they were and she didn't want to harm any more than she had to. She sketched a forest in the hallway and drew the matter from the inner wall.

There were shouts and swearing, but when she looked up, thick pine branches stuck through the hole in the wall. She shoved through them, allowing the very center of the newly created forest to fade, while bullets cut through the foliage and slammed into tree trunks. She drew further on the wall across from her. A hole appeared, exposing a room.

White overhead lights. Examining table and naked figure pinned down. Girl. A man standing over her.

Bingo. She leapt across the hall.

The man pulled a syringe out of the girl's arm and a huge explosion rocked the building.

Vallon went flying.

CHAPTER 27 — MEWLING MASSES

"It's begun."

Jason ran his hand over the landsat close-up image of the warehouse and environs. A forest surrounded the warehouse now, and though it looked like it had been standing for a few hundred years, it was *wrong*. It felt—*artificial*—*plastic*.

He looked up at Amundson from the image flattened on Amundson's desk with the help of a paper weight, a box of paper clips, a stapler, and an empty water glass. Amundson stood by the window looking down on the evening-grayed streets of Seattle. To the far west, the sky was red with sunset over the Olympic Mountains. The day was ending and so were other things—like Vallon's hope for freedom. She'd be in his hands by the end of the day if the plans went ahead like he and Amundson had made them.

"Alert the installation security," Amundson said, and the third person in the room, Amundson's lovely Eurasian pet agent, Moore, sent a text message that would be picked up regardless of what Vallon and her little Gifted friends might do to the installation's phone lines.

A flicker out of the corner of his eye brought Jason's gaze around to the other diagram flattened on the top of Amundson's desk. This one was weighed down with Amundson's name plate and another glass in addition to the edge of the landsat image. On it were the architectural designs of the warehouse's rebuilt interior and exterior security specifications. Something flickered and changed. The outer fence, followed in quick succession with the warehouse wall.

"They've been breached."

Amundson nodded. "Tell them. Protocol number one is to be put in action."

Moore hesitated, and not for the first time Jason wondered what Amundson had on her that she helped him. Protocol one called for gassing the intruder, hopefully enough to incapacitate them quickly. She nodded and sent the message.

Jason turned his attention from the landsat image to the warehouse schematics. Another flicker. "They're in the containment room."

But the outer wall flickered and felt strange under his fingers. The inner wall, too. "Something's wrong. Containment's not working."

"Fucking Gifted," Amundson said and crossed to his desk, studying the schematic as if he had a hope of reading what had changed. "I'm not taking a chance they'll win this little bout. I'm not having a bunch of half-trained Gifted children running around the countryside!"

He picked up his cell phone and stabbed a number. "Hello, General," he said, and Jason froze.

The only general they were dealing with was Adjutant General Reginald McReedy, responsible for Washington's National Guard and HS advisor to the state governor.

Moore shifted in her chair and Jason met her gaze. She was still an inscrutable beauty, but something about her eyes hinted of terror. So she wasn't doing this by choice at all, and she didn't like where this was going. He turned back to Amundson, who was exchanging pleasantries.

"It's not that bad yet. There's still plenty of time to contain them." He hoped.

But Amundson just waved him away.

"How close are your men to being in place?" He listened, nodded. "Our emphasis has got to be on containment. The bastards have broken in. We can't take a chance on these terrorists getting loose."

Another listen. A nod and then: "All of the researchers signed waivers when they signed on to this job. The security detail knew there were dangers, given what the subjects could do and any necessary countermeasures."

Another nod. "I appreciate that."

He hung up and turned to Jason. "Those bastards are going to have the surprise of their lives if they think they can walk right into my installation and out again."

§

Concrete and paint chips and bits of wood rained down over Vallon where she'd tumbled into a corner. Her ears rang and her head filled with the roar that had effectively deafened her. A shooting pain ran up and down her right arm, the end of a long sliver of wood impaled there. She stuffed the vellum in her pocket, gritted her teeth, and yanked it free. The pen, thankfully, she'd managed to hang onto.

Blood ran down her arm in a constant, dripping flow. Super. She needed to drain her power like she needed the proverbial hole in the head, which Amundson would be all too happy to give her. The bastard was flipping shooting at her. At least his National Guardsmen were. And the explosion was close, too. Too close.

[Xavier?] Please, please, please let him be okay.

[Here, *Bela*. And you are unharmed?]

[Just shaken. Don't come inside. I need you there as my back up.] No need to tell him about her arm. She cut the link and picked herself up. The trees she'd created in the corridor had mostly faded away when her concentration was lost, but the end of the corridor where the gunfire had come from had not been quite so lucky. Whatever ordinance the Guardsmen were using, it had cut through the walls and exploded only after entering the building. This one had happened to lodge in the corridor. She stumbled to the hole into the other room, sickened by the destruction and the fact that Amundson was prepared to take out his own people.

The man she had seen was no longer in the room. She clambered through the hole in the wall, then stumbled at the thick coppery smell. Something was wrong. She glanced up at the camera on the wall and knew she had to get going. Another boom sent a shudder through the building and emphasized her need for haste. Given Amundson's disregard for life, her entrance into the building could be all he needed to order that all the children be killed.

She hurried to the table and stopped. Her stomach dropped. Young girl with the budding womanhood of the fifteen- or sixteen-year-old. She had sweat-blackened brown hair and cornflower blue eyes that stared sightlessly at the ceiling. The syringe lay discarded on the floor beside her. Vallon's chest tightened with the need to cry. All that potential lost because one man was afraid of what he didn't understand.

Amundson had done this. He would do anything to stop the children from being freed. She would stop him. Had to. She -reached- and pulled out the vellum one more time. Spread it on the table next to the unknown girl's head and erased the walls between the rooms that held the captive children. As the walls faded, she ran, leapt over the remains of the wall into the next room, but the life essence of the pony-tailed girl faded and winked out. She was too late. Ran for the next room and found the same. The light in the red-haired boy's eyes flickered out.

"No! Dammit no!" Fury filled her. She leapt into the next room and found herself face to face with the man she had seen with the syringe. White coated, narrow face, sallow skin. With him was a dark-haired woman with South Asian coloring, also in a lab coat. Doctors? Didn't matter. The woman held a syringe to the arm of the young girl on the table—Vallon's girl!

"How dare you!" Vallon screamed. She grabbed the power from the ley lines under her feet and sent it bursting up through the floor. It inundated everything in the room in an eerie, amber glow. The woman screamed. The man tried to run, but his legs wisped away just as the woman's face streamed apart at the edges. The table melted under the girl, just as the forms of the two people collapsed.

The echoes of the woman's scream turned to mewls and filled the room, filled Vallon's head with a sound that she would never forget. She cut off the flow of power—too late. She stood in a lightning-scented room with the girl freed of her bonds and trying to find her way from the table between two pulsing bloody masses spread on the floor. Vallon went to her and carried her to a clean space of linoleum.

She was young, long-legged and slim hipped as a colt, brown eyed and brown skinned, with a sweet scent of cardamom and warmed amber that made Vallon think of sweaters and hot chocolate in winter. Her eyes were wide with comprehension and shock, and bruises and blood spatter covered her arms and the thin hospital gown she wore. She had tightly curled hair in a modern afro that showed off her high cheekbones.

"You okay?" Vallon asked, holding her shoulders. The girl's Gifted presence burned into her and sent her afterburn jangling, her legs wobbling for a moment.

"You!" The girl's wide eyes went wider. "I *know* you. I dreamed about you—or something."

Vallon shook her head. "Not a dream. I'm Vallon. I'm from the AGS. We'll have to figure out what it was some other time. Can you walk okay?"

The girl took a wobbly step. Another. "I'm Keira. I'll manage." Then her eyes filled with tears. "You didn't get to the others in time, did you?"

Vallon hesitated, but there was no time for niceties. She shook her head. "We still have a chance of getting the kids upstairs out, though."

She -reached- and the glow of their massed presence still gleamed. They were still alive so far.

"Come on." She scanned the room, pulled open a cupboard, and found a second thin surgical gown. Tossed it to the girl. "Better put that on as a robe, I'm thinking."

Keira pulled it on as Vallon led her through the adjoining rooms while trying to shield the already shocky girl from the sight of her dead friends. The walls reformed behind them. Then they were back to the hallway. And she was fighting back the déjà vu image of just what she'd done. She poked her head through the hole into the hallway and a bullet slammed into the wall beside her, shattering concrete shards in all directions. She fell back, wiping her own blood off her face.

"You're cut," Keira said, dabbing at something on Vallon's forehead. Vallon found the wound—a deep slash on her brow.

"Only a flesh wound, but we're cut off from going this way." Because she was *not* going to do something like she'd done in Keira's room again. She was not a killer. It wasn't what she'd signed on to the AGS for.

Another boom rocked the building and she could hear distant screams. Was Amundson purposely shelling his own installation, or were they hitting the warehouse by accident?

Xavier. The other Gifted outside. She turned her sight beyond this room and the next and *saw*.

National Guard pulled up on the road, lethal equipment turned in the warehouse's direction. But as she watched, something was launched and was followed by a terrific explosion that tore up the earth on one side of the warehouse. Three of the bright flares of Gifted were gone. She staggered back.

She looked at the two unmarked walls of the room. If she broke through one of them, it would take them to another room that might give her better access to the outside. She could get Keira out to a chance at safety. Xavier could get her out while she came back for the other kids.

"If you're thinking about getting me out and leaving the others, it ain't going to happen." The shock had left Keira's gaze and she had her arms crossed over her chest. She was all of thirteen or fourteen, but she had a stubbornness in the set of her chin that Vallon recognized from too many years of looking in her own mirror.

"But it's not safe here. There are guns and bombs."

"Ye-ah. And there are bad people with guns out there, too."

Someone tried the door to the room. Locked, thank God, but the heavy-looking metal door rattled on its hinges. They were coming from both directions. She had to make a decision.

Go out or go for the kids. Keira glared.

"Fine! All right?" She grabbed the vellum and saw Keira's eyes light up as she sketched a stairwell that ran up through the floor. Counters, ceiling, and wall between the rooms melted away into a misted spiral stairway that swiftly solidified.

"Holy cow." Keira's eyes were round again. "That's not something they teach in the academy."

"Right. So I broke the rules. Now come on." They raced up to the next floor, the stairs already fading under them, and found themselves in what had to be a fifty-foot-long narrow hallway. Three quarters of the way down, two security guards turned towards them.

CHAPTER 28 — CORDITE AND GRILLED CHEESE

The rumbling of the National Guard vehicle engines had died away to be replaced by the sounds of military machines of death—ordinance and explosions they were using on the land around the warehouse and on the warehouse itself. The sunlight had finished fleeing the sky, leaving the heavens gradually absorbing the darkness under the trees that Vallon might have abandoned, but Xavier had rebuilt. He leaned against the trunk of a cedar, half watching the direction and distance of the bombs—so far they hadn't come near to him—while most of his attention was on the bright flare of Vallon's presence in the dark hulk of the warehouse.

He did not like his role of watcher. He liked it less now, when his physical condition made him good for not much else. He flexed his jaw and his fists tight. At least from this vantage he could back Vallon up as she'd asked.

In the coming darkness, floodlights lit up the exterior parking lots except for the area Vallon had changed. So far, no one had remarked on that dark wedge in the fence. Blessedly, the unGifted didn't see it as an anomaly.

Overhead, the night-bruised sky had already shown the first few stars, all hidden now in the brilliance surrounding the warehouse. Grey smoke trailed up against the deep blue.

So far she was okay. He'd watched in horror as Gifted flares went out inside the warehouse and had tried to content himself with the fact that Vallon was strong and resourceful. She'd proved that so many times, but this time seemed even more precarious with the weight of the United States government against her. Every part of him ached to go after her, but in his depleted condition, he was more apt to be a liability. But sitting on the sidelines had never suited him well. Of course, when he *had* finally taken a side, look at where it had got him. The irony of it was not lost on him.

A watcher again. Sitting on the sidelines simply holding the shielding forest in place, when at full strength he could have wiped the National Guard and the whole warehouse away.

Not that he would. Though he'd killed on the orders of the Council before, he would not use power to destroy. That was an edict that tradition said flowed right back to the beginning of the Council and the time of the Diaspora. Destruction, so the edict of the mighty First Cartos, Lazar, said, brought destruction back onto the destroyer.

Vallon's presence shifted through the warehouse, now joined with a second Gifted, so she had rescued one of them, but they were not free yet and the cluster of Gifted that were the children still were held stationary, while around them the halls and rooms of the warehouse were filled with massing numbers of unGifted. They were coming for Vallon, and he'd felt her rage and revulsion at what she had already done to protect the girl. The trouble was, in his condition he was not sure he could deal with them from this distance and still hold the protective forest that hid Francis Drake's Gifted, who massed in the forest as if they planned to attack.

The Gifted might not hold as much power as he did, but that could be for a number of reasons, not least of which was lack of training—something he was thankful they lacked, given their lack of understanding of who and what they were. But they had learned without the Council's guidance the benefits of working together. The Gifted had fallen back from the edge of the warehouse fences and now their essences came together in two masses. They drew power from Pangea—were going to do something.

"Great Mother Pangea, please let it not harm Vallon." His words disappeared into the darkness, but here in this Creation-made forest, surely she was listening. Surely she would hear him when her children were fighting for their lives.

But from what he had learned of Francis Drake, the man could not be trusted. Not the way he had used Vallon and Fi and so many other Gifted and partially Gifted before—or tried to.

There was movement in the warehouse. Vallon's bright flame wavered. UnGifted closed in on her position.

Dark streaks flared in her essence. She was injured—wounded!

That was it. He left his tree and started through the last few feet of forest. [Vallon! *Bela!* I am coming.]

[Don't you dare! I'm fine. They just got me in my shoulder and I'm bleeding like a stuck pig.]

[You must leave now. The Gifted are massing and I hear the clank of the National Guard again. Something is happening.]

[Give me five.]

She cut him off and he swore. He was an actor, not an observer. Did she mean five seconds? Five minutes? Five hours?

He fretted at the entrance to the funnel of fence that led to the wall. His head spun from lack of blood pressure when he moved too fast. Landon Snow had almost completed the depletion the Council had started. Much more blood loss and he would be totally useless.

He ground his teeth and turned his attention back to Vallon. She was close to the mass of students. At least there was that, but for all he could tell, she was trapped in a different room and the unGifted had cut her off.

A sick feeling of despair caught in his stomach that he would not tolerate. Five seconds, then. He could not wait five minutes.

[*Bela*, I am coming.]

§

The pain in her shoulder left Vallon almost nauseous and afraid to breathe as she leaned against the office desk with her head back. The room was small, a researcher's office, she supposed, based on the anatomy posters on the white-painted walls and the library of books on human physiology.

A clatter of desk drawers and the patter of feet, and Keira dropped onto her knees beside Vallon. "I've gone through the desk. There's nothing there. No bandages, no rags, not even a tissue."

Beyond them the wall rang with pounding where once there had been a door. Vallon had wiped it away so they were safe for the moment until the men thought to shoot their way through. Of course, they were also cut off from escape, and the too-frequent explosions in the building seemed to be coming closer.

She closed her eyes for a minute, but the red through her eyelids seemed to telescope into darkness far too easily.

She needed to get moving and get the kids out before Amundson's men had cut through the confusion and come up with a solid plan. She tried to get up, but movement sent blood gushing down her arm. She needed something to stop the bleeding or she'd be no more able to use the power than Xavier was. Less, probably.

"The bottom of your gown," she choked out, her eyes clamped shut against the darkness that ate at her vision. She didn't dare pass out or they were both dead—or worse, captive. "Keira, I need you to tear a strip off your gown and wad part of it up. Press that into the wound. Then I need you to take the rest of the strip and tie it over my shoulder to hold the wad in place. You got that?"

She squinted her eyes open and Keira was already struggling with the hem of her gown.

"Scissors. In the desk, I'll bet."

Keira scrambled to get them just as the pounding on the wall stopped. Vallon opened her eyes. That could not be good. Keira had found the scissors and was carefully cutting a strip.

"Come here."

Keira obeyed and Vallon grabbed the strip and tore it off the gown and quickly wadded it up.

"Another one," she ordered and Keira obeyed, copying Vallon's process.

The thud, thud, thud of rapid gunfire came through the wall, and the wall where the door had been began to shudder. Plasterboard dust clouded into the room. Amundson's men had found their solution.

She scrambled to her feet with Keira's help. The kid was good, she had to give her that. Thoughtful gaze and a quiet mouth, efficient in how she moved.

"What do you think? We're close to the kids. What's the best way to get to them?"

Keira pursed her lips and looked around, then her gaze distanced for a minute as she -reached-, and cleared when she returned. She staggered against Vallon.

"Sorry. I needed to orient myself, and the darn drugs and the bleeding they did to me makes it more difficult."

Vallon nodded and braced herself on the desk to turn. The damned wound stung like a bitch and seemed to steal the strength from her legs and arms. She had been shot by the men in the corridor before she could drag Keira in here to cover. Thankfully the bullet had hit her left shoulder above her already injured arm. "Through there, then."

Keira nodded. "Are you sure you can do it?"

"Watch me." Vallon managed a grin and scrubbed her bloody hands on her clothes, then spread the vellum, -reached-, and began to draw, reshaping the walls so they created a closed corridor right through to the kids' holding room. A bullet broke through the wall behind her, carrying the acid tang of cordite, and ripped past, barely missing Keira.

Vallon grabbed her and stumbled as the pain and weakness hit her. A stream of bullets barely missed her and the cordite became a sickening miasma—or maybe that was the pain in her arm as she choked back bile and grabbed Keira to keep her down. Behind them, the single bullet hole was being chewed open by more gunfire.

"Come on!" Doubled over, the blood flowing down her back and arm, she shuffled forward when all she wanted to do was curl up and sleep for a million years.

[*Bela*, I'm coming] cut through her half daze.

[No! Stay back. It's too dangerous.]

But he'd already cut her off, damned man. Had to be a hero and go rushing in. It had got him shot in New Madrid, and would likely do the same here. She should know. She cradled her injured arm as they burst in among the other schoolkids, and she let the corridor wisp away, returning to intervening rooms. That might have bought them some time. They might not know where she and Keira had gone.

The room was a barracks—that was the only way to describe it. Lines of cots covered with flimsy-looking grey blankets were bolted to the floor. An open doorway let in the sound of dripping water and the scent of institutional soap and shower. At one end of the room, a series of long narrow tables showed where the meals had been served. The scent of grilled cheese sandwiches and ketchup still hung in the air. Beyond the tables, what appeared to be a narrow anteroom led to a solidly locked door.

Keira was surrounded by the sea of kids. There must have been forty of them. They were all shapes and sizes, but they were young, eleven and twelve years up to about Keira's age. There were none of the juniors and seniors she remembered bullying her when she was in the academy. None who might have the power and the training to help with the escape.

"Where are the others? The older kids?"

Keira's gaze held steady, but the rest of the kids looked away. "I'm it," she said. "Most of the older ones were killed when they tried to escape when we first arrived. Then a few of us tried to do something from inside."

A young boy with tawny skin and brown hair stepped up beside Keira. "Those they didn't take downstairs, they took away. They never came back."

A few of the younger kids cried silently and Vallon knew there had to be older brothers and sisters involved, as well as people these youngsters knew and admired.

It meant it all fell to her and she just wasn't sure of her strength. She seriously needed a chair right now. Or a bed. Well, maybe a bed and a doctor. *Cut it out, Drake. You can't have any of those things, at least not yet.*

"Okay," she said. "We all want to get out of here, so you are all going to need to do exactly as I say."

The clang of a door and the sound of heavy footfall said she had no time to say anything. Amundson's men were here.

CHAPTER 29 — BLOOD LINKS

She was being just like Vallon. She was.

The cool ocean wind might be streaming in from the northwest carrying the scent of the tide, but it couldn't displace the gunpowder and smoke that came off the warehouse that she and the others stood beside. Well, not quite beside. They stood outside the fence within the cover of cedar and spruce and pine trees that the ashes of roses scent said Vallon had made and the spicy, incense scent said Xavier held.

They stood in a circle, linked by their hands, and Fi felt the others like a not-quite-comfortable pop and fizzle through the touch of their palms. On her left was a woman named Drew, who had worked with Francis Drake for a long time. On her right was a man named Jake, who had been rescued with his children. His wife had died. What held them all there was the knowledge this needed to be done. Like Vallon had said, Amundson had to be stopped. Or at least *this* had to be stopped. The kids inside the warehouse had to be freed, and so did the agents held prisoner in Amundson's HS headquarters in Seattle. They couldn't chance splitting up and being taken one by one, so they had to work together. Forty-eight Gifted, most of whom were Francis Drake's men, sprinkled through with rescued AGS agents. He had split them into two groups with the intension of having them work together on the two parts of the project—as he called it. She stood in the smaller one, charged with stopping the National Guard and the research station, while the other, larger group, would address the Seattle HS office building.

And she was part of it right from the beginning—not dragged into it by Vallon or anyone else. *She'd* made decisions about what she thought was right and wrong and whose side she was on. She was out here of her own volition because she might not have the power and training Vallon had, but she did have something to give, and that was important. Each of them was important because they added to the whole.

That was a little bit too much like what her mother had always told her, but her mother wasn't here and forcing her. No, this was different.

"It's time," said Francis Drake from his place in the circle. He looked tall and strong, like the father she'd never known. He was someone who was trying to make things right. To get their people out and stop the unGifted from doing this.

It was like everyone took a breath together. Everyone closed their eyes and there was only the flare of their presence and the ocean wind in her face and the shiver of anticipation.

"Draw the power up," Francis said.

She -reached- into the earth and drew up the perfumed power until it filled her like when she was a very young child and had spilled her mother's perfume bottle all over her clothes. The rose-scented power shifted and took on the scent of each of the Gifted in the circle.

"Send the power through to me as the focus," Francis called.

Fi obeyed, the rose scent flowing like a river from her hand to Drew, into her from Jake, until their scents mingled and all there was, was a spiced mélange of power that took on Francis' scent of almond. She rode with the power, following it down into the earth again as Francis aimed it like a weapon.

A weird whine cut the air, and she opened her eyes. Something like a candle trailed across the sky. Then the forest beyond where they stood exploded with light. The concussion threw her backwards into a tree trunk. She landed in a heap, momentarily blind and deaf. Then someone to her right started screaming. A woman. She forced herself up, and smoke covered everything. The forest, the scene, looked so far away and sounded like they were at the end of a tunnel. Someone was administering first aid to the woman while Francis was yelling through the smoke. Trees flamed beyond him, turning the scene even bloodier than it was.

Something warm on her leg and she touched it and brought her hand up. Red. Blood. She was bleeding and she couldn't see what had caused it. Suddenly the pain cut in and she gave a small cry.

"My God! You're bleeding!" Jake said, suddenly materializing beside her and catching her arm. "Medic! We need a medic here!"

Fi pulled away. She couldn't wait.

She had to find Vallon. She might be hurt. She might be the woman screaming. She -reached- for her friend, but Vallon didn't answer. Her

Gifted flame and the scent of ashes of roses was there, but it was streaked with grey. Not healthy. She was hurt. Fi spun around, seeking.

There. Through the trees, but Jake had caught her arm again. He forced Fi to sit on the ground and wait while someone else bandaged her leg, and all the while Fi knew she had to be gone. Had to find Vallon. Help her.

Francis Drake hauled her up to standing. "You okay to do this thing?"

This thing. This thing? Her head was so muzzy she wasn't sure what he was asking; he *had* been looking for Vallon at one time. She nodded.

"Good girl." He nodded at Jake to help her into the circle where they all joined hands again. There were more flights of those firework birds and more booms. The earth shook under her feet so she staggered into Jake and Drew. Their circle was smaller, but they reached for the power again and Francis drew in what they collected so his Gifted presence grew larger and then he dove into the earth and aimed the power towards the hulking presence of the warehouse and the people beyond, who were shooting at them. Across the circle, the flames in the trees turned Francis Drake's face crimson as he seemed to exhale and pour the power back into the earth.

They kept flowing into him, but something wasn't right. The expression on Francis's face—was it just the light, or had his eyes taken on the same look as her mother's just before she attacked Seattle?

Fi staggered, but neither Drew nor Jake released her hands.

Fi followed the aimed power as it breached the earth like a geyser, pouring up around the warehouse and the armed men. UnGifted winked out. Trucks and weapons faded. But not all. A cadre of soldiers still fired at the forest and the sagging warehouse. What was he doing? She tried to spread the power in that direction, but Francis pulled it back into a narrower flow. The warehouse walls melted like butter under the sun. Within its walls, the candles of unGifted flickered and faded, then winked out. Concrete, brick, metal, and mortar all began to break apart and wheel into a giant, grinding maelstrom.

But in the midst of the whirlwind, glowed Vallon. With her, the mélange of Gifted children. What was Francis Drake doing? He could hurt them. Why had he left some of the soldiers still shooting?

This didn't make sense. It didn't make sense at all. Why take a chance on injuring the children and Vallon? Why leave the soldiers at all?

Because Francis Drake can't be trusted. Vallon's voice cut into her brain.

No, he can't be trusted. Whatever he was doing, it wasn't in an effort to rescue Vallon and the children. It was like he was trying to get them killed. If Vallon was killed, it would rid him of someone he hadn't been able to twist to his bidding. If the children were killed, it would lead to a war that wouldn't end because the Gifted would be out for revenge. Was that what he wanted? A war?

Surely a war wouldn't last that long, because the Gifted could simply wipe the unGifted armies off the map.

And leave the Gifted, no doubt under Francis Drake, in control.

It made too much sense even to her pain-muddled brain. She couldn't let this happen.

Fi tried to pull loose again, but Drew and Jake held on.

"Stop! We have to stop. This isn't what it looks like." No one stopped. She tried to stop the flow of power through her, but the circuit was complete. Power was sucked up through her and then channeled to Vallon's father.

She had to stop it somehow. She struggled in Drew and Jake's grasp, but they held on too tight. The warehouse whirlwind now rose eight stories high. She had to make him stop.

She leaned down and bit Jake's hand and sank her teeth in. He bellowed and released her and she turned and managed to rip loose from Drew, then stumbled and tumbled to the ground. The power flow, interrupted, stopped, and the warehouse and column of National Guard reformed. The encircled Gifted staggered, but Francis Drake's horrible gaze impaled her.

"What have you done?" he roared.

"You can't do this! You're going to let those children die. And Vallon!"

Francis Drake advanced on her. "That's ridiculous! I was trying to help them. Give them a chance to get out during the destruction."

She scrambled to her feet and almost fell when her injured leg gave under the afterburn fatigue.

"No you're not. Vallon was right. You want a war, and what better way to get the Gifted to fight than if their children die under an assault?"

The sky lit up with another explosion and she whirled around. A direct hit on the warehouse sent a column of red flames into the sky.

"Vallon!" she screamed and started to stagger through the trees toward the flaming building.

From behind her, all she heard was Francis Drake yelling.

§

The sound of heavy footfall rang too loud from the anteroom to the students' holding room. The children started to scream and flooded towards the far end of the room—not that that would help them if the soldiers let loose a volley of bullets. The copper stink of fear hung in the air. Vallon turned to face the new threat, but she knew she couldn't keep on going much longer. The blood loss from her shoulder was telling on her like a heavy weight that made her knees shake. So were her hands, dammit. She fumbled the vellum out of her pocket and pulled out her pen. Let the floor soften in the anteroom and hold the men. She reached for power and it rammed into her so hard her legs gave. She tumbled to the floor and hit her head on a cot.

What the hell? The air reeked with almonds. The walls began to sag, then came apart. From the anteroom came a man's gut-wrenching scream, too swiftly cut off. A powerful wind ripped through the room and the cots strained against the screws that held them to the floor. All of the bedding ripped loose.

The ceiling groaned and tore apart, piece-by-piece, ripped up and above them into a roaring whirlwind. The bedding followed it, but not before the corner of a sheet whipped her face. She staggered back towards the children.

"What's happening?" Keira yelled.

What indeed? Power didn't act like this. It could melt the matter and transform it. To create a tornado required intention, and the almond scent told her everything she needed to know.

In a tornado, there was a very good chance she and the children would be killed. That had to be her father's intention all along. Kill the kids and he'd have created a very strong motivation for the Gifted to keep fighting. Give them their kids alive and there was far greater chance of them heading for cover wherever they could to keep their children safe. Her father was nothing if not ruthless.

"We have to get out of here." Because he'd already set the warehouse up as a target, and the whirlwind was tearing at her clothes and hair and she felt like she could get lifted up without too much more effort. "Get the kids organized. Get them holding onto something." What, exactly, she wasn't sure.

The floor wavered and faded under them and a cot ripped loose and was dragged towards the center of the room. Its shift jarred other cots and they tore loose as well, becoming a shifting, dangerous sea of furniture.

She had to get them out of here. Undoubtedly the lower floor would also be affected, but it would be that much closer to the ground and outside.

Using one of the still-stationary cots, she swiftly sketched on the vellum and then stole from the streaming power to do her bidding. The taste of almonds was bitter in her mouth as she poured it into an opening in the floor and stairs. It took everything she had to hold them in place. The blood loss was telling. She closed her eyes. "Keira, take a look and tell me what you see down there. Be careful."

Keira dropped to her knees and peered carefully over the edge. "Corridor. There's no one there."

"Good. So get them down." Vallon's knees gave so she knelt on the floor, her forehead slowly sinking towards the vellum.

Just a little longer. Just a little longer. The children started down, hesitantly at first and then in a flood. She closed her eyes for a moment.

"Vallon?! Come on. We're down."

Vallon stirred at Keira's voice. She didn't remember the kids all going. She didn't remember laying her head on the vellum, either, but good thing she had. The cot was shaking loose of its moorings. The vortex hauled one, another, another, up through the even larger hole in the ceiling, and the vellum shuddered under her cheek. She grabbed the vellum and pen and went to stuff them in her pocket when suddenly the maelstrom stopped. An instant of absolute quiet.

Then the power collapsed in on itself, unmaking everything it had made. Cots slammed into place. Ceiling closed. Floor closing up at her feet, stairs fading. She leapt for them, felt the tear of her matter ripping through the floor, landed on the stairs—

And fell through to crash onto the children.

She landed on her shoulder and the room exploded into bright light and pain. She curled in on herself, but soft hands and falling water disturbed her. And her name.

"Vallon! Vallon we have to get out of here. I can hear voices. There're people coming. Vallon, wake up, Please!"

Vallon groaned and rolled over and looked up at Keira, who had frightened tears streaming down her face.

"Who died?" Vallon groaned and tried to sit up—just moving took her breath away. She swallowed back the pain and tried to smile but didn't feel like her effort was that successful.

"I thought you did," Keira choked out.

"Sorry. Still here. How are the kids I landed on?"

"Okay. Bruised. Scared."

Vallon stood, with Keira's aid. From down the hall came voices, getting louder. She closed her eyes and -reached-. One room between them and the outside, though the wedge of 'safe' zone she'd created in the fence line was a long ways away. If she was stronger, she could create a path through the outside rooms, but the way her hands were shaking, she wasn't sure she could last that long. Better to get them outside and then deal with the fence and whoever was there. She explained her plan to Keira and then led off down the hall until she reached a door into a room that shared the warehouse's outside wall.

She pulled the door open and leaned in to check for safety. Then the sun went nova behind her.

§

The Seattle towers glittered back at Wolf Amundson like pillars of hope in a night-bound world. Northward, the battle for America hopefully was finished as swiftly as it started, and then it would simply be a matter of collecting the Gifted that Landon Snow had so kindly catalogued. Then it would be over. America would be safe and all the cities of America could slumber as peacefully as Seattle looked from this height.

He closed his eyes a moment, then studied the reflections in the night-darkened floor to ceiling glass. He sat in the HS boardroom on the fourteenth floor of the tower that housed Seattle Station. Behind him around the boardroom table, his elite core of agents, Page, his E.A. Moore, and Jason Bryson all monitored the situation in Anacortes. The voices of the agents conversing with the National Guard communications officers and with the warehouse placed a quiet murmur over the hush of the air conditioning. Moore sat rigidly with her back against the wall, awaiting his orders, next to the bank of phones she monitored. The woman's delicate face was drawn and pale, as if she knew her days were numbered by the number of days the rest of the Gifted survived. Actually, she was right. The years he had had need of her as his mole inside the AGS were over. Her Gifted brother, snuggly kept where Amundson could easily decide whether he lived or died. Moore had done everything in her power to make sure he lived.

And now her efforts didn't matter.

The last of the room's occupants hung over a map of Anacortes as if his life depended upon it. Jason Bryson had changed in the short time Amundson had known him. His eyes had turned from intelligent consideration to the gleam of a zealot, and his face had transformed to the blotchy ruddiness of the fanatic. If this battle against the Gifted was important to Amundson, it was life breaking to Bryson; and it was not clear why, except he wanted the Drake woman for some reason.

Bryson was one to keep an eye on, for an unknown purpose meant that he could not be wholly trusted. But in the meantime, he *could* be a useful tool. And when he lost that usefulness, well, then, there was the need to understand just why Jason Bryson could do what he could do.

Their gazes met in the reflection, Bryson's jet-black gaze meeting Wolf's ice-blue, and for a moment it felt like a test of wills, as if Bryson knew just what Wolf was thinking. But Wolf held his ground and finally Bryson looked away, back to his maps of the battle. So far they knew the Gifted were there, they just didn't know what they were going to do.

"There's more change," Bryson said into the quiet room.

Wolf swung his chair around. "Where?"

"There're walls changing. It looks like they're going for the research section."

Wolf sat up. He was not letting those subjects be taken. They posed too much danger. "Alert the doctors. They're to deal with probable breach of containment. Use final protocol."

Moore jerked in her chair and her knuckles went white on the chair arms. Then she went still as her Eurasian mask of inscrutability smoothed back in place. It was one of the things he admired about her, but it made her predictable.

"Orders sent, Sir," said the broad-shouldered, dependable Page.

Whoever was intruding into the facility wouldn't find what they sought when they reached those subjects, but it would lure them deeper into the installation, just as he'd planned.

Bryson reported changes in the research section walls and then an attempt to leave.

"We have them pinned down, Sir," Page said.

"Good. Tell the National Guard to aim for those coordinates."

The room went totally quiet and all eyes reflected in the glass at him.

"Just do it. I know what I'm saying." Wolf shifted his chair to catch Page's eye and nodded. The man obeyed.

"They report a direct hit into that quadrant."

He closed his eyes, imagining the smoke, the blood, the mayhem. Maybe he'd dealt the blow he needed right there, if the Gifted had gone in enmass.

"We've got change. It looks like they're headed for the subject quarters upstairs. They've created a stairwell that will join corridor 2C."

"On it, Sir." Page spoke into his hands-free phone. The others worked quickly over their keyboards. Bryson, focused on the schematics, jerked upright. He looked around the room. "Something's happening."

Wolf turned to him. "Well? Report, mister."

Bryson shook his head, then he shot to his feet and glanced in Moore's direction. "Change. Here. While we're focused on them, they're attacking us here!" He looked around the room as if he saw something there, but there was nothing. Only a terrified looking man and the rest of Wolf's agent's staring.

Wolf glanced at Moore, and the tension in her body said that maybe Bryson was right. Could it really be happening like this and he wouldn't even know it?

He wasn't taking a chance. "Grab your equipment on battery power. We're going out."

He stood and led them to the elevator, pushing past the other agents in the offices. He didn't want a panic slowing their exit. Avoiding the elevator, they plunged into the emergency staircase.

Sixteenth floor. Fifteen. Fourteen. Their feet clattered down the stairs. "Report, Bryson. What's happening?"

"I can fill you in, Sir," Page said. They caught one woman and one of the test subjects in cross fire. They think they hit the woman."

Thirteenth floor.

Jason stopped dead on the stairs and faced Wolf. "That's got to be Vallon. She wasn't to be harmed."

Around them, was that a haziness to the walls? His heart sped up a little, because a haze wasn't natural.

"Bryson. If there's change happening here, wouldn't we be better off talking about this after we're out of the building?" He caught the other man's arm and started leading him down the stairs.

Twelfth floor. Eleventh. Tenth. Ninth.

There was gum on the stairs, and on the railings. At least it felt that way, the way his feet and fingers kept sticking.

And that wasn't natural, and jeezus-god, get him out of here.

"We have to go faster. It's happening," Jason said.

"Then stop it, damn it." Wolf demanded.

"How the hell am I supposed to do that? I don't have the Gift."

"Moore!" Wolf roared and turned to the woman who brought up the rear. "What can you do about it?"

"Sir?" Her dark eyes flashed hatred in Bryson's direction that was quickly hidden away when she turned to Wolf.

"Stop this change. I'm ordering you."

She looked around, then shook her head. "I might be able to slow it down a bit, but there's too much power involved. There's no way I can stop it."

"Then fucking slow it down enough that we can get out of this fucking building."

Her gaze fell. "Yes, Sir."

Wolf turned and kept going. Eighth floor. Seventh. Sixth, Fifth.

Almost livable if one leapt from a window.

Fourth, and the air seemed filled with smoke, the stairs—he'd never liked these fake waterfall courses.

What? There was something the matter with his mind. He was running down a miniature waterfall, but he wasn't sure why. With him were a team of agents and Jason Bryson, with rolled up maps and charts under his arm.

They reached the bottom of the waterfall and burst into the street. He turned to see a miniature park, replete with mock Mt. Rainier and a series of waterfalls running down its side into pools caught amidst thick foliage. The water gave back rippled reflections of the florescent gleam of Seattle buildings.

Bryson stood beside him.

"Sir, their attack was successful."

"Attack?" Wolf looked at the man beside him. Jason Bryson looked shocked and a little defeated. "We're the ones attacking."

"Sir, they just took out the entire HS headquarters. That's where the building used to stand."

Amundson looked from the park to Bryson and to the small cadre of disheveled men and women standing not too far from them. They looked oddly out of place. So oddly he did a double take, and Page and Bryson followed his gaze. A group of disheveled men and women staggered up out of a hole in the side of the faux mountain.

"Are those…" he started to ask, because they looked like AGS agents he'd had arrested and held for interrogation.

"Run!" Moore screamed and started to follow her own advice.

The agents did, scattering through the park and disappearing down side streets, but two long strides and Page caught Moore's arm before she could escape. Wolf waved three of his remaining men to pursue the escapees. Then he turned to Moore and shook his head. Beyond her the park yawned like a huge hole in the city, and he'd been changed with it. That was the only explanation for the empty place in his brain. Creatures like this woman had done it.

"You know what this means for your brother," he said.

Moore snarled up at him and spat.

Wolf's arm shot out in a resounding slap that sent her reeling back into Page's arms. "Secure and sedate her. We have work to do. Give the Guard the coordinates of the dorms. Tell them to increase fire. I want everything dead in that installation."

§

Xavier pushed through the last shield of trees around the floodlit warehouse. Vallon was there. Vallon was wounded. Explosions continued to go off in the forest around him, though why the armed troop had not moved in to surround and protect the warehouse he couldn't fathom. The wind off the ocean lay cool on his skin and carried the scent of brine and almonds.

Almonds?

He stopped. *Almonds?*

Kata power burst skyward around him in a bright gold geyser of power that churned into a whirlwind. *Kata* power tainted by almond. The power bled into his depleted blood and out again, tearing at his strength and reawakening desperate hunger and debilitating weakness. His legs gave and he went down on his knees, his belly.

He grabbed for a tree branch to haul himself up. He had to reach Vallon. Help her.

The power poured around him, but his blood was too thin for the *kata*. He reached deeper for the lavender-scented *heret* and dragged the blue-gold power into him. After only a day, it still was not enough to deal with his depleted veins. He swore and clung to the tree trunk, punched his thighs with his fists as the geyser ripped power from him. High above in the night sky, moving lights told of small planes and a helicopter, circling.

He was Cartos; more powerful. But this was not just Vallon's father. This was him augmented, just as Rebecca Murdoch had been similarly augmented. And he had barely defeated her when he had been at full strength. Francis Drake was doing something just as wrong.

Not moving the magma core of a mountain. No, Francis Drake was using the power not to defend against the attacking soldiers, but to attack. The guardsmen flickered and went out like candles. Their equipment melted away. The warehouse, though, was caught in the wind and was being torn away in a manner that could injure or kill any living Gifted or Cartos.

What was he doing when Vallon and the children were still inside?

Unless he wanted the Gifted to think he was helping the children by attacking the warehouse.

If they were killed in the battle, Drake would say it was a tragedy that would never have occurred if the unGifted hadn't held them prisoner. The Gifted would be furious, and that was what Drake wanted. The true war would begin then, just as Vallon thought.

He would not have innocents pay such a price, nor Vallon.

He went to his knees, dug his hands into the muddy ground, and -reached- deep for the saffron-tinged blue-gold *platiqua* that snaked deep in the earth.

[Mother Pangea, hear me, your faithful servant for so many long, lonely years. Let me use your power and protect the woman I love now that I have found her.]

The deeps of the earth seemed to rumble around him. He siphoned off *platiqua*, careful not to get caught in the current that could sweep him away. His blood heated in his veins. Power frothed, but not the way it would normally. This was a faint shadow on a sunless day, but it was enough that he pulled back from the mother's breast and stood, as the whirlwind ripped loose the trees around him, ripped at him.

But this time it could not steal from him. With the *platiqua* in his veins, he ran for the warehouse. Reached its metal sides and sent a bolt of power into it. The wall melted away and he ducked inside just as everything suddenly went quiet.

He stopped. Drake's whirlwind was gone and yet the man still lived, the Gifted still banded around him. Vallon was to his left, but coming this way. He headed for the door.

A roaring explosion wrenched the building. Metal screamed. The floor shuddered and heaved and tossed him to the floor. The roof caved in towards him.

He used the *platiqua* to hold it away, scrambled up into dust and smoke and the stink of burning. The doorway was not there anymore. It lay splintered on the floor, debris piled deep beyond the opening. Smoke streamed in and was sucked out through the opening he had created.

Vallon. Where was she?

There. Still to his left.

He sent power surging into the wall, created an opening that smoke and heat surged through. The entire place was burning. The explosion had been big enough. The guardsmen must have seen Drake's attack as just that, and had decided to finish the job. Kill everyone in the warehouse and there would be nothing worth the Gifted's attack. But the Guardsmen were fools if they thought that. Already he could feel the angry power building. Drake had what he wanted, now.

The children…

He plunged into another room, this one filled with blinding smoke. The heat sent him back a step. An inferno raged beyond the room. Flames licked in the door, but Vallon was here, somewhere.

[*Bela?*] Please let her be safe. Please, Mother Pangea. His heart beat a tattoo in his chest.

Silence for too long. He opened himself and saw the brilliant glow of her presence, a small cadre of smaller flames around her. He started towards them, but debris blocked his way. Cut through it with the power and was on his knees beside her.

She lay still on the floor, her blonde hair ruddy in the flame's light, her skin carrying a false color of life, and he thought he was dying. His heart slowed. Blood flowed from a wound in her chest in a heavy black stream.

"*Bela.*" He lifted her up. "*Bela*, you must live for us."

She hung limp and his chest filled. He closed his eyes. "Please, *Bela*. We have just found each other. You cannot leave so soon."

Was that movement, a sigh? Surely her breast drew a deeper breath.

She coughed. Coughed again and her great brown eyes flashed open. "The children?"

He shifted her so she could see the small band of young ones through the smoke, huddled against the wall.

"Keira?"

One of the older boys just looked towards the burning hallway.

She closed her eyes and tears flowed down her cheeks. The building shuddered as something gave way somewhere. Another explosion, but smaller. Xavier stood up, Vallon in his arms.

"Can you walk?"

The children nodded as one.

"Then come."

The *platiqua* was fading and he knew that he would pay a price, but they had to get out of here first. He -reached- and blasted a hole in the wall, shifted Vallon's fence indentation to shelter the opening, and a blast of ocean air hit their faces. He urged the children out—only ten of them—and stepped out with Vallon.

Smoke streamed across the stars. Red light filled the sky, and overhead, the moving lights of helicopters and small planes circled and circled. Spotter planes? Media? Either way it was not good. One would report anyone escaping the area, the other would send the events of the night into the world and unGifted consciousness. There was no chance of unwriting these events on the world.

He staggered into the woods, the children stumbling after like small ducklings. The pine and cedar perfumed the air and seemed to cleanse the smoke away.

"Vallon. *Bela*," he whispered. "You must stay with me."

The wound was so bad. It flowed faster as he walked. He needed to get her someplace safe, needed to get her medical care.

The trees thinned around him, just as a figure came charging through the trees towards him. Beyond lay the derelict house that had been Francis Drake's temporary headquarters.

"Vallon! Vallon!" Small, blonde Fi came stumbling up, smoke black on her face and clothes, tears in dark runnels down her cheeks. "She's alive, right? I can feel that she's still alive." She caught Vallon's hand and held on as if her life depended upon it.

"She lives, but the blood loss is grave."

Fi looked up at him wild-eyed. "I'll give her my blood. I'll do anything. It was all my fault. I shouldn't have believed him."

She swiped at her tear-filled eyes.

"I do not think you did that, Fiona." He motioned behind him with his head and kept walking towards the derelict structure and the Cayenne that sat in front of it. He at least had a medical kit there.

"But I helped. I believed him. At least at first, I did. And so I helped him."

He reached the car and settled Vallon on the ground, then pulled out the medical kit. Fi hovered over him. The children were like filthy wraiths on the ground.

"Fiona." His use of her name momentarily stopped her recriminations. "If what you say is right, you helped me save them by breaking Drake's circle. Now please help again by seeing to the children. Check them for burns or other injury while I see to Vallon. And if you can let their parent's know they are here, that would be a good thing."

He glanced up at her, to see if she heard.

"I think they already know," she said, looking towards the trees.

He followed her gaze and saw Gifted filtering through the darkness towards the children, beyond them a towering column of flame was eating towards them. So the forest had caught, too. He truly needed to get Vallon out of here.

The medical kit yielded thick bandages that he used to fill the holes in her shoulder and chest before binding the bandages in place. Then he immobilized her arm across her chest and found her looking at him with huge, defeated eyes.

"I couldn't stop it," she said, her voice hoarse with smoke. Her words broke and her eyes filled and he pulled her into his arms where they clung to each other. At least she was here. She had a chance to survive—if he could get her the medical attention she needed.

"Nor could I, *Bela*. Sometimes there are things we are doomed to repeat as a race."

Around them the Gifted were arriving, some shouting for joy as they found their child or children. Most collapsing in despair.

"How many?" Vallon asked him and struggled loose to face him.

He knew what she asked. "Ten. There were ten with you in the room."

She slumped in his arms, her eyes closed, her breath hitching. Then she swallowed. "There were forty when I found them."

"Yes. And there would be forty bodies in the rubble if you had not intervened."

But he could see the toll the news took on her. She seemed to shrink in on herself.

"Vallon?" Fi returned to crouch on the gravel beside her. "Vallon, I'm so sorry. I should have believed you. I shouldn't have listened to your father. I'll never be like you. I know that now. Maybe I'll always be that child you think I am."

Vallon opened her eyes and turned a bleak look on her friend. There was no warmth in her eyes. There was nothing, as if her heart had been burned out.

Fi fell back from the chill in Vallon's gaze. "Please, Vallon. Please forgive me."

"How can I forgive you, when I cannot forgive myself?" Vallon shook her head and looked at Xavier. "There are soldiers coming. We should leave."

The hollowness in her eyes frightened him. This was not the deeply caring woman he had come to love. This woman looked like she struggled to find a reason to live. But she was right, also. The National Guard was advancing.

He stood. "There are soldiers coming this way. I suggest you take your children and leave."

"No! We must stand and fight or else we will be hunted down forever!" Francis Drake's voice cut through the darkness as he climbed over the fence into the parking lot.

"We're too few," one of the Gifted said.

"Not so," Drake said. "There are more of us, survivors of the second group, and they were successful in their mission. The HS building in Seattle is no more. With luck, they got Amundson."

A small cheer went up.

"Then it's over?" someone said with hope.

"What he has started will never be over," Xavier said. "Drake wanted a war, and now he has it."

The tall blond man confronted him. "What we want is the freedom that your kind have. We want to be our own society. But then, you can't understand. You already have it and you and your kind think you can just exist on your own and watch and not be involved. But that time has come to an end. All Gifted must stand together against the unGifted. Your presence is proof of it."

"My presence says nothing but that I am a lovesick fool who wants his love safe." He turned back to the Cayenne and picked up Vallon, carrying her to the car to slide her into the rear seat. "And now I will do exactly that. Go someplace safe. Pray there is some place in the world that will be safe after this night."

He glanced at Fi, who stood beside Vallon's closed door and caught her shoulder.

"You can come with us, if you want to."

Her wide blue eyes turned up to him. "I can? But Vallon doesn't want me anymore."

"Not true, little one. Vallon is angry at herself that she could not save all the children. That is all it is."

Those sad blue eyes said she did not fully believe him.

"Climb in, little Fiona. Vallon needs you. You have tried very hard to stop a war tonight. Now we must go, if we are not to be trapped by it." He opened the door and she scrambled in beside Vallon as he went around to the driver's side.

He climbed in and keyed the engine on. Its purr rumbled through him and he turned off the headlights. Beyond the car, the few Gifted whose children had survived headed along the water's edge, presumably towards safer places. He wished them well, but there was nothing he could do to help the swell of refugees who would be trying to leave America. Not by himself and not now. Now he had Vallon to worry about. He urged the car forward through the Gifted who readied themselves to fight. Along the road towards the highway, the headlights showed a column of what could only be more National Guard coming to do battle.

He turned the Cayenne the other way and opened up the engine, heading north along the coastline. He'd cut inland farther north. Now he just needed to get as far away as possible. He glanced at Vallon in the rearview. She was collapsed behind him against the driver's side door, her eyes open and staring out at the passing fence posts. From the other side of the back seat came Fiona's soft sobs. Hopefully, when they got beyond the Canada/US border, they would have a better chance of coming to grips with what had happened. Then they could determine their next course of action.

From behind, the night sky was filled with flames.

EPILOGUE

The heat and the dust were eating Gregor Gleason alive. The pain of his wounds had long ago turned to a white noise of screaming nerves his mind had stopped registering. But the heat of the frying-pan-flat desert through the shattered windows of the car left him parched and unsteady and sure as hell hallucinating, because behind him came a long line of dark suburbans and police cars with red and blue lights strobing ineffectually in the sun's full-on glare. Just as bad as the heat was the horrible dust that came billowing in his windows whenever he slowed. It set off his coughing and *that* was painful.

Since the little episode on the highway, he'd learned the virtues of shallow breathing.

Sweat made the steering wheel slippery under his hands. Or maybe that was blood from when he'd torn off part of his shirt to stuff the cloth in his chest wound. He couldn't actually remember anymore, and that wasn't good. It was like everything was starting to shut down in his brain until the only things he could hold onto were the coordinates Landon had sent when he'd dialed him on the special phone, and the grim reality of the road before him. Just drive straight and he might get there. If he got there, he might survive.

But the desert stretched forever ahead of him, shimmering with heat and with no sign of life. Just where was Landon leading him and all these others, and there was something the matter with the fact he was leading these other vehicles. His poor wounded brain just couldn't quite fathom what, but he should be there any time. Any time, but the desert stretched empty for miles before him and the dust and the vehicles chased him like they would chase him right off the continent and into the Pacific Ocean.

He would almost relish it after the heat and the dust. Seattle would be so lovely this time of year. He would miss its lovely Indian summer. He would miss the rains, too. Most of all, he'd miss the purpose of the AGS and the knowledge he was helping America.

Apparently, America didn't want his help anymore.

A whiff of baby's breath got up his nose and he slowed, the dust flowed over his car and set him coughing again, but this had to be it. Landon's little hideaway.

And suddenly the dust was gone. Green lawn stretched left and right of him in a wedge of life in the desert landscape. He slammed on the brakes and turned the battered car aside. The car slid to a stop and behind him, grey vehicles slipped through the green space like ghosts and were gone, chasing something that was no longer there. A ghost, like he felt.

He collapsed back in his seat until small, efficient hands reached over to unbuckle his seatbelt.

"Welcome to the place that isn't there and the headquarters of Gifted resistance," Landon Snow said.

ABOUT THE AUTHOR

Author of the unique Cartographer Universe series, Karen L. Abrahamson writes poetry, short fiction, and fantasy, romance and mystery novels, as well as non-fiction for newspapers and magazines. In her words, "a bad day of writing is still better than the best day working for a living."

A born wanderer, she currently lives in the Metro Vancouver area of Canada with two Bengal cats who channel James Dean's attitude. When she isn't writing she can be found with a camera and backpack in fabulous locations around the world.

To learn more about her, visit her website at www.karenlabrahamson.com

To find more of her writing, visit www.twistedrootpublishing.com.

ALSO BY KAREN L. ABRAHAMSON

The Cartographer Universe (in chronological order)
The Warden of Power

The Cartographer's Daughter

The American Geological Survey Series:
Afterburn
Aftershock
Aftermath
Afterimage (coming Spring 2014)

Terra Incognita
Terra Infirma
Terra Nueva

Other Novels by Karen L. Abrahamson
Ice Dragon
Emberstone
Mutable Things

Novels by Karen L. Abrahamson writing as Karen L. McKee
Ashes and Light
Shades of Moonlight
Judas Kiss
Second Spring
A Different Nightmusic
Shadow Play

TO READ MORE OF VALLON DRAKE AND
THE AMERICAN GEOLOGICAL SURVEY,
TURN THE PAGE FOR THE FIRST CHAPTER OF
AFTERIMAGE
BOOK FOUR IN THE SAGA OF VALLON DRAKE AND THE
AGS.
Coming Spring 2014

CHAPTER 1 – BREATH AND COPPER BLOOD

The pain drilled into Vallon Drake's chest until the night-bound world of the moving vehicle reduced to Fi Murdoch's supporting arms around her and the simple act of breathing. Breathe in, in a painful rush and she would stay alive, but the pain hazed the world. Breathe out, and for a moment relief flooded in. If she could hold her breath forever. If she could just breathe differently, shift her body, but something cold and hard and jagged in her side stabbed her each time she moved and sent fresh blood flowing warm and sticky down her side.

If she could just stop breathing.

But that was impossible and even now she struggled to get enough air.

The pain was a constant nagging reminder of what she had done. Not what she set out to do. She'd lost the children—not all, but most of them, including Keira—trapped and lost in the explosion that had done this to her. She'd failed.

But that was the least of it. She could deal with failure and grief. It was part of life.

The SUV dipped and swayed as it sped down the highway, taillights of other vehicles painting bright red slashes on the darkness. Fi's whispers drilled into her, begging Vallon to stay with them, and just why should she? Just what good was she to anyone after what she'd failed to do and what she'd done? It was the unclean feeling that ate at her worse than the thing in her side. All her life she had sworn to use her power to protect life. To preserve it.

Except this time she hadn't.

Two mewling puddles of melting life, white research coats around them.

Yes, she'd been trying to protect Keira but that didn't make it right and in the end the girl hadn't made it out of the facility had she? Too many lives lost and she was responsible right back to the fact her father was still alive. She jerked back from the memory and the thing in her side stabbed her from within, a reminder again. And payback. She choked back a moan, but Fi must have heard her. Her arms tightened around Vallon and seemed to trap her here with the pain. Xavier, too. His dark gaze reflected back at her from the rearview mirror as he somehow expertly guided the Porsche Cayenne through the darkness with just one good hand. It was his will that held her. His will that would not let the pain cut the rest of the way through her chest. That would not just let her release her breath for good. Those dark eyes held her.

The question was whether he was right. Yes, she loved him. So much it filled her up and made her wonder how she had survived for so long without him. But since his appearance she had only dragged him into trouble, first with her people in the American Geological Survey, then with Homeland Security, and now with his own secret Cartos Council, whose sanctions he had ignored to come back to her.

There was no question: Vallon Drake was not good for Xavier de Vargas. Actually, it seemed that she wasn't much good for too many people. Sure, she might have stopped a few disasters, but the people closest to her were always the ones who paid. Like Xavier. Like Fi.

Like all the innocent Gifted who were going to die at the hands of Wolf Amundson, they would be better off without her. It was her fault Wolf Amundson gained the excuse to take over the AGS.

Not much you can do about that, now, pigeon. She could hear Landon's voice. Landon, her mentor, who had turned out to be a traitor, too, just as her father Francis Drake had turned on her. It suggested she was fatally flawed—either too much like the two of them, or something about her made them make horrendous decisions. And that made the absence of breathing that much more attractive. She couldn't hurt or influence anyone else if she quit breathing.

She leaned back in Fi's arms wondering whether she had the strength to make it so.

§

The white lines on 15 led on into the darkness and nothing. Trees pressed in from either side and made it hard to breathe. Or maybe it was the twisted feeling that strangled in Xavier de Varga's chest. It was a new feeling, for always before he held himself still and breathed through the dangers. But this time the woman he loved lay dying in the back of his vehicle and all he could do was drive.

Drive and pray to Mother Pangea. It had been years since he felt this desperate.

His hands gripped the leather steering wheel harder regardless of the pain in his flayed hand, guiding the powerful Porsche Cayenne around other highway traffic as fast as he dared, but not fast enough as far as he was concerned. He glanced into the rearview mirror where Fi Murdoch cradled Vallon against her. Fi's face was ashen and tears streaked her face as she stroked Vallon's face. Vallon, well, if Fi was pale, then Vallon was the color of ashes from the injuries she had sustained trying to rescue the Gifted children from the warehouse-turned-research-facility north of Seattle. The wound in her arm bled, but she could recover from that, the wound in her chest, though, that was another matter. She'd been caught in the explosion that killed most of the children and some projectile had buried itself in her flesh too deep for anyone but a skilled surgeons to fix—or a healer. But at least her eyes were open, huge and dark and luminous with pain as she struggled to keep breathing. The sound of it burbled over the humming of the Cayenne's wheels. The coppery scent of blood negated the vehicle's new-car-new-leather smell.

"How is she?" His voice sounded rough and desperate, even to him.

"Awake, at least." Fi's tear-stained voice was barely a whisper. "You can't leave me like this. We just found each other, Vallon. We just fixed things between us. You promised you'd be there for me. You hear?" She stroked Vallon's hair and hugged her.

Sentiments he echoed. After a long life wandering the world on missions of the Cartos Council, he finally had found the woman he loved. His *Bela Menina*. He could not lose her now. It was impossible. Unacceptable. Not to be allowed. Because she was all that mattered. All his work for the Cartos Council was useless—a futile endeavor given how they left so many of their young progeny to wander the world with little to no guidance except edicts of what not to do or suffer the consequence— and he was the one sent to spy on the youngsters and to mete out those consequences out. A useless enterprise. More meaningless the more he thought of it. The Council had lost touch with what they were for, and with the very people they were supposed to guide and support. He caught Vallon's eye in the rearview mirror again. The only good thing arising from his years of work was that he had stumbled upon Vallon Drake.

"Stay with us, *Bela*. We will be at the border soon. There is a rest stop ahead and we must clean ourselves and the car. We must plan on there being photos or drawing of at least Vallon and possibly myself at the border, given our friend, the detective, seems to have teamed with your Amundson."

Vallon shook her head, her ghostly face grim. "Not my Amundson. Don't use his name in association with any Gifted." Her voice was a hoarse gasp and whisper.

The Gifted—those Americans with the Cartos talent to rewrite the landscape using only their mind and vellum and pen—had mostly been employees of the American Geological Survey, an ultra secret department of Homeland Security charged with the protection of America from possible terrorists with similar talents. But the Gifted were not the whole story. Unbeknownst to them, but theorized to exist, were others with the Gift. The Cartos, an older, powerful group of people with the same talent. Xavier was one, and the first to confirm their existence when he went against the Council's orders and revealed himself to Vallon. And became a hunted man.

"Well, Amundson is our first problem. He will surely have the borders closed to us. Normally I would simply transmute across, but that is beyond all of us at this time." Loss of blood had left him and Vallon each too weak and Fi had neither the skills, nor the training needed.

The sign for the last rest stop before the border came up and he took the exit into the parking lot. Orange-colored streetlights turned the night amber and late September insects formed clouds around the glowing globes of light.

Praise the Creator, the parking lot lay empty. He leapt out and went around to the rear passenger door. Fi was trying to get Vallon fully upright. Xavier reached in and swept Vallon into his arms. For a woman who was a force of nature in everything she did, she felt too small, too light in his arms, even though she was five foot eight. He placed a kiss on her forehead.

"Come, *Bela*. We will get you bandaged up a little better." He prayed to the Creator that it was possible.

Cradling her against him, he strode to the washroom building, Fi bringing up the rear. Once inside, he locked the bathroom door, then settled Vallon on the sink counter. The fluorescent lights and the washroom stink just made her condition even more clearly dire. Her white t-shirt and jeans were dark with blood from the wound in her shoulder and the one in her chest. Fi had tried to keep pressure on them, but just moving from the car to the washroom had sent a bloom of new red down Vallon's side. She swayed where she sat and Xavier swore and leaned her back against the wall.

Much more bleeding like this and she was not going to make it. That much was clear. She needed a physician quickly, but he had no connections to any physicians in this area. He had such medical assistance across the border in Canada, but getting there was the problem. So risk taking her to a doctor who would likely turn them in to Homeland Security, or risk the border and Vallon bleeding out in the interim?

He explained the risks to the two women.

"Get her to a doctor," Fi said from where she leaned, exhausted, against the wall, her leg seeping from her own injury. But Vallon, closed her eyes and shook her head.

"The border. We have to cross. If we stop for help, we'll all be caught. You have to get to safety." She swallowed and opened her eyes to look at them. "You two are the most important people in the world. Fi, I'm so sorry I've used you in the past. I shouldn't have. Xavier—how could I have found you only now?" Her eyes filled with desperation and she reached a blood-stained hand for him.

"Stop it!" Fi, shed her fatigue and stepped between them. "You stop it, Vallon Drake. Just stop it, now! You are not going to die because we won't let you, so you just quit acting like you are! You hear?"

The ferocity was surprising coming from the meek, pixy of a woman. But at this moment her gaze was clear, not the muddled mind caused by the abuse of Fi's mother. She tossed the Cayenne's medical kit on the counter and opened the top then faced Xavier like a ferocious mother lion. "I don't know how to do all this stuff. You do."

With more light and more time than he had had at the battle to free the Gifted children he pulled up Vallon's bloodied shirt and carefully bandaged the wound. Inside it he could just make out the angry end of some kind of shrapnel, but he didn't dare pull it free for fear of increasing the blood flow. So he padded the wound as best he could and then started tightening bandages around her torso.

Vallon sagged against the grey wall.

"*Bela*, I am so sorry. It must be done."

She sucked in a breath and nodded, but her pallor was too great. No matter Vallon Drake's will to live, how long could her body continue to lose such amounts of blood? She was covered in it. They all were. Not exactly the way he wanted to face the border. For himself he could pull on his coat to cover the blood, the women, however, could not.

"We need to get you two clothes."

Fi shook her head. "We don't have time. A doctor first and then clothes. Or we wash them out here as best we can."

Xavier nodded, and Fi pulled off her shirt. Water ran red as she washed it. Vallon was too badly injured to care and her shirt too blood covered to ever wash clean. She began to slide down the counter to the floor so Xavier pulled her into his arms, cradling her with his warmth.

"Come," he said. "We need to move."

Vallon was too still, too cool in his arms. Her usually fiercely strong arms hung almost limp around his neck and the copper-penny scent of blood masked her ashes of roses scent. There was no option. He had to get her medical help. The question was whether he could find a doctor between here and the border crossing, and if not, if she could hold on until he could reach his contact on the other side.

If Homeland Security didn't find them first.

§

Blood. Blood on his hands. Copper-scented blood caked in his manicured cuticles, on his shirt and soaked into his moccasin soles.

Landon Snow stood next to the operating table, the body that was once Gregor Gleason, deposed Chief of the American Geological Survey, in a pool of blood in front of him. Around him gleamed the chrome and white painted surgery room where previously he had held Xavier de Varga prisoner. At least that venture had been moderately successful.

Sorrow and the fatigue of long labor slumped Landon's shoulders forward over the messy remains of Gregor's open chest cavity. Whatever the man had been through to reach Landon, the wounds he'd borne had devastated too many critical organs for Landon's relatively meager surgical skills to heal. Gleason had required a whole team of thoracic surgeons and even then his chances of survival would have been slim. For him to be dependent upon only Landon had basically sealed his fate.

And so Landon had failed him.

He held up his bloodied gloved hands, wiggled his fingers and felt his gorge rise. Why, he wasn't quite sure. These hands had been as bloody with Xavier's blood and that had been the result of his efforts, not trying to save the man like this had been.

Torture, a part of him whispered. *You tortured a man and inserted a tracking device as if he was an animal. All because you had to know how to find the Others.*

Gleason's drying blood slicked his fingers. He had been a good man—not a particularly Gifted agent, certainly not in Vallon's league—but he'd been committed to his country and keeping it safe. He'd been a moral man. A man strong with ethics who truly cared.

And he was dead because of Amundson.

"I'm sorry, old friend. I truly did everything I could." It was the truth. When Gleason had driven into Landon's hideaway, the police hard on his heels, Landon had run out to Gleason's vehicle only to find the ex-head of the American Geological Survey collapsed over his steering wheel, seated in a pool of his blood. Somehow, with only Landon's assistance, Gleason had walked into Landon's research facility, his breath a burbling, gurgling wheeze. He'd collapsed unconscious on the surgery table, leaving Landon to administer anesthetic and attempt emergency surgery.

When he'd cut open Gleason's chest, he'd almost immediately sewn it up again. Whatever type of ammunition had hit Gleason had ricocheted around inside his chest, torn up his lungs and yet somehow missed his heart and arteries. To try and find enough flesh to mend was an impossibility. How the man had driven all this way into the Nevada desert and then walked inside, was a testament to the strength and fortitude that had been Gregor Gleason.

Lost now. As were the connections Gleason had to the politicians who might stop what was coming at the hands of Wolf Amundson.

Landon sighed and sought a needle and thread on the tray of surgical instruments. Swiftly he sewed up the chest cavity and stood there shaking. From the body rose a faint scent of Gleason's old spice scent through the stink of charnel house. He bowed his head.

"Creator, take this man from the dust he will return to and transform him into the gold he always was." He stepped back from the table and filled a basin with water, then gently began to wash his old friend.

Watch for *Afterimage* coming Spring 2014.

FANTASY, ROMANCE AND HIGH ADVENTURE FROM TWISTED ROOT PUBLISHING

If you enjoyed this book, you might enjoy other
titles from the Cartographer Universe available from
Twisted Root Publishing in your local bookstore or
wherever e-books are sold.

www.karenlabrahamson.com

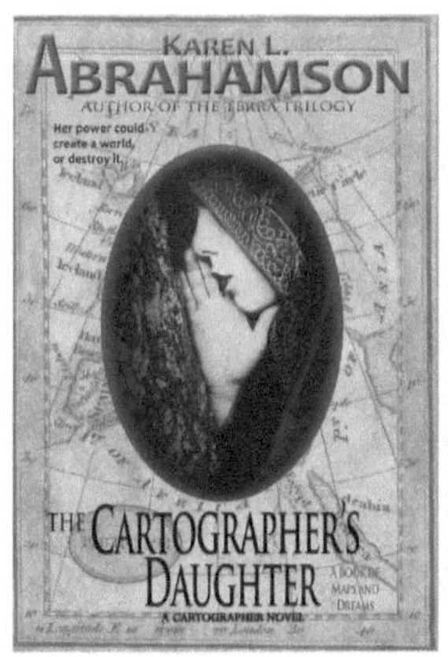

9 781927 753248